Also by Michelle Gable

A Paris Apartment
I'll See You in Paris
The Book of Summer
The Summer I Met Jack
The Bookseller's Secret
The Lipstick Bureau

MICHELLE GABLE

THE
BEAUTIFUL
PEOPLE

A NOVEL

GRAYDON
HOUSE

**GRAYDON
HOUSE®**

Recycling programs
for this product may
not exist in your area.

ISBN-13: 978-1-525-80503-5

The Beautiful People

This is a work of fiction. Names, characters, places and incidents are either the product
of the author's imagination or are used fictitiously. Any resemblance to actual persons,
living or dead, businesses, companies, events or locales is entirely coincidental.

® is a trademark of Harlequin Enterprises ULC.

Graydon House
22 Adelaide St. West, 41st Floor
Toronto, Ontario M5H 4E3, Canada
www.GraydonHouseBooks.com
www.BookClubbish.com

Printed in U.S.A.

For Elaine, Caryn, Laura, and Aileen

Always the Beautiful People

Happy 2024

AUTHOR'S NOTE

Slim Aarons was famous for photographing the rich and fabulous, whether in Palm Beach, Acapulco, Vail, or Gstaad. After getting his start in the Army, capturing the horrors of WWII, Slim vowed to stay on the "sunny side of the street" and spent his long career documenting "attractive people doing attractive things in attractive places."

This novel fictionalizes the early '60s jet-setters he photographed, but most characters are based on real people, including Lilly and Peter Pulitzer, Wendy Vanderbilt, Enrique and Julia Rousseau, and, of course, Slim Aarons. The protagonist of this book, Margo, is a work of fiction, though as Slim's assistant, she does much of the same work (and must abide by the same rules) as her real-life counterparts. Most circumstances (and parties!) in this novel are based on facts as well, including the meteoric rise of the Lilly Pulitzer brand, but I shifted the timeline and minor details in several instances to fit the overall story arc.

Slim's work greatly inspired this book, and where a specific image can be associated with a scene, I've listed the photograph's title and editorial number at the end of the novel. Slim sold his catalogue to Getty Images in 1997, and all can be found on their website. If you stumble across any photographs you find particularly resonant, I'd love to hear from you!

Thank you so much for reading *The Beautiful People*. Now, strap in and get ready to ride with the jet set. I hope you love the trip.

PART 1

From the moment you cross over the drawbridges over Lake Worth from West Palm Beach...you enter what amounts to an island of privilege, in many ways the most remarkable one left in the country.

—Cleveland Amory, *The Last Resorts*

1

PALM BEACH / FEBRUARY 1961

Gogo Hightower arrived in Palm Beach expecting an engagement, not to be left flat on her rear at the Bath & Tennis.

Everything in her life—the carefully selected schools, the hobbies, the debutante ball—was supposed to lead to the ring, to Mrs. Crim Pebley III. Mere hours ago, Gogo had gazed up at the ballroom's curved beams and iron chandeliers, imagining she might have her wedding here. The ceiling was designed to resemble the hull of a capsized Spanish cargo ship, so maybe she should've seen it coming.

Now Gogo was marooned, alone at a table while employees scurried about collecting soiled napkins and lipstick-stained glasses. The luncheon ended forty-five minutes ago, but she couldn't compel herself to move, not until a small man with a tight black mustache tilted his head toward the exit.

Gogo didn't need to be asked twice. She snatched her purse from the table and her gold peau de soie heels from under a chair. The matching gold beret was gone, disappeared after she chucked it at Crim's head. Oh, well. There'd be other hats.

With the detritus of a once snappy outfit in hand, Gogo exited the room between a pair of six-foot-tall champagne glasses and staggered down the pink satin–lined hallway toward the front desk. She borrowed the phone and left one message, and another, before venturing outside, where she spent several minutes contemplating the deep end of the pool. She'd never heard of anyone successfully committing it this way and would probably only ruin her dress and traumatize a half dozen children in the process.

Gogo turned away from the pool, and collapsed onto a chaise. She draped an arm across her eyes as Crim Pebley's face flashed through her mind, torturous pictures of the happy times they'd once shared, from hunts in Virginia to dances at the Burlingame Country Club. They had fun together, and they had plans. One day there'd be a wedding, and a white clapboard house. They'd raise a passel of children and follow this dream to happily ever after, the end. Now Gogo's future was smashed to bits. Her life was over, at only twenty-one years of age.

2

Gogo heard the whoosh of a door and the clack of heels on concrete. "Darling!" sang a voice. She opened one eye, and a second. "Why are you in *repose*?" It was her best friend, Dolly Fritz.

Gogo jumped to her feet and wrapped her arms around Dolly's neck, nestling her face in her thick black hair. "Thank God you're here," she said. It was a great stroke of luck. Dolly acted like an older sister—protective, forever coming to Gogo's aid—but was not always available. She often disappeared into her own world, or Europe, for days or even weeks at a time.

"I guess I don't need to ask how Sibley's wedding was," Dolly said, wiggling out of Gogo's hold. "But what's with the decorations?" She crooked a thumb toward the building. "The hallway looks like a birth canal."

Gogo nodded. It was a lot of pink, now that she mentioned it.

"Truly awful." Dolly shook her head. "Anyway. I apologize for the delay. I was watching Fitzroy and he absolutely refused to go down for his nap."

Gogo released a small gasp. Fitzroy? *A nap?* For a millionaire hotel magnate, Dolly could be disorganized. Distracted. Prone to misplacing people and things. Her father died when she was fifteen, leaving a teenage girl in charge of several major properties throughout Northern California. Where fiction had Eloise at the Plaza, San Francisco had Dolly at the Huntington, except in this case, the child was running the show. That was more than ten years ago, but sometimes Dolly still acted like the baby heiress she'd once been. "You're babysitting?" Gogo asked, just to check. "You're watching a live human child?"

"An ocelot," Dolly said. "Which is a type of jaguar, I think?" The Fuller Callaways had gone to Miami to see about a yacht, and asked Dolly to watch him for the day. She was the only person they knew presently in Palm Beach.

"Oh" was the only response Gogo could gin up, although in some ways, this made sense. Her friend *was* the sort of generous that could get a person's hand bitten off. "Is that why you didn't come to the wedding? The ocelot?"

Dolly shook her head and plunked down on the end of a chaise. "I called in sick at the last minute," she said. "Sick of attending the same event twelve weekends in a row, but I left that part out. Now I wish I'd gone. I can't believe Crim dumped you at a wedding. That is too low, even for him."

Gogo wrinkled her nose. *Even for him?* If Dolly didn't care for Crim Pebley III, it was the first she'd heard of it.

"Well, go ahead," Dolly said with a sigh. "Tell me what happened."

Gogo hardly knew. One minute she was drinking pink champagne, and the next Crim had whisked her outside, where the rush of daylight was harsh, like stepping into a cold shower. Gogo squeezed her eyes shut as Crim began to speak. Though he'd intended to wait until Monday to have this discussion, Gogo was too handsy on the dance floor, forcing him to spit it out. Crim couldn't marry her. Instead of the engagement she'd expected, they were breaking up.

"It was that quick!" Gogo said, her voice climbing to new

heights. "I feel like someone dropped me off the side of a building."

"Poor thing," Dolly cooed. She patted the chaise, instructing Gogo to sit back down. "He could've waited a couple more hours."

"Or not done it at all!"

Dolly opened her handbag, and angled it toward Gogo, offering one of the balled-up tissues littering the bottom of her purse. For all her wealth and breeding, Dolly could be a terrible slob. It was as though no one had ever taught her how to take care of things. "If you're not going to dry your tears," she said, when Gogo refused, "dab your face. It's very red and shiny. Are you using new moisturizer?"

Gogo swiped a tissue. "Don't be mean! My skin is extremely sensitive." She'd spent hours, full days of her life, rubbing Mum in her pits, dousing herself in Arrid cream, and in general applying any product that promised to alleviate sweat and/or hide red splotches. Usually her efforts made things worse, this time no exception.

"What else did Crim say?" Dolly asked. "Surely he gave you a reason."

Gogo bit her lip as the tears came rushing back. "He claims I'm not a serious person. That I don't have ambition!" To make a good home *was* Gogo's ambition, but Crim didn't think this counted for much.

"Listen, sugar," Dolly said. "I appreciate that this is upsetting, but it's for the best. Crim Pebley is a real second stringer, if you catch my drift."

Gogo didn't catch her drift, not at all. If Crim was junior varsity, what was she? Anyhow, what did California's Prettiest Millionaire know of second stringers? Dolly was beautiful, independently wealthy, and, as opposed to Gogo, her stepfather was not currently under federal indictment for securities fraud. She truly had it all.

"I've never understood the appeal," Dolly went on. "I'm convinced you only wanted to marry him so you'd have an excuse to leave home."

Gogo shot her a glare. She *loved* Crim. Getting out of her mom's house was simply a fringe benefit.

"I'll give it to you straight," Dolly said. "You're not mourning Crim Pebley but the life you thought you'd have. You pictured toting a bunch of rug rats between a massive Victorian in Pacific Heights and a swanky pad in New York. Every season you'd come to Palm Beach."

"I did," Gogo sniffled. "I did picture that. It's so lovely here, don't you think?" Dolly pulled a face, and Gogo took immediate personal offense. "What possible objection could you have? Look around!" She flung her hands overhead. "The flowers, the sunshine, the ocean. Everything's perfectly manicured, clean at all times. Did you know it's the only place in either hemisphere where there's a daily garbage collection?"

"Bully for them," Dolly said and crossed her arms. "Palm Beach is duller than dieting. It's all automobile people here now, so many Dodges and Fords. And everyone is so *cheeky*. One woman initiated legal proceedings because some neighbor didn't invite her to a party."

"She probably just wanted to be included…"

"Palm Beach is a stupid, man-made, made-up place where the poodles outnumber the humans, and every other door is marked *private*. I fail to see what's so great about that."

"It's so pleasant," Gogo insisted. "There are no juvenile delinquents, or gangsters. No strife at all. Crim's father told me that there isn't any tension between the rich and poor."

"Only because there are no poor. I suppose he made a similar statement regarding race relations?"

As a matter of fact, he did, but Gogo intuited that she should not raise this point.

"Palm Beachers keep *those* people," Dolly said, "in West Palm Beach, on the other side of the bridge. Along with tradesmen and teachers. Anyone who believes in working to get ahead. Say what you will about San Francisco, but it has a personality. On the West Coast, society is still playful and fun. That's why no real writer has ever written about Palm Beach."

Gogo noodled on this but remained unconvinced.

"Listen, Gogo," Dolly began.

"Please call me Margo. Gogo Hightower is dead."

Dolly lightly rolled her eyes. "Fine. We are officially done with Gogo Hightower *and* Crim Pebley the third." She removed the tissue from Gogo's hand and returned it to her purse. "I've had plenty of broken engagements. There's no need to get worked up. Think of it like passing from one season to the next."

"But those engagements were ended of *your* own accord," Margo said. Also, no one would accuse Prince Gonzalo de Borbón of Spain or King Baudouin of Belgium of playing second string.

"That's neither here nor there," Dolly said. "The relationship is over and it's time to move on. First things first, you need a place to stay. Should I send someone to fetch your belongings from Crim's?"

"I'm staying at the Colony," Gogo—*Margo*—said. "Do you think the Pebleys will keep paying my bill?"

"The Colony?" Dolly tucked her chin into her neck. "You weren't staying with Crim?"

"Their home is undergoing extensive renov—" Margo stopped, and her cheeks flamed. How had she not seen through this embarrassingly thin excuse? "Oh God." She clapped a hand over her face. "I'm such a dope."

"What a little weasel," Dolly muttered. "When's your flight back to San Francisco?"

"I don't know. Crim took care of the travel arrangements."

Dolly exhaled sharply. "This is quite the pickle," she said. "Could your mother wire you the cash to get home?"

Margo shook her head. There'd been money once, enough that her family managed to cling to the outer limits of San Francisco society, but whatever social and actual capital they'd managed to accumulate was now kaput. It had happened so fast. Last year, the *Examiner* anointed Margo the Deb of the Year, describing her as "strawberry-haired, tiny-waisted, and marvelously photogenic." Then the Feds busted her stepfather, he hightailed it to Rio de Janeiro, and their house of cards fell.

"There's *nothing*?" Dolly said. "As in zero dollars?"

"You should've seen the house," Margo said. "There's hardly a painting or piece of furniture left. Mom's sold it all for Sandy's legal defense. I hope she's paying the lawyers directly." They were down to their final few cents, and Margo hated to think of Sandy squandering their money on cachaça and Brazilian prostitutes.

"Hmm," Dolly said. "Forgive me if this is an indelicate query, but what were you planning to do next?"

"Marry Crim."

"Oh, sweet Jesus. Who knew you were such a gambler?" Dolly stood. "I'll get you back to San Francisco, but you must come up with a long-term plan. You can't return to Antoinette's house and sit around praying for the best."

"I know that," Margo snapped. The idea of living with her mother, no exit route in sight, was giving her cramps. "Maybe I could model?"

"Ha! You're three feet tall."

"Some people think I'm *marvelously photogenic*," Margo sniffed.

"Huh. That gives me an idea." Dolly paused, putting a contemplative finger to her lips. "Yes. I just might have a way to get you out of this mess." She smacked her hands together and pulled Margo to her feet. "Chop-chop," she said.

"Really?" Margo said, so relieved she was practically levitating. *This* was why Dolly had been her first call. She always had the answer.

"Don't worry, sugar," Dolly said. "The Doll will take care of you. That's what big sisters are for. Now, slap a smile on that mug and let's go change your life."

3

Dolly parked her turquoise convertible in front of a small cottage. Margo peered through the window, frowning. This didn't seem like a life-changing kind of home, but she had to trust her friend.

They stepped out of the car. As they approached the house, a man opened the door. He was tall, gangly, and tanned. Probably in his midforties, though Margo couldn't tell for sure. "It's the Doll!" the man said. "In all her glory! I'm thrilled to see you."

"Oh, Slimbo, wonderful as always." Dolly wrapped him in a hug. "Gogo, I'd like to introduce you to someone. This is the great Slim Aarons. Slim, this is my dearest friend in the world, Gogo Hightower."

"I actually go by Margo—" she said as Slim shut the door behind them.

"When it comes to photographing the jet set, Slim is *it*," Dolly said, digging her red-tipped claws into Margo's arm, an encouragement to pay attention. In Dolly's grossly misinformed opinion, Margo sometimes acted lost at sea. "The man's a genius, a miracle worker."

"How fascinating," Margo said and batted her eyes, hoping

her manufactured bubbliness was enough to mask her skepticism. This man's wrinkled blue oxford and boyish cowlick didn't exactly scream high society. "I hadn't realized we were in the company of someone so esteemed. Where might I have seen your work?"

"Name any magazine of importance," Slim said with a smirk.

"He took that picture of me in front of the Palace of Fine Arts," Dolly said, and something clicked. Margo loved that photograph. In it, Slim managed to capture the true essence of Dolly—stormy and moneyed and powerful, with the countenance of a glamorous, thickly browed American eagle.

"That's a remarkable image," Margo said, truthfully. Though they were finally getting somewhere, she remained flummoxed as to how a talented yet rattily dressed photographer was going to make a difference in her life. Maybe he'd snap her picture and put it in a magazine or newspaper. Ask the editors to give her one of those honorary titles, like Palm Beach's Most Eligible Bachelorette. Of course, Margo wasn't from Palm Beach, and the only press she was destined to receive would employ words like *jilted* and *failed debutante*.

"Thank you for the compliment," Slim said. "It's always nice to meet a fan."

He led them into the kitchen, where a gamine, dark-haired woman was cleaning a high chair. Dolly introduced her as Slim's wife, Rita. She'd just put their two-year-old daughter down for a nap.

"Alright, Doll." Slim leaned against the counter. "I'm dying to find out why you so desperately needed to see me."

"My friend has found herself in a jam," Dolly said, getting straight to the point. "You're in one, too, and I have a solution for you both. I'm envisioning a union." She laced her fingers together. "A plus B equals Z."

"I don't recall having any problems."

"I can think of a few," Rita chimed in, with the hint of a Boston accent.

"I'm referring to the fact that your assistant quit," Dolly said.

"That's merely a temporary hiccup," Slim said, and his wife let out a squawk.

"Ha!" Rita said, tossing her rag into the sink. "You keep calling it 'medical leave,' but the woman had a *baby*. She's not going to come back to work for you."

"Then, it's settled," Dolly said. "Slim needs an assistant and Gogo—*ahem*, Margo—needs a job. The two of you shall work together, like the Good Lord intended. This is so invigorating. I forgot how much I love charity work."

"Oh gosh, what a fun idea," Margo stuttered. She didn't know what was required of a photography assistant, but it surely demanded terrible acts of effort, the likes of which she was not fit to undertake. It was time to weasel her way out of this, and fast. "While working for Mr. Aarons would doubtless be a *delight*, I fear that I'm not the gal for the job. I have very poor arm strength, for one."

"Gogo Hightower!" Dolly gave her a gentle whack to the head. "This is not open for debate. In case you haven't noticed, your options are nil." She made a "zero" using both of her hands.

"I have *some* options," Margo protested feebly. "I can find a job in San Francisco?"

"Get real," Dolly said with a snort. "San Francisco is all finance and shipping and canning. Nothing for women, unless you want to apply to be a chambermaid in one of my hotels. But honestly, you wouldn't make it through the interview process." She closed her eyes. "Gogo. *Margo*. Please see the situation for what it is. You have no money, no man. Nothing but determination and your sad little dress."

"Hey!"

"I'm not letting you turn down Slim Aarons," Dolly said and opened her eyes again. "Working for him would provide income *and* put you in rarefied air. You can't comprehend all the notables he's shot." She rattled them off. C. Z. Guest, for one, and Marilyn Monroe. Howard Hughes, Joan Collins, Gary Cooper, and every single Kennedy. The list went on and on.

"And the Pebleys?" Margo said with a gulp.

"God, no," Dolly said. "Slim's clients wouldn't invite the Pebleys to poodle-sit."

"Doll. Enough. You can cut it with the sell job," Slim said, lighting a cigarette. "If I'm going to hire a new assistant, I need a serious gal. A professional. She ain't it."

With that, Margo's hackles rose. Why did people keep insisting she wasn't serious? In addition to her flawlessly executed debutante season—*Deb of the Year, if you please*—she'd completed one full semester of higher education. All Margo wanted now was to get married, buy a house, and start a family. She was serious as death. "Mr. Aarons, I'm a diligent and hardworking person," Margo said, uncertain why she felt obliged to defend herself with this very rumpled man. "I attended *college*."

"Interior design school," Dolly said, unnecessarily. "Also, you quit last month."

Slim chuckled and Margo began to panic. One disgrace per day was more than enough, and now she was about to be rejected for a job she didn't want.

"I had every intention of finishing," Margo said. "But there were unforeseen circumstances." Namely, her first semester check had bounced, as had the second, and she returned to campus after Christmas break to find the college bursar and a luggage trolley in her room. Margo's roommate—Crim's sister—witnessed the scene, which might've explained at least some of what'd just happened at the B&T.

"I'm responsible," Margo went on. "In addition to being

very dedicated to my studies, I spent my entire life looking after horses. Other people's horses," she hastened to add, since she only ever leased them, though one could argue that made her *more* dependable.

"Admittedly, my friend isn't presenting the most compelling case," Dolly said, stepping between them. "But Gogo has what it takes. You like your girls to blend in, right? I've seen this one mix it up with royalty and the social elite. She'd be equally as comfortable with the Duke of Windsor as with Truman Capote, or George Hamilton, or Paul Newman."

Margo peeped over Dolly's shoulder. "I'm sorry, did you say Paul Newman?"

"I love ya, Doll, but your friend doesn't read as especially 'interested,'" Slim said.

"Hold on a minute…" Margo pressed her lips together. Perhaps there *was* a solution in all this, something she could untangle from the horrors of genuine industry. Accepting this job would prove to Crim that she was serious. Better yet, if Slim Aarons truly hobnobbed with the Beautiful People, maybe she'd find a better, richer man. Margo inhaled and stepped around Dolly. "This sounds like a tremendous opportunity," she said. "I'd be honored to work for you, Mr. Aarons."

Slim's jaw dropped, more theatrically than Margo deemed warranted. She'd offered to *help*, not light his house on fire. "I don't recall asking you," he said, measuredly, fixing his glacier blue eyes on her face. The color was intense, like radiation. "Also, I sense you'd be a liability. So, thanks, but no thanks."

Rita groaned. "Good God, Slim! Gogo is what you've been looking for. Plus, she has Dolly's stamp of approval. What else do you need?"

"That's true. I'll vouch for her," Dolly piped in. "I'll vouch for Gogo Hightower any day of the week."

"Margo," she reminded everyone.

"Stop being such a bullheaded monster," Rita said.

Slim glanced at his wife and his shoulders loosened. His face was one-third less outraged. This Rita character clearly wielded great influence. Margo would have to remember that.

Slim smoked the rest of his cigarette before continuing. "Can you wake up in the morning?" he asked.

Margo rattled her head. "Um. Yes. I do it every day."

"Can you tolerate hours in the sun?" The answer was no, but Margo nodded eagerly. "If you work for me," Slim went on, "there will be travel but no time for leisure. That means no tennis, no hair appointments, no minibar tabs. No shopping, no dry cleaning, no days off, no boyfriends, no sightseeing, no cameras." He lit another cigarette. "You're not going to run off on me, are you?"

"Never." Margo smiled tightly. She would absolutely *run off* the first chance she got.

"Her boyfriend left her high and dry," Dolly said. "Her stepfather blew the family fortune. She can't run off because she doesn't have any money, or anywhere to go."

"Hmm. I do prefer to hire people who are a bit desperate," Slim mused, and Margo wanted to melt into the floor. "Listen, kiddo." He pushed himself from the counter. "Working isn't a death sentence. Even the best families run into money troubles on occasion. I admire what you're doing. Most people in your position would off themselves instead of taking a real job."

"Haven't ruled it out."

"You're hired," Slim announced, thwacking one of his big, meaty mitts on her shoulder. It was like being slapped with a porterhouse steak. Meanwhile, Rita Aarons clapped and whooped.

Margo didn't know whether she was happy or sad. Mostly she was grateful, if not a little afraid, wondering what the hell she'd just gotten herself into.

4

Margo stared up at the hotel, mouth hanging open, no words to say. Slim had relocated her, and was footing the bill, but he'd failed to mention Margo would be staying on the *other* side of the bridge.

Though it had Palm Beach in its name, *West* Palm Beach was a different bag altogether—a place for teachers and tradesmen, just as Dolly had said. Whereas Henry Flagler had developed Palm Beach for plutocrats to vacation in privacy, he'd created West Palm Beach for the help.

"What's wrong, kid?" Slim asked and lit one of his ever-present cigarettes. "Not good enough for ya? The Pennsylvania Hotel is very nice. Advertises itself as 'Breakers West.' It was *the* place to be in the twenties."

Margo glowered. *Breakers West?* Fat chance of that. And the twenties happened four decades ago. "It's splendid," Margo croaked. She was in no position to complain. "But how am I going to get to work if Palm Beach is over...there?" She gazed forlornly across the water, toward the *right* side of the lake.

"There's a bus," Slim said, and it was all Margo could do not to weep.

"Okey doke!" she said, trying to appear full of mirth and not terror. "Can't wait to see the inside! Thanks for the ride. I'll take it from here." Slim offered to help with the luggage, but Margo might as well get used to a life without bellmen and porters.

She bid Slim farewell and limped toward the entrance, suitcases in hand. With its elegant ivory facade and manicured grounds, the hotel seemed decent, and its beautifully tiled mezzanine did whisper of some prior heyday. But it didn't take long to spot the blemishes—threadbare rugs, scuffed marble, narrow, dimly lit halls, and her room, however tidy, possessed all the charm of a cardboard box.

Margo released her suitcases to the ground and plopped onto the bed, which could've doubled as a wooden plank. This was a ghastly situation, but she'd have to make the best of it. Dolly was right. Margo had no options, and Slim Aarons might be her only chance to claw her way into high society, into the good life he shot.

With every drop of her soul, Margo *believed* her rightful place was among these people, whether on the arm of Crim Pebley, or somebody else. It's what newspapers, friends, even her mom had been saying her whole life. No matter what it took, Margo would make herself invaluable, first to Slim, and then to everyone else in his orbit, and return to the path on which she belonged.

5

Margo met Slim outside the Everglades Pharmacy on her first day of work.

"Good afternoon," she said. "Lovely day, isn't it?"

"What in God's name are you wearing?" he barked.

Margo glanced down. Breezy professionalism had been the idea, but apparently white silk culottes and a matching short-sleeved jacket didn't cut it, despite the lively coral blouse poking out from underneath. "Is this not appropriate?" she asked, deflating.

"You look like an eighteenth-century sailor boy. Hold on a minute. Are those *stockings*?" He leaned down to examine her legs. "For the love of Christ, not even Jackie Kennedy wears hosiery in Palm Beach!"

Red spilled across Margo's cheeks. She had not anticipated such sartorial scrutiny from a man who'd worn a moth-bitten blazer two days in a row. "I apologize if I hit the wrong note," Margo said as she adjusted the bobby pins in her criminally straight hair. "I tried my best. This outfit was rather spendy, for the record."

"I don't give a damn about the price tag," Slim said. "You're supposed to blend in, be part of the crowd. That's the key to this gig." He slid a cigarette between his teeth.

Grimacing, Margo remembered the advice Dolly had given last night on the phone. *Be uncommonly helpful. Don't be afraid to break a sweat.* "Thank you for the reminder. Would you like me to hold something?" she asked, gesturing to the silver suitcase in Slim's left hand. He also had a blue-and-white-striped canvas bag beneath his right arm.

"I prefer to carry my own equipment."

"Oh. Okay." *Don't forget to smile, so you don't come across as so perpetually bewildered.* "Let me know if you change your mind!" *And for God's sake, Gogo, know when to shut up.* Instead of speaking another word, Margo smiled, stretching her lips as far as they would go.

"Are you alright?" Slim asked, craning. "You look as though you have a bad case of gas."

All at once, Margo's face fell. She'd been at this job ninety seconds and was a certified wreck. The *San Francisco Examiner* called her "charming" on three separate occasions, but where was that charm now? Maybe it'd vanished, along with her money, social standing, and everything else. "I'm fine," she said to the ground. "Just peachy."

"Glad to hear it. Now that we have that out of the way, it's time to work." Slim jerked his head to the left. "Come on. Let's stroll."

⸺

"No lights, no props, no stylists, no problems," Slim said as they hurried along, past the boutiques and art galleries and jewelry stores. Worth Avenue was considered the most affluent shopping street in existence, with the best of New York, London, Paris, and Rome, all in one place. But Margo didn't have time to browse. Slim was over a foot taller, and she needed to take three or four steps for every one of his.

"I work in natural light only," Slim continued. "If it's good enough for Rembrandt, it's good enough for me. Also, I never use makeup people, and I don't spend a nickel on retouching." For someone who chronicled the Beautiful People, his process was exceedingly bare-bones. In addition to the no-makeup, no-hairdresser business, Slim carried only his Leica, a few lenses, and a light meter.

"And what will we be shooting?" Margo asked, quickening her pace. As they flew by Saks, she peeked inside to see a woman trying on a blue mink over pink Bermuda shorts. "Portraits of important people?"

"Portraits?" Slim stopped abruptly. He seemed offended, but Margo couldn't work out why. "Anyone can do a portrait. I'm a *storyteller.* People hire me because I understand them. I'm able to show the world how they imagine themselves to be."

"Oh. Okay," Margo said, still befuddled.

"I'm an *environmental* photographer," he went on, "which means I shoot my subjects in their natural habitats—their offices, or living rooms, or gardens. By the pool or on the golf course. Accompanied by their goddamnned dogs. My photography reveals something about the subject through their background. It represents not only how they want to be seen by the world but their literal place in it. You can look at one of my pictures and know it was taken in Palm Beach, or Bermuda, or Mexico."

Margo grinned, genuinely this time. "That all sounds *wonderful,*" she said. "So many photographers these days seem fixated on torturing the world with visions of desperate children or pets."

"I've had enough of that," Slim said. "I started my career as a combat photographer. I've seen concentration camps and bombed-out villages. I've been shot at, and slept in the mud. Now I prefer to stay on the sunny side of the street."

Margo's smile spread. Maybe everything would be fine.

"Well, here we are," Slim said.

Margo looked up at the familiar, British Colonial–inspired facade and froze. "We're shooting *here*?" she said as all prior cheer whooshed out of her. "At the Colony?" This had the makings of a proper nightmare. Margo wanted to come back, but not so soon, or as anyone's *employee*. People who saw her get dumped were probably lunching beside the pool at that very moment.

Slim released the world's heaviest sigh. "We're shooting a patio fashion show. Is this going to be a problem, Miss Hightower?"

"No." Margo vigorously shook her head. "No problem at all."

"Good. I need to be able to rely on you," he said. "I need to trust you because my clients trust *me*. They see me as one of them, which is how I'm able to get into places that don't ordinarily allow photographers. The Colony, for example. The Everglades Club. They invite me to their parties and into their homes. Without trust, we have nothing."

"You can trust me," Margo said. "I'll do my job perfectly. I'll blend right in."

He scanned her outfit again, dubious. "One last thing," he said. "I'm a perfectionist and working for me will not be easy. You're going to love me and you're going to hate me, depending on the week. In the end, the good *should* outweigh the bad, but I can't make any promises. We'll have to see when we get there."

6

They stood beside the kidney-shaped pool. As Slim surveyed the scene, Margo shifted from one foot to the other, waiting for instructions as the sun beat down. Ten minutes in, she was covered in sweat and had a pebble in her shoe.

"First reaction," Slim said, and Margo threw him a confused look. "Oh, for Christ's sake. What do you *see*? Do you have any sense for a scene?"

"Well, I only just started..."

Despite the mirrored aviator sunglasses, Margo could tell Slim was rolling his eyes. "This isn't difficult, Miss Hightower," he said. "Use your *eyeballs* and find something for the lens to latch on to. Does anything or anyone catch your attention?"

Margo wasn't a big ogler, but she'd do her best. "Let's see..." she said, taking in their surroundings, from the white tablecloths to the white rattan chairs, to the temporary runway on the other side of the pool. Beyond the stage and beside a flagpole, a dark-haired woman in a navy blue bikini sat on a lounger, sipping champagne. She had a nice figure, and an even nicer life, from what Margo could tell.

"Her," Margo said, pointing listlessly as she ached for what might've been, what could be still, if she played this right.

"That's who I noticed, too," Slim said, already zipping across the patio, arm extended. The woman stiffened when he first introduced himself, but soon softened into his smiles and charm. Slim waved Margo over and they got to work.

Could Margo move the chair forward two inches? Scooch the silver champagne bucket back? Place the umbrella a foot to the left? *Wait*, put it three and a half inches to the right. Straighten all the silver clips keeping the tablecloths in place.

"Won't the tables be out of the shot?" Margo asked, and Slim once again rolled his eyes.

"What did I say about backgrounds?" he groused. "*Environmental* photography?"

Margo decided it was best to heed Dolly's advice and shut up.

Slim instructed the woman to lie on her hip so the sun hit her legs at the best angle. He borrowed a pink cloche from a lady eating a diced shrimp salad and plopped it onto the model's head. "Dangle your arm over the back of your chair," he told a man in a white jacket, soon to be known as one of the background elements.

As the model reapplied her lipstick, Slim untucked a corner of her blue-and-pink towel and draped it from her chair. After each modification, he stepped back and sized it all up, then tinkered with everything six or seven more times. This must've been what Slim meant when he called himself a perfectionist.

While Slim shot, Margo got to the hard work of standing around while avoiding sweating to death. He'd been right about the pantyhose, and the *sailor-boy costume*, which was now soaked through. Margo scuttled backward, inch by inch, until she reached the shade of the patio. Using a nearby chair, she removed the rock from her shoe, then closed her eyes in sweet relief.

"Hey, Jimmy," said a voice. "You didn't tell me you were bringing a date."

"Gotta love the Colony. They won't put a water glass on your table unless you beg, but they'll stock it with a pretty girl."

Margo's eyes flew open. In front of her stood three trim, pleasing men—two in lemon-colored trousers, one in pink. They were attempting to sit at the very table she was presently leaning against.

"I'm sorry!" Margo said and jumped. "I wasn't..." Her voice trailed off. As the men took their seats, Margo inspected their hands. No wedding rings. She smiled, pushing back chunks of her damp, sweaty hair.

"I'm never going to complain about a cute girl," one of the men said. He sized her up, and an inquisitive smile crept across his face, as though he remembered meeting her but couldn't place where.

"My name's Margo, by the way," she said, praying none of them knew Sibley or Dean, or had attended their wedding. The men didn't seem visibly mortified on her behalf, which was a good sign. "Do you guys live around here? I'm from California, but I like Palm Beach so much I just might stay!" She giggled nervously as the men exchanged baffled glances. All those debutante lessons and not one about how to flirt under a time crunch.

"We'd love for you to join us," one of the men said. "But, er..." He peered over his shoulder. "I think someone wants you?"

Margo looked up and spotted Slim on the other side of the pool. He was red-faced and screaming her name. After a hasty goodbye, she clambered back across the patio, embarrassed and furious and mystified as to how proper working folks kept jobs from interfering with their lives.

"You don't have to keep telling me you're sorry," Slim said as he heaved his silver suitcase onto a table. "Next time you need shade, tell me first. From my vantage point, it looked as though you were flirting."

"Ha. Never!" Margo quacked. She'd been apologizing on and off for the past ninety minutes. But now the fashion show was over, the woman in the blue bikini was gone, and Slim no longer seemed peeved. Margo was ready to put this long, awkward afternoon in the rearview mirror.

"I'm curious," Slim said as he rooted around in his case. "What made you choose interior design school?"

Margo mulled this over. "I suppose it was the desire to make my world beautiful," she said, and this felt true enough. "I liked learning about patterns and surfaces and repetition of themes. How to turn an ordinary room into something the neighbors would envy." Also, what else was Margo going to do? She couldn't see herself as a teacher or nurse.

"All good reasons." Slim snapped his case shut. "I think we're all set for the day. Hopefully there will be one or two decent ones. Guess we'll see when they come back from the darkroom."

Margo shivered. Just thinking of a darkroom cooled her by ten degrees.

As they skirted the pool on their way back to the hotel, Slim asked Margo how she'd liked her first day of work.

"How was my first day," Margo repeated, an old trick from her debutante days. It gave you time to come up with a response. Unfortunately, she didn't have one. Phrases like *overwhelmed*, *physically depleted*, and *moderately confounded* all came to mind. "Well, Slim." She took in a breath. "It was fantastic. I can't wait to see what's next." Dolly would be so proud of her shiny attitude, and that she made it through her first day without dissolving into the concrete.

"Glad to hear it," Slim said with a smile probably best categorized as a smirk. "And if you thought that was terrific, you're in for a treat. Tomorrow we have a party at Lilly and Peter Pulitzer's house."

"As in the prize?" Margo said, after chewing on this for a second. She understood she was meant to be impressed but wasn't sure why.

"Well, yes. But no one thinks about them that way. Peter's not even in publishing." As they walked through the lobby, Slim gave her some context. Instead of joining the family business, Peter had dropped out of Stanford to buy and run a liquor store and bowling alley, which he later sold, investing the proceeds into several hundred vacant acres along the Florida coast. When the federal government purchased a large swath of this land to build I-95, Peter was left with a fat bank account and a four-hundred-acre citrus grove. Oranges were his primary business now.

As successful as Peter was, his wife, Lilly, was the true family gold mine. Her mother was an oil heiress, and her stepfather an heir to Carnegie Steel. Together her parents had the largest real estate holdings in South Florida.

"You can't get any higher than the Phippses in Palm Beach," Slim said. "Around here, there's a real divide between the Old Guard and the new, and the Phipps family is the only one that dominates both, with Peter and Lilly the top dogs of the younger, hipper set. They're the Bohemians, the swingers, the perpetual good time. The island's very own Tarzan and Jane."

"They live *here*?" Margo said. *Tarzan and Jane* sounded wild, but most people she'd seen so far were quite buttoned-up. "In Palm Beach?"

Slim chuckled. "Oh, Gogo Hightower, you have much to learn."

"It's Margo, actually…"

"Peter and Lilly Pulitzer don't merely live here. They *are* Palm Beach."

7

The Pulitzers' two-story yellow clapboard house didn't seem like much from the road, but the interior was sprawling, a chaotic riot of color, chinoiserie, and kitsch.

Victorian wicker lived beside Asian screens in rooms carpeted with fiery Spanish rugs. Each nook and alcove they passed defied everything Margo had learned about room composition in her point-five years of school. This must've been what her professor meant by a departure from postwar decorative restraint.

Slim and Margo cut through a dining room. Its main features were ceramic elephants, papier-mâché parrots, and a veranda that faced Lake Worth. In the living room, beside a wet bar, a dapper, dark-haired man played a grand piano. Margo was one toe out the door when she did a double take, nearly toppling a plaster cat in the process. "Is that...?"

Slim bobbed his head. Dutch Elkin—the band leader and newest, hottest man on the scene. Dutch and his ten-piece orchestra played New York's St. Regis supper club five nights per week, and gossips loved his tragic backstory—orphaned as a newborn and adopted, Daddy Warbucks style—as well as the fact that he was so damned attractive. The Pulitzers must've been big-time if Dutch Elkin entertained at their afternoon parties.

"Try to keep pace," Slim said, and Margo glanced back, accidentally catching Dutch's eye. He winked but kept playing.

They walked into the kitchen, which was all whirring blenders and cigarette smoke and booming conversation. Five women in flipped bobs sat in a leather banquette, firing off barbs and bon mots and complaints.

My gardener didn't come this morning. Third time in a row!

Is anyone making martinis?

I despise what the Jet Age has done to travel. Now all sorts of curious people can afford to come here for the winter!

A lady in white sunglasses and a very serious beehive opened a refrigerator stocked with only champagne. She grabbed a bottle and passed it to a group lounging on an exotic, Moroccan-inspired couch-bed. A dog lapped noisily from an oversize porcelain bowl nearby, splashing water across the floor.

Two little girls with sun-streaked hair ran past, followed by a tall, deeply bronzed woman in hot pink pants and a matching headscarf. Margo was so shocked by the woman's bare feet that she almost missed the black-and-white animal perched on her shoulder. She let out a small, squeaky scream, but only Slim turned to look.

"Was that a *monkey*?" Margo said, a hand over her thundering heart.

"His name is Goony," Slim replied, casual as every day. "He's a colobus. Let's head outside." He nodded toward the patio. "We have some people to shoot."

—

As Slim used his great height to periscope over the crowd, Margo waited for direction, her heels sinking into the grass. Today she wore a red broadcloth patio dress with a red-and-white gingham ruffle, which was marginally better than the

sailor-boy fiasco, but only by degrees. Unfortunately, she didn't
have a surfeit of options.

Studying this backyard overgrown with banyan trees, ferns,
and fat, lush gardenias, Margo realized the only group she
blended in with was the mariachi band. Until this week, she'd
never considered what living in San Francisco had done to her
fashion education. Margo could wear the hell out of a coat, but
this was a land of pink dresses and flimsy sandals and even bare
feet. Dolly always said that West Coast society was more fun,
but Margo questioned how well she really knew Palm Beach.

"Are you looking for anyone in particular?" Margo asked
Slim, raising one foot and another as two hedgehogs trooped
by. Standing around for hours seemed to be the crux of this
job, and while Margo wasn't looking to break her back or anything, she didn't want to be bored out of her skull.

"Yes and no," he answered, ever helpful.

Slim moved deeper into the party, and Margo followed, her
eyes glued to the grass, and the animal feces and rotted man-
goes littering the ground. When he reached the middle of
the lawn, Slim removed the camera from its case and slung it
around his neck.

"What do you see?" Slim said. "Give me your two cents."

"Um..." Margo said, squinting into the crowd, recalling
what he'd taught her at the Colony. *The trick is finding something
for the lens to latch on to...what draws your eye.* In the sunlit haze
of white sunglasses and light, floaty clothes, one person stood
out. It was the woman from the kitchen, with the monkey and
spill of black velvet hair.

"Her. In the pink pants," Margo said. "The one on the patio,
swaying to the band." Objectively, she wasn't the most beautiful woman at the party, but she was tall, and assured, and threw
off an energy, a magnetism nobody else did.

"Got it on the first try. *Again.*" Slim fiddled with a something or other before continuing. "This is why it's helpful to have someone like you by my side. The right kind of girl can appreciate other women far better than a man ever could."

"Thanks," Margo said, warily. "But it wasn't hard. Do you know her name?"

"Oh, Miss Hightower. Despite your best efforts, sometimes you really do announce yourself as a yokel," Slim said, shaking his head. "*Of course* I know her name. Everyone does. That, my dear, is Lilly Pulitzer." He lifted the camera and the shutter clicked.

8

Lilly danced through the crowd. Spinning and flitting, she pulled each person in for a hug and a kiss before releasing them back into the swell. From Dorothy Spreckels Munn to Alice Topping to Marjorie Merriweather Post, Margo tried to remember the names as Slim fired them off.

Even from a distance, Lilly's personality was as overflowing and abundant as her hair, and people shone with delight whenever she approached. "Hello, girls!" she called to a group, waggling a hand overhead. She swiped three pigs in a blanket from a silver tray and complained to the universe that she's constantly dieting, *but it never works!* Slim kept shooting, yet Lilly didn't notice.

After making her rounds, Lilly plunked down, alone, at a table festooned with abandoned wineglasses. She lit a cigarette, and it smoldered in her hand, unsmoked, as she stared out toward the water, her pink headscarf flapping in the breeze. Her expression was serious and pensive, two hard dashes between her brows. Though she suddenly appeared older than her thirty or so years, Lilly was undeniably pretty with her thick bangs, deep tan, and sun-kissed cheeks.

"She's probably waiting for her husband," Slim said, when he caught Margo gawking. Peter was due to arrive from his orange groves, and usually landed his seaplane with a great splash beside the dock. Women around here agreed Peter Pulitzer was *divine*, easily the dreamiest man in Palm Beach. "Even Rita has the hots for him," Slim added as he leaped up onto a chair. He lifted the camera, targeting Lilly again.

At last, she clocked him. "Slim!" Lilly shouted and stubbed out her cigarette. "Get off my furniture!" Slim snapped away and Lilly raised both middle fingers. "How do you like this angle?"

"Excellent!"

"Do you ever put that blasted thing down?"

"Not when there's a perfect subject right in front of me."

"Your taste is extremely questionable," she said. "I'm just a frumpy old Palm Beach matron."

Margo couldn't believe her ears. *Frumpy?* This from the woman who exceeded her half of the Tarzan-and-Jane persona. Margo peered down at her flat chest and pale legs. Why did her mother and the *Examiner* let her think she was such a hot number?

"I'm going to ban cameras from my house," Lilly said as she pushed herself up from the table. "Photographers, too."

"I don't like photographers, either," Slim yelled back. "That's why I'm a storyteller."

"You're so full of it!" Lilly said with a laugh. She whirled around and stamped across the lawn, toward a diminutive brunette in a white-and-pink-striped top.

"That's Flo Smith," Slim said as Lilly wrapped an arm around the woman's waist. "She's a former model, and a close friend of Jack Kennedy's. They dated, way back when. You should write this all down when you get back to the hotel. You need to keep track of these people."

According to Slim, Flo's husband, E. T., was once ambassador to Cuba but his chief calling was as a member of Palm Beach's most coveted golfing foursome. "The initialed ones" consisted of E. T., the VP (Johnson), the AG (Bobby Kennedy), and of course, JFK. Almost everyone Slim named that afternoon was a *former* something, but he never said what any of them did now.

As Slim stalked closer to the women, Lilly tugged on the brim of Flo's straw hat. Their faces weren't visible, and Margo spent several minutes trying to figure out why Slim was still shooting, until she finally absorbed the whole composition. Flo's stripes, Lilly's scarf, and the pool stretched out behind them. The dappled greens and blues on the water matched the colors of Lilly's tunic. Everything in perfect harmony.

A certain knowing crashed over Margo like a wave. Already Slim had opened her eyes, to this house, these people, this pool shaded by orange trees. Why would anyone choose New York, or Crim Pebley, God forbid, when they could live carefree and in perpetual summer like the Pulitzers in Palm Beach? *This* was the life Margo wanted, and if bare feet and monkeys were acceptable, maybe they'd be more forgiving of a failed debutante from the West Coast.

9

Antoinette picked up on the third ring. "LaSalle residence," she said, and Margo winced. How could it be the *LaSalle* residence, when LaSalle had flown the coop?

"Hi, Mom," Margo said, steadying her breath, swallowing away the lump in her throat.

"Oh. Hello." Antoinette sounded confused, as though she was trying to pair a face and a name. "How are you?"

It was the strangest ordinary question Margo had ever been asked. "I'm doing well," she lied. "Sorry it took me so long to call. You were probably expecting me home by now?" It'd been ten days. Ten days that were nothing and forever at the same time.

"You never mentioned when you were going to return," she said. There was a hollowness in Antoinette's voice, like she'd been sapped of all sentiment and thought. Then again, maybe the emptiness was literal, the echo of a home stripped bare. Even though it'd been more than six months, Margo could still see the advertisement in the *Examiner.*

LIQUIDATION SALE
PRIVATE ART COLLECTION
Priced for Quick Sale

I just want to gauge the interest level, Antoinette had said at the time. *See how much we could bring in if we need to sell a few items.* But then friends and strangers traipsed through and bought it all, picking up Margo's life on the cheap while she wept upstairs like a child. These were only *things*, but growing up alone, in that quiet, drafty house, she'd imagined the statues as pets, the girls in the paintings as friends. *The Sisters* once hung over her bed, its doe-eyed girls in white staring down, the little sister with an arm around the bigger sister's neck. It felt like a promise, a hope.

"Sorry if I forgot to mention my travel plans," Margo said now, despite knowing she hadn't forgotten a thing. When it came to Antoinette LaSalle, it was easier to play along. "Anyhow." She took in a big drink of air. "I wanted to tell you… I'm going to be in Palm Beach a bit longer than planned."

Margo expelled the rest of the story in one long stream. *Crim and I broke up and I took a job as a photographer's assistant and it's going swimmingly which is why I haven't had a chance to call.* "It's so much more tolerable than I expected!" Margo chirped. "Slim Aarons is very talented, albeit crotchety at times. But I'm learning a lot and he shoots *all* the most important people. Not only in Palm Beach but around the world." *Breathe, Margo, breathe.* "It's amazing that a grump who talks with his hands and doesn't have an inside voice can be so widely considered brilliant!" Margo hesitated, entertaining the possibility that Antoinette might've fallen asleep. "Mom. Did you hear me?" she asked, just to be sure. "I've taken a job and the engagement is off."

"Yes, I heard." Her mother yawned. "Honestly, Gogo, was the engagement ever really on? Did you even have a ring?"

"Not technically. No matter, I think it's the best thing that could've happened to me. I've learned that it's a *much wider field*, if you know what I mean." Margo nearly had herself convinced.

"Hmm. We'll see. Though it's not all that difficult to do

better than Crim Pebley. Listen, I'm glad you called. What do you want me to do with your things?"

"My *things*?" Margo asked. "What things?"

"Your clothes and books. I sold the house. You need to get it all out."

The information stopped Margo cold. It couldn't be. She must've misheard. "You sold our house? Tell me that's not true."

"It is," she said, sleepily.

"But. Wait. You can't." Margo could barely get the words out. "Why? It's all we had left." All they had left of her dad, was what she meant. He'd died in the war, when Margo was a baby, and Antoinette hadn't kept anything to remember him by. Not a dog tag or photograph or sweet tale. Margo's only connection to this ghost of a man was the home he once owned, and that would be gone, too, because of Sandy. She wanted to scream.

"You're acting like a child," Antoinette said.

"That was our home. Where are we going to live?" Margo's pulse boomed in her ears. San Francisco had been her backup plan, the worst-case scenario. Regardless of what happened, she could go home and regroup. Margo didn't love living with her mom, but Sandy was gone, which was an improvement. If everything went to shit, where would she go?

"*I'm* moving in with Sandy's sister," Antoinette said. "Until he clears up this mess and gets back on his feet."

Margo twisted her mouth, wondering about these feet. Though Antoinette blamed their recent financial and social difficulties on Sandy's federal indictment, the ground had long been shaky, his stance perpetually unstable. They pretended otherwise, but Margo knew the score. She didn't miss the small clues, like her mother's effortful flashiness. Antoinette always wore more makeup and jewels than everyone else, as though trying to prove something.

"Mom. Let's think about this for a moment. I'm earning

money right now." How much, Margo didn't exactly know, but she had to do *something*. "Do you want me to ask Dolly for the name of her lawyer? I'll bet it's not too late to back out of the sale."

"Margo. Knock it off," Antoinette said. "You're a grown woman. You need to figure out your situation on your own." She exhaled and Margo could practically hear her rub her tired, sagging face. "I'm sorry, but selling the house is my only option. Lawyers are expensive and I must defend these scurrilous accusations against your father."

"Not my father," Margo said. For more than a decade, Antoinette had been attempting to pass Sandy off as a father figure though he was even less interested in the prospect than Margo was.

"I'm not going to argue with you," her mom snapped. "Now, please tell me where you'll be living, so I can send your stuff."

Margo felt like she'd stepped out of body and was viewing herself from a great distance. No fiancé. No money. No home. Her life had become a melodrama so absurd she almost couldn't believe it. It was all too much to take in, and the anger, hurt, and astonishment bubbled up into a laugh. "Where do I live?" Margo said. "Now *that* is the question."

"Is this amusing for you?" Antoinette said.

"It *is* funny, you have to admit." Margo wiped the tears from her eyes. Where did she live? The answer was nowhere, or maybe the Pennsylvania, but Margo couldn't have her clothes and childhood memories shipped to a West Palm Beach hotel. "Just send it to the Huntington," she said. "Dolly can store it for now."

"Easy enough," Antoinette said with another yawn. "It's getting late. I'd better go."

It was only nine o'clock in Florida, and California was three hours behind, but Margo didn't bother pointing this out. "Alright, Mother. Good luck with everything."

"Same to you," she said, and they both hung up without another word.

10

Slim had already yelled at Margo three times that day.

First, when Margo banged the car door against the curb. *If there's a dent, I'm going to dock your pay.* She then had the temerity to pick up his camera case when he preferred to carry all equipment himself. *Did I ask you to do that? I'm not an invalid!*

Now they were on Lake Trail, the tree-lined public footpath that separated Lake Worth from the swimming pools and patios of the island's grandest homes, to shoot Charlie Munn, the man known as Mr. Palm Beach. He had shown up on a bike, and when Margo wheeled it out of the way, Slim blew his lid again.

"Only you would remove a *bike* from a bike path," he griped. "What the hell did you think we were going to shoot?"

Margo drew a blank. The sunshine? Palm trees? The yachts docked along the trail? Mr. Palm Beach was seventy-plus years old and dressed head to toe in white, from his slacks to his polo shirt, to his fedora trimmed with black. That he might not be compelled to document his exercise on film did not seem unreasonable. "Something less...outdoorsy?" Margo tried.

"We are literally outdoors!" Slim said.

"I don't *have* to ride the bike," Charlie said. He passed her a sympathetic look, and Margo shriveled inside. She didn't need one of the most prominent men in Palm Beach thinking she was a dolt.

"Then, come up with an alternative!" Slim said to her.

After giving Slim a weak smile, Margo stepped onto the trail. She wasn't great with numbers, but in her estimation, there were probably fifty people ambling along, another dozen or so weaving through on bikes. When did the world get so damned crowded?

"Whatever you decide, we should get going," Charlie said. "I think it's about to rain."

They began with shots of Charlie guiding his bike down the trail for a real "how do you do, fine sir, I've just arrived" mood. As Margo led him along, she envisioned all the catastrophes that could befall them. Sprinklers might turn on or they'd get pummeled by a pedicab. Charlie would break a leg or lose a spleen and she'd ruin Palm Beach for the man who'd been coming for half a century.

Margo couldn't muff this up. She was homeless and down to her last chance. If Slim fired her, had she even earned enough to rent her own apartment? What would one cost, anyway? Margo didn't know what her salary was, or when she might be paid, and couldn't ask because money wasn't something nice people discussed. On top of all this, Dolly had personally vouched for her, and Margo refused to disappoint her.

After several back-and-forths on the path, Charlie set his bike aside. He borrowed a rod from a tourist and caught two fish from the lake. As the clouds moved in, Charlie grew anxious about the potential for rain. Weather wasn't like this in the old days, he claimed, before they started draining the Everglades. "We should wrap up," he announced. "Do you have what you need?"

"You gave me more than enough," Slim said, jovially, shaking Charlie's hand. "With you, it's always a piece of cake!"

Charlie thanked him and lunged up onto his bike. Margo crossed her arms and watched as he pedaled off, wishing that Slim might one day use some of his renowned charm on *her*. Together, they walked back to the road.

"You're awfully tetchy," Slim noted, using the hood of some-one else's car to pack up his camera and film. "I do hope you'll perk up before we arrive at our next destination."

"Two shoots in one day?" Margo said, her voice teetering. The Charlie Munn shoot had been quick, but managing Slim's perfectionism and inevitable beefs necessitated an extensive amount of mental and physical concentration, and Margo was already spent. "Where is this next shoot?" she asked. "Is it out-side? Should I bring a hat?" She peered up into the sky. It was sunny again. "What happened to Mr. Munn's clouds?"

"You won't need to worry about clouds," Slim said, as a grin stretched across his face. "Not where we're going."

"So, inside then?" Margo guessed, slack with relief.

Slim shook his head. "Even better. I'm taking you to the sunniest place in Palm Beach."

11

Behind the big, fancy shops on Worth Avenue, through a maze of interconnected courtyards, lived a world of mossy green fountains, scalloped awnings, and bougainvillea dangling from red-tiled roofs. Tucked in amid the quaint shops was a yellow door. Slim stopped in front of it and pointed to the sign overhead.

Pulitzer Groves Fruit Shop

"Peter's store?" Margo asked.

"The shop belongs to Lilly," Slim said, and flung open the door.

As they entered, Lilly was crouching nose to nose with a curly-haired white sheepdog. "SIT!" she was saying. The dog smiled and wagged its tail. "SIT… SIT… SIIIIT… Alright then, don't." Lilly hopped up. "See if I care." When she spotted Slim, her face burst into a smile. "Slim-o!" She ran over and threw her arms around him.

Margo glanced around. Impossibly, the two-room shop was more helter-skelter than Lilly's home, with candy-colored dresses dangling from the ceiling, and dozens of citrus-filled wicker baskets scattered across the floor. Green and yellow pillows were tossed about, and in the corner, two brunettes chatted on a pink couch.

"Margo?" Slim said. He and Lilly stared at her expectantly. "Are you paying attention?"

"I'm sorry." Margo rattled her head. This wasn't the first time he'd called her name. "Pardon my distraction. I was mesmerized by this fun space!" She walked toward Slim, pushing several towering paper flowers out of her way.

"As I was saying, Lilly, I'd like to introduce you to my new assistant, Gogo Hightower."

"Thank you, Jesus. Finally, he hired someone." Out of nowhere, Lilly swooped in, wrapping Margo in a tight embrace.

"It's nice to meet you," Margo said, voice muffled, her cheek squished against Lilly's breast. "My name is actually Margo."

"I'm so glad you're here," Lilly said. "Maybe Slim will stop acting like such a grump." She stepped back and flicked her waist-length, minky-black locks behind her shoulders. The front of her hair was teased into a bouffant so high she could've hidden a toddler in there. "Look at you! You're cute as a button! I love the freckles. Tell me everything. How did you come to work for Slim? What were you doing before?"

"Being a failed debutante mostly," Slim said and opened his lighter.

"Lilly is one of those," piped in one of the girls from the couch. "Never even attended a ball."

Lilly cackled. "For your information, I had a party every year, and one of those, I'm sure, was my coming-out. Debutantes are such bores anyhow." She turned back to Margo. "I'm so sorry Slim hoodwinked you into working for him. But I have a feeling you'll like it here."

Margo gave a light laugh, relaxing for the first time since

she'd arrived in Palm Beach. What she'd witnessed at the party was not a mirage. Lilly's charisma was even stronger close-up.

"And where is Tarzan today?" Slim asked as he ticked through a rack of dresses.

"Out in the wilds of Okeechobee," Lilly said and looked at Margo. "Slim thinks Pete and I are the *most* uncivilized people he's ever met. He reviles my constant lack of shoes." She stretched out a leg and wiggled her dirty toes. "Never mind all that. What can I get you?" Every word she said came out in rapid fire, and Margo could barely catch up between sentences. "I have water, and juice. There's gin somewhere. Girls!" She flipped around to face her friends. "This is Slim's new assistant, Margo. Be polite!"

"Helloooo," one of the women drawled. "I'm Wendy."

Margo needed no introduction, having recognized that sable hair and big doe eyes from the society pages. This wasn't just a girl called Wendy, but the socialite Wendy *Vanderbilt*. Margo did her best not to gape.

"Welcome to Chez Lilly," Wendy added. "Never mind the *Pulitzer* on the door."

"I've told you a thousand million times," Lilly huffed. "I am not changing the name. Who cares about Lilly, the dim housewife? Pulitzer stays."

"You're so damned stubborn. Typical Scorpio."

"And you're such a Pisces."

"You mean artistic and intuitive? Empathetic?"

"Impractical. Oblivious," Lilly said, merrily. She gestured to the second woman. "And this is my dear friend Julia Rousseau. She and her sister Bibi own Salon Français, across the way."

During her short stay at the Colony, Margo had met three different women who'd flown all the way from Texas to shop at Salon Français, which sold French ready-to-wear and custom-made clothes. Nothing had a price tag, and you weren't supposed to ask.

"Nice to meet you," Margo said, and Julia returned a blank stare.

"Don't mind her. She's in a state," Lilly said. "It's not personal. Let me get you a drink."

Lilly scuttled to the back of the shop to cut up some oranges. As Slim wandered, Margo studied the birdcage-shaped bamboo dress racks that hung from the ceiling. Each one held a dozen or so sleeveless shifts in every color under the Palm Beach sun— blue dresses with plumerias, red dresses with hibiscuses, and large white seashells set against orange-and-red stripes.

"You're going to love our juice," Lilly called out. "The Indian River citrus district has the best oranges and grapefruit on the planet." She took a bite of an orange and watched as the juice dribbled down her wrist. "Checking out the merchandise, are you?" she said when she noticed Margo browsing. "Snag any dress you want. On the house!"

Margo smiled, unable to imagine wearing one of these confections on the briny, foggy San Francisco streets. Not that she'd be returning to San Francisco anytime soon. "Sorry if this is a silly question," Margo said, "but do you sell these dresses? The sign outside says it's a fruit shop."

Slim looked up sharply from where he stood near the window, but Lilly saved her with a rich, generous laugh.

"Slim hasn't told you anything, has he?" She walked back to the couch and wedged herself between Wendy and Julia. "It started with fruit, but eventually my little enterprise took on a life of its own. The story is a *hoot*."

After giving birth to three children in four years, Lilly explained, by age twenty-five she wasn't doing much. Though she adored her babies, Lilly had to wonder, was this all there was to life? The tedium of motherhood threw her for a loop.

"I wasn't sleeping," she said, "I wasn't eating—admittedly this had its advantages—but my parents and husband were beside themselves with worry, and they sent me off for a Bloomingdale's cure. Precisely what I needed."

Wendy bobbed her head with great understanding, but Margo was all turned around. Bloomingdale's? How did shopping fit into this? Julia must've been confused, too, because she'd replaced Slim at the window, and was staring through it, brow furrowed.

"At Bloomingdale's, they told me to get a hobby," Lilly continued. "Peter always has more fruit than he knows what to do with and I thought to myself..." She lifted a finger. "Deluxe fruit baskets!"

Soon Lilly was trucking around in a beat-up station wagon, delivering her wares and befriending every maid, butler, and cook in Palm Beach. They raked in thirty thousand clams in two months and Peter's surplus was solved. He convinced her to open this shop, where Lilly was struck by another idea.

"Not all fruits are pretty enough for a basket, so I took to selling the juice from the bruised ones," Lilly said. "Two business lines in one go. How do you like that? Pretty impressive for someone with such a pea brain. Anyway, it's all been such a kick. Work is so much fun, don't you think?"

Was work fun? Margo asked herself. This didn't seem right, but Lilly *was* happy. She was effervescent, positively bubbling with life. Maybe she was onto something.

"In typical fashion," Lilly prattled on, "I solved one problem, and a new one reared its head."

Juicing was murder on Lilly's clothes. Tired of slumping around stained like a slob, she bought out the five-and-dime's inventory of loud fabrics and asked her seamstress to whip up some dresses. Nothing fancy—two side seams, two darts, and three holes, the same frock every girl learned to make in home ec. She was only camouflaging her own clumsiness, but before long, Flo Smith wanted one, likewise her pal Dysie.

"When I asked Peter if I could hang a few in the shop to sell, he told me to make eighty. I told *him* he was out of his mind," Lilly said with a giggle. "But I did as he suggested, and it took off like zingo. Especially once Jackie Kennedy was photographed wearing one."

"The First Lady?" Margo snuck a peek at one of the racks, struggling to imagine Jackie Kennedy in a bold daisy print.

"Lil made it out of an old curtain," Wendy said. "Imagine if fancy pants knew."

Lilly sprang to her feet. "Oh, Jacks wouldn't care. We've been thick as thieves since we were girls. She's much more fun—and naughtier—than the press makes her out to be." She swished past Margo and resumed juicing. "Slim!" she hollered, pouring out two small paper cups. He poked his head out of a storage room, like a burglar seeing if the coast was clear. "Juice is on!"

Slim marched across the store, and finished the drink in one gulp. He returned to his hiding place and Lilly beckoned Margo over, Dixie cup outstretched. "Delicious," Margo said, after taking a sip. The citrus pinched her tongue. As she took another, Julia let out a torrent of curse words. She shouted something in Spanish, hit the window with both hands, and stormed out of the shop.

"Poor dear," Lilly clucked, shaking her head. "Her husband is one of the Cubans trying to overthrow Castro. She's a tad stressed because she hasn't heard from him since he left for training in Central America. But you know how revolutions go. They always last longer than expected."

Margo nodded, despite not knowing how they went at all. Was this the Bay of Pigs debacle she'd overheard Palm Beach men complain about when she was staying at the Colony? It was somehow tied to the president's inexperience and bravado and his tendency to play both sides. Margo didn't follow. Mainly, she was struck by the fact that everyone in Palm Beach claimed to be friends with Kennedy but none voted for him.

"I keep telling Jules," Lilly said, "nobody should fret about Enrique Rousseau. He's the type to get into a million scrapes but end up fine, like an aristocrat from a Nancy Mitford novel."

"Listen, gals, I hate to break up a party," Slim said as he emerged once more from the storage closet. "But I was hoping that my assistant might provide some...what do you call it...*assistance?*"

Margo had been so wrapped up in Lilly's story, she'd forgotten they were there to work. "What do you need?" she said, hurrying over. Slim handed her a curly pink wig and told her to haul a tan wicker mannequin onto the shop floor.

"That'll never fit you," Wendy joked as Slim yanked a pink-and-white rose print from a rack.

He didn't acknowledge Wendy's crack. "A little to the left," he said as Margo pushed the mannequin into a beam of sunlight. "Back two inches. Bring over that basket of fruit." After getting the mannequin into place, Slim guided the rose dress over its head. He added the wig and a pair of pink earrings he'd fished out of a tray of enamel jewelry.

That large red flower? Stick it behind the couch. Put the nesting dolls on the coffee table, on the corner. Margo followed each instruction and waited for the next. By now, she understood that Slim knew what he wanted, and wouldn't stop until it was perfect, no matter how many hours it took.

"Okay, Lil, time for you to get in the picture," he said at last.

"Absolutely not. You told me you were photographing the *shop*. I'm so bloated today." Lilly patted her stomach as if to prove something. Unlike her two friends, she wasn't wafer-thin, but Margo never understood the appeal of skinniness. She'd love to have curves instead of being the sort of girl who would forever pray for her boobs and hips to grow in.

"I shoot people first, and places second," Slim said. "What are you so worried about? I've never made a woman look bad."

"The man has a point," Wendy offered.

Sighing, Lilly slipped into a pair of gold sandals. "You do seem to get us somehow," she said. "Fine. But this gal is going to block most of me." She stepped behind the mannequin and wrapped both arms around its waist.

"Excellent," Slim said. "All you have to do is stand there. Your face will do the rest."

Lilly threw back her shoulders. She stood perfectly erect with her lips pursed, her eyes daring Slim to make a wrong move.

Slim began to raise the camera to his face but then stopped. "Hmm," he said, pondering. "Hmm."

Margo saw it, too. Lilly was beautiful, but in danger of being dulled by the vibrancy of the shop. She needed something *more* to stand out among it all.

"I was thinking," Margo said, and Slim looked at her with great alarm. "Maybe if we…?" She put both hands on her hips and felt the tube of lipstick she'd hidden in the front pocket of her Bermuda shorts. "What about a swipe of this?" she said, holding up a tube of watermelon pink. Was it gauche to share lipstick? Probably, but not as gauche as telling another woman she could use some makeup. Well, it was too late now. The horse was out of the barn, and she might as well ride it.

"Brilliant idea!" Lilly said to Margo's relief. She lobbed the tube to Lilly, and bit back a smile.

As Lilly applied the lipstick, Margo snuck a glimpse of Slim. He wasn't yelling, or scowling, which was tantamount to applause. Maybe Lilly was right, and work *was* fun, or maybe it was only this shop.

"Are we almost finished?" Lilly asked after thirty minutes

had passed. "Though I do *adore* your company, I need to make some deliveries."

As Slim started to answer her, the door flew open. A dashing, sun-drenched man stepped inside, illuminating the already sunny store, like somebody had finally remembered to pull back the drapes.

12

Peter Pulitzer patrolled the shop, saying hello, giving hugs, teasing his wife about the excessive number of cellophane-wrapped baskets scattered around the room. Margo watched, not sure what she was looking at. With his close-cropped dark hair, deep tan, and impish smile, Peter was criminally handsome, but he was also…grubby?

"Quite the specimen, isn't he?" Slim materialized behind Margo. "Bet the man who jilted you doesn't seem so intriguing now."

"He's…he's…something else," Margo said, still figuring this out, surprised the "dreamiest man in Palm Beach" would walk around filthy, apparently covered in mud. "Where *was* he?" she whispered.

"Peter's extremely hands-on with his orange groves. He and Lilly both work harder than they need to. God love 'em."

"Slim!" Peter called out, swiveling the spotlight of his attention to their side of the room. He strode over and gave Slim a convivial thump on the back. "Sorry I missed you at the party," he said. "Rather, I'm sorry you missed me since I wasn't there. Lil was absolutely furious."

"Not me!" Lilly sang as she undressed the mannequin. "Your business required tending to, and that's that."

"It really couldn't be helped," Peter said, and added something about a late freeze and needing to flood the roots with warm water. "I must keep my top customer in business. She's a real tyrant." He winked at his wife, and she blew him a kiss. "In any case, I was thrilled to hear you were back in town. I need to get you out in the new speedboat—" Peter stopped. His eyes jumped toward Margo. "Jiminy Christmas! Where are my manners? I'm Peter Pulitzer. You must be the latest victim of the Slim Aarons machine."

"I am," Margo said, extending an arm, curious whether he'd washed his hands that week. "Margo Hightower."

"A handshake?" Peter flashed a white grin. His teeth were so immaculately straight they could've been designed by the same people who did the hedges in Palm Beach. "Does this look like a damned boardroom?" As he brought Margo in for a hug, she smelled his sweat, and the mud, and the distant odor of cigarettes.

"God, Peter! She's wearing white!" Lilly said. "Meanwhile, you look like you just crawled out of a mine."

"I think Miss Hightower can take care of herself," Peter said and let go. "She'll have to, in order to survive Slim. It's great to meet you, Margo. Whereabouts are you from?"

"California. San Francisco, to be specific," Margo clarified, because when people heard *California*, they imagined ocean breezes and sunshine—a bigger, rockier version of Palm Beach. Meanwhile, on any given day in her hometown, the temperature could swing forty degrees in either direction and a person might need to change outfits three times for one walk.

"Those are Peter's old stomping grounds," Lilly chimed in.

"I was in Palo Alto," Peter said, and a cloud passed over his formerly sunny face. "Which is different but equally bad. God,

I hated that place. California is a shapeless nightmare designed to outrage anyone who likes order or beauty. And San Francisco?" He flubbered his lips. "To quote Rudyard Kipling, the place is inhabited by perfectly insane people. No offense."

"Um, well…" Margo wanted to protest, but what could she say? She loved San Francisco and certainly didn't view it as a *shapeless nightmare*, but it *was* gloomy as hell. Why would anyone choose to stumble around in relentless drizzle and fog when they could be here, awash in a permanent summer?

"Knock it off, Peter. You barely lived there a year," Lilly said. "Someone needs to train you how to have a normal conversation."

"You've done your best, darling. But I find it impossible to play proper WASP."

"You're right on the impossible part," Lilly said.

"Ah, it's all in good fun." Laughing, Peter rolled up his sleeves, revealing ropy, bronzed forearms, and—*could it be?*—a panther tattoo. Margo tried not to rubberneck, but it was too late. "Uh-oh," Peter said. "The expression on your face. I hope I haven't offended you."

"No doubt she's offended by that hideous ink," Lilly said.

"Not at all! The tattoo is terrific," Margo said, skin on fire. "I was only staring because…you're so tan!"

So tan? Margo could've smacked her own face. Where was a good old-fashioned Florida hurricane when you needed one?

"It's settled. You've won your way into my husband's heart." Lilly slid up beside him, resting a hand directly on the panther. "For years he's been competing with George Hamilton for deepest tan in Palm Beach and now someone's officially *decided* it. He'll find a way to claim you're an expert."

When everyone laughed, Margo's shoulders relaxed.

"I'm glad we've come to this unanimous conclusion," Peter

said with another blazing smile. He squeezed his wife, then kissed her on the head.

As they batted around a few more jokes and playful barbs, Margo watched, decorum and "blending in" be damned. A light seemed to surround Peter and Lilly, a halo, as though they were religious figures in a Raphael painting. Margo hadn't been to church in ages, and she wasn't particularly keen on the High Renaissance, but if life could be like this, she'd happily join the religion of Pulitzer, and spend every day praying at the altar of Palm Beach.

13

As they walked away from Lilly's store, *something* fluttered in Margo's chest. Maybe this was excitement, or what people called exhilaration. It felt not unlike the first whispers of a crush.

"Do you have a passport?" Slim asked, breaking into her thoughts.

"Of course I have a passport. Why?"

"Could you be ready to leave at a moment's notice?" Slim pivoted to face her. "Are you able to pack light?"

"Sure, I mean, I try…"

"Good," Slim said, and flicked a butt into the street. She'd never understand how he could run his mouth nonstop without losing his cigarette. "We're going to Acapulco," he announced.

Margo blinked. "We're leaving?" she said, filling with a sick, clammy panic. "When?"

"Two days."

"But we just got here…"

"*You* just got here."

"The season isn't over."

"The *season*," Slim said as they turned from Via Mizner onto

Worth. "Like you're a Palm Beach socialite. We're not here for parties and charity balls. We're here to work."

What about Lilly and Peter, she wanted to know. *What about this new life I'm trying to start?* Everyone on Via Mizner was going to forget her by the end of the week.

"Good Lord," Slim said. "You must be the only person iffy on Acapulco. I've got bad news for you. That's going to be a high point. It's all downhill from there."

"We're going somewhere *after* Mexico?" In that shop, progress had been made, and here he was, pulling it back.

"My work takes me all over the world, Margo. You know this. I have eight assignments for *HOLIDAY* magazine in the next nine months."

"What about your family? Don't you live in Palm Beach?"

"No, I don't live in Palm Beach," he scoffed. "I let a house every season, but technically we live on a farm in Katonah. That's Upstate New York."

Margo knew Slim traveled on assignment and assumed he might bring her along every now and again, but she hadn't counted on it being a regular occurrence, or that it'd happen right away. How was she going to meet a husband if they were constantly on the move?

"Acapulco," Margo said, acclimating to the idea. Surely the Beautiful People were there, too, she reasoned as Dolly's voice rang in her head. *Pretend you're happy. There are no obstacles! Act like you have it all worked out.* Margo inhaled and put on her debutante face. "Gosh, Slim, that sounds neat. Everyone wants to go there these days. How long will we stay?"

"Now, that's the spirit. We'll be there about ten days, and then it's on to Chicago."

Margo shuddered. Acapulco was one thing…but *the Middle West?* This couldn't be right. Slim Aarons was famous for his dazzling locations, so there must be a different Chicago, a more glamorous place from which the American version got its name. Like Vienna, Virginia, or Naples, Florida, or Venice Beach.

"Chicago," Margo repeated. "Do you mean the one in…?" She clamped her eyes shut. "French Africa?" She'd once known a girl from Algiers, Illinois.

"God help the youth in this country," Slim moaned, dropping his head all the way back. "Chicago is in *America*, in the state of Ill-i-*noise*. Dolly was right. You don't get out much."

"She said that?"

"Listen." He stepped toward her, and Margo fought the urge to retreat. "If you're planning to stick with me, it's not going to be all Acapulco cliff divers and Colony Hotels. Some of us gotta work for a living and I need to keep my portfolio diverse. There are too many editors who think I'm only suited to swell, watery places."

"They probably meant it as a compliment?"

"The Midwest is a beautiful region, and if Chicago isn't up to snuff, you'd better quit now. I'm not carrying around any mopey deadweight." Shaking his head in disappointment, Slim marched toward his car.

"I'll be there!" Margo scrabbled after him. She didn't want to quit, *couldn't* quit. He was her only chance. "I'll go to Acapulco, Chicago, anywhere else you name."

If Slim's family spent every season in Palm Beach, at least she had a promise to come back. In the meantime, Margo would throw herself into the work. She'd return to Palm Beach smarter and tanner and with tales of Acapulco. She'd return to Palm Beach and pick up right where she'd left off.

14

KATONAH, NEW YORK / MARCH 1961

Margo sat in her makeshift bedroom, on the second floor of the two-hundred-year-old white farmhouse Slim owned near Bedford, New York.

Though they'd been back a week, Margo still didn't have the words to describe Acapulco, not that anyone had asked. It'd been hot and dry, certainly. Unforgiving and exhausting, too. An ideal spot for anyone who enjoyed cactuses and the constant presence of sand between the teeth. The sun shone 340 days per year, and Margo had the peeling skin and ruined silk blouses to prove it.

The work had been *grueling*. Because Slim's family wasn't there, he was free to follow the jet set round the clock, from morning swims to lunches at the beachside go-go restaurants to the five-to-seven parties everyone attended each night. Alcohol was cheap in Mexico, likewise cocaine, and maybe this explained why they all partied like the world was about to end.

Slim was a teetotaler, never anything stronger than ginger ale, yet his energy was boundless. Meanwhile, Margo possessed whatever was the opposite of *pluck*. As they slogged from one location to the next, she undoubtedly projected the aura of a Chihuahua recently chucked off a boat.

Margo hoped these travels would give her something to talk about, a worldliness to flaunt back in Palm Beach. While the place was chockablock with a classy, international set—New York power brokers, Italian bankers, sulky French movie stars, duchesses, industrialists, and, always, Kirk Douglas—none of them even so much as glanced her way.

Sure, she could say she'd been to Las Brisas, a walled-in resort so exclusive that it had its own power grid, police force, and water supply, but she could never admit that she'd arrived via Mexican Jeep, which was to say, atop an ass. After hitching her donkey to a post, Margo had spent the next five hours blocking sun and wind to make the conditions perfect for Slim, while occasionally wading into a pool fully clothed to remove pieces of fuzz or a leaf.

Margo did have a bank account now, which was *some* progress, she supposed. Then again, Slim was her cosigner, so the money wasn't all hers. Last week, as they stood in front of a teller at Country Trust Company, Slim handed Margo ten dollars and explained that each week, he'd pay her an "allowance" of five dollars and deposit on her behalf. Their timing was perfect, the teller said. The bank was offering new accounts an interest rate of 3.25 percent, *and* a set of silverware. Slim would hold on to that, too.

The whole endeavor left Margo feeling like a child. What did women without husbands, or fathers, or male bosses do? Hide money in their shoes? Margo thought of Dolly, who had multiple bank accounts available at her discretion. Multiple accounts *and* a new boyfriend, apparently. An American State Department employee she'd met in Paris. Some girls had all the luck.

Margo didn't *mean* to complain, but she was in the dumps, and had nothing to do but ruminate while they waited for the images to come back. Only one place in North America had the equipment to handle Kodachrome film, and processing it took up to ten days. Of course the fussiest man in existence would use the world's fussiest film. Margo couldn't wait for this part of her life to end.

———

The sack landed with a thud on the doorstep shortly after one o'clock on a sunny afternoon. Slim had taken his daily lunch of tuna fish on white bread and was trolling his six acres on a riding lawn mower, long legs bent, knees up at his ears. Knowing he'd want to get started, Rita called him inside, and the two got to work.

Kodachrome film came back as slides on two-inch cardboard mounts. Because Slim used dozens of rolls per day, this meant hundreds of tiny squares to sift through. As he spread the images across the light table in his workroom, Margo went dizzy, completely walleyed.

"How do you pick the ones to send to *HOLIDAY*?" she asked, staring at approximately fifty pictures of the same blonde. She knew most of these would end up in a storage box, joining the others in the room. An ACAPULCO box stacked on top of ARIZONA MILLIONAIRES or HOLLYWOOD A (or B, or C).

"Editing is elimination," Slim said. "First, we exclude the ones that are obviously wrong." He pushed aside several featuring a blonde woman wearing a pink gingham bikini at the Villa Vera Racquet Club's swim-up bar. "Then you sort through the rest as many times as necessary until something about an expression strikes you and you say, 'Yes! That's who she is!'"

Margo nodded, pretending like she understood.

"I use Kodachrome," he went on, "because of the saturated colors and minimal grain. The superior sharpness and detail. Look here." He pointed to the woman again, and Margo noticed a mustache-like line of sweat above her top lip. Now, *that* was interesting. She hadn't seen it before.

They moved on to photos of a socialite standing in her private pool at Las Brisas. Louise Anne was radiant, as though staring into the heavens instead of Slim's lens as he crouched on a wall overhead. From this angle, Louise Anne's white off-the-shoulder bathing suit gave the impression of a wedding dress, the effect amplified by the floating hibiscuses surrounding her. Margo had picked those flowers from a hillside nearby, and somewhere out of frame, she was nursing a tweaked ankle and bee sting.

"This is incredible," Margo said, examining one image. "I was standing right there. I watched every snap, but I never saw this." Slim had captured something invisible to the naked eye.

"It's funny, isn't it?" Slim said, smiling in that smug, prideful way that usually drove her nuts. "The same person can be shot from infinite positions yet show something new every time. The images that do come back never tell the full story. Your eyes play tricks on you, and so does the camera. What you see is almost never what you get, which is why it never hurts to look more than once."

15

PALM BEACH / APRIL 1961

They were back in Palm Beach, for one last stint.

Margo had assumed they wouldn't return until next season, so Slim's decision was a gift. She vowed to remember this the next time she had a blister, or Slim got on her very last nerve.

Yes, Slim, whatever you say! I'd be thrilled to comply!

The season was already petering out when they arrived. Everyone seemed to move more slowly, the parties were fewer, and even Slim's shoots had a casual, laid-back feel.

"If you play your cards right," he joked, "I may introduce you to the concept of free time."

Sure enough, after a morning spent photographing the Colony's early birds—children splashing in the pool, a group of gray hairs shooting backgammon—Slim told Margo to take the rest of the day off. It's what she'd been waiting for. A chance to visit Lilly's shop.

Palm Beachers rarely left home before noon and Worth Avenue was empty as Margo meandered along, rehearsing what to say. Something about browsing, and shopping, and just happening past. It had to sound casual. Entirely off-the-cuff.

Margo veered down the Vias' cobbled walkways. As she approached Lilly's yellow door, her eyes skipped over to Au Bon Goût, the we-have-everything shop. The best way to convincingly portray girl gone shopping, Margo realized with a happy jolt, was to actually shop. She could wander into Lilly's store, holding someone else's bag.

Her timing was perfect. At that very moment, a woman in a silk shirt and pink Bermuda shorts was unlocking the Au Bon Goût's door. Margo slipped in behind her. Curiously, several women were already inside.

Margo felt all eyes on her as she moved through the store. She paused and pretended to contemplate a cabbaged-shaped soup tureen, nearly choking at the three-digit price. These people really did have money to burn, and Margo was suddenly worried about the meager twenty-two dollars in her purse. So much for an "everything" shop. "Everything over one hundred bucks" was a more accurate name.

After checking all shelves and tables in the shop, Margo spied a basket of pot holders beside the register. The price was right, but she wasn't about to purchase something that asked in hand-printed script, Who Invited All the Tacky People? Just as Margo was about to give up, her luck kicked in. Next to the pot holders sat a pile of linen napkins—two for five dollars. Margo snatched up a pair.

"Hello," she said, setting the napkins onto the sales counter. "I'd like to purchase these, please." She clicked open her purse.

The woman nodded and plopped them into a bag. After handing the bag to Margo, she opened a large leather-bound book. "Last name, please?"

"It's Hightower, but I wouldn't be on your mailing list. It's my first time in the store."

The cashier gasped. Her face went white, and goose bumps skittered along Margo's arms. From somewhere in the shop, a door opened and closed. "How did you get in here?" the woman said. "Are you a member?"

"A member?" Margo repeated, and the room began to spin. "A member of *what*? I'm here to shop."

"Au Bon Goût isn't for tourists." The cashier slammed the book closed and ripped the bag from Margo's hand. "You can't ramble in and *buy* something." She asked Margo to leave, but Margo was frozen, unable to move.

"My goodness," someone said. "What on *earth* is going on?" The voice kicked Margo back to life, like a dart to the rear.

"*Shit,*" Margo said, probably out loud. She turned and found exactly who she'd expected. It was Wendy Vanderbilt, accompanied by a bouffanted and befuddled Lilly Pulitzer.

"Margo, did you try to purchase something? Oh gosh, you poor dear. This is a members-only store." Wendy's voice was all sugar, which did not sweeten her sneer. "Don't be embarrassed," she said, rubbing Margo's back. "This is Slim's fault. He needs to give his assistants a better lay of the land. If you're looking to do some shopping, there's a thrift store nearby."

"Oh, for Christ's sake." Lilly stepped around Wendy. "Ora, dear, please give me the bag," she said. When Ora objected, Lilly slapped a hand on the counter. "Enough! This is a damned store. You're not manning the gates of St. Peter. Just put it on my account. The girl is with me."

16

"Don't give it another thought," Lilly said, looping an arm through Margo's as they marched away from Au Bon Goût. "The membership deal is a hustle. It wasn't like that until recently. For no good reason, they decided to charge one hundred dollars per year for the privilege of walking through their door. Everyone thinks it's dumb, but we play along because it's owned by a friend."

Lilly's assurances slightly lessened her humiliation, but Margo still had the sense of floating, of her body being separated from her brain. This faux pas was the opposite of "blending in," and if Slim caught wind of it, he'd fire her on the spot.

"I feel terrible for intruding," Margo said.

"Absolutely do not. Alright. Enough about that goofy place." Lilly detached from Margo and threw open the yellow door. Unlike Au Bon Goût, her store hadn't been locked. "Let's discuss more important topics," she said, kicking off her sandals. "Namely, the pictures you and Slim took of me the last time you were here. I'm afraid to ask. How did they turn out? Were they terrible?" She winced. "I told him I didn't want to be photographed that day."

Margo laughed at the idea of Lilly as anything short of glowing. When Slim narrowed down the images to the best few, there she stood, looking big and earthy and magnificent, like some kind of tropical queen. From the wallpaper with its orange and lemon slices to the pink flowers, the entire frame was filled with color and light, but Lilly's piercing dark eyes and knowing expression warned that a new season might start any day.

"The images are the best of Slim," Margo told Lilly. "I'm positive they'll end up in a magazine. They're that good."

"Phew, what a relief!" Lilly said, pretending to whisk sweat from her brow. "Some people always look terrific in photographs. Wendy, for example. And Peter! But I'm a damned wild card."

Margo didn't see how this could be true, but assured her, again, that she had nothing to worry about. Lilly smiled, and they stared at each other for several dragged-out beats. Showing up at Lilly's was the culmination of Margo's plan. What was she supposed to do next?

"Well, here are your napkins," Lilly said, holding out the bag.

Margo took the bag, her face rotating through several shades of red. "Thank you. Sorry to have, uh, caused any inconvenience."

"Do not apologize. It's always fun to stick it to Ora. She's so damned uptight. Anyway." She patted Margo's shoulder. "Back to the grind! So lovely to see you. Please remind Slim to bring by the photos." With that, Lilly disappeared behind a dress rack.

Margo slunk out of the shop, a pair of droopy napkins in hand. Lilly had been kind, delightful as always, but Margo couldn't shake her unease. She hoped she hadn't just pushed Palm Beach's inner circle further out of her reach.

17

Four days later, Margo found herself up the creek once again. She'd rung Dolly for a chat—on her own dime, no less—and was told in no uncertain terms to get bent.

"You need to move your stuff out of the Huntington," she'd said.

"My stuff?" Margo repeated, feeling as though she'd been knocked on her head.

"I hate to spring this on you," Dolly said and paused, presumably to release a long stream of cigarette smoke. "But Don's moving here from Paris and needs to store his antiques. You can't freeload forever!"

Margo's mouth hung open. She was tongue-and-brain-tied. This was not the Dolly she adored, the one who was generous, who'd dropped everything when the contents of Margo's home had been sold. *That* version of Dolly Fritz literally picked Margo up off the floor.

"Let's get you out of here," she'd said, upon finding Margo balled up in a closet. "We have better places to be." She then ferried Margo back to the Huntington, where they ate ice cream and got drunk on champagne for a week. Dolly told her to come back, anytime. She could live there if she needed to, free of charge. The offer had an expiration date, it seemed.

"Oh, okay," Margo said now. Her soul was flattened, but this was about more than the fate of the few items she still owned. Everything was changing, and for the worse. Dolly had never moved a man into the Huntington before, and this wasn't even the son of some robber baron, or a minor royal from a third-tier kingdom. Don MacMasters was a no-name bureaucrat Dolly had known for approximately one week. The whole arrangement stunk, but saying this out loud might sound like sour grapes. And so, with her eyes brimming and jaw clenched, Margo promised to work it out and hung up the phone. She wept for ninety minutes straight.

Although hours had passed, the gloom stuck to her like a bad smell. Slim noticed as soon as she opened his car door. "What's with you?" he asked, throwing the car into reverse before she was fully inside.

"Almost just lost a limb," Margo said. "But don't mind me!"

"Stop complaining. I saved you from having to take a bus," Slim said, and they punched out onto Flagler Drive. "Have you ever thought about putting your bed against the wall so you can wake up on the right side of it for once?"

"Very droll," Margo grumbled, turning toward the window.

As Slim drove them across the bridge, Margo rolled the conversation around in her mind, trying to decide what bothered her the most. Was it the unwelcome elevation of Don Mac-Masters? The displacement of Margo and her stuff? The fact that her very last option was gone and spent?

"You're going to have to tell me what's wrong," Slim said as he turned from Cocoanut Row onto Via Sunny. "You're grinding your teeth, and I don't pay for dental work."

"Well, Slim, I'd love to tell you what's wrong, but I hardly know myself." Margo fiddled with the hem of her blouse for several minutes before continuing. "I talked to Dolly earlier today," she admitted. "She has a new boyfriend. Works for the government. A civil functionary. Evidently." She made a face.

Slim chuckled. "I heard something along those lines."

"He's moving to San Francisco. Seems a little fast but…" Margo sighed. "Anyway, I've been storing my personal effects at the Huntington but *Don* needs the space now." What had Dolly said those months ago, on that dreadful afternoon at the B&T? *The Doll will take care of you. That's what big sisters are for.* Where was this big sister now? "He's quite the antiques aficionado. Needs every last centimeter of space."

"So the glum mug is because you're worried about your personal junk?" Slim said, and Margo flinched.

It did sound awfully selfish when spoken out loud. *Who cares about the love life of my dearest friend when I don't have anywhere to put an empty jewelry box with a broken ballerina?*

"Not that I mind moving it," she insisted, "but I don't know the first thing about finding storage in San Francisco." Storage was the immediate dilemma, but the problem was bigger than that. It was like Dolly had kicked Margo out of her life, same as a bunch of old clothes and horse blankets.

"How much stuff are we talking about?" Slim asked, pulling up to a valet stand temporarily erected outside a client's estate.

"It's not a lot," she said. "Clothes, books, that kind of thing." Margo wasn't the sort of girl who'd earned a lot of trophies, and her bedroom furniture was long since hocked. "Honestly, I should just tell her to set it on fire. The items aren't worth the effort of moving somewhere else."

"Have it shipped to Katonah," Slim said and kicked open his door.

"Wait. Back up," Margo said, scrambling out of the car. "You're willing to house *my* belongings, at *your* house? Is this a prank? Or is Dolly paying you?"

"Margo." Slim locked eyes with her over the car. "I know that I can be difficult, a borderline pain in the ass."

"I wouldn't call it borderline."

He smirked. "You're not a breeze to deal with yourself. But I like you, kid. We're a team. As long as you're with me, you have a home, and I'll suffer the presence of your mounds of crap."

"Oh, Slim." Margo brushed away invisible tears. "That is really the sweetest thing you could've said."

"That's enough of that." Slim flapped his hands as though shooing a swarm of flies. "Can we focus on the job at hand? In case you were curious—though that doesn't sound like you— here's what we're shooting today." He slid an invitation across the roof of the car.

OUR FAMILY TREE IS GROWING!

Margo glanced up, confused. Babies weren't usually Slim's bag. He signaled for her to read on.

Name: Baby Girl
Weight: 6,000 pounds
Arrival: April 8, 1961

Please come celebrate at my parents' home
on Lake Trail, six o'clock sharp!

The baby was a yacht, and they were there to photograph the christening. Margo let out a groan and Slim laughed.

"I feel the same," he said, slamming his door. "But they're paying me to shoot them with their precious boat, so that's exactly what we'll do."

On the lawn behind the house, people swilled cocktails beneath a huge white tent, enjoying a clear view of the *Baby Girl*, who was docked several yards away. The christening was about to start and a beauty queen hired to do the honors stood near Margo and Slim, whispering to herself that it would all be okay.

"I spent all week practicing," she told Slim as the owner donned a skipper's cap and shouted for everyone's attention. "I've broken too many bottles to count, but I'm still so nervous!" The owner handed her the champagne, but despite all her practice, it still took three tries for her to break the thing. Slim managed to capture a few shots. Tepid applause ensued.

Following the ceremony, guests ate from a seafood buffet and watched a forty-minute film of other people's yachts cruising the Bahamas at a turtle's pace. The movie had all the intrigue of a celery stalk and Margo was comforted to discover that the high life could also be dull.

As they loitered just outside the tent, Margo yawned once, and again. Slim passed her a look. She peered over her shoulder to hide a third yawn and spotted two men walking up from the water. One had a shock of white hair, its brightness matched only by the other one's teeth. When they noticed Margo, she flipped back around.

"Slimbo!" Peter said as the men arrived next to them. Margo's shoulders hiked up to her ears.

"Peter! Excellent to see you," Slim said. "And the esteemed Jim Kimberly."

Peter's companion was the trim, steely heir to the Kimberly-Clark Kleenex fortune, an infamous playboy, sportsman, and self-styled swashbuckler who carried his own roll of toilet paper wherever he went.

"What do you think of the new arrival?" Slim asked the men. "If I recall correctly, the SS *Baby Girl* is a bigger vessel than what either of you own. You must be seething with envy."

Peter snorted. "Hardly. The thing is an eyesore."

"Not to mention an egregiously expensive way to compensate for the deficiency in one's pants," Jim added.

"Don't you have a ninety-footer that can cross the Atlantic?" Peter said.

"Yes, but I'm not compelled to tell everyone about it."

"Ah. Yes. The devil's in the details. Hey, look who it is," Peter said, turning his attentions to Margo. "The California girl. It's great to see you again. I'm glad Slim hasn't chased you off yet."

"California girl? I like the sound of that," Jim Kimberly said, stepping around Peter to shake Margo's hand. His skin was dry, and unsettlingly soft. The toilet paper was jammed into his armpit.

"Margo Hightower," she said, reluctantly, between her teeth. Margo once overheard a woman say that Jim Kimberly gave her the willies. She now understood what that meant.

"Miss Hightower. The pleasure is all mine," Jim said, though her pleasure had not been mentioned or indeed experienced. Smiling like a demon, he looked straight past Margo, over her head. "You've built a hell of a life for yourself, Slim. A job that involves photographing beautiful women while accompanied by a different woman half your age."

"Give it up, Kimberly," Peter said. "You do realize no one's paying you a royalty every time you act like a lech?"

"Just admiring the inventory." Jim gave Margo another very thorough up-and-down. "Jesus Christ," he said with a whistle. "How do you find these girls? I think you told me once. Always a thoroughbred from a good family, is that correct?"

"Yes, that's what I've said," Slim mumbled, and Margo pulled her chin into her neck. *Thoroughbred* was a compliment, given her dicey distaff line, but she didn't want anyone comparing her to a horse. At least he had the decency to act embarrassed about it.

"You sly dog," Jim said. "Doesn't your wife mind?"

"It's not about *me*. A pretty face puts people at ease," Slim said as he retrieved a brass zippo from his coat. The GOOD LUCK stamped across it was almost worn off. "It helps distract subjects so I can make decisions about how I'm going to work, without anyone getting in my way."

"I'll bet she's a distraction," Jim said with a snicker. "Man, oh man. Well. It's a good job, if you can get it. But you've gotta be careful with those thoroughbreds. Sometimes they get their own ideas about things. And all that pampering and inbreeding…" His eyes slid toward Margo's and her body curdled like old milk. "It can make them insouciant and difficult and *impossible* to train."

18

After swiping a black-and-white-swimsuited Barbie from the floor, Margo shoved Howdy Doody's monkey beneath her arm and scanned the room for the remaining Mr. and Mrs. Potato Head pieces. Eventually, she'd have to explain to the neighbors why a toy popcorn popper had ended up in their yard. Who knew babysitting required both physical labor and mild diplomacy?

Margo never expected that watching Mary Aarons might become part of her job, but Slim had called that morning, desperate. Rita was golfing and he'd forgotten that he was scheduled to meet an editor for lunch. Could Margo please, oh please, look after Mary at his place? She'd be napping for most of it.

"If you don't want to do it for me," he'd said, when Margo hesitated, "do it for Rita."

That was all it took. Margo had liked the scrappy, high-energy Rita from the moment they met. Tall and slender like Slim, she once modeled swimsuits for *Sports Illustrated*. She also had stories for days, but unlike her husband, Rita's temperament was calm and reasonable and she didn't come at a person like a freight train.

"Fine," Margo had said. "Can I use your washing machine?"

If she was going to babysit, at least Margo could save a few pennies on laundry, and it'd be nice to return to the hotel with a bagful of clothes that smelled like Palm Beach.

"We have a washing machine?" had been Slim's response.

Mary was a pleasant child—polite and serious and not prone to tantrums, as opposed to her dad. The past two hours had flown, and now she was down for her nap, giving Margo the opportunity to dry her clothes and tidy up. Before long, the cottage was gleaming, and Margo scattered some plastic mustaches in the hall, so Slim wouldn't get the wrong idea and want to use her as a housekeeper.

As she passed back through the kitchen, someone knocked on the front door. Margo leaned across the sink to peek through the window and saw a figure wearing white trousers and a white polo shirt. Peter Pulitzer.

Margo pulled back. Her heart skipped seven or eight beats. Should she answer the door? Of course she should. It'd be rude not to. Peter was Slim's pal, and he and Margo were on friendly terms, too. He'd gotten Jim Kimberly to leave her alone at that terrible yacht party, after all, by saying he overheard some friend of theirs bragging that he'd beaten Jim in golf.

Get it together, Margo chided herself. Finally, and with a deep inhale, she opened the door. "Greetings!" she sang. "Welcome to Slim's."

Peter's forehead jumped in surprise. "Margo! Hello. I wasn't expecting you." He craned his neck, searching behind her. "I'm supposed to pick up something from Slim. He's not around, is he?"

Margo shook her head. "He went to lunch. Rita is out, too. One of them should be home any minute. You're welcome to wait, or..." *Or, what, Margo? What?* She could be such a dope sometimes.

"I could wait a few."

As Peter consulted his watch, questions clacked around Margo's head like ice in a cocktail shaker. Should she invite him in? Would that be weird? Or would leaving him outside be more uncouth? Margo wished someone would tell her what to do.

"So. What'd you think of the *Baby Girl*'s debut?" he asked her from the front step.

It took Margo a second to catch up. "Oh! The boat was beautiful, one of the biggest I've seen." She'd never been asked to opine on a yacht, and Margo hoped she was doing this right. "Seemed like a great party. The buffet smelled delicious!" Margo smiled, and Peter gave her a crooked, funny look, like he expected her to go on. "What?" she said. "What is it?" Margo ran her tongue over her teeth, checking whether there was something between them.

"Nothing." Peter laughed dryly. "When people bring up the size of someone's yacht, it's not usually done in a *nice* way. And commenting on the smell of the food? Un-ironically? I was sure you were going to make a remark about...I don't know...the scent of hot new money. It's nice to talk to someone who isn't completely jaded. Wow, I must really hang out with some terrible people."

"I'm sorry," she said. "I don't really know what I'm talking about."

"I'm the one who should apologize—for introducing you to Jim Kimberly. He's weighing the benefits of divorce, which means he's on the prowl."

"It's fine," Margo assured him.

"Again, I'm sorry."

"It's fine."

Peter smiled and continued to stand there as Margo's eyes darted around. She prayed for Slim or Rita to show up, but the street was quiet, save a lone man walking his poodle. "You mentioned picking up something from Slim?" she said. "If you tell me what it is, maybe I can help?"

"Right. I almost forgot. Slim printed some pictures of my

wife? I hope you know what I'm talking about because I don't have a clue."

"I do, actually. I saw them earlier." Margo wracked her brain, trying to remember where. In the living room? On Slim's desk? Maybe they were on the kitchen table, beneath Slim's newspapers. "You're welcome to come in," she began, her offer stopped dead by the whir of a police siren.

Peter whipped around as a car raced up to the curb. Two uniformed men stepped out looking ten kinds of serious. Until now, Margo thought the Palm Beach police force only ever parked cars at big parties.

"Hi, Elmer. Hi, Roy," Peter said as the officers walked to the door. "What appears to be the problem?"

"We've had a complaint from a neighbor," one said as he flipped open his pad. "About women's panties flapping in the wind." He zeroed in on Margo.

"I have laundry drying in the yard?" she said as her cheeks pinked. Couldn't he have led with anything else? Pajamas? A robe? "Is that what you mean?"

"Miss, are you aware there's a city ordinance against hanging one's laundry out to dry?"

"There's what? An ordinance? What?" She glanced back toward the cottage.

"You've broken a law, and we'll need to write you a ticket."

Margo felt sick. "Please, Officer, don't give me a ticket," she pleaded. "I'll take it down." The officer stopped writing, but only because a long, sad wail emanated from inside the house. "Miss, I believe that's a child crying," he said.

Mary. Up from her nap.

"I'm going to head out," Peter said, backing away. "Let Slim know I was here. Boys, please take it easy on Miss Hightower. She clearly wasn't aware of the ordinance, and her hands are full as it is."

19

Tomorrow they would fly to Chicago, which meant Margo had one more chance to get it right, one more day to leave an impression that did not involve flashing lights or breaching private shopping clubs. Lilly still needed the photographs, and Margo offered to drop them off.

"You *should* be the one to do it," Slim said with a cackle. "Since your untimely arrest prevented Peter from picking them up." Margo hadn't been arrested, and she managed to talk the men out of a ticket, but Slim nonetheless considered it one of the funnier things he'd heard in his life. Multiple times per day he cracked himself up by "apologizing" for neglecting to tell Margo she shouldn't toss her underwear all over his yard.

Determined not to flub this last errand, Margo marched down Worth, photographs in hand. The season was over, and many of the shops were shuttered, their awnings drawn in until late November. City workers were uninstalling the streetlights, most windows were dark, and the Vias' fountains no longer gurgled. On Via Mizner, the only sign of life was Lilly, perched on a stepladder outside Salon Français.

"Hello!" Margo called out. "I have your photographs."

Lilly hopped down and wiped her hands on her dress. Instead of her customary florals or pinks, today she wore blue-and-orange diamonds set against yellow. Her season was changing, too. "Thank you for bringing these over," she said, taking the envelope. "My head is spinning. I have so much to do. Including, now, closing up Julia's shop."

Lilly gestured to where an awning had once been, and mentioned freedom fighters, and taking Cuba back, and Margo deduced that the counterrevolution was about to commence. "Julia is in agony over her husband," Lilly added, "and who can blame her? Everyone says it will be a bloodbath."

There was no real way to answer that. "How…scary," Margo said.

"It is. And I wanted to find some way to lighten her load. Anyhow." Lilly ripped open the envelope. Her face brightened as she flicked through the pictures. "Wow. Wow. Wow. Slim really knows what he's doing."

"I told you they were great."

"It's funny. Anyone who saw these would think I'm running a dress shop, not a fruit stand." Mouth twisted, Lilly tapped the stack against her palm. "You know, I think I could do something with these, but *what*?"

"Maybe an advertisement?" Margo said.

"Hmm, maybe," Lilly said, tucking the images in the front of her dress. "A puzzle for a later date. There are other things to think about right now." She looked at the shop and then back to Margo. "Listen, I hate to put this on you, but Julia and Bibi left their shop in wretched shape. Do you happen to have an extra hour or so? I could really use the help."

"I have all afternoon," Margo said, a thrill rising in her chest. Slim would want her to offer, but more than that, it was an opportunity to wipe her slate clean. Everyone talked about first impressions, but last impressions were important, too, and

Margo was about show Lilly that she was the most generous and helpful person in Palm Beach.

—

But first, cocktails.

"Any Palm Beach proprietress knows," Lilly said as she mixed a concoction of champagne, grenadine, and vodka known as a Russian 75, "when you close after the season, it's critical to get rid of the perishables. We can't let all this good booze go bad." She laughed. "I hope you're not too scandalized."

"Slim is the teetotaler, not me."

Lilly rolled her eyes. "Slim Aarons and his damned ginger ale."

"If he can get through a war without liquor, he never needed it in the first place," Margo said, quoting her boss. Slim didn't care for nightlife, in general. *After you've heard Louis Armstrong in Rome, where do you go from there?* It was such a Slim Aarons thing to say.

"How'd he get such a fun wife?" Lilly said and handed her a glass. Margo took a sip and the champagne danced on her tongue. "Does Slim ever allow you to cut loose while you're traveling?"

"Definitely not. But he did let me try the local drink when we were in Acapulco." Margo hadn't expected to like slurping alcohol out of a sawed-off coconut, but when it came to Things Margo Enjoyed in Acapulco, Coco Locos were on the list. That is, if she'd had a list, or enough to put on it.

"Acapulco!" Lilly exclaimed, setting her drink on the counter. "That's right. How was it? I've been dying to go but haven't found the time." She opened a cabinet and pulled out a roll of clear plastic bags. "It's the hottest of spots."

"*Hottest.* You're right about that," Margo said, then hesitated, biting back all the grievances bound to pour out. No one liked a complainer, and she could find some way to give Acapulco a little shine. The white-sand beaches *were* lovely—not that Margo personally experienced them—likewise watching the blue sails cut through the horseshoe-shaped bay. "The skies are really beautiful at night," Margo tried. "The stars are incredibly bright, and all the city lights kind of tumble down the hillside toward the harbor, like a veil." Margo smiled as she remembered. Maybe Acapulco did have a few good traits. Like Slim said, it never hurt to consider something a second time.

"No wonder everyone's gaga over the place," Lilly said. As Margo held out the roll of bags, Lilly tore them off, one by one, and began to wrap the remaining dresses in the shop. "Did you see the cliff divers?" she asked, about the famed men who scaled a 135-foot rock face in bare feet, then hurled themselves into the choppy blue waters below. "Swear to God, they're the reason I'll never be able to see Acapulco. I'd spend the entire time convincing Peter not to try, lest he end up splattered across the rocks."

"He wouldn't be allowed," Margo said. "It's a family trade, and they have a union."

"That would only make him *more* determined." She handed Margo six bagged frocks and together they moved them into storage. "Son of a gun," Lilly said, shoving the dresses to make them fit. "We've done a crap ton of work and I don't have so much as a buzz." She slammed the closet door shut. "It's an untenable situation. Time for a break. You and I need to top off."

—

An hour later, they sat on the floor, sorting through a pile of fabric swatches and buttons. Margo was getting shifty and uncomfortable in her cotton weave pants. She didn't know how Lilly could stand it in a dress.

"Margo, you are too much!" Lilly howled, when Margo offered to finish sorting so Lilly could do something more upright. "I'm wearing one of my Lillys and I designed these bad boys precisely so a woman can mess around on the floor with her kids. Why do you think I cut them so high?" She leaned to the side, demonstrating how the slits went all the way to her hip joint. "The idea is *ease*. You step in and zip it up as far as you can reach, and voilà! You're ready for the day. You don't even need to bother with a bra or panties."

Lilly flipped the hem to show the dress's lining and Margo suppressed a gasp. Had she been *bare bottomed* all along? The thought was both horrifying and exciting, like a juicy piece of gossip. "How…innovative…" Margo said, suddenly parched. She sipped the remnants of her Russian 75.

"It really is, if I do say so myself. I can't wait to make more this summer, when I'm not inundated by a constant stream of people tromping into the shop, demanding juice."

"Is it weird?" Margo asked. "Being here when others are gone?" Though preparations were everywhere, Margo couldn't picture Palm Beach in full hibernation.

"For me, the worst part of the year is right *now*," Lilly said. "Everyone is cranky as they eke out their days, attending the last, sad parties and making sure they've accrued enough time to prove *intent of domicile* for tax purposes. By the time it's all over, most people are itching to go."

"What about you?" Margo said, pushing aside a pile of buttons. She was starting to feel the buzz, from the alcohol and the revelation about Lilly's lack of underwear. "Do you ever get stir-crazy?"

"It can get dull," she admitted. "My tendency toward boredom is why my shop exists, but it never lasts long. Around here, the unpleasant blows away eventually." She smiled, almost dolefully. "For me, Palm Beach is more of an emotion than a place."

Margo nodded. She understood what Lilly meant. It was beginning to feel like an emotion to her, too.

"There are a few downsides." Lilly jumped to her feet and Margo followed, wobbling on the way up. She grabbed a mannequin for balance. "I always miss my friends. Wendy and Dysie and Flo, of course. Julia and Caca. I hope that Cuban fiasco turns out alright." She released a long sigh.

"Caca?" Margo repeated, taking a beat to remember where she'd heard the word before. It was in Mexico, she realized. A result of being forced to spend so much time on or around donkeys. "I'm sorry, isn't *caca* Spanish for…?"

Lilly snickered. "For *shit*, yes! That's what I call Enrique, Julia's husband. Half the time I forget that's not his real name." As the story went, when Lilly first met Enrique Rousseau, he was acting like such a pill that she called him *Caca Caliente*, as in *hot shit*, and the name stuck. "It's really too appropriate," she added, chuckling to herself. "This is a man who went to a revolution with a houseboy, his own tent, and a three-month supply of cigars. Those old aristocratic Cubans are an amusing bunch." Lilly paused. Hands on her hips, she cast about the room. "Looks like we're about done here. Truly, Margo, I can't thank you enough."

"It was my pleasure," Margo said, woozy, wondering what time it was, and whether they allowed drunks on the bus.

"You're a hell of a gal." Lilly threw an arm around her shoulders. "A real gem. Wendy and Flo are my best friends, but they'd never get their hands dirty like this. You and me, we're both doers. We're practical and want to achieve tangible things." She gave Margo an extratight squeeze and let go. "In Palm Beach, there's a long-standing tradition of us old-timers 'adopting' the newbies and showing them the ropes. I know you're leaving, but you must come see me the minute you get back. It's good for me to have someone like you around."

Margo was too stunned to speak. All at once, her worries about ordinances and memberships vanished, packed away for the season, maybe for good. Lilly might not remember this conversation seven months from now, but Margo would take her up on her offer, first chance she got. There were many glorious places in Palm Beach, but none so promising as under Lilly Pulitzer's wing.

PART 2

I hope you boys will all have a very good time on your vacation. But do not go to Palm Beach—that den of iniquity.

—Rev. Endicott Peabody, headmaster of Groton School, 1884–1940

20

PALM BEACH / NOVEMBER 1961

"Oh, you fucker!" Lilly yelped. She was kneeling on the floor beside a safe-deposit box. "Why won't you cooperate?"

"Maybe you grabbed the wrong key?" Wendy said from the pink couch.

Lilly jammed the key in several more times, but it refused to budge. "You're probably right. Good Lord. I'm too dim to break into my own petty cash. Pea brain strikes again." She sprang to her feet. "Go to hell, you damned thing!" she said and pitched the key across the room.

"Hello, Margo," Wendy said, and Margo gave a small startle. "You really managed to shimmy in here, didn't you? Like a ghost." Margo stood in the open doorway, queasy from nerves. "Oh, I, uh…" Would Lilly remember what she'd said, about "adopting" her, that Margo should find her the minute she returned to Palm Beach?

Lilly whirled around. "It's Margo! Back for another round!" she said as her enormous gold hoops swayed back and forth. "What are you doing standing there, half in and half out of the shop? Come in, come in." She made large sweeping motions with her hands.

Margo moved tentatively into the shop, scanning the floor for an available path. The place was more cluttered than ever, like someone had chucked a hundred baskets through the door and run.

"What are we up to today?" Lilly asked. "A little pre-Christmas shopping?"

"Not at Au Bon Goût, I hope!" Wendy said.

Margo tried to laugh. "I've learned my lesson," she said.

"If you are shopping, I hope you'll take some of this merchandise off my hands," Lilly said. "As you can see, we're a stitch *overstocked*." It wasn't only the baskets. The bamboo racks were so crammed with dresses Margo couldn't distinguish one print from the next. "This is all Peter's fault, naturally. He thinks I'm a multinational corporation and is always pushing me to do more, more, more. Now I'm drowning in fruit baskets and shifts. I'll probably have to advertise myself. *Oh God!*" She put a hand to her forehead. "So much work!"

"You need a break, sweetie," Wendy said, patting the couch.

Emitting a big puff of air, Lilly plopped down beside Wendy and folded her legs beneath her rear. "Surely this feels like a time warp to you, Margo. You've been out living your life, and I haven't left this shop."

"You were in Capri this summer," Wendy pointed out. "And the Adirondacks, for some reason."

"You and Slim must've been all over the world," Lilly said. "Didn't he mention Greece? Wendy!" She bumped her arm against Wendy, who had returned to her magazine. "We're having a conversation. Don't be rude!"

Wendy sighed and rested the magazine in her lap. She looked at Margo, sleepily, with her big doe eyes.

"Uh, yes, there was a trip to Greece," Margo said.

"But did *you* go?" Wendy asked, and Margo prickled, wondering how she'd guessed.

Margo *hadn't* gone to Greece, and it remained a subject so sore she could use a painkiller. She'd instead spent the summer bouncing between Katonah and the Midwest, snapping dubiously named characters (Bathhouse Carter, Joe Bananas) and full-of-themselves magazine publishers, like that unctuous Hugh Hefner. Margo had attacked every shoot with gusto, squelching any vexation with the promise of Greece. Then it came time for the trip, and *HOLIDAY* would pay only for Slim. Margo stayed behind in Katonah, writing captions as her belongings arrived, box by box, from the Huntington Hotel.

"Unfortunately, I didn't make it to Greece," Margo said with a smile that no doubt read like a grimace. "But we did see some nice homes outside Lake Forest, Illinois?" At one estate she'd almost contracted pneumonia after wading in a murky, brackish pond to move around some lady as she sat in a boat overflowing with roses.

"Oh, I love Chicago," Lilly said. "So, Wen, whaddaya think? Shall we fill her in on everything she missed?"

"Not much has happened, honestly," Wendy said with a yawn.

"Well, *you've* managed to lead an interesting life." Lilly cranked her head in Margo's direction. "Have you heard? Wendy is dueting with George Hamilton. The actor? He's such a beefcake. Unfortunately, it means she's not presently with my brother, Dinny, but I consider that a temporary situation."

By Lilly's telling, between Dinny Phipps and George Hamilton, Wendy had ripped through a roster of men, from Prince Albrecht of Liechtenstein to Arthur MacArthur, son of the general. She'd also spent several *hot and heavy* weeks with Rhadamés Trujillo, and while Margo didn't particularly want to have a dalliance with the son of the dictator of one of the bloodiest regimes in history, at least Wendy had options.

"The girl has left a trail of broken hearts from New York to

Palm Beach," Lilly said. "One day she'll recognize Dinny is the only man she needs. They'll get married, and we can become sisters!"

"I think you and I are better as friends," Wendy said flatly.

Somebody *rat-a-tat-tatted* on the window. The women glanced up to see Julia Rousseau peering through the glass. After blowing them a kiss, she bustled across the Via to unlock her shop.

"Now, that's one change since last season," Lilly said. "Julia's husband was safely evacuated from Cuba, and Caca and his friends are no longer preparing to instigate a revolution, thank God. Not that their troubles are over. That's why you caught me breaking into the petty cash." She gestured toward the locked cabinet. "Julia is a tad short on funds while Caca gets his sugar business up and running. With the supply from Cuba cut off, everyone will make a mint, and the Rousseaus will be swimming in it. They'll be the toast of the town, just like they were back home."

Wendy made a face. "Personally, I think Julia's a social climber. I have some qualms about those 'high society' claims."

"Oh, Wendy, you're always so suspicious," Lilly said. "Caca and Julia are both from tip-top Cuban families. They're due to be admitted into the B&T, any day. The Kennedys aren't even allowed in there."

"We'll see," Wendy said. "Social climbers always show their true stripes, mainly because they never make it more than halfway up the ladder before falling off from exhaustion. It's great for the economy, though." Yawning again, she flicked a page. "I need to get back to New York."

"Gosh, so sorry to have bored you," Lilly teased, and nudged Wendy's leg with her bare foot. "Anyway. Who wants to get some lunch? I'm starved." She turned to Margo. "You'll come with us, yes? Please say you will."

A smile spilled across Margo's face. She couldn't believe how

quickly Lilly was including her. Maybe the "adoption" was un-
derway. "I would love to—"

"Oh my God! I can't believe it!" Lilly hopped up and Margo's
eyes followed her path to where Peter entered the shop. "What
are you doing here?" Lilly said and kissed him smack on the lips.
"It's not Monday, is it?" She looked at Margo. "He can only abide
the office for a maximum of one day per week. What a life!"

"In fact, it is Wednesday," he said, beaming, eyes crinkling
at the corners. "I had to come in for a meeting and thought we
could grab a bite at the Colony, but it appears you're busy." He
swiveled around to face Margo and his lips drew into a wider
grin. "Hey, it's Slim's right hand. Good to see you again."

"We're not busy in the least," Lilly said. "We were about
to break for lunch, but you can take us *all* out. Your very own
harem."

"It'd be my honor," Peter said.

Lilly was already collecting her things—a handbag, her cigarettes, a single gold bangle. "What's this meeting?" she asked.
"Is it about sugar?"

"An even worse folly." Peter smiled sheepishly. "There was a
transaction I needed to make. I'll tell you all about it at lunch.
It's best if you hear it sitting down."

—

"The suspense is killing me," Lilly said as they strolled along.
Though Christmas was more than a month away, Worth Avenue was decked out with golden baubles, crystal garlands, and
fat red ribbons tied around the trunks of palm trees. "I have to
know *now*. I'm happy to sit down." She squatted, and Margo
couldn't believe how low she was to the ground. "I'll sit right
here on the street."

Peter yanked her to standing. "You're such a goof. I *could* tell
you," he said, his tone so teasing his words seemed to dance.

"But I've had a fabulous life and would like it to continue for a few more minutes."

"PETER!" Lilly tossed her hands up into the sky, but Margo could see it was all show. "What did you buy this time? Wait. Is there a way you can hide it from me? Like a lover or something?"

"She'd be pretty hard to hide," he said. "I purchased a Lotus Seven."

Lilly stopped. She narrowed one eye. "What. On earth. Is a Lotus?" she said. "How much did it cost and why did you buy seven of them?"

Peter laughed. "It's a car. And I only bought one. I guess we can categorize this as 'good news.'"

"Hardly. Why do you keep buying so many damned cars when you prefer to fly?"

"The Lotus isn't for driving. I'm planning to race it at Nassau Speed Week," he said. "This is a little your fault. I'm always trying to convince you that I'm still dashing and adventurous after all these years."

"I'll take alive over dashing any day," Lilly said. "Gah! I just know you're going to croak in some dramatic fashion. Plane crash, eaten by a shark, possibly both. I'll be the most tragic figure to ever exist."

Wendy lit a cigarette. "It's better than dying of a heart attack," she said. "Or cirrhosis."

"She gets it." Peter hooked a thumb toward Wendy. "What about you?" he asked Margo. "Do you think racing cars is foolish?"

"I, um, don't really have an opinion," Margo said, surprised to be pulled into the conversation, surprised they'd remembered she was there.

"Come on!" Peter gave her a friendly wallop on the back.

"You can do better than that. Pick a side. I promise you won't get in trouble."

"Leave the poor girl alone." Wendy took a drag of her cigarette. "She only just arrived in Palm Beach and is still getting her bearings. Lucky break that her first day back she's dining at the Colony. What are the chances?"

Wendy's tone was pointed. More than pointed. A freshly sharpened spear. Margo recalled what she'd said about the social-climbing Julia Rousseau and could only imagine what Wendy might say about *her*. As much as she wanted to lunch with two Pulitzers and a Vanderbilt, as much as she wanted to wedge her way into Lilly's everyday life, Margo couldn't risk getting under Wendy's skin so early in the game.

"Wow," Margo said, inspecting her bare wrist. "I didn't realize how late it'd gotten. I need to find Slim. No lunch for me today, I'm sorry to say."

"But you have to eat *sometime*," Lilly said.

"You do seem very *hungry*," Wendy noted, looking her up and down.

"I wish I could, but Slim is such a bear when I don't check in!" Margo trilled. "Have fun! It was nice to see everyone!" She pivoted on a heel and scurried away.

21

"How soon can you get here?" Slim spit into the phone.

"What time is it?" Margo asked. With the receiver lodged between her shoulder and ear, she walked toward the window. The cord stretched just long enough.

"Who cares what time it is?" Slim said. "I need your help. I promised Rita I'd watch Mary while she golfed."

Margo drew back the shade and studied the new pool deck below. Construction was coming along. "Am I babysitting again?" she said. "You really need to keep better track of your schedule." She hoped this wouldn't be a regular occurrence. Mary was a sweet child but working for Slim Aarons was supposed to be glitzier.

"Not this time. Mary's a regular chatterbox," he grumbled. "And I can't let Rita find out that I forgot again. What I need is for you to run an errand on my behalf."

Margo softly groaned. Did Slim appreciate that any errand she might run would require two to three buses, minimum?

"It involves dropping something off at Lilly Pulitzer's house," he added, and Margo perked right back up.

In short, Slim had printed hundreds of copies of the man-

nequin images from last spring, which Lilly planned to mail
to her Christmas card list to entice her friends into buying her
dresses. Slim promised to deliver the pictures last week, but
the days had gotten away from him, and the Christmas clock
was ticking.

"Okay..." Margo checked the time. "I can be there in thirty
minutes. Will you let me borrow your car?"

"My *car*?" Slim balked. "I thought you hated to drive?"

"That's not true." Margo liked driving fine, she simply wasn't
licensed. This was a technicality, she figured, given how often
she used to tool around in Dolly's white Jaguar. "I haven't been
behind the wheel in a while," she said, "but I'm sure it's one of
those tasks that comes back to you, like riding a bike."

"That's not very comforting..."

"Slim. You're asking me to do *you* a favor," Margo pointed
out. "And this would be more expeditious than syncing multiple bus routes."

"Fine," he said. "I'll call Lilly and tell her the plan. Whatever you do, don't overstay your welcome. Remember, this is
a job. And these are not your friends."

⁓

"We're in the kitchen!" Lilly called out, after a maid let Margo
inside. "Just come on back, Slim."

"It's Margo, actually," she said, following her memory, and
the scent of something simmering on a stove.

"Even better!"

"I have your—" Margo took two steps into the kitchen and
promptly tripped, careening into the champagne fridge.

"Whoa, easy there," Lilly said with a quick laugh.

"I'm so sorry," Margo said, glancing back to the pair of
tanned legs splayed across the tile. "I didn't see you there." She
was mortified but, also, what kind of grown adult sat on the
floor? Especially a floor that was routinely trampled by chil-

dren and pets. But Margo was the interloper, and the mistake was hers, and she apologized a few more times for good measure. "I'm sorry," she repeated.

"It's perfectly fine," the woman said as she pushed a dollop of baby food through the rosebud lips of the boy on her lap. Taking in the scene, Margo's brain went hazy. She began to lose sensation in her arms and legs.

Lilly spoke and stirred an enormous vat of chili, but Margo heard nothing through the whooshing in her ears. All she could think about was how Slim was going to flip his lid when he realized he'd sent Margo on an errand that put her in the same room as Jackie Kennedy.

"I'm sorry for interrupting," Margo said, avoiding so much as a glimpse of the First Lady. *Pretend she's not in the room.* "Should I come back later?"

"No, and you're not interrupting at all. We're just chitchatting. Jacks needed a breather," Lilly said, and Margo accepted that ignoring Jackie wasn't a viable option. "The photogs have been relentless. Palm Beach is supposed to be a *reprieve* from the hoi polloi, but this place feels no more exclusive than Coney Island."

"Their bulbs and big lenses," Jackie said, her voice a whisper. "Some days, I really can't take it." She set down the Gerber's and lifted John-John from her lap. As he teetered away, she pulled a cylindrical gold case from her purse, and removed a cigarette. "Don't tell the press." She flashed a devilish grin.

"The reporters are absolute vultures," Lilly said. "I don't know how you stand it."

Jackie took a hard, intense draw on her cigarette. "It is quite frightening to lose your anonymity at age thirty-two," she said. "Though I'm used to it." Cigarette still burning between her fingers, she began to gnaw on one of her nails, all of which were short and ragged, bitten down to the quick.

"I would've bolted by this point," Lilly said.

Jackie laughed softly. "I bolt, on occasion," she said. "But it's always temporary. Jack needs his wife, and that is my job. You must think our marriage is terribly Victorian." Jackie reached out, snagging John-John's britches to guide him back to her side. He wasn't skilled at walking yet and landed with a thump on his rear.

"You could've *only* married Jack Kennedy," Lilly said. "Anyone else would've bored you to death." She dipped her finger into the chili to sample a taste. "And I couldn't have married him because he's too conventional, and cares too much what his family thinks."

Margo watched all this in silence, her mouth slightly ajar. As the aroma of ground beef and onions wafted around them, all she could think was, *Jackie eats beans?*

"That's why Peter is perfect for me," Lilly went on, wiping her hands on her yellow-and-white gingham shift. "He didn't go into the family business. He does his own thing and lets me do what I want. He's also not too hard on the old peepers."

"Peter is extremely handsome," Jackie agreed. "Every woman is a little bit in love with him. But honestly, Lilly, how do you stand all that sweat and dirt?"

"I'm not prim and proper like you. We're opposites, remember?" Lilly looked at Margo. "Jacks was always so studious, but I wanted to have fun. She stayed in her room with her nose in a book, while I zipped about, befriending absolutely anyone who'd tolerate me."

"What a curious way to say you were trying to rule the world," Jackie teased, in that soft, whispery voice. Until today, Margo had assumed it was a put-on. "It's a miracle that I liked you at all. Usually I find feminists beyond exhausting."

"I'd hardly call myself a feminist. Look at me. Barefoot in the kitchen."

"You're always barefoot," Margo piped in and was treated to laughter not only from Lilly Pulitzer but also the First Lady of the United States.

Margo was about to attempt a follow-on comment, something witty, if possible, when Lilly whipped toward her. "Where are my manners?" she said, and Lilly's demeanor shifted. There was a stiffening, as if she'd only just realized she wasn't among friends. "Poor Margo's been standing here, waiting for us to finish giggling so she can take care of business. Did you have something for me?" She nodded toward Margo's hand.

"Oh. Right!" Margo extended the envelope toward Lilly. Her fingers had left round greasy prints behind. "Slim asked me to drop these off."

"It's about damned time," Lilly said and ripped open the package. "Thank you, Margo. You're an absolute lifesaver." She turned to Jackie. "Margo is Slim Aarons' latest assistant."

"Slim Aarons?" Jackie's face brightened, proving that Slim Aarons had this effect on absolutely everyone. So much charm, wasted on a man. "I adore Slim! He's shot my husband's family for years."

Margo nodded, thinking of the picture of Jackie in Slim's hallway, taken at the April in Paris Ball in '58, when Jack was only a young senator from Massachusetts. In the photograph, Jackie wears pearls and elbow-length white gloves, and has a ruby-red satin wrap on her lap. She smiles into Slim's lens adoringly.

"It's my favorite photograph ever taken of Jackie," Slim had said, when he caught Margo staring. "In so many pictures she seems hard, but not here. It's all in her eyes. They're soft, loving, and open. That's the real Jackie Kennedy."

"Remember my dressmaking hobby?" Lilly handed Jackie a photograph. "My seamstress went wild with the latest batch, and none of them fit. She forgets I'm thick in the middle, even though I diet constantly." Jackie nodded in solidarity as Lilly continued, "Now I'm overrun with frocks in a *fruit* shop, which is *no bueno* this time of year, and Peter decided to further complicate my life by advertising my baskets in every major newspaper in Florida. The orders are flooding in, and I've got to make room for all the damned citrus. Thought I'd send these photos out to the ladies, along with handwritten notes, to lure them into the shop and get the dresses off my hands. What do you think?"

"Lilly," Jackie said. "This is incredible. You're going to sell out in a blink. If you don't, give me a ring, and I'll scoop them up."

"They would hang on you."

Jackie shrugged. "I have a good tailor." Sighing, she pushed herself to standing and ground her cigarette into an ashtray. "I should get back to the manse. Let's go, darling boy. See how your father's doing." She swept her son onto her hip with one surprisingly toned arm. "Jack hurt his back."

Lilly made a face. "Again?"

"He can't even pick a piece of paper up off the floor," Jackie said. "His mood is unbearable."

"I'm sorry, love. I'm not much of a churchy type, but I'll pray with everything I've got that he recovers soon. For your sake, at least." Lilly smiled, but her mouth was strained. There was something in the air that Margo could not pick up. "He'll be fine," Lilly said, and squeezed Jackie's hand.

"That's what people tell me," she said, sighing again. "I suppose my only choice is to believe it."

22

DECEMBER 1961

If there was one place to find Palm Beachers on the other side of the bridge, it was at the Palm Beach Kennel Club.

"Greyhound racing?" Margo said, top lip curled, when Slim told her where they'd be working that night. "You know that's illegal in California?" Sandy LaSalle used to complain about it all the time, though it struck Margo that he always found somewhere to watch. Had he gone to Nevada? An underground track? It probably wasn't worth thinking about.

"What a helpful piece of information," Slim said, rolling his eyes. "Luckily we're in *Florida*."

When they arrived at the Belvedere Road oval, the grandstand was packed with smartly dressed men and women staring at any one of the five televisions and speaking a language Margo could not comprehend. *Lengths* and *posts* and *5–2 favorites. Hemmed in at the first turn.* Something called a *quiniela.*

"I'm going in on Pat's Flyer," someone said as he bumped Margo's arm. His friend wanted Screen Play, maybe Best Policy.

There were too many people, and too many words. Not even Slim could take a decent picture in this crowded, shadowy place, and Margo sensed they weren't truly there to work. Slim had gone in on the next race, placing his money on Crocadoll.

"What's wrong?" he asked, cigarette dangling from his mouth. "You're very pale."

"I'm always pale."

"That's not true. Normally you are red."

"I'm sorry. I'm a little…" Margo waved a hand in front of her nose. "Overwhelmed."

"Overwhelmed?" Slim scrunched his face. "At a dog track? I hope you weren't like this when you met the First Lady."

"It's not the same," Margo said. Ever since she'd told Slim about the encounter, he'd acted like she'd purposefully done something sneaky, like rob a bank, and he was going to personally catch hell for it. Margo had been out of her depth, certainly, but hadn't committed any sins that she knew of. "I'm sorry," she said. "This place is getting to me."

"Oh, here we go. Time for the customary Margo regroup," Slim said, twirling a hand overhead. "Go take a minute. I don't need you attracting any bad luck."

"Thanks," Margo said, bolting from the oval before he could think twice.

Exhaling, Margo stepped outside just as a long black car pulled up to the curb. She paused, watching as a man in a dark suit lunged out of the back seat. He was polished, buffed like a gem, and his thick, dark hair was combed with such precision, the grooves could be seen from a distance. As the man drew closer, Margo's heart caught. It was Dutch Elkin, in the Brylcreem and flesh.

"Why, hello there," he said, and Margo swore he was emanating actual heat. Finally, she understood the term *weak in the knees.* "What's a pretty girl doing out here all alone? Celebrating a big win? Recovering from your losses?"

"Neither," Margo said with a jittery smile. "It's kinda crowded in there."

"I feel that. Have we met before?" he said, looking Margo up and down. "You're very familiar, but I'm embarrassed to say that I can't recall. Trust me, it's not you. I'm known as a bit of a scatterbrain."

"Margo Hightower. I think we ran into each other…" Margo squinted, feigning deep contemplation. "At a party at Lilly Pulitzer's last season?" It was strange how something could be true but also very much not, depending on how it was said. "You were playing the piano? We didn't really have an opportunity to talk…"

"Ah. Well. That explains it. My head's so gummed up when I'm working, I barely remember my own name. I'm Dutch Elkin. As far as I know!" He put out a hand. As Margo shook it, she noticed a scar slicing through his left eyebrow. "In case you were wondering, I'm a musician," he added, "which explains the aforementioned piano."

"Oh, neat," Margo said, pretending this was new information, that she hadn't a clue he was the leader of a ten-piece orchestra with a recently released album tearing up the charts. When it came to Dutch Elkin, she knew an embarrassing number of details. His mother had died in childbirth, for instance, and his father by suicide shortly thereafter. Baby Dutch was raised by his mother's good friend and her husband, the son of a railroad tycoon who'd run for president three times.

"Well, Margo Hightower," Dutch said, "I ought to get inside, but I hope you're in Palm Beach for a while, and not just passing through."

"A few more weeks," Margo said. If she was passing through, a dog track on the other side of the bridge would've been a weird place to stop, but she didn't mention this, given he was here, too.

"Excellent." He grinned. "So maybe I'll see you inside?"

"Maybe so," Margo said with a nod.

"If we don't find each other in there—" He took her hand and gently brushed his lips across her knuckles. "I'll make it a point to run into you somewhere."

23

Margo pushed open the yellow door. "Hello?" she called out, craning over the baskets and dress racks. "It's Margo. I'm here to help!"

Ever since Margo proved herself capable of not crashing cars or irrevocably offending First Ladies, Slim had been quick to send her on errands. Usually this meant picking up some old coot's prescriptions from the pharmacy, but today her task was Lilly. Peter's advertisements had left her inundated with gift basket orders and she had only a few days to get them out.

"Hello?" Margo said again, venturing all the way in. Christmas music played from the radio. The lights were dimmed, and the shop felt homey and smelled of citrus. "Lilly?"

Margo snaked through the glut of baskets and crates, following the beacon of Lilly's sky-high bouffant until she found her on an upturned bucket, tying a sage green bow around a wicker box.

"Oh, thank *God*," Lilly said. "I was about to give up and burn down the place for the insurance money. Can you believe this goddamned mess? What is with men? Somehow their version of 'helping' causes forty-eight new problems."

Margo pulled up a stool and Lilly went through the instructions. She'd determined the most efficient route from A to B, *so just follow along and we'll be out of here in a jiff.* It was a more focused Lilly than the one who'd closed Julia's shop last spring. There were no cocktails this time.

The task was simple, but Margo struggled to concentrate. The damned Christmas music was making her nostalgic, for no reason that she could work out. Margo had always been an afterthought in her home, and Christmases were not meant for her. Sure, there were grand years when Sandy was flush, with two-story trees in the foyer and velvet dresses and, once, a live pony under the tree, but that was another lifetime ago.

Last year's holiday was the bleakest on record. Sandy had split for Brazil, and Crim was in Palm Beach, supposedly securing his grandmother's ring. For an excruciating ninety minutes, Margo sat with her mom at the long, shiny table that fit up to sixteen, chewing through a very tough roast, distracting herself with visions of wedding dresses and the joys *next* Christmas would bring.

Now it *was* next Christmas, Margo realized with a start. There was no Crim, no Antoinette, not a plan in sight. When she tried to conjure how a Palm Beach holiday might look, her mind went blank.

"I don't think you've ever told me," Lilly said, jerking Margo back into the room. "How did you end up as Slim's assistant? Do I recall a busted engagement?"

"Something like that." Margo tugged on her bulky V-neck cardigan, wondering why she'd dressed for Bedford or San Francisco instead of Palm Beach. The shop was stuffy, and she was already working up a sweat.

"Well, that man is an idiot, if you ask me," Lilly said. "You're cute as all get-out. But, really, he did you a favor. Every girl should have one broken engagement. It gives her some experience and makes future beaus work harder, knowing she might split. Anyhow, I suspect you won't be single long. That's meant to be a reassurance, by the way. Not a threat."

Margo forced a laugh. "I hope you're right. It's not easy to meet people, with Slim's schedule," she confided, halfway surprised she'd said this out loud. But Lilly was so open and gracious, she practically drew the words out.

"Dealing with Slim on a daily basis could qualify as an Olympic event. No matter. Lucky for you, I *love* setting people up. Granted, there are a lot of olds around here, and unless you have a penchant for retired farm-equipment manufacturers, the pickings are thin. What's your type?"

"Oh gosh." Margo hemmed and hawed. She didn't know whether Lilly was truly serious, but answering "correctly" seemed critical. "Well. Um. I ran into Dutch Elkin at the racetrack the other day..." Margo gulped, hoping he didn't sound too out of the blue, or too out of reach.

"Dutch is a hunk," Lilly agreed. "Unfortunately, there aren't too many of him around."

"Yeah, I figured..."

"Though I'm very resourceful. I introduced Slim's last assistant to *her* husband."

Margo nearly fell off her stool. "You did?"

"You bet. He's Dysie's cousin and it was love at first sight. Slim barely forgave me for that. Hmm." She tapped her chin. "Let me think on it. I'll come up with somebody great. You're too darling to be single, and, Lord knows, you can't spend the rest of your life following around Slim."

—

A few minutes after nine o'clock, Lilly hopped to her feet and announced it was time for a break. She heaved herself onto the couch and patted the cushion beside her. Margo sat down in what she'd come to think of as Wendy Vanderbilt's spot.

"We're making progress," Lilly said, lighting a cigarette. She offered one to Margo, who shook her head. As much as she'd tried, Margo could never get the hang of smoking. She always felt like a bumbling fool, and there was nothing glamorous about hacking up a lung. "I love how Peter complains that I take too much fruit, yet his little schemes are what's generating the demand. Look at this place!" She flung out a hand. "Slim printed all those splendid photos and they're sitting in my kitchen, collecting dust. I haven't had a second to mail them out."

"You could do a postholiday sale?" Margo suggested. That's what the stores in her neighborhood did when they were overstocked. It was the only time of year Antoinette gave her money to shop.

"That sounds like a lot of work," Lilly said.

"Oh, sure. I just thought—"

"Not to worry. I'll handle it in my usual way. Have fun and trust the solution will present itself, eventually." She turned to smile. Unlike her husband's straight white teeth, hers were crooked, and mildly overlapping, as though she had a few spares. "This can't be how you anticipated your evening might turn out," Lilly added, "but I'm eternally grateful."

"I don't mind at all. I like being in the shop," Margo said, and meant it. Even though her back ached, and her hands were dry, she loved the crackle of the cellophane, the scent of the fruit and, most of all, the warm presence of Lilly.

"Tell me, Margo," Lilly said. She took a drag of her cigarette and released a long stream of smoke. "If you weren't working for Slim, or marrying the wrong man, what would you be doing right now?"

"Oh gosh," Margo spluttered, picking shards of dried wicker off her kelly green double-knit pants. "I suppose I'd still be at interior design school?" Was this true? If Sandy's schemes hadn't collapsed, would Margo have stayed, or would she have married Crim and left to set up house? When she pictured her former classmates traipsing back and forth across campus, the notion she might be with them almost made her laugh. It felt like a version of Margo Hightower that was never meant to be.

"Interior design school?" Lilly said. "How fun. I love decorating, but of course, most people find my style offensive to good taste. Did you get a degree and everything?"

"Not exactly. I went for a semester, but…had to leave."

"No way!" Lilly thwacked Margo on the leg. "Me, too! I went to Finch for one semester, but ack! It was so dull. I couldn't stand it. So, I bailed. Went to work as a midwife's assistant in Appalachia."

Appalachia? The revelation knocked the wind from Margo's chest. Most Palm Beachers believed they lived in a wild and woolly place. This is the last frontier, they'd say, citing the Everglades, and bobcats, and man-eating alligators. The bravado always made Margo roll her eyes, and she couldn't imagine any of them living in Appalachia, Lilly least of all.

"You think I'm batty," Lilly said. "And you're right, but I longed for something different, and that's what I got. Days spent riding a mule through the knobs—that's what they call hills—delivering medicines and supplies, occasionally assisting in a home birth. I was never going to do it long-term, but it scratched the itch I had at the time."

Now that Margo thought about it, maybe Lilly was the one Palm Beacher who could make it in Kentucky, or wherever Appalachia was. She already had a predilection toward bare feet, and at that very moment, most of her friends were decked out in their finest, hobnobbing at Ta-boo or the Everglades Club, while Lilly was here, packaging fruit. What had she said, all those months ago? They were both doers. They wanted to achieve tangible things. This was true about Lilly, and Margo hoped it was about her, too.

"I don't think you're batty at all," Margo said. "I'm impressed. You do so much that you don't have to. Assisting in home births. Running this shop."

"I wouldn't call this a charity project. I'm somewhat trying to make a profit. Despite how it must appear."

"Yes, but you have a husband, children, a house on Lake Worth." *A place to spend your holidays.* This was probably getting too personal, crossing some line, but Margo couldn't stop herself. She was desperate to understand how someone with everything wasn't satisfied, why she'd be willing to exert such effort when she didn't have to.

"Sadly, children have terrible profit margins," Lilly said with a wink. "You wouldn't believe how often they demand to be fed. Multiple times per day! My weekly grocery bill rivals the GDP of a small country."

"Yes, but, you don't need to worry about it. You have, um, ample resources..." Margo cringed, hoping this was an acceptable way to talk about money.

"I'm loaded, is what you're saying. Livin' in fat city. You're right, though. My life is great, and I do occasionally fantasize about giving up the hassle of commerce to spend my days drinking bourbon by the pool. But—gah!—I'd get so damned bored. Without the shop or some other thing to keep me busy, I'd end up at Bloomingdale's, same as before."

"You've mentioned Bloomingdale's a few times," Margo said. "I know it was the impetus for the fruit business, but what was so great about it, if you don't mind my asking?" She couldn't comprehend how a shopping trip had such a lingering effect. This was a woman who made her own clothes with fabrics bought at the five-and-dime.

"Oh gosh, where to start? Before Bloomingdale's, I was a

namby-pamby, not in control of my own life. I let everyone else tell me what to do. Took me a while to recognize that I needed to be the boss."

Margo cocked her head, taking this in. "But the kids, and the house…" she said. "Aren't you the boss of all that?"

Lilly snorted. "Hardly. Women like me, we're not *really* in charge of these things. The proof is in the pudding. Even though I'm constantly at the store, my house runs as smoothly as it ever did. There are maids, and tutors. Nannies and governesses. Tennis and riding instructors. Even a cook. Everything is always perfect when I walk through the door, just as I'd hoped and feared it will be. But this shop… It could only be run by me. And isn't that magnificent?"

"Wow." Margo blinked. "I'd never thought about it like that." Was it—God forbid—boring to be rich? What did a wife do when her days weren't filled with a thousand small and medium tasks?

"Bloomingdale's was the best thing that ever happened to me," Lilly went on. "I think it was the regimen. Reminded me of boarding school."

"I must be missing something," Margo said, but her words were broken up by the clap of the door. Both women stretched over the baskets to see who had the gall to enter despite the CLOSED sign in the window.

"Come back tomorrow!" Lilly sang. "Ten o'clock. Noon!"

"I don't know, kid. I'm awfully busy," a man said. The voice was so familiar it sent goose bumps crawling along Margo's skin. "Maybe you can help a guy out. I *heah* you've got the goods."

"Son of a bitch," Lilly said with a laugh. "What the hell are you doing here?"

Margo poked her head up, like a gopher out of a hole. It was Jack Kennedy. She almost died on the spot.

"Can't you see we're *closed*?" Lilly said, sauntering up to his side. "Guess you don't have to be able to read to attend Ha-vahd."

"I've never cared much for rules." He flashed his million-watt smile. "I'll make it quick. My wife loves your dresses, and I live to make her happy. Since she couldn't pick a pattern, I'll take one of everything ya got."

Lilly looked over to Margo and wiggled her brows. *The solution will present itself, eventually.* For Lilly, maybe it really did.

24

Margo threw her purse onto the dresser and dashed to the phone. She didn't consider herself a gossipy type, but in the last two weeks, she'd met both the president and the First Lady and had to tell *someone*. Dolly picked up on the third ring.

"Dolly!" Margo said, beginning to cry. How she'd missed that husky, smoky voice. "Thank God! I thought you were avoiding me. You've been impossible to reach, but I wasn't about to give up. I must've tried fifty times." This was no exaggeration, but Margo was bubbling with so much excitement that she was willing to forget the unanswered rings and all the messages left over the past nine months, none of which Dolly returned. Even her mother always picked up for their last-Sunday-of-the-month calls. But Antoinette wasn't Dolly, and her friend did this sometimes. She vanished without warning, and it was never personal.

"Great timing," Dolly said. "I was *just* about to leave. How are you? How's Slim?"

"Slim is the same as always. Never mind him. You won't believe who I met tonight. Or the other week!" Margo described everything, from tripping over the First Lady, to John-John, to the smoking. "If you ever notice a lackey standing around with a lit cigarette, it's hers! She makes them hold one in case she needs a puff."

She told her about the president coming into Lilly's store and buying every dress. "Jack is as handsome as you'd expect," Margo clattered, "and I found Jackie positively enchanting. Her manner of speaking is so unusual. It really draws a person in."

"Sounds like you're having fun," Dolly said with a short, perfunctory laugh. "Do the Kennedys know that half the people in Palm Beach *swore* they'd leave the country if he were elected? Now they happily shake his hand while griping about his politics, and accusing him of being an amphetamine freak behind his back."

"They're worse about Bobby," Margo said, "on account of him being a dangerous, leftist radical. All the Kennedys are fair game, aside from Rose, whom everybody adores." She plopped onto the bed, swelling with warmth. Talking to Dolly was like visiting home.

"I'm happy it's going so well," Dolly said, and Margo could hear her smile through the phone. "You've really turned things around. I'm proud of you! Listen, I should go—"

"Wait!" A flutter of panic rose in Margo's chest. *Now or never*, she thought, with a hard swallow. "What are your plans for the rest of the month? I was thinking of going back to San Francisco for Christmas. It would be nice to get together? We haven't seen each other in close to a year!"

"You want to come to San Francisco?"

"I thought I could stay at the Huntington," Margo said. "If you have a vacancy, that is. I can pay for it myself. I've saved a decent amount because Slim doesn't let me do anything. At this rate, I'm in danger of becoming independently wealthy!"

"The Huntington," Dolly repeated. She hesitated a moment.

Several moments. An entire afternoon, just about. "I'm sorry, that doesn't work. I'm spending the holiday with Don."

Margo felt herself deflate. She'd partway expected this, but that didn't mean she couldn't wish it'd gone the other way. "The thing with Don is serious, then," she said.

"I'd say so. I'm going to marry the man."

Margo stared at a smudge on the wall. No matter how many times Dolly got engaged, she never expected her to go through with it. In some ways, she *counted* on it. When Margo was little, her mom was the only person she could depend on, but Sandy LaSalle had taken that away. Then Dolly swooped in, just in time. If her friend slipped into forever with Don, where did that leave Margo?

"Hello?" Dolly said. "Is something wrong with the phone? I must've missed your excitement and well wishes."

"The phone is fine. I'm just...surprised." Margo's voice was strangled. "Don MacMasters must be some catch if you're finally settling down. It's hard to imagine anyone more appealing than King Baudouin."

"I want a real person," Dolly said. "Not a king."

Margo nodded. *You've never met Don in person*, she reminded herself. *You don't know what he's really like.* All she'd seen were grainy pictures, and maybe Don didn't photograph well. Dolly rarely looked like the force she was.

"Well, I'm very happy for you both," Margo lied. She hoped that saying it might make the sentiment real. "Once you're married, do you think you'll travel a lot? Because of Don's State Department job?"

"Don is no longer with the government," Dolly said.

"Oh, really? What will he be doing now?" Margo was attempting neutrality but could sense Dolly tightening, closing like a zipper.

"If you must know, he's opening an antiques shop in San Francisco," Dolly said, "specializing in French furniture."

Margo squeezed her eyes shut, as if in pain. Opening an antiques shop sounded like a Sandy LaSalle–type gambit, if her mom had the money for it. Margo envisioned a parade of fly-by-night enterprises where Don made only revenue and Dolly paid all the bills.

"Don is a wonderful man," Dolly said with great emphasis. "And it's time. I want to be married. Have kids. I can't put it off any longer. I'm going to be twenty-seven this year."

"Twenty-seven isn't that old…"

"Try to be happy for me, Gogo. Try to understand."

"I'm happy for you," Margo choked out. "I wish you all the best."

After they said their goodbyes, Margo hung up the phone, feeling at once empty and cold, as though someone had flipped her over and dumped out everything good. For so many years, they'd both been alone, and Dolly was her salve, her comfy corner of the world. It was only a single conversation, and maybe Margo was overthinking it, but Dolly's *goodbye* felt like a permanent farewell. A statement. She didn't need Margo anymore, if she ever did in the first place.

25

For the first time since Sibley and Dean's wedding, Margo was not the worker bee at someone's house party, but a guest. Technically the hosts had invited Slim and Rita, and Margo was *their* guest, but at least she wouldn't have to worry about lighting or wind or lugging multiple heavy objects from one room to the next.

The event was a Christmas party with a *Bachelor Father* theme, though Margo wasn't sure what was so festive about a situation comedy featuring the misadventures of a single father and his manservant raising a teenage niece. The decorations didn't clear things up, either. When guests walked in, a butler greeted them with white-and-red leis flown in from Hawaii. Chinese lanterns hung from the pergola and antique cars were parked on the lawn.

Though she had the lei, and a cocktail, Margo didn't know the hosts, or the guests, and felt glaringly out of place. Slim and Rita were off doing the twist and Margo had nothing to do aside from stand around near the dance floor, smiling blankly into the void, while everyone around her discussed Christmas plans. Lucky jerks.

Thirty minutes passed. Forty-five. An hour. Margo wasn't working tonight, which meant she didn't have to stay. She could take a bus back to the hotel, and spare Slim the hassle of driving her home. It was a mistake to think she could show up at a stranger's house and simply fit in.

As Margo turned toward the house in defeat, someone grabbed her arm. "Where do you think you're going, Missy?" Lilly said, whirling her around. "Merry Christmas!" She planted a kiss on each of Margo's cheeks. "You're adorable in Christmas plaid, but we *must* get you into a Lilly. What do you think of the latest number?" She twirled to show off a red-and-pink, floor-length Lilly adorned with large white butterflies.

"It's terrific, of course. And I'd love a Lilly," Margo said, observing the man behind her. He was tall and dapper with olive skin and slicked, thinning hair. "But I'm shocked you have any left to sell."

"Isn't that the truth? Whew! The president stripped me clean." Lilly buckled her knees and pretended to pass out. "I'm going to have to find a new fabric supplier. Woolworth's is absolutely fed up with me buying all of their stock." She looked back and pulled her companion into the conversation. "Enrique, you remember Margo, don't you? Slim's assistant. The one who absolutely saved my life."

Margo extended a hand. "We haven't met," she said, throwing on her best and most dazzling debutante smile.

"You haven't *met*?" Lilly smacked her forehead. "Enrique Rousseau, this is Margo, as she just pointed out. Sheesh. Nobody needs me here at all."

The name took a minute to register. Caca Rousseau, live and in person. It felt like meeting a minor celebrity, and in fact he *did* call to mind an aristocrat from a Nancy Mitford novel, exactly as promised.

"The pleasure is all mine," Caca said, and kissed Margo's hand. "Slim's assistants get more enchanting all the time."

The comment was compulsory, but it pinked Margo's cheeks, and she wondered with a faint desperation if she was ever going to outgrow this habit. She already appeared younger than her years and having the complexion of a rashy kid didn't help.

"Oh, brother," Lilly said with a titter. "Trying to charm everyone you meet. Don't mind him, Margo. You know how those well-heeled Cuban refugees are, always playing the part of dashing romantic heroes."

"It is *you* who decided we're romantic figures," Caca said, mischief jumping in his eyes. "You who thought we were so brave, escaping the Red takeover, sailing to America in boats packed with fine French furniture, and money sewn into our clothes. Alas, the Americans have realized we're intent on staying, so the enthusiasm has died. You are no longer willing to be charmed by us."

"Poor, poor Caca Caliente," Lilly said, pouting.

"It *is* very difficult to be me," he teased. "Especially when beautiful, ambitious women waste parties by talking business. Nights like this I wish I hadn't survived the Revolution."

"Not funny!" Lilly gave him a light whack to the chest. "We were discussing Talisman," she said to Margo. "His and Peter's sugar venture."

"It is not Peter's business. It is my business. He is helping me find the money."

Lilly rolled her eyes. "In any case," she said, "I was offering my counsel, but Cubans absolutely loathe listening to women. Meanwhile, I'm so good at selling, I'm completely out of my best product."

Margo smiled but couldn't imagine a scenario in which the president would buy all of Rousseau's sugar. *The invisible hand is a crock of shit*, Sandy LaSalle used to say. According to him, there was no single "market" because rich people had their own. There might be a nugget of truth in there, somewhere, if Margo understood economics.

"Lilly, *tata*, you have a brilliant mind for business," Rousseau said, patting her head, his gold watch jangling on his wrist. "But let's not get ahead of ourselves. Before we can *sell* the sugar, we need to *plant* the sugar. Small details, no?"

Caca babbled something about financing, and Lilly shot back. Margo barely knew how her own bank account worked and pretended to listen while examining Caca's face. He wasn't catalogue-model attractive, but had an allure that came on slowly, the more you looked.

"I'm just asking you to listen to me for one second! Is that so difficult?" Lilly said, throwing her arms over her head. Caca stepped away from her, and she stepped closer. They did this several more times, until Margo was forced to ask herself whether she was still part of the conversation.

"When those two get going," a voice behind her said, "it's impossible not to play the third wheel." Margo spun around and came face-to-face with Peter, dressed in a half-baked Santa costume (top half only), a drink in each hand. "One of these was supposed to be for Lilly, but she's clearly occupied. Care for a cocktail? Your choices are a gin gimlet or a Mai Tai."

Margo checked Lilly and Caca, who were several yards away, screeching and hollering—good-naturedly, of course—and speaking dramatically with their hands. "Sure, I'd love one," Margo said, reaching for the Mai Tai.

Peter moved it away. "Please. Allow me. It's not too often I get to play chivalrous gentleman," he said, smiling, his white teeth glowing against his deep tan. "Those shoes look like they hurt. Whaddaya say we take a load off? Follow me."

26

Peter sat on one of the lounge chairs by the pool, Margo the other. She locked her ankles together and prayed her rear wouldn't break through the plastic strips.

"I hope you don't feel obligated to babysit," she said as they both stared out across the pool. Here she was, alone with Tarzan at her first Palm Beach party. It seemed like trespassing. "There must be gobs of people you need to see." She tilted her head toward the dance floor, on the other side of the hedge.

"Perhaps, but a pretty young woman should never be left alone in Palm Beach." Peter wielded another of his high-voltage smiles. "I can't believe the buzzards haven't swarmed. Where is Jim Kimberly anyhow?" He made a show of looking around.

Margo laughed. "I thought you two were old pals?"

"We're the best of friends," Peter said, "which is how I know he's such a wolf. What were those two talking about over there, anyway?" He dipped his head toward Lilly and Caca, who remained engaged in an extremely spirited debate. "Talisman?"

Margo nodded. "She's giving him advice, though he doesn't seem very receptive."

"No. He wouldn't be. A man like that," he said. "My wife is

something else. She fancies herself a business mogul now that she's sold out of baskets and dresses. Not that she's wrong." Shaking his head, he fished around in his pocket for a cigarette. "Only Lilly Lee could turn a hobby into a major enterprise. That woman was gifted with the ability to spin anything into gold. I'm so damned proud, I could burst into tears."

Speaking of tears, there was a knot of them in Margo's throat. She'd never heard a man talk about his wife that way.

"I'll bet ya that by next season," Peter went on, "all of Palm Beach will be decked out in Lilly Pulitzer shifts. You should pick one up, before you leave. Bring the style to…" He squinted. "Where'd you say you were from?"

Margo sipped her drink. The ice had melted, but the pop of lime was strong. Had it been from one of Peter's trees, or did he stick to yellow and orange fruit? "San Francisco," she replied. "You know, *the shapeless nightmare?*"

Peter groaned and threw back his head. "What a jerk! Don't take anything I say seriously. I hope I didn't offend you."

"Not at all." Margo gave a quick smile. "The city is great, but it has its drawbacks. It can be…" She searched for the right word. "Confusing. It's part of California, but…*different*. The weather is awful, of course."

Peter leaned forward, elbows on his knees, a cigarette burning in his left hand. "As Mark Twain said, *The coldest winter I ever spent was a summer in San Francisco.*"

"Exactly. I love it, but it's the sort of place that can really mess a person up."

Her mother, for example. Possibly Dolly Fritz. In some ways, it made sense. The city was founded by misfits and criminals and settlers who arrived via wagon train, after potentially consuming several family members along the way. Margo couldn't explain this to Peter, of course, lest he mention the *perfectly insane* people again.

"I think it's because there's such a wide gap between the promise of California," she said instead, "especially Northern California, and what it delivers. It's a far cry from Palm Beach, where everything is so lovely, and reliable." She pictured the island's clean avenues, the awnings, the neatly trimmed hedges.

"Plenty of folks find those traits off-putting."

"Oh, I'm aware," Margo said. "My best friend…" *Former* best friend. "She thinks Palm Beach is a tacky, 'made-up' place. Can you imagine? She's from San Francisco, too, if that tells you anything."

"To be fair, she has a point," Peter said. "A person could argue that Palm Beach is the most compelling place made with money. In other parts of the world—San Francisco, for example—cities and bridges and roads were constructed out of necessity. Here, they were built as luxuries. For years, people were perfectly fine to do without. One person's *lovely* is another's *unnatural*."

Margo remembered what Charlie Munn had said, the day they photographed him on Lake Trail with his bike. On top of his draining-of-the-Everglades concerns, he had an entire speech about how in Palm Beach they used to walk on dirt roads and shoot their own dinners, relaying this in a manner that suggested he considered it a preferable existence. "I never thought about it like that," Margo said now. "On the other hand, all that planning means it'll never qualify as a *shapeless nightmare*."

"You do know that the man who developed Palm Beach was born in Northern California?" Peter asked, and Margo looked at him, surprised. "It's true. The Mizner brothers were a couple of shysters who spent their early years swindling gold miners, marrying ninety-year-old widows, and picking up felony convictions before taking their tricks to Palm Beach. They're responsible for the style around here—whatever you think that's worth—but they also fueled the Florida boom with a host of schemes. Bank fraud, interlocking directorates, and insider trading. Then, of course, they blew it all up."

"Hmm. Interesting." Margo took a tense sip of her Mai Tai. She was probably the only woman at the party familiar with the term *interlocking directorates*, and wasn't proud of it.

"That's why there's something a tad *off* with every one of Mizner's buildings," he said. According to Peter, Addison Mizner was famous for his refusal to follow a plan. He built houses that were significantly larger or smaller than what a client asked for and often forgot full rooms, staircases, and kitchens. "Don't let the carefully curated impression fool you. Things can seem grand from the outside but be very convoluted once you open the door." Suddenly, Peter hopped up. "Your glass is empty. Let's get another drink." He reached down and hauled Margo to her feet.

"Well, well, well," a voice said, and Margo yanked her arm out of Peter's hold. "What do we have here? The last two people I'd expect to see buddying up on loungers."

"The incomparable Wendy Vanderbilt," Peter said, as Wendy stepped in front of them. "Lilly didn't tell me you'd be here. I thought you were in New York?"

"Decided to stick around," Wendy said, the ostrich feathers on her dress flapping in the wind. "You are too funny, Peter. You'll talk to absolutely *anyone*. Hi, Margo. I wasn't aware you knew the Scotts."

"Oh, sure…" She glanced around. Were the Scotts the people who owned this house?

"Anyway. Enough chitchat." Wendy slid her arm through Peter's and snuggled into his side. "Shall we find Lilly? We need to rescue poor Enrique from your wife's incessant 'help.'"

"Did someone say my name?" Now Lilly had materialized on the pool deck, leaving Margo to wonder if there was some rich person's portal she wasn't aware of. "Everyone needs to stop yammering about how magnanimous I am. It's exhausting."

"You really are magnificent, darling," Peter said, and kissed her cheek. "I'm glad you've joined us and, more importantly, given poor Rousseau a break."

"There *are* more pressing matters than Talisman Sugar Corporation. I wanted to introduce Margo to someone," Lilly said. She whistled and snapped her fingers overhead. A man broke away from a group on the lawn and walked around to their side of the hedge. His presence cast a long shadow, even at night.

"You two have met, right?" Lilly said, and Margo's mouth went dry. Somehow, Dutch Elkin was more attractive than she remembered. Taller, too, but not gangly like Slim.

"Hey, gorgeous," Dutch said, narrowing in on Margo, his eyes dancing in the low light. "I'd ask how you're doing, but what I really want to know is, where ya been my whole life?"

27

Everyone vanished, as though they'd been raptured, and Margo and Dutch were the only ones left. Margo wished the others had stuck around for a minute or two so she didn't have to carry the conversation herself.

"Look at you," Dutch said, sizing up her red-and-green-plaid taffeta dress. "From the dog track to Lake Worth, you clean up nice."

"Likewise," Margo said, though he was mostly the same. Sharp suit. Slicked-back hair with a hard part. The small but eye-catching scar in his brow. Dutch Elkin was the definition of suave and suddenly Margo questioned her ability to hold his attention for more than three seconds.

"I can't talk very long," he said, possibly saving Margo from herself. "I'm scheduled to play in about five minutes."

Margo smiled and said she understood because of course she did. Working at other people's parties—maybe they had more in common than she guessed.

"Listen, I don't like to pussyfoot around, so I'll cut to the chase. I'd love to take you out," he said. "I'm finishing the year with a bunch of gigs on Long Island, so if we're going to make this happen, it'll need to be soon." Dutch removed a pen from the inside of his coat. "Are you going to be around for Christmas?" he asked.

"Well, um, my plans are still up in the air," she said.

"I'm well acquainted with *that*." As a waiter walked by, Dutch grabbed a napkin from his tray. "Where are you staying? Here in Palm Beach?"

"Um, yes. Sort of." Margo looked away. "Not directly in Palm Beach," she added meekly. "The Pennsylvania Hotel? It's in West Palm Beach." She might as well admit it so he'd appreciate what kind of lowbrow, other-side-of-the-bridge girl he was dealing with.

"I'm not in Palm Beach, either," he said. "Isn't it nice to be out of the fray?" Dutch gave her a wink, though his *out of the fray* was nothing like hers, based on what she'd read in the *Palm Beach Daily News*. In his case, it meant his adoptive parents' massive estate on Hobe Sound. Jupiter Island had been built in response to the increasing popularity of Palm Beach, and it was therefore quieter, and decidedly more exclusive. "How about next Thursday?" Dutch scribbled something and handed the napkin to Margo.

She stared at his blocky print.

La Petite Marmite the 28th * 8 o'clock!

"Next Thursday. How 'bout it?" Dutch capped his pen and slid it back into his coat.

"I'd love to but—" But *what*? Margo didn't understand the niggling inner voice that told her to decline. This was what she wanted. Plus, she and Slim were going to Austria in a few weeks, so her clock was ticking, too.

"Excellent. It's a date." Dutch studied her for a minute and shook his head. "God, those freckles." He brushed a finger down her nose. "Cutest thing in the world."

With that, he pivoted and strode off.

Margo marveled, watching him go. Lilly really was capable of spinning anything into gold, just as Peter had said. She'd thrown Dutch into her path at precisely the right moment, and now Margo had a date at the most fashionable restaurant on Worth. Being forced to stay in Palm Beach for the holidays might turn out to be the luckiest break, if not for one very large snag. Margo's time was not her own, and to go out with Dutch, she'd have to convince her keeper to let her out of the barn.

28

At five o'clock on Christmas day, with a bouquet of red and purple anemones in hand, Margo walked from the bus stop to Slim's, so deep in rumination she was almost hit by three separate cars.

He'd been generous enough to invite her to the cottage—*of course you'll spend Christmas with us! Where else would you go?*—and Margo couldn't storm in and start breaking rules. She needed a pretense for this date.

Dutch wants to teach me to play the piano. Ludicrous. Slim would never buy it.

It's just a friendly get-together. Aren't I allowed to have friends? Too transparent, too whiny.

You wouldn't want me to reject a potential client, would you? This was closest to the bull's-eye, but not quite right. Margo needed to come up with something, and fast. The date was in three days.

"Merry Christmas!" Rita said when she answered the door. "Margo! Why the dickens did you bring flowers? They're beautiful, but that's too generous, especially given how little my husband pays you. Come in, come in." Rita shut the door behind them. "Dinner's about ready."

They proceeded toward the dining room at the back of the

house. About halfway there, Margo heard Slim chuckle. Someone else laughed and shouted, "It's true!" and Margo halted in her tracks. She'd assumed there'd be only one other person at dinner, and that was not the voice of a three-year-old girl. She threw Rita a worried glance.

"That's just Peter," Rita said. "Lilly's at her parents' tonight, and you know the deal. They hate him. He's not allowed on their property. Etcetera."

Margo jiggled her head. Who didn't like Peter Pulitzer? He was one of the most winsome people on earth. "They hate him?" she said, to confirm, because she could not accept it. "Why?"

Hand on hip, Rita considered this. "I'm not exactly sure. Maybe because they got married so young? Or he never graduated college? They're not keen on orange groves? Who knows?" She shrugged and hooked an arm through Margo's. "In any case, good luck to us. With those two at the table, you and I will never get a word in. I hope you didn't have anything important to bring up."

—

"I must tell you, Margo," Peter said.

The sound of her own name made Margo jolt. For the thirty minutes they'd been at this table, she'd been stuck in her head, debating how and when to wedge Dutch into the conversation. "I'm sorry, I didn't hear that," she said, dabbing the corners of her mouth with a napkin.

"I was saying that, as much as Slim sings your praises—"

"I wouldn't go that far," Slim interjected.

Peter slopped a spoonful of green bean casserole onto his plate. "I think my wife appreciates you most of all," he said and took a sip of wine. "You've been so helpful. An absolute godsend. She swears she couldn't have gotten through the holidays without you."

"A godsend?" Rita's brows shot up, as though someone had kicked her shin. She looked at Margo. "What on earth does Lilly have you doing over there?"

"It's nothing." Margo slapped the air. "Just helped get some baskets out."

"According to Lilly, this girl saved Christmas. That's in addition to closing Julia and Bibi's shop at the end of last season. The way she tells it, you're part guardian angel, part lucky penny."

"How strange," Rita said, her eyes darting back and forth between Margo and Peter. "I thought Margo had a job, one that keeps her rather occupied." She dealt Slim an intense, winnowed glare but he was cheerily dicing up ham, oblivious. "How much is Lilly paying you? Gosh, I hope it's not more than what my husband does."

"Don't worry," Peter said, reaching for the bottle of wine. "Lilly may not be giving her cash, but Margo will be appropriately compensated. My wife is hell-bent on taking her under her wing. First and foremost, this means setting her up."

Slim dropped his fork and it clattered on his plate. "What do you mean, *set her up*?" Now he was all ears.

"You're not *that* old, Slimbo," Peter said with a smirk. "Surely you've heard of dating. Going steady? Perhaps they called it *courting* in your era. In any case, Lilly wants to find Margo a beau. Unfortunately, her first thought was a real stinker. I *am* sorry, Margo. I was able to save you from Jim Kimberly, but Lilly dragged me away before I could rescue you from Dutch."

"You didn't need to rescue me," Margo said as all eyes in the room flew in her direction. She took a sip of water before continuing. "He asked me to dinner. La Petite Marmite, on the twenty-eighth?" Her voice sounded high and strangled, but she was in it, and had no choice but to carry on. "Slim, I know the rules. You said no boyfriends, but it's only one date and if we're not working that night, I'd like to go." Margo closed her eyes, bracing for impact.

"No," Slim said. "Absolutely not."

"I agree," Peter piped up.

"I think that's a *fantastic* idea," Rita said. Whatever was bothering her a minute ago had faded away and she was back to her good-natured self. "Dutch is a sweetheart, and Margo needs to have fun occasionally, lest she get so fed up she quits."

"Margo has enough to focus on without fretting over whether some stupid boy is paying enough attention to her."

"But it'd only be one date," Margo pleaded. "He's leaving at the end of the week."

"Why didn't you say so? In that case…no."

Rita whipped Slim with her napkin.

"On the same page, buddy," Peter said, raising his glass. "Dutch Elkin is trouble. Thinks every pretty girl is his for the taking. I'll make sure Lilly finds a different and better way to repay Margo."

"Money is always welcome compensation," Rita offered.

"This conversation is over," Slim said.

He lit a cigarette, as did Rita, and Peter glugged the rest of the wine. Margo focused on her ham while the room remained silent, the cigarette smoke hovering like a low-lying cloud, held up by the thick layer of tension in the room.

Finally, Rita ground out her cigarette and rose to her feet. "Time for dessert," she announced. "Margo, would you help me dish it up?"

⌣

"I'm going to tell you two things," Rita said, hacking at the butterscotch pie with a knife. "First, Dutch seems like a nice kid, and I will personally ensure that you have your date. Second, stop doing favors for Lilly Pulitzer."

"Why?" Margo said, holding her plate in midair. "I don't

mind. Actually, I enjoy it. Lilly's so fun to be around. She makes everything more radiant somehow."

"She is incredibly *effervescent*." Rita gave the word extra bite, as though bright, brilliant shininess was bad. "I get the attraction, and you're not the first to be drawn in by Lilly Pulitzer's vast charms and even greater fortune. But these folks are a unique breed. They see the world differently."

"How so?" Margo asked as Rita launched a piece of pie in her direction. She moved the plate to catch it.

"They don't have to think about money, for one. If the world economy went into free fall, their biggest worry would be how to live off the interest from their nest eggs, instead of the interest from the interest." Rita snorted. "Yet, *some of them* still manage to get free labor."

"Not having to worry about money doesn't really seem like a *downside*," Margo pointed out.

"Are you listening? These people *like* recessions. They think it restores the dollar and makes employees work more joyfully. They don't understand the value of *anything*, and that includes people, and will think nothing of using someone if it serves their own purposes."

"I thought *these people* were your friends," Margo said. "I thought some of them join your holiday dinners."

"They're *clients*, which is different," Rita said, slicing up the last wedge of pie. "Don't get me wrong. Even Slim gets sucked in sometimes. It's very easy to do and I'm constantly reminding him that they're not to be trusted. It's not intentional, they play by different rules, and what you see is not what you get."

"I don't know, Rita," Margo said, carefully. Palm Beachers openly disdained Bostonians and maybe this was coloring Rita's view. "Obviously, I haven't met everyone in Palm Beach, but Lilly is so open. She always says what she means."

"What she means, or what she wants you to hear?" Rita

licked the knife and tossed it into the sink. "These people are razzle-dazzle and loads of fun, like a magic show. But you have to proceed with great caution, Margo. You need to keep both eyes open. Watch for the sleight of hand and know that they have a thousand tricks up their sleeves."

29

It was past midnight. Christmas was over, but the holiday remained undone. Margo knew how to put a bow on this day but was having a hell of a time finding the fortitude right now.

At last, she closed her eyes, and picked up the phone. She asked the operator to put her through to Mrs. Edgar Mapes of San Francisco. However shaky their relationship had been, Antoinette was her mother, and Margo needed to wish her a Merry Christmas. It was nine o'clock in California. Margo hoped it wasn't too late.

"Hello, Mrs. Mapes," Margo said, when Sandy's sister picked up. "Merry Christmas. This is Gogo Hightower. Is my mother there?"

Pauline answered, "Hold on, please," and Margo's heart clenched.

When Antoinette finally came on to the line, Margo was so tense she might've strained a stomach muscle. "Merry Christmas!" she sang. "I know it's not the last Sunday of the month, but I was thinking about you and wanted to hear your voice." She paused, but the line remained silent. "Hello? Mother, are you there?"

"Yes, I'm still here."

"Oh. Okay." Margo felt as though she'd been gently smacked. "How was your holiday? Did you have fun with Pauline and Edgar?"

"It was fine," her mom replied, which was as much as one might expect.

"Glad to hear it. I spent Christmas with Slim's family," Margo said, though Antoinette had not asked. "We had a nice evening."

Overall, it *was* a nice evening, Rita's ominous warning notwithstanding. If she'd said to be wary around Wendy Vanderbilt, *that* would've made sense, but Lilly was one of the warmest, most welcoming people Margo had ever met, and Rita's only evidence about her dubious character was that rich people were rich, which was more of an endorsement than anything else. In the end, Margo decided Rita's words added up to a whole lot of not much. The woman had voluntarily married Slim, and thus her head wasn't always on straight. Margo would believe what she saw for herself.

"Rita made ham," Margo told her mom, unnecessarily. "And butterscotch pie."

"How splendid," Antoinette said, and Margo heard the click of her lighter.

"We don't have to stay on the line long," Margo said, letting them both off the hook. "But I wanted to check in during what must be a difficult time. Being without Sandy, living in someone else's home…" Also, the Edgar Mapeses were unpleasant on their best day, the human embodiment of coal in a stocking. "I hope you're doing okay."

"Not really," her mom said without missing a beat.

Not really? It was the most honest she'd ever been. Until now, every time Margo pushed back on Sandy's antics, or reminded Antoinette that he was really putting them through the wringer, her mom erupted in rage, furious at Margo for blowing things out of proportion. Had Antoinette finally recognized the size of the problem?

"I'm sorry," Margo said. "Do you want me to visit? Lend some moral support? We have a trip coming up, but maybe after that. Slim would give me the time off. He's not a complete ogre." Margo went to laugh but didn't have the energy.

"That's very sweet, Gogo." Her mom sighed. "But what would be the point?"

To give you company, Margo thought. *To spend time together. You are my mom.*

"Okay, understood," Margo said with a sigh of her own. "Please call if you need to. For the next few months, I'll be in and out of the Pennsylvania Hotel in West Palm Beach. You can leave a message with the front desk if I'm not around."

"Thank you," her mom said, and the women said goodbye, their conversation ending just as quickly as it'd begun.

Margo flicked off the light. As she pulled the covers up to her chin, a strange, new sensation washed through her. One might call it a revelation. She'd had thousands of conversations with her mom over the years, but for the first time, Margo finished one feeling sorry for *Antoinette*, instead of herself.

30

Rita made good on her promise. Margo was allowed to go out with Dutch.

"But only one date," Slim took great pains to clarify. "That's it." Margo thanked him profusely and didn't bother to push. She hoped for more than one, of course, but Dutch was leaving town and no second date had been offered. If and when that happened, it was a headache for another time.

Now Margo sat across from him at La Petite Marmite, her belly tight with nerves. Dutch was semifamous. He was talented, and leading-man handsome. He'd served in the Army, for the love of Christmas, and lived in New York. What did Margo bring to the table? The question had haunted her all week.

After Slim gave his reluctant okay, Margo rang Dolly for advice—*please, what do the smart and worldly discuss?*—only to learn that her friend had absconded to Mexico with Don. Without her ace in the hole, Margo was forced to recalibrate. The next day, while Slim shot some muckety-muck from Cincinnati at the Everglades Club, Margo excused herself to the powder room and made a beeline for the golfers' pavilion, where she eavesdropped on the knickers-clad men tromping in and out.

People were still talking about Joe Kennedy's stroke, and what that meant for the rest of the Kennedys and the nation at large, since—obviously—Joe ran the show. A few men deliberated whether being forced to admit Black members into their clubs was a form of government mind control. Something about "the damned Constitution!"—she didn't follow. Though she'd managed to collect a handful of scraps, Margo lacked the glue to put it together. Sadly, to keep up with Dutch, she'd likely have to read beyond the gossip pages. He'd lived abroad, after all.

"That's a great dress," Dutch said, peering at her from over the menu. "Very saucy."

"Thanks," Margo said, a fierce blush overtaking her face. She hadn't been certain about the outfit when she walked into the restaurant and was less so now. The skirt was cherry-red and adorned with fat polka dots, the colors reversed on top. Dolly had once called it *a real Friday-nighter*, and her mom swore up and down that Margo looked fabulous in red (*never yellow or pink, not with your skin tone*), but tonight she worried it was too loud, too "look at me." Margo wished she had the shape and coloring for a Lilly.

At Rita's suggestion, Margo ordered the shrimp scampi and a Kir Royale, the restaurant's signature drink, and Dutch chose a steak cooked medium rare. As the waiter walked off, Margo surveyed the room's red carpeting, gas lamps, and white ironwork. La Petite Marmite was more faux French Quarter than French-inspired, forcing Margo to consider whether Palm Beachers were really such experts in style. It was an uplifting thought and she felt herself loosen. There was no reason to agonize over a few polka dots.

"I'm so glad you were able to fit me into your schedule," Dutch said, craning forward, the candlelight dancing on his lightly stubbled skin. "A girl like you must have her dance card full."

"It was my pleasure," Margo said. She smiled, and Dutch smiled back. Her voice got all tripped up in her chest as she wondered, *what next?* "So..." Margo cleared her throat, and recalled what Antoinette drilled into her head. *Always aim the spotlight on your date. Men love to talk about themselves.* "You played the piano so beautifully at the Scotts' Christmas party. How did you get into the business?" she asked.

A funny look crossed Dutch's face, as if he'd just come to in a strange place. "Oh, right! The party. So. How did I get into the business?" He pondered this. "I can thank my parents first, and then Uncle Sam."

Margo was fully apprised of Dutch Elkin's background, but she listened intently, her eyes wide and engaged. Because his father was a crooner of some acclaim, Dutch assumed he'd sing, too. He was enrolled in Yale's music program when a stint in the military changed everything.

"I was stationed in Panama," Dutch said. "Bored as hell, and so I joined the Army band. They assigned me the goddamned glockenspiel." Chuckling, he shook his head. "I thought, *Christ, this won't help with the ladies,* but if I'm going to do something, I'm going to do it well." He gathered up the best musicians in the armed forces and formed a jazz orchestra. They played all over Panama City and were the hottest ticket in town.

Dutch spoke the same way he played the piano—animated, and with great passion, leaning into every beat. One minute his eyes would be glassy as he basked in a memory, the next his brows jumped in excitement. As he approached a turning point, he'd hunch down, then spring forward with a laugh, smacking his knee. Throughout it all, he couldn't stay still, constantly drumming his fingers on the table, tapping his feet.

"Eventually, the owner of the St. Regis saw us play," he said.

"Afterward, he handed me a card and told me to call the next time I was in New York. I did, and now I'm at his supper club five nights per week."

"Fascinating!" Margo said, proud of her ability to effect surprise. The situation struck her as funny. Normally, in Palm Beach, she pretended to know more than she did. "What do you usually play during your shows?"

"A bit of everything," Dutch said, and by everything, he meant the gamut, from show tunes to movie themes to top-40 songs. His goal was to give people what they wanted, and make sure nobody sat down, even if it meant keeping two thousand songs in his head at a time. "To be perfectly honest..." He looked around, as if checking for spies. "All this success is as shocking to me as it's been to everyone else. When I started out, they called me a throwback and said I'd fall flat on my face. Deep down, I suspected they were right, despite my conviction that people were tired of watching TV and listening to jazz records on their couch. I knew folks wanted to get out and dance but doubted whether I had the chops to make it happen. You should've seen me at my first performance. I took months of acting lessons, but my body was pure jelly."

"Acting lessons?" Margo said. "Why?"

"It *is* a performance, but really, I needed to figure out who I was."

Figure out who he was? Margo batted the idea around in her head. "How did you manage to do that?" she asked. It'd never occurred to her that people could determine this for themselves. All she'd been taught was how to follow rules and live up to expectations, nary a mention of forging new paths.

"I thought of all the band leaders I've admired throughout history," he said, "and decided I didn't have to be any one thing. A little of this, a smidge of that. I can make anyone happy if they tell me what they need." He leaned back in his chair and smiled. "That's all there is to it. And what about you? You've got a flashy occupation, too. Have you always been interested in photography?"

"Oh, I'm not interested in—"

"A fellow creative. I love it," Dutch said as the waiter dropped off their plates. "Isn't it amazing that we have these...these..." He gazed up at the ceiling, searching for the words. "Outlets, I guess. Sometimes I find myself so pent-up with frustrations and the general ups and downs in life, and playing music is the *only* way to get it all out. You feel?"

Margo nodded. Did she *feel*? Yes and no. Mostly what she felt was discombobulated. She'd never heard a man discuss his emotions like this.

"I think you're the first woman I've met who's into anything creative, aside from decorating her own home." He glanced up, eyes sparking. "I find that incredibly appealing."

"I'm only an assistant" had been at the tip of her tongue, but Margo couldn't say this *now*. She couldn't confess that she wasn't *interested in photography* as much as she was into not being destitute.

"Maybe we can trade services one day," he said. "You teach me how to use a camera, and I'll teach you a song or two on the piano."

"Sure, yes, that'd be terrific," Margo said and gobbled down some scampi.

"You know what else is great about you?" Dutch cut into his steak and took a bite. Margo held her breath, waiting for him to swallow. "The other thing I like about you," he said, pointing at her with his fork, "is that you're not one of them..." He jerked his head backward, toward the other people in the restaurant. "You're an outsider, just like me."

"An outsider?" Margo said. "You grew up summering on Jupiter Island!"

"I grew up spending the *season* on Jupiter," he said. "During the summer, I usually went fishing, somewhere in the West. That's how I earned this scar." Dutch pushed back his eyebrow hair and explained that, when he was fourteen or fifteen years old, he went fishing with a family friend named Ernest Hemingway—maybe you've heard of him?—and walked away with the better catch. Hemingway was so livid that he beat Dutch upside the head with a fishing rod. "I deserved it," he added. "I was pretty smug."

"Hemingway," Margo repeated. "Right. Okay. Real everyday stuff. I can see why you consider yourself an outsider."

"Look. I know how it seems. But even though I was *around* all the glitz, it was *their* world, not mine. I lived with the Whitneys, and they treated me like a king, but I was never formally adopted. It felt like they could take it away at any time."

"Oh, Dutch." Margo placed a hand on her chest, picturing the lost boy he'd once been. She *knew* that little boy. He was not so different from her.

"Anyway," he continued, "if you want the truth, I prefer being an outsider. It means I don't have to give a fuck—excuse the French—about last names or pedigrees or how many generations so-and-so's family goes back. By all accounts, my mom was the same way. She came from old money, and my dad was Jewish, so when they got married, she was kicked off the social registry. According to Marie—Mrs. Whitney—her reaction was, 'who cares? It's a lousy phonebook!' All that to say, I have the freedom to hang out with people I dig." He gave another stomach-flipping smile. "People who are new, and different. Including promising young photographers."

"I don't know how promising I am," Margo said, looking away with a small smile, unable to believe her luck. Had she met the one man in Palm Beach who wouldn't care where she came from?

"Oh, you're promising alright," Dutch said. "I have a feeling about you, Margo Hightower, and I'm rarely wrong about these things. You're like a great album that hasn't been released, one that is going to take the world by storm. Thank God I discovered you first."

—

Only the dessert plates remained, scraped clean, aside from the tacky puddles left by the ice-cream cake. Margo was buzzy-headed from the Kir Royales, and from Dutch. This felt like more than a date. It felt like the start of something.

"Austria is next?" Dutch said, reaching into his jacket. "I've never been, so you'll have to take loads of pictures. I want to hear all about it. After that, it's back to Palm Beach, yes?"

"Yes, though we'll go to Katonah in between," Margo said quickly. She'd never met anyone who spoke so much without stopping.

Dutch laid a pocket-sized calendar on the table. "What works?" he asked, stubby red pencil poised in the air. "You pick the date, and I'll put it in my calendar. No matter where I am in the world, I'll come right back here to take you out."

"Um, well," Margo began, her pulse racing. It was a thrilling yet inconvenient turn of events. *Only one date,* Slim had growled. *That's it.*

"How about the last Friday in January?" Dutch said, penciling it in. "That should give you enough wiggle room, don't you think?"

Oh, Lord, was she ever going to need to wiggle. As her brain whirred, deciding whether to go ahead and jump, a couple appeared at their table. It took Margo a second to comprehend that it was Lilly and Peter, tanned and resplendent, she in a towering purple turban, him in a pink button-down shirt.

"This is the best thing I've seen all week," Lilly said, clasping her hands together. "The two cutest people I know."

"That's a helluva compliment coming from the most adored woman in Palm Beach." Dutch got up to give Lilly a kiss and Margo stayed in her seat, more jumbled than she'd been five minutes before. Why were they here? Was this a coincidence, or had they come on purpose? Lilly had set them up, but only Peter knew about the date, since she'd inadvertently told him over Christmas dinner.

"Nice to see ya, pal," Peter said, shaking Dutch's hand. "Lookin' good, Margo." He gave her a wink. She did not know what to do with it.

"I love romance," Lilly said, still bubbling with delight. "I love *love*. Are you two already head over heels?"

"You really are a mover and a shaker, Lil," Dutch said with a laugh. Margo closed her eyes and tried not to die. "It's only our first date, but from where I'm sitting, the future is dazzling."

31

Slim's farmhouse was exactly how Margo remembered it—cozy, cluttered with photographs and memorabilia, last summer's magazines still stacked on the bench by the door. It was noticeably quieter, though, without Rita and Mary, who were still in Palm Beach. Margo and Slim would join them once the Austrian film came back.

They had started their trip at Lech am Arlberg, a charming town tucked into a sunny mountain pass in the westernmost part of the country. Lech was isolated in that way rich people liked. No trains served the area, and while Slim and Margo had taken a bus from Langen, celebrities, diplomats, and European royalty drove up from Innsbruck or Lindau in their Mercedes. Its remoteness guaranteed exclusivity—the hoi polloi wouldn't make all that effort—and allowed people to crow about how much friendlier and more relaxed it was compared to Gstaad or St. Moritz.

Lech was also smaller than the bigger-name resorts, consisting of only a few hotels and chalets, some shops, and one baroque church. Nearly everything that happened in town could be viewed from the Hotel Krone, where Slim and Margo set up shop. Each morning, between nine and ten o'clock, skiers in brightly colored sweaters and pants descended upon the square. After dropping the kids off in ski school, they flagged down their own instructors determined to perfect the "Arlberg technique," whatever that meant. At the end of the day, they all skied off the mountain, right onto the street.

Après-ski meant gathering at the Krone's Ice Bar, which faced the Lech River and the chalet-dotted slopes. Over the course of a week, Slim snapped hundreds of pictures of people sipping cocktails as they snuggled beneath plaid blankets, or sat in the blue chairs with yellow straps that Slim found in summer storage.

"Margo!" Slim yelled one afternoon from the roof of the Krone. "Find out who owns that white VW van, and who owns the red car."

Margo peered over the edge to the driveway below. Slim wanted her to locate the owners of the two vehicles, borrow the keys, and swap their placement. Fifteen minutes later, several dozen people watched as Margo parked a van sideways on a short, snowy hill. She hadn't known it was possible to sweat in twenty-two degrees Fahrenheit, but at least Slim got the shot.

Because it sat high in an open valley, Lech had the best sun of all the resorts, but night fell hard and fast, at five o'clock on the nose. By five fifteen, the hotels were filled with flushed, red-faced skiers. They drank and listened to yodelers and ate beef goulash while sleigh bells jingled outside.

In Lech, Slim introduced Margo to a new challenge. The afternoon light was spectacular, but ski resorts were the hardest to shoot. The images had to say *Austria* even without one of Margo's captions. Done the wrong way, Slim explained, all that white could be too bright, or not special enough. Snow didn't appear much different from one continent to the next, and they wouldn't have the usual tricks at their disposal, like the ability to rummage around someone's castle for a few eye-catching personal possessions to throw into the shot. There weren't any flowers, either, only woodsy, snow-covered buildings and people doing interesting things in the right-colored clothes.

After Lech, they traveled to St. Anton, which was more crowded and on a different part of the mountain, so it only received an hour of direct sunlight per day. Slim felt good about what they'd shot in Lech, so they made quick work of the place and headed back to the States.

Back at the farm, they read newspapers and ate meals prepared by generous neighbors while Slim regaled Margo with tales of his *classic New Hampshire childhood*. How nice that he was able to experience a Huck Finn lifestyle, but Margo was concerned about *right now*. A hundred times, over a dozen tuna fish sandwiches, she wanted to ask, *what if I went on another date? Would that be so bad? Did you even notice the first?* But it was too risky a proposition, doubly so without Rita around. Instead, Margo was forced to stare at the ticking clock, waiting for the slides to be done.

—

Margo considered herself a warm-weather girl, but the final images from Austria were almost enough to change her mind.

"Slim," Margo gasped, holding the first one up to the light. From the roof of the Krone, he'd captured the frozen river and the Ice Bar, the colorful ski rack, and the lot with Margo's precariously parked car. The hazy sunlight and softly drifting snow gave the photo a dreamy, ethereal quality, making the ski chalets and the Omeshorn mountain resemble a fairy tale. "You can do anything, can't you?"

"That's why they send me all over the world," Slim answered, pretending to grumble, as he visibly puffed up.

One set of slides showed Princess Luciana Pignatelli in sea glass–colored stretch pants, a matching green-and-black sweater, and a silk scarf draped around her neck. Slim shot her in profile as she pulled skies from a rack, flakes of snow dusting her tawny hair. Next came pictures of a bartender shaking a drink, and snow bunnies reclining in green-and-red-striped loungers. Each image was better than the last.

Maybe Dutch was right, about art and creativity expressing emotions and thoughts that couldn't be said. Until now, Margo hadn't grasped that a single photograph might encompass both a complete story and a moment in time. It was past and present, a memory and the creation of something new.

"Maybe one day you could teach me how to do this?" Margo heard herself say. Slim looked up, eyes popping out of his skull. "I mean…" She shook her head. "I could never do *this*. But maybe, one day, you can teach me how to use a camera?"

The words had come from nowhere, but they felt true, like they'd been there all along. Maybe it was Dutch, or maybe she wanted to be accepted in the same way everyone accepted Slim. Perhaps it was both plus something else altogether. *Was* she a creative, deep down?

"I hired you to be my assistant," Slim said. "My *tuttofare*." He'd used this word many times, and it was supposed to mean his "do everything," a gal Friday type. But an Italian prince in St. Anton said that in practice it was used to describe a handyman or errand boy.

"I know I'm only an assistant," Margo said, trying a different route. "But don't you think I'd be more helpful if I understood how it all worked?"

Slim put down the slide he was studying. "You've developed quite the list of demands these days," he said. "First, a date, and now, a photography lesson? What's next? The deed to my house? You can't pick up a camera and call yourself a photographer. Do you appreciate all I went through to get here?"

Margo did appreciate it because he'd told her at least twelve times. Slim enlisted in the Army when he turned eighteen and was sent to work as a hydro dipper in the photography department at the military academy at West Point. *I dragged prints through chemicals for months before anyone let me touch a camera!*

"I wasn't claiming I could be a photographer," Margo said. "I was only asking for a chance. Anyway. Message received. I won't bring it up again." She put the lid on a box of slides and moved to the next one.

Slim let out a long, weighted sigh. "Let's focus on this for now, shall we?" he said. "And maybe, one day, I'll let you try the camera. But you must remember. Unlike the people we shoot, life is not yours for the taking. Nothing will be handed to you. You must earn every last thing."

32

PALM BEACH / JANUARY 1962

"The third meeting of the International Cuban Rescue and Relief Committee is hereby adjourned," Lilly announced, pounding her fist on the table like a gavel. "You are dismissed."

The women stood and pushed in their chairs. Flo Smith, the host, buzzed about, ensuring no one forgot her purse or hat, while Margo remained blended into the corner. They were supposed to be shooting a feature for the *Saturday Evening Post* about prominent Palm Beach hostesses, but Flo had sprung this meeting on them last-minute, and it was taking far longer than the *fifteen minutes, tops* she'd promised. Margo didn't understand what this "charity work" was about. As far as she could tell, the agenda was:

- Smoke
- Gossip
- Discuss the merits of the sugar business

Of course, Margo had long since learned that in Palm Beach it was gauche to have a party for the sake of having a party. Anytime more than three people gathered, they were mandated to donate to an orphanage or fund research for some obscure disease because, when it came to charities, you couldn't step on the Old Guard's toes.

Finally, all the guests aside from Lilly had filtered out, and Slim directed Flo onto the patio. He instructed Margo to pick up the dog, and Flo's son to gather his favorite toys and bring them outside. The eight-year-old returned with a tennis racquet, basketball, and twelve-gauge shotgun.

"Why are we doing this, Slim?" Flo complained. "I'm tired. Organizing shit is hard work. Also, I'm fairly certain I look like melted death."

"He's immune to logic," Lilly warned, as she draped herself across a chaise. "The easiest way to get rid of him is to do what he says."

"How's this?" Flo flipped her chair around. "You can shoot the back of my head."

Slim refused to react. "Do you remember the first time you invited me to lunch?" he said, fiddling with the camera. "You told me not to bring my Leica, so I thought I'd hit the jackpot. Finally, I'd made it socially."

"Keep dreaming!" Flo teased. She'd made a quarter turn and was peering over her shoulder. Already he was drawing her in, like a magnet.

In his recounting, Slim assumed the luncheon was for him, until he spotted Jack Kennedy tramping across the dunes in rolled-up chinos and a sports shirt, Jackie on his heels. "I should've realized the score, when the party consisted only of beautiful women for Jack, and men over six feet for his wife," Slim said and raised the camera. "Too bad for Jackie that I'm the type of tall man you know."

"She's not as picky as you'd think," Flo said.

"You're such a naughty girl," Lilly said, an arm flopped over her face. "Always trying to tempt people to stray."

"It's not about tempting anyone," Flo said as she angled herself more toward Slim. "Man is by nature not a monogamous creature. All you can do is accept it or choose to go with a woman. I tried that, and it didn't really do it for me."

Everybody laughed, and Flo's ratty white poodle writhed and twisted out of Margo's hold. It scurried over and leaped into Flo's lap. Flo stroked its head and settled into the shoot, precisely as Slim planned.

———

Thirty minutes later, they'd finished, and Flo disappeared into the house for a nap. Lilly was on the lounger, snoring gently, while Slim packed up his lenses.

Now or never, Margo decided, as she picked the dog hairs from her overblouse. The second date was hurtling toward her, and Slim was always more reasonable when people he admired were within earshot.

"Hey, Slim," she began. "I'd like to address a potential..." Margo paused, swallowing her words. She felt like she was standing at a fork in the road, but both paths were blocked.

"What is it, Margo?" Slim snapped his suitcase shut. "Are you going to ask to take my job again?" He looked at Lilly, who was just coming to. "This one wants to become a photographer," he said, crooking a thumb. "Can you stand it?"

"It's not that. I mean, yes, I'd like to learn, but..." Margo searched for the words. "Do we have a shoot next Friday? I was hoping to have a night to myself. If it's convenient for you."

Lilly hopped to her feet, her nap fully shed. "Friday night? Ooh-la-la. Do we have another date with Dutch Elkin?"

"No," Slim barked. "We do not. She isn't allowed to date."

Lilly thwacked his arm. "Don't be such a despot. Peter and I saw them together at Marmite and they were adorable." She swung her head back toward Margo. "Though I do have some notes. For your next date. A way to…" She waggled her fingers. "Spruce things up."

Spruce what up? Margo had thought the date had gone well.

"She isn't allowed to date," Slim repeated. "You married off my last assistant. If you were planning to do it again, you didn't need to wait until she was actually capable of a few things."

"I will *not* let you get in this girl's way," Lilly said, and turned toward Margo. "You come see me at the shop tomorrow, anytime. Well. Anytime after ten but before four. Though not between twelve and one forty-five. I'll fix you up."

Margo glanced at Slim, but his face was unreadable, wiped clean of all expression. He'd never looked so blank, and it chilled her to the core. "What are you *fixing me up* with, exactly?" she said, her voice thin as a spider's web.

"Heavens, Margo, I can't spoil the surprise!" Lilly said and giggled. "If you want to snag someone like Dutch, you'll need to go against your natural inclinations and listen to me."

33

Never had a person been so nervous to patronize a fruit-and-dress shop.

Margo wanted to spend time with Lilly—always—but wasn't keen on learning the specific ways in which she'd apparently muffed her date. Maybe he'd only asked for a second date to be nice. She imagined Lilly and Peter watching, observing, commenting, while she clattered away, oblivious. The idea made her physically sick.

Try to be happy about this, Margo reminded herself. *Lilly wants to help.* Also, Slim had encouraged her to go, which was a damned miracle, especially because he knew this was about Dutch. Luckily the only thing more important than his rules was the jet set itself, and giving in to Lilly Pulitzer's whims was part of the job.

As soon as Margo popped open the door, Lilly burst out from behind the register and wrapped her in a robust, hardy hug. "Wendy! Look who it is!"

"Ciao," Wendy answered, without losing focus on her magazine.

"Boy, do we have a fun project ahead of us today," Lilly

said, a glint in her eyes. She snatched Margo's hand and hauled her over to one of the dress racks. "Our goal is to make you as appealing as possible to Dutch. He's an interesting man who's seen it all."

Margo forced a smile, telling herself this comment didn't have to sting. She agreed with it, even. "Yes, too true," she said. "I've asked to have two newspapers delivered to my hotel room each morning, to keep up with current events."

"What a clever idea! But I was referring to your appearance." Lilly exhaled. "Let's get the tough part over with first. I tell you this with only love in my heart, and *I'm sure* it's just a California thing, but your clothing choices are—shall we say—all over the map."

Wendy snorted. "Oh, Lilly, you and your projects. You love taking in strays. Started with your husband and kept going. I love that about you."

"I live to be helpful. Margo, darling, the problem is that sometimes you read as stuffy, other times, juvenile. From staid suits to picnic dresses. And whatever this is." She swept a hand, indicating Margo's green dress. "It's mind-boggling but we're going to change all that."

Margo's first reaction was to take offense. She'd bought this dress specifically for Palm Beach and thought the gold rope belt gave it a Lilly Pulitzer oomph. Then again, its color had been described as "clown green" in the catalogue and she'd never seen Lilly wear a belt, not a single time.

"I hope you're not taking any of this the wrong way," Lilly said as she sorted through the racks. "It was a fun quirk at first, but when I saw you at PM the other night, I had to step in. This is Dutch Elkin we're talking about. He lives in New York, amongst the most fashionable women alive."

Wendy set the magazine down, of her own accord. "You have a date with Dutch Elkin?"

"They already *went* on a date," Lilly said. "This is for the next one."

"Goodness, Margo." Wendy let out a whistle. "I'm impressed."

"First things first, we need to find Margo a point of view," Lilly said. She studied a sand-dollar print for a second before choosing peonies instead. "What do you think?" She held it up to Margo's face.

Margo smiled, attempting to exude *something*. Confidence, joie de vivre.

"Hmm. Not quite right. Don't worry. We'll make this work." She returned to the dresses, rummaging with greater intensity. There was a tremendous amount of grunting and throwing back of the head. Just as Margo suspected. She'd never pull off a Lilly Pulitzer print.

"No yellows," Wendy chimed in, sounding like Antoinette.

"The issue isn't Margo," Lilly said. "It's the patterns. Woolworth's isn't giving me diddlyshit these days. It's like they came up with ten designs and can't find it within themselves to go an inch further. I need a new supplier. Peter has banned me from cutting down any more curtains."

"I keep telling you to go down to Key West," Wendy said. "Take it from an artist. That's where the true creatives and artisans are these days."

Wendy was an artist? It was the first Margo had heard of it.

Lilly blubbered her lips. "You're probably right," she said. "Alas, our girl can't sit around and wait for me to find a new supplier. Luckily she's got youth and good looks on her side, and that covers a mountain of ills."

Margo barely had time to contemplate what these *mountains* were before Lilly began pitching dresses at her, one by one. Seconds later, Margo was dripping in shifts, a clash of prints screaming back at her from the shell-encrusted mirror.

Lilly peered over her shoulder. "Which one strikes your fancy?" she asked.

Tucking a piece of hair behind her ear, Margo took herself in. She'd developed a mild tan over the past year—a staggering turn of events—and her hair was now more blond than strawberry. These were improvements, but Margo still viewed herself as too washed-out for a Lilly. Also, she didn't have enough of a figure to make dancing purple elephants seem like anything but a costume.

"What?" Lilly said, sensing her unease. "What's wrong? You don't like any of them?"

"The dresses are great. I'm afraid that... I don't have the right shape?"

"Right shape?" She pulled a face. "What are you talking about? That's the beauty of a Lilly. Literally anyone can wear it."

"Maybe the girl is onto something," Wendy said, moving to her hip as she swung her legs up onto the couch. "She probably wears that new junior petite size all the designers are introducing." She flipped her gaze to Margo. "You must be relieved that everyone's minimizing their lines. Are they doing it for brassieres, too?"

Lilly shot her friend a glare. "Here's an idea. Instead of squawking from the peanut gallery, why don't you help? This fits perfectly within your foundation's mission." Wendy had a new charity organization to promote the adoption of "elegant casual" attire at Palm Beach parties. Equally Chic's core belief was that people could have style without sequins and bow ties.

"Sure, why not." Wendy bounded to her feet. It was official. Margo was a charity case. "Personally, I like this one," Wendy said, holding up a green-and-blue pansy print. "It'd look fab with your eyes."

"You're definitely on the right track color-wise." Lilly sidled up to Wendy. "But what about this butterfly print? The

blue is perfect for her skin tone, and butterflies are my favorite. Colorful, fun, flitting around." She glanced back at Margo.
"What do you think?"

"It is a great pattern," Margo said, warming to the idea. The
print was cute on the hanger and, miraculously, no worse when
held up to her skin. Margo had been told her whole life that
her face couldn't handle bright colors, but maybe it could, in
the right circumstances.

"SOLD!" Lilly shoved the dress into Margo's hand. "I love
it when a plan comes together. Your very first Lilly, free of
charge."

"Oh, no, I couldn't."

"Maybe we can write it off on Equally Chic's books!" Wendy
chirped.

"No tax man needed," Lilly said. "Consider it repayment for
the gift basket debacle. I won't have it any other way."

Margo smiled, cautiously, as she folded the dress in half. Lilly
hadn't offered a dressing room but asking to try it on seemed
like an insult. "Thank you. That's incredibly generous," she
said. "I can't wait to wear it." *See, Rita? I am getting paid.* Not
that she'd been looking for compensation.

"Now that we've settled that, let's move on to the juicy stuff.
When's date number two?"

"Oh, um. Next Friday? Nothing has been solidified yet. I
need to request the time off. Slim can be a little…"

Lilly waved her away. "Slim is Slim. All bark and no bite.
You think he would've learned his lesson. He needs to give
his assistants a break if he doesn't want them flying the coop.
Let me talk to him."

"No. Please," Margo said, filling head to toe with a damp,
dark dread. She could hear him now. He'd rant about the gall
of Margo, sending Lilly Pulitzer to do her dirty work, and he
wouldn't be wrong.

"Good Lord, it's not going to be that bad. I do have *some* couth," Lilly said with a laugh. She rubbed Margo's shoulder. "It's going to be fine. First of all, you're an asset to Slim, and don't ever forget it."

"I'm not sure he'd agree…"

"You're an asset," Lilly insisted. "Don't worry, I'll get him to come around. Some people think I have influence in this town, and what's the point of having it if I never get to use it?"

34

"I'm downstairs," Slim said into the phone.

Margo jiggled her head. Were they supposed to go somewhere? Was she late? *Shit.* Had Lilly said something to Slim and in his fury, he'd hightailed it to the other side of the bridge? "Um, hello, Slim," she said. "I wasn't expecting you this morning. To what does this pertain?"

"IT PERTAINS TO ME BEING IN THE LOBBY."

"Should I change? I'm wearing a—"

"Get your ass down here RIGHT. NOW. I don't have all day."

Margo hung up the phone and slipped into a pair of Keds. She hurried down to the lobby, where she found Slim leaning against the front desk, holding a brown leather case.

"Hello." Margo dropped her key with the front desk clerk. Already she could feel Slim sneering at her white sneakers and shorts. "Sorry if you don't like the outfit," she said, in a foolhardy attempt to cut him off at the pass. "But you didn't give me much time to change."

"I hope I'm not making you late for a tennis match," he said and pushed off from the counter. "Let's go."

Margo followed him outside, across the busy road, and to a park on the other side of the street. Maybe everything was fine, she reasoned. If Slim was mad, she would've heard about it by now.

Finally, he stopped and set the case on a picnic table. He snapped it open and removed a small, box-shaped camera. "Today I'm going to teach you how to shoot."

Margo squinted, confused. "That's not your camera," she said, wary. There had to be some catch. Slim believed he'd done a great service by hiring her at all—which, fair enough—and she hadn't earned further generosity.

"You think I'm going to train you on a Leica?" Slim scoffed. "Do you know what aperture is? Shutter speed? How these affect a photograph?"

"Well, no..."

"Let me introduce you to a Brownie."

Despite working for Slim for over a year, Margo still didn't know much about the profession, other than Brownies were what housewives used for family shots, and what Slim recommended whenever somebody asked for photography advice. Rita said it was because he was so afraid of competition that he tried to squelch amateurs right out of the gate.

"This camera is about as basic as it gets," Slim said. "There's no light meter. Only two shutter speeds and one aperture setting." The aperture dictated how much light the lens allowed through to the film, Slim explained. Different apertures could change which elements of a photo were in focus. The Brownie was set to f/11, which meant the opening was on the smaller side. It allowed for a larger depth of field and better focus.

Margo was hopelessly lost.

Slim told her to think of the camera like a human eye, with the lens as the eyeball, the shutter the lid. Aperture was the iris, and the film was the retina. It might've been a useful comparison, had she understood how eyes worked.

"This is the front," he said, then showed her two viewfinder windows, one for portrait, one for landscape. "The big circle in the middle is the shutter window. When the shutter is open, light from whatever you're photographing passes through the lens. This reflection forms an image, which is projected onto film at the back of the box. That's the exposure. The longer the shutter is open, the more light gets onto the film."

He rotated the camera and showed her the control lever used to adjust the shutter speed. Forty for one-fortieth of a second, and eighty for one-eightieth. There was also a letter *B*, but Slim said this was beyond Margo's comprehension. A chart instructed which speed to use, based on weather conditions—clear sun, hazy sun, cloudy bright, or cloudy dull. "Assess the weather and use the numbers in the middle column," Slim said.

He showed her how to load the film, and how to advance it by turning a knob. When the number *1* appeared in the red window, the film was properly loaded.

"Next you have to compose the picture," he said, and clicked the camera closed. "And decide whether you want to shoot vertically or horizontally. Okay, time to practice." Slim placed the camera in her hand. "What do you want to shoot?"

Margo checked the scene. She saw a mother pushing a carriage, and a man lying in the grass. In front of her was Lake Worth, on the other side were glimpses of Palm Beach's lakeside estates, and the red peaks of the Royal Poinciana's roof.

"I do have plans later in the week," Slim said, impatient, as he lit a cigarette.

"Hold on." Margo recalled what Lilly had said. "Don't I need a point of view?"

Slim tightened his mouth. The comment pleased him, but he'd never admit it. "You should probably learn how to operate it first," he said. "Few things are worse than not being able to take the picture you want because you don't know how. My advice is to ease into it. Shoot an object that is not moving."

"Fine. A palm tree."

"And, what's the weather?"

Margo consulted the chart. "Based on the weather, the setting says *80* or *40* plus *F*?" Slim rolled his eyes deep into his skull. "What? I'm following the chart!"

"*F* stands for filter. You don't need to worry about that. Put it on *80*," he said, and Margo flicked the lever. "When you shoot, you must remain perfectly still. One-eightieth of a second might sound fast, but it's relatively slow, particularly in daylight. The slightest movement will blur the image."

Margo picked a vertical orientation and held the camera near her waist. "Now gently squeeze the shutter button," Slim said.

Margo tensed her body and gritted her teeth. She wasn't going to let this camera move a hair. As she pressed down, the shutter clicked, and the camera jerked wildly to the right. "What the hell?" she screeched, and Slim sniggered.

"While you're learning, hold the camera against your body, or put it on something solid." Slim took the camera from her and wound the film. The number *2* now showed in the red window. "If you forget to wind the film," he said, "it'll take two photographs on the same frame, and ruin both."

Margo fared better with the next shot. She trained the lens on a seagull and managed to keep the camera stationary. By the time she reached the last frame, Margo was almost having fun. Slim was neither yelling at nor mocking her, which she took as a very good sign.

"Thank you for showing me," she said, handing the camera back. "Hopefully I didn't waste the entire roll."

"I reckon you will have done alright." He wound the film until the backing paper passed the window, then opened the camera and traded the old roll for a new one. "We'll get this developed, see how it turns out. If you did a decent enough job, you might get a second lesson."

"Gosh, did someone forget to tell me I was assigned a fairy godmother?" Margo said, pretending to look around. "Maybe it's time for me to play tennis, or start a minibar tab."

Slim's face went to stone. "I'd caution you against pushing the envelope. I've let you break one rule. *No cameras.*" He lifted the Brownie. "I'm not going to allow you to breach two."

It dawned on Margo why they were here, in a park, on the other side of the bridge, when Slim could've been literally anywhere else. Lilly must've said something about Dutch, and instead of blowing up he'd picked distraction, and feigned munificence. If Slim gave Margo an inch now, she couldn't ask for one later. She'd traded date number two and hadn't known.

Outrageous, Margo thought, boiling, quietly furious, though some part of her was flattered. If he was working this hard to keep her away from Dutch, Slim Aarons really viewed her as an asset, just like Lilly said.

35

Margo was trying to keep up with current events, just as she'd promised herself, just as she'd told Lilly. Unfortunately, there was a lot going on in this world. Major events happened *every day* and Margo was presently behind by more than two weeks. It was time to either pay the piper or wave the white flag, and with the morning off, Margo decided she should probably do something with the free time. She opened the first newspaper and perused the headlines, already bored out of her skull.

John Glenn Becomes First American to Orbit the Earth

Senator Kennedy Urges Peaceful Coexistence with Communism

Hope to Curb Castro Sags

Several colleges—the University of Georgia, of Alabama—were being forced to admit Black students, and it hadn't previously occurred to Margo that people saw desegregation as a choice. She couldn't understand why some folks were so upset that others wanted to be treated like humans.

U.S. Expands Economic Aid to Counter Communist Influence in Asia

Freeze Strikes Second Blow at Ravaged Citrus

There was a hubbub in the Dominican Republic—something about a junta—but Margo couldn't get through more than a paragraph without wanting to take a nap. These reporters really had a knack for making death and destruction seem bland.

Margo switched to the *Palm Beach Daily News*, known as the Shiny Sheet because of the paper it was printed on. One might call this gossip, but whatever was going on at the Everglades Club or the Society of the Four Arts *was* news. If Margo wanted to be part of Palm Beach, it was critical that she knew who was due to arrive at the Breakers, and who'd left, and the details of the roaring twenties party held in the Findlay Galleries penthouse. Notably, Wendy had done the Charleston on a table, in a short, fringed dress. She was also spotted at Russell and Mary Alice Firestone's "twist-and-swim soiree" with Lilly's brother, Dinny Phipps. The *New York Times* should hire these writers, Margo thought, if they could make Wendy Vanderbilt read as lighthearted and fun.

Margo flipped through several more papers, her eyes barely landing on each page. Just as she was about to call it a day, a headline jumped up and wrapped its fingers around her throat. Margo read the words again, unable to latch on.

DOLLY FRITZ IS WED IN MEXICO

Impossible. Absolutely no way. Margo closed and opened her eyes, but the words didn't change.

Dolly Fritz, who has been in society headlines for years as San Francisco's most beautiful, richest, and most eligible heiress, was married over the weekend in Mexico to a San Francisco antiques dealer.

According to the article, the couple wed in Mexico City, with Mrs. Ann Coleman Woolworth serving as the bride's attendant. The snub stung. As much as Margo considered Don the opposite of a catch, she would've been there, had Dolly asked.

Stomach roiling, Margo examined the photograph of the happy couple as they cut their three-tiered wedding cake. Dolly wore pearls and a short-sleeved dress with a full skirt. Her eyebrows were thick and dark, and she'd affixed a bow to each side of her chin-length bouffant. Don stood behind his new *wife*—the word made Margo gag—smiling in a manner customarily reserved for little boys putting frogs down their classmates' dresses. Also, his face was puffy, as though fresh off a three-day bender, and there was no delineation between his chin, jawbone, and neck.

Thirty minutes later, still horrified beyond measure, Margo found herself reaching for the phone. She dialed without a thought in her head and Rita came on the line with a singsong hello. "Have you heard about Dolly?" Margo said, breathless, the taste of sick in her throat. "She's married. Does Slim know? I can't believe it. I always assumed she'd come to her senses."

"Wait. Slow down," Rita said. "Dolly Fritz got married?"

"Yes! To that horrible man. Has Slim said anything?"

"Not specifically. I think he was expecting it, though. He's been calling everyone in his book, trying to find a soul who's heard of him. Hasn't had a stick of luck."

Margo tweaked her mouth and got a bit hot behind the eyes. It was awfully sweet of Slim to ask around like that. "Well, that's just great," Margo said. "Slim knows everyone, which means Don MacMasters probably isn't even his real name. Oh, Rita. This is a disaster!" Poor Dolly. Her mom had been after her money for years, and now a man was doing the same thing.

"Let's not jump to any conclusions," Rita said. "Slim took Mary to the beach, but I'll talk to him when they return. Sweetie, please. There's no reason to hyperventilate. Hang up the phone. Slim and I will call you as soon as he's back."

Margo set down the receiver, sad and angry and more heart-broken than she'd been a year ago at the B&T. For the first time in her life, she understood the urge to punch something. Thankfully, her violent impulses were thwarted by the trill of the phone.

"That was fast!" Margo said, picking up before it completed the first ring. "I don't mean to be histrionic, but we must in-tervene! Can we arrange to have him arrested? Is that what Interpol does?"

"Interpol? Uh-oh. What's going on?"

Margo's heart skipped multiple beats. "Slim?" she said, de-spite knowing it wasn't her boss. No doubt about it, the voice belonged to Dutch.

"It's not Slim," he said. "And I'm not sure whether to take that as a compliment or insult."

Margo forced a laugh. It felt like someone had knocked the wind out of her. She wasn't built to withstand so many simulta-neous emotions. "I'm only kidding," she said, unconvincingly. "I thought you were someone else. What are you doing? How are you? Are you in New York?"

"I am, for another few days, and then it's down to Miami for a benefit," he said. "That's why I'm calling, actually. I was hop-ing you might be able to sneak away and meet me for dinner. I know we'd calendared something for the end of the month, but this might be our only chance. My manager keeps agree-ing to gigs without consulting me first."

"Yes!" Margo said. "Absolutely. I'll meet you in Miami." It was possible that Dolly's news had sapped her of logic and com-mon sense, but with the right timing, an out-of-town date was the perfect solution. Margo wouldn't need Slim's approval or be forced to slink around Palm Beach.

"Well, that was easy. I love a woman who's sure of what she

wants. I'll be there Monday and Tuesday nights. Which is better for you?"

"Tuesday is perfect," Margo said, amazed by her luck. Slim
was attending a *square dance party* that night, hosted by Marjorie
Merriweather Post Hutton Davis May, heir to the Post Toasties
fortune. Every Tuesday during the season, Mrs. May invited
Palm Beachers to the garish pink-and-brown faux Mediterranean villa she'd christened Mar-a-Lago for an evening of
hoeing down. Famously, people dreaded the dances. The food
was abysmal, no one was allowed more than two drinks, and
every machination was conducted with the sort of precision
that would make a fascist dictator blush. But a person couldn't
decline an invitation from her and expect to be invited anywhere else. For once, Margo was grateful to be left out.

"Tuesday it is," Dutch said. "How about drinks and an early
dinner? Since I've got a gig that night. Six o'clock?"

"Perfect!" she said again. The earlier the better. Margo didn't
love taking the bus at night.

"It's a date. Six o'clock. The Castaways Hotel. The place is
famous. You won't be able to miss it."

36

"I'm going to need you to buck up," Slim said as they marched across the pool deck of the newly built La Fontana Cooperative Apartment Homes on North Flagler Drive.

Margo said there was no bucking needed and then promptly tripped on a long pink carpet. Nearby a sign read FASHION SHOW TODAY! It was a benefit for Wendy's charity, though what she needed the money for was anyone's guess. Eliminating sequins and bow ties from Palm Beach events didn't seem especially capital-intensive.

"You're not acting like yourself," Slim went on, "which is really saying something. I'm *used* to you being all over the place."

Margo shot him a glare. *All over the map* was how Lilly had described her wardrobe, and hearing it again might really make her paranoid, if she'd let it. Either the two were talking behind her back, or she *was* that erratic. There was no good explanation.

"I appreciate that the Dolly situation has gotten you all worked up," Slim said, "but I had nothing to do with it, so I don't understand why you're angry with me."

"I'm not angry. I'm confused as to why you don't care that

Dolly married that creep," Margo explained for the seventh or eighth time. They'd already squabbled in the car on the way over. Not only had Slim failed to call when he and Mary got back from the beach, he'd greeted the news with no more than a shrug. Sure, he'd attempted to get the scoop on Don, but in the end, people made their own decisions, and sometimes their decisions were bad. What could he do?

"Dolly chose a very bad husband," Slim agreed. "But I gather that's not why you're really upset. I assume it's the marriage in general that's gotten your goat."

Margo stopped. She whirled around to face him. "This is *not* about Crim Pebley, if that's what you're implying."

"What the hell is a crimpebley?" he said, screwing up his face. "It sounds like an English dessert."

"My former almost *fiancé*? The one who left me at the B&T?"

"Oh. That guy." Slim lit a cigarette. "Why are we talking about him?"

Margo turned on a heel and kept walking toward the check-in table, but it was not hard for Slim to keep up.

"You're mad," he said. "Because you mistakenly believe she should make major life decisions with you in mind when she hasn't been thinking about you at all. That's human nature, Margo. People look out for themselves."

"What a depressing way to view the world," Margo said. "Anyway, this isn't about me. It's about her getting duped. She settled for a *State Department aide* after dumping Prince Gonzalo *and* King Baudouin, who is the most attractive man on earth."

"Gosh, you're hurting my feelings," Slim tried to joke, but Margo refused to bite. "Stop. Stop moving. Look at me." Reluctantly, she pivoted back around. "Here's what you're not seeing," he said, gesturing at her with his cigarette. "In many ways, this union makes sense. Dolly would *never* marry a king or a prince, because it would mean attaching herself to *their* lives.

She doesn't want to be a princess or queen consort. Dolly Fritz needs top billing, and it is a rare man who doesn't mind sitting in his wife's shadow. Our egos always get in the way. It's one of our worst qualities."

"But what about the Pulitzers?" Margo said. "Lilly is wildly successful, and Peter is always going on and on about how proud he is."

"You can't compare anyone to the Pulitzers. Peter is happy to let Lilly shine because he likes to do his own thing. They're both one of a kind, which makes them a perfect match. As for Dolly…" He ground his cigarette into a potted plant. "She's married, and there's no going back. My suggestion? Play the dutiful friend for when she eventually needs a shoulder to lean on."

"I'd love to, if she'd respond to any of my communications…"

"Oh, Margo." He shook his head. "Listen, there's a chair in the front row with my name on it. Why don't you take a load off? I'll let you know if I need your assistance. In the meantime, watch all the pretty dresses and be glad for your friend. Dolly got what she wanted. Not many folks can say that."

⁓

Margo sat in a folding chair, her thighs sticking to the seat. She'd rather be helping than watching, because it would give her something to do. On the other hand, it was a million degrees, and at least she was in the shade.

"Hello, hello," Lilly said, slipping in beside her. She tore off the SLIM AARONS sign formerly taped to the back of Margo's chair. "Oh, honey, don't let them confuse you for Slim. You're far more attractive." She balled up the paper and chucked it aside. "How fun is this? We're in the audience today. Working girls getting their well-deserved time off!"

"Do you have any dresses in the show?" Margo asked, fanning her face with a program, hoping to wave away some vexation. She was still steamy, hot with frustration, despite the acknowledgment that Slim did make one or two decent points. She hated his wizened-old-professor act, especially because he was so damned good at it.

"No Lillys today," Lilly said. "Not until I find a reliable fabric supplier. But my girls are modeling some children's wear, so a few Pulitzers are on the clock." She shifted in her seat, her long tresses tickling Margo's shoulder each time she moved. "Oh, here come the models! Hell's bells. They call those shift dresses?"

Margo rattled her head, trying to clear her mind of Dolly and focus on the model strutting past. She wore a black shirtdress festooned with hand-painted gold medallions.

"I think these are from Belk's," Lilly observed, her tone even, though not necessarily indifferent. A woman stopped in front of them and demonstrated how the club collar of her navy blue sheath could be worn up or down.

"A new twist on tennis whites!" the announcer declared when it was time for the sporty lines. The pieces were embroidered with gold and green flowers, and racquet bags bore jaunty slogans, like I'M SET! ARE YOU GAME? And Love 40. When it came to tennis, Margo preferred 40 Love, but supposed this wasn't really about keeping score.

The show paused. A tiny, blond-bobbed girl peeped her head around a screen. A second head followed. It was Minnie and Liza Pulitzer, both wearing sunshiny yellow. Liza whispered in Minnie's year, and Minnie whispered back. Margo couldn't help but smile. The girls were plotting something.

A moment or two later, as the evening gowns lined up, the girls clasped hands. They bounded toward the runway, but someone reached out just in time, yanking them back. Margo recognized that arm. It was tanned, and ropy, and had a prowling panther tattoo. Minnie and Liza weren't the only Pulitzers working, it seemed.

Grinning, Peter lovingly chided his daughters for their naughtiness, then squatted to retie Liza's bows. The scene was so touching Margo's bottom lip began to quiver. She snapped her head away, sending her sunglasses flying.

"Admiring my little monsters?" Lilly said, leaning down to retrieve Margo's glasses.

"Oh. I. Uh," she stuttered, unsure why his sweet act had thrown her for such a loop. "They're just gorgeous!"

"They're marvelous kids. All three of my children are, and Peter is great with them. It's a miracle, given his childhood. He never really learned how to be loved." She crossed one leg over the other and fixed her eyes on the runway. "He frustrates the dickens out of me sometimes—what man wouldn't—and I have to remind myself that he's had a tough life. Plus, it isn't easy to be a man in Palm Beach. They get so lost down here. It is a woman's world, after all."

"A woman's world?" Margo said, befuddled as she threw Lilly a sideways look. "In Palm Beach?"

"Oh, sure. In case you haven't noticed, the place is run by the Old Guard, which is to say an autocratic widow matriarchy." She laughed through her nose. "Meanwhile, so many of the younger gals are founding companies yet still have kids, cook every night, and play bridge. The men feel inferior."

"I hadn't thought about it like that," Margo mused. Now the models were coming out in fur stoles, leaving Margo momentarily envious of whatever internal systems they possessed that prevented them from sweating to death.

"The men have a tendency to be insecure," Lilly added. "That's why so many of them call me and Julia and Bibi the *tradesies*. They can't *stand* our success and want to take us down a notch."

"Why don't the men start businesses?" Margo asked.

They were in a tricky situation, Lilly explained. Americans praised people who worked hard and looked down on those who didn't, the exception being if you had enough money to do nothing. "If a man doesn't work in Detroit or Chicago or even New York, he's shunned, but in Palm Beach, it's the norm. They don't have to work. They don't even know whether they want to, and so they flail around, thoroughly confused about what expectations they're supposed to live up to."

Margo thought about this, remembering the impression she'd had at that first party, at Lilly's house. Former ambassador, former steel magnate, former press secretary to this person or that. At the time, it seemed like the only person actively employed in Palm Beach was President Kennedy.

"Without societal expectations," Lilly said, "they forget how to behave. Men lack a woman's intellectual curiosity, so they struggle to find interests, other than booze and golf and gambling. It's easy to burn out living like that."

"But what about Peter?" Margo said. "He has his oranges. He's not burnt-out."

"He's better off than most, but he still lives here. It's a strange, strange place." She folded her hands in her lap and muttered something about how they didn't need to showcase so many muffs in Palm Beach. It was the precise opposite of the ideals Wendy was promoting. "Not that you asked for my advice," Lilly said. "But when it comes time to settle down, I highly recommend you *don't* choose anyone who grew up in Palm Beach."

Margo nodded, thinking of Dutch. He'd grown up visiting the area but, by his own account, never really belonged. She thought he overplayed his so-called outsider status, but maybe not being raised here was what he meant.

Dutch. The name sent a happy chill up her spine. Smiling, Margo rotated to face Lilly. "I have a date with Dutch Elkin on Tuesday," she said, and the relief in telling her was instant and all-consuming, like she'd taken one of those calming pills for ladies. *Mother has enjoyed sustained tranquilization all day!*

Lilly whipped in her direction. "Get out!" She gave her a slight push. "That is tremendous news. I told you that Slim would come to his senses."

"Actually…" Margo's gaze slid to where Slim stood, to the left of the stage. "He doesn't know. I'll tell him eventually, but Slim has been preoccupied, and I haven't—"

"Say no more." Lilly pretended to zip her lips. "Your secret's safe with me. I like to gossip as much as the next gal, but I'm the queen of discretion. I've kept a million secrets. You can trust me with *anything*."

37

A waitress in very short shorts led Margo toward Dutch, who was seated in the far corner of the restaurant.

Margo tried to appear smooth and confident as she moved through the room, despite having to duck to avoid the ratty nets dangling overhead. With its scuffed wood paneling and cracked red vinyl booths, the Wreck Bar meant what it said. The overall decorating scheme was evidently whatever washed up on shore last week, but Margo wouldn't have to worry about anyone from Palm Beach seeing her here.

"Well, hello, sunshine," Dutch said, standing to greet her. When he sat back down, he left behind the scent of Brylcreem and aftershave. "You look terrific."

Margo smiled. Even though 80 percent of the people in this restaurant were in bathing suits, she didn't feel out of place. A Lilly really did work for anyone, and in any situation. "Thank you," she said and wiggled into the booth. "What a fun place! Is that...?" She leaned forward, squinting through a porthole window. "A human foot?"

"That's the pool's deep end," Dutch said. "The idea is that we're underwater. Isn't it great?"

"Um. Sure." *Great* wasn't the description she'd pick.

"I come here whenever I'm in Miami. It was built by Jimmy Hoffa and his Teamsters and is a real gas when things get going."

"You mean dancing?"

"Yes, but also guests are encouraged—borderline *required*—to join in with the band."

Margo bobbed her head. Well, that explained the tambourine on the table.

She skimmed the menu. Shrimp cocktail was Margo's best bet, but she'd had the scampi on their first date and didn't want him to think of her as the shrimp girl, especially on the heels of Wendy's jab about *junior petite* sizes.

"I'm so glad we could make this work," Dutch said. "For the record, I called you three times before you picked up." He held up his last three fingers, middle to pinkie. "How impressed were you that I figured out where you were staying?" He flashed a grin. "I'd like to claim top-notch detective skills but in fact I dragged the information out of Rita Aarons."

Margo stared at him, confused. She could've sworn *she* was the one who'd told Dutch about the Pennsylvania when they spoke at the Christmas party. Why had he called Rita?

"Man, that woman was hacked off," Dutch continued. "Read me the riot act about how lucky I was that she picked up instead of her husband. Which floored me because, Slim?" He flung his hands into the air. "That guy is cool as a cat."

Margo blinked. "Sure. If the cat was rabid, and on fire."

Dutch cackled. "He must loathe phone calls."

"Depends on who's making them." Margo sighed. God, she was tired of consulting Slim on every last thing, tired of rules and budgets and eating cottage cheese and ketchup one to three times per week.

The waitress sashayed over, and Dutch ordered a bottle of champagne. "Yes, sir," she cooed. After asking about his latest gig, the woman gave him a very appreciative up and down before flicking her eyes toward Margo. *Is that all ya got?* her face seemed to say.

As the woman walked away, Dutch smiled at Margo, and she smiled back, fiddling with the paper napkin, weighing whether now was the time to mention current events. She'd been reading all those damned papers, yet Margo couldn't bring herself to ask what he thought about requiring tests to vote.

"Congratulations on your album," she said instead, because men loved to talk about themselves. "The papers are raving!"

"That's what folks have been telling me but for all I know, it could be pans from coast to coast. I don't keep up with any of it. My ego can't handle a drop of negativity, so I stay away."

"You don't read the news?" Margo said, and her body sank, as if buried beneath a thousand partially read newspapers. Had she done all that wretched studying for no reason at all?

"Don't look so alarmed!" Dutch laughed. "I read the regular news sometimes, but none of the gossip, or entertainment junk. There are too many lies, and my skin is delicate as an onion's."

"Wow. I didn't expect that," Margo said, still rolling the information around in her head. "Well, according to everyone, it's a hit."

"Mighty kind of you to say." Dutch glanced up and winked at the waitress, who'd returned to pour them each a coupe of champagne. "For now, I'm trying to enjoy it all. Cheers," he said, and Margo sipped the champagne. The taste was unexpectedly decent for a place that longed to be a shipwreck.

"Anyhow, enough about me." Dutch took another gulp. "You've hardly told me a thing about you, beyond your photography aspirations. Who are you, Margo? Where'd you come from, before you dropped into my life, like a dream?"

Margo smiled thinly and set down her glass. Here it was. The question she'd dreaded. There were a dozen ways to begin. "I grew up as an only child," she said, which was a safe enough start. "With my mother and stepfather, in Pacific Heights. That's San Francisco."

"Is your family still there?" he asked, no sign of judgment on his face.

"Technically. But the situation is…in flux." Margo stopped to collect her thoughts. Dutch said that he didn't care about reputation or social standing. His own mother was kicked out of the social registry, which he seemed to take as a point of pride. If there was a time to risk his opinion of her, it was now. She'd kept things from Crim and look how that'd turned out. "My mom is in San Francisco, but she's living with my stepfather's sister," Margo confessed. "They had to sell the house because he's… Gosh, this is difficult to say out loud." She cleared her throat. "My stepfather, the man who raised me? He's wanted by the Feds."

Dutch smacked his hands on the table, and the silverware clanked. His face lit up like he'd seen Marilyn Monroe. "Hot damn!" he said. He was—could it be—*excited*? "This sounds like a hell of a story. Tell me everything."

Margo explained as much as she could. Through a series of stock transactions, mergers, and shifty business combinations, Sandy LaSalle had gained control of several dozen companies over the past decade. He left many insolvent and looted the rest, enriching himself by many millions of dollars in the process.

"Sandy swears it's all a complicated business matter and people can't grasp high finance," Margo said, already lighter without the burden of silently carrying these things. "Emptying the family bank accounts and cavorting with women in Rio seems pretty straightforward, but I'm no expert."

"The man is a shyster, it's obvious," Dutch said. "Was it hard for you when he left?"

Margo had to think about this. "Hard only because it was

embarrassing, and I felt bad for my mom. But we were never close." Most of the time, Sandy treated her like someone else's pet he was forced to occasionally watch. Despite their fifteen years together, Margo never got to know the man. He lived in her memories as a caricature, a cartoon figure claiming to be the son of a Russian czarist army general as he strutted around in a ladies' fox stole. "I always got the impression he was putting on an act," Margo said. "How much my mom saw or understood remains a mystery."

Margo pictured the elaborate Christmases, the endless parade of blue velvet jewelry boxes. When Antoinette attempted to sell the necklaces and bracelets and big, fat brooches to fund Sandy's defense, most pieces were fakes. It wasn't a startling turn of events—Sandy was all preview, no show. Once he promised to buy Margo a pet elephant, then rented one for her eighth birthday, which was as close to a vow as he'd ever kept.

"If you don't mind my asking," Dutch said and picked up his fork. Their dinners had materialized, as though they'd dropped from the sky. Margo hadn't noticed the saucy waitress return, which she took as a good sign. "What happened to your real father?"

"Wow, you're digging deep, aren't you?" Margo pulled off her yellow headband and ran her fingers through her hair. "The short answer is that I never met him. He left for the war when my mother was pregnant, and died in the Pacific. My mom met Sandy when she went to the Philippines to pick up his personal effects." At the time, Sandy was running a casino catering to Japanese soldiers—the declared enemy, Margo realized now.

"Aw, hell," Dutch said, his eyes brimming. Despite all his swagger, this man was soft on the inside, and it only made her like him more. "That's a drag. I know from experience that it's hard not to take a parent's absence personally. It can make a person feel abandoned."

Margo cocked her head. Abandonment wasn't a word she'd ever used to explain the gaping hole in her life. Did she wish she'd been raised by her father? Yes, of course. Did Margo mourn him, though? Not really. Was it possible to miss what you never had?

"Most people think I hit the jackpot," Dutch went on. "Because I grew up with the Whitneys, in the biggest homes on the East Coast. But that doesn't change the loneliness. You get it, though. We're in similar boats."

As she went to speak, to say how sorry she was for all he'd been through, Dutch threw up a hand, signaling the waitress for a check. Margo had only eaten two bites of her meal. She thought their night was just getting started.

"We'd better go," Dutch said and gave the woman his Diner's Club card.

"Right. Your gig." She'd been so caught up in their date she'd forgotten they were both supposed to be somewhere else.

"You're so easy to talk to," Dutch said as Margo gathered her belongings—headband, purse, a clip-on earring that'd been hurting her left lobe. "You're a fantastic listener but have plenty of your own stories. That's very rare."

"Yes. Well. Sandy LaSalle is all stories. Lucky me."

"You're also the first girl I've taken out in ages who's never seen me play," he said. "Makes me feel like maybe I have more than one thing going for me." He smiled sheepishly. "I know it's stupid."

"Um. No. Not stupid at all," Margo said, flummoxed yet again. She *had* seen him play. He'd been playing the piano the first time she laid eyes on him, and at the *Bachelor Father* Christmas party, where she and Rita watched him perform five or six songs. When he finished, he thanked them for sticking around.

"Here you go, Mr. Elkin," the waitress said as she returned

with his card. "It's a pleasure to see you again. Make sure you're always seated in my section. I'll give you the *most* service."

The woman toddled off, tight and sleek in her very short shorts. Margo checked Dutch, shocked to find him concentrating on *her* instead of the woman's rear. "I want to do this again," he said. "And again, and again, a hundred times more."

"Me, too," Margo said, her little heart pattering like a team of runaway horses as she imagined a world where this might happen, where they'd openly dine at the Everglades Club, or Ta-boo, no questions asked. They'd be a bona fide couple, attending parties and balls and twisting with the Pulitzers, and Slim couldn't say bunk. Margo would finally be her own person and he'd no longer be in charge of her life.

38

Slim blew into the hotel like a hurricane, full of wind and spitting debris.

"There you are," he said, dropping cigarette ash all over the lobby.

"There *I* am? I've been waiting," Margo said. Last week, he'd given her a second photography lesson and today was supposed to be the third. "You're ten minutes late," she added, crossing her arms.

"Change of plans." Slim pushed his aviators on top of his head. "I had a client request, but promised to golf with Rita."

"*Again?* You really need to—"

"Nope!" He sharply raised a finger. "I didn't forget. The client thing just came up, and I can't say no. You wanted to shoot today? Excellent." He held out the camera bag. "Welcome to your first solo assignment."

Margo made a small choking sound. "You want me," she said. "To do a shoot. All by myself? I've only taken pictures of seagulls and trash cans. Is this a good idea?"

"It's an atrocious idea," he conceded. "Do you think I *want* to play golf with Rita and her girlfriends? I do not. But I won't turn down certain people, and if I can avoid letting down my wife, I will do it. That woman puts up with so much."

"She really does," Margo agreed.

"Here. Take it," he said, shoving the camera at Margo. She accepted the case, hands trembling. "Luckily the person who requested my services is the one person who wouldn't have a fit seeing you show up in my stead. Lilly Pulitzer is going to Key West to find some new prints. Or inspirations for prints?" Slim shrugged. "Regardless, she could only go today, and understands that calling at the last minute means getting the C team. She wants documentation. That's it. In other words, very low stakes."

Margo swallowed. Her mouth was bone-dry. This couldn't be low stakes, not with Lilly Pulitzer involved. "And you can't reschedule?" she said.

Slim tossed his hands into the sky. "Why do you make everything a thousand times more difficult? This isn't brain surgery, Gogo. Photography is 25 percent ability, 25 percent luck, and 50 percent hard work. And you're only shooting patterns."

"But you won't be around to tell me what I'm doing wrong!"

Shaking his head, Slim put one of his meaty mitts on her head, like a benediction. "Don't overthink it," he said. "It's only photography. Not the end of the world. You've got this, kiddo. Do your best. That's all anyone can ask."

❧

Margo met Lilly on the tarmac at the West Palm Beach airport. Peter would be flying them to Key West, Lilly explained, pointing to the white-and-gold-and-green plane parked beside them.

"How…efficient!" Margo chirped. She knew Peter flew all the time, but he didn't seem earnest or serious enough to pilot other people around.

"Don't worry," Lilly said, laughing, as she took in Margo's expression. "He hardly ever crashes."

"What a relief."

Peter poked his head out of the plane's open door. "Hi, Margo," he said, looking tanned and relaxed as a summer's day. *Too* relaxed, frankly, for someone about to hoist her into the sky. He had on a white-and-blue-striped Izod shirt, for heaven's sake. Like a fraternity boy on summer vacation.

"Let's get a move on," Lilly said, twisting her long, thick hair into a knot on top of her head. "Peter's not really trained to fly at night."

"Is air travel the only option?" Margo asked as Peter helped her up and into the back of the plane. He smelled like some combination of cigarettes and soil and citrus. Margo also detected a hint of whiskey but chased the thought away.

"Some people take a boat," Lilly said. After pushing the passenger seat back into place, she sat down beside Peter and pulled the door shut. "That's how Mom and Memsie always get there. Of course, they'd never let Peter fly them, not in a hundred thousand years!"

"Oh," Margo said, and Peter started the engine. She fastened her seat belt. "Wow, there are a lot of buttons and levers and compassy things up there!"

"And I know how to work most of them." Peter glanced back, nearly blinding her with one of his sparkling, impish grins. "Ready for takeoff?" he said.

Margo nodded and tried not to weep.

As they taxied down the runway, Margo slipped on her sunglasses and sent up a prayer. If they crashed, she hoped the newspapers would spell out her name instead of announcing the crash killed three people: Lilly and Peter Pulitzer, and a guest.

39

"Most of these homes were built by ship carpenters," Peter said as they strolled Key West's winding brick paths. "They're made of mahogany and saltwater cypress. You'll have noticed the peaked roofs. That's to run off the rain."

Margo had noticed the peaked roofs, as well as the widow's walks, wide porches, and shutters, the Spanish-lace woodwork and delicately turned spindles. Downtown Key West was charming and unique, and busy as a beehive, with workmen hammering and sawing on every street.

"This isn't a walking tour, Peter!" Lilly shouted. She was several yards ahead. "Stop trying to murder Margo with boring facts. She's here to work."

Two hours in, Margo hadn't taken a single snap, not with Lilly tearing through the town at a breakneck pace. One second she was two blocks ahead, and the next, she'd vanish, reappearing minutes later with some fresh item of inspiration—an apron, a swatch of fabric, a pair of pants. By the time Margo thought about taking out the camera, Lilly would've crammed the new purchase into an old crinkled Gristedes bag, already on to the next thing.

"Wait here," Lilly said, when Margo tracked her into yet another store. "I'll be out in a jiff. We'll have plenty of time for pictures later. We can find somewhere scenic to lay it all out." The first rule of photography was giving the subject what they wanted, and Margo didn't protest.

Now she leaned against a building, while Peter smoked a cigarette a few yards away. Five minutes became ten and then twenty, which Margo spent alternately reviewing the Brownie manual and using it to fan her face. She'd have to take a minimum of one roll of film today or Slim would never trust her again.

Twenty-five minutes later, Lilly exploded from the shop, a wad of fabric balled in her hand. "You guys!" she said, scrabbling up. "I think I've found the solution to all my problems in life." She splayed her fingers to show what she'd discovered.

"This might be a boneheaded question," Peter said, walking up. "But what's so special about it?"

Thank God Margo wasn't the only one who didn't understand how a dancing daiquiri pot holder was going to solve anything.

"Are you kidding? This print is outlandish, exceptional, utterly rare. Even better…" Lilly flipped it over to show the label on the back. Key West Hand Print Fabrics. "Their factory is in town, and they have thousands of original prints. Hurry! Let's go!"

Within seconds, they were hurtling across Key West, past sunburned tourists and buzzed military men, until they reached the factory on Front Street. Lilly shot through the open door, thwacked her bag onto a hard surface and asked, "Is this your shit?"

It was, and she wanted to see the rest.

—

Peter handed Margo her ice cream.

"Sorry we're having to kill time," he said, licking drips of strawberry marshmallow from the side of his cone. Margo had picked vanilla, because it was an easy choice, and wouldn't stain her Lilly. Now she wanted something more adventurous. Peter probably thought she was a dud. "My wife prefers to shop alone. Trips like these, it's a lot of waiting around. I'm used to it, but I know you were hoping to get a few pictures."

"It's fine," Margo said as they reached the end of the block. They took a right on a cobblestone street. The ocean lay straight ahead. "I'm sure we'll get to it, eventually."

"So, did I hear correctly?" Peter said. "You agreed to another date with Dutch? That's quintessential Elkin, hoodwinking nice girls in cities worldwide. Never trust a guy who wears a suit for a living."

They walked several steps in silence, Margo licking her ice cream as she sorted out her thoughts. How many times would she have to tell Peter that Dutch was a terrific companion, all gentleman? "I thought you two were old pals," she said at last. "Between him and Jim Kimberly, it sounds like you keep very dubious company."

Peter chortled, gamely. "Both are fine if you're not dating them. Usually I avoid romantic entanglements with my friends," he joked.

Margo finished off the rest of her cone. "For the record," she said, "Dutch has been chivalrous and kind."

Indeed, their night had ended like a fairy tale. Dutch took Margo's hand and led her outside, where a shiny black car idled, ready to ferry her back to the hotel. With the ocean winds whipping around them, Dutch brushed the hair from Margo's face and leaned in for a kiss. His lips were soft, just how she imagined they'd be, and she'd floated back to West Palm Beach as if on a cloud.

"You *are* aware of all the women he's dated?" Peter said. Before Margo could answer, yes, she read the gossip pages, he ticked off several names. Liza Minnelli. Charlotte Ford. Susan

Kohner. Gary Cooper's daughter, Maria. "He's the sort of man who makes a broad fall in love with him and then never calls again. I don't like seeing girls I respect get mired in it." He swiped Margo's crumpled napkin from her hand and threw it into a trash can. "Do you think I'm overstepping?" he asked, peering back over his shoulder.

"A little bit?" Margo said.

He exhaled. "Forget I said anything."

Now they were standing in old Mallory Square, where nineteenth-century commodores once hunkered down to defend against pirates. Resuming the role of self-appointed tour guide, Peter explained that years ago, the town leaders banded together and reimagined the old docks as a tourist hub, and turned the warehouses into playhouses, art galleries, and museums.

Peter went on and on, but Margo was stuck one conversation back. Did she care that Dutch had dated Liza Minnelli? Not really. Miss Minnelli didn't seem too reliable anyhow, though she didn't love Peter's girl-in-every-port implication. Then again, if Dutch were such a cad, Lilly wouldn't be encouraging her to go out with him and Wendy surely would've launched a verbal grenade about his copious romantic escapades, had there been one to throw. Still, Margo wished she'd heard from him at least once in the past week.

"And this is it." Peter lunged up onto a concrete barrier and spread his arms. "The southernmost point in North America! We are closer to Havana than mainland Florida."

Margo stepped up beside him and stared out across the water, toward the naval ships in the distance. The briny, fishy stench was strong, and for a second, she thought of San Francisco, if San Francisco were perpetually sunny and plus forty to fifty degrees. Suddenly Dolly's face appeared in her head. Margo's breath snagged.

"Margo..." Peter checked her face. "Is everything alright?"

"Yes. Fine. Everything's grand," Margo stammered. She closed her eyes and cleared all thoughts of Dolly, of *Mrs. Mac-Masters*, from her mind. "So, um. How's the citrus industry these days? Booming, I'll bet, with your number one client doing such brisk business!"

How was the citrus industry? Margo wanted to die. Was she a bad conversationalist despite all that training?

"*Booming* isn't the word I'd use," Peter said, cautiously. "The recent freeze has been murder on the fruit. I'm hardly able to give any to Lilly. If she were smart—which she is—she'd switch to a dress-only trade—" He stopped to examine Margo. "You look cute in yours by the way."

"Oh, thanks." Margo blushed fiercely. Was Peter flirting with her? Of course not. She shook the ridiculous thought away.

"That was a bedsheet originally bought for Liza's room," he added, reaching into his pocket for a cigarette. "But decent fabric never stays in my house for long. Anyway, how's work going for you? You've been with Slim for quite a while. Must be some kind of record."

Margo's first inclination was to say no, and what did he mean, but it was *quite a while* by any measure, especially when it came to a woman rapidly advancing in age. "It's been a year," she said, lightly astonished. "Some days, I could swear only a minute has passed, others it's an eternity. He's a tyrant but does let me try new things on occasion." She held up the camera.

"Trying new things is the only way to stay young," Peter said. "Not that you'll have to worry about that anytime soon."

Margo smiled. It was funny how she didn't know Peter very well, but his presence felt casual and lived-in. He lent a certain ease to conversations, and Margo was never on high alert like she was around someone like Wendy.

"How do your parents feel about your job?" Peter asked.

"Most of the Old Guard still seems to believe that 'proper' daughters aren't supposed to have jobs or their own lives outside the home."

The Old Guard. That's what Slim had called the Phipps, and Margo wondered whether they didn't like Peter because he let his wife work. As for Antoinette's and Sandy's views on her occupation, she was unable to conjure a world where they gave a damn.

"I don't think they have a strong opinion, either way," she said.

"Better than the opposite, I guess. I hope that when my daughters are adults, they'll do what they want, not what they think we expect. Luckily they have Lilly as a role model." Peter flicked his cigarette into the sea. "We should get back," he said. "My wife probably owns the damned store by now." Squinting against the sun, he chuckled. "That Lilly. She is nothing but surprises and left turns and coming out of the clear blue. Sometimes I wish I had a playbook, so I'd know what to expect."

40

Lilly burst out of the factory storefront, arms loaded with fabric, hair falling out of the knot on her head. The timing was perfect, as though Peter and Lilly were set to the same clock.

"What'd I tell ya?" Peter said, conspiratorially, as he leaned toward Margo. "Cleaned out the whole store."

"The place is a gold mine!" Lilly said. "Look at these fabrics! Just look at them! I bought three thousand yards on the spot."

Peter rolled his eyes though they all knew he didn't mean it. The man was bubbling with pride and Margo got a little teary at the sight. Suddenly, an idea popped into her brain, and a thrill swelled in her chest. Slowly, Margo unlatched the camera bag.

"Can you handle these patterns? I'm mad for all of them." As Lilly showed Peter the swatches, Margo removed the Brownie from its case. She checked the chart and sky. The film was loaded, courtesy of Slim.

"I'm going to take a few shots…" Margo said with a dry swallow. "If you don't mind."

Neither Pulitzer heard, or maybe they didn't care. Margo placed the camera vertically against her hip bone and walked backward several paces, and several more, narrowing in on the pink and blue bangles adorning Lilly's wrist, the purple tigers and yellow monkeys spilling from her hand. Margo was trembling like an earthquake but pressed the shutter anyway. *Click.*

"This is great, Lil," Peter said. "But three thousand yards? How do you propose we get it home?"

"That's why I brought along some muscle." Lilly playfully pinched his arm. "We'll grab as much as we can, and they'll send over the rest." She spun around. "You!" she said to Margo, widening her brown eyes. "You're my good luck charm! You magically got the holiday inventory off my hands—"

"Well, the president deserves some credit…"

"And now I'm stocked for the next—" she flapped a hand "—God knows how many years. Eek! This is so exciting. Get ready, my loves." She dumped the rest of the fabric into Peter's waiting arms. "I was only playing before, but now Lilly Pulitzer is in serious business."

Margo spent the plane ride back all jangling nerves and jiggling feet, praying not for a safe landing but that the roll of film she shot would pan out.

In Key West, Margo had been struck by a jolt of energy—*creative inspiration*, if she could be so bold—and hoped she could summon it one more time. She wanted to capture Lilly as she arrived back home, triumphant and ready to unleash her new designs on Palm Beach. Margo thought about Dutch and how anxious he'd been in his career until he'd decided to trust himself. *You can do this*, Margo told herself. *You already have.*

Peter landed the plane with a bump and a clang, and they taxied for what seemed like three seconds. When the door opened, Margo gulped down all her fears and hopped out in front of Lilly. "Let me get a few of you deboarding from the successful trip!" she said, flabbergasted by her own brazenness.

She must've been feeding off Lilly's excitement, the buzzing in the air that felt like change.

After advancing the film, Margo told her subjects to come out of the plane.

"Ready for me?" Lilly said, peeping through the door. After getting Margo's okay, she reknotted her hair, gathered up a pile of fabric, and leaped down. *Click.* Had Slim ever photographed a woman jumping from a plane? Margo didn't think so. She might've done something new.

Next, she shot Peter exiting, then shot them both as they navigated the oily gray puddles on the tarmac. Lilly led and Peter followed, holding on to the back of her dress with one hand, a bundle of fabrics tucked beneath his opposite arm.

Trailing them from a short distance, Margo removed one roll of film and put in another, just in time to capture Lilly at the pay phone, placing an order for Key West Hand Print's entire stock. Peter watched in admiration so unchecked it approached worship. Margo prayed these images would turn out, so Lilly could see how he was looking at her, how they *both* looked to the rest of the world.

41

NASSAU, BAHAMAS / MARCH 1962

"I need to show you something," Slim said, reaching for his camera case, which rested between them on the ferry terminal's bench. "I want you to see what you did."

"What did I do?" Margo asked, a knot in her throat. If Slim had uncovered some proof of her date with Dutch, he wouldn't confront her in public, Margo reasoned, not when they were en route to the glitziest party yet. That weekend, over one thousand guests were due to arrive in the Bahamas to celebrate a new resort, on the recently established "Paradise Island," which was previously abandoned and riddled with hogs.

"I had these printed locally." Slim handed Margo an envelope. "Take a look." Sucking in her breath, Margo opened the envelope and removed several photographs. They were her images, the ones she'd taken last week in Key West. Slim tapped a picture of Lilly bounding from the plane. "This one really stood out."

In the photograph, Lilly lands with one foot on the ground, her back foot kicked up, a flip-flop barely hanging on. Watching from the plane, Peter tells his wife to be careful, that the tarmac is slick, but he's not looking at the asphalt. His eyes are glued to his wife's high, round derriere. The famous Lilly side slits reveal the start of its curve.

"What do you think?" Slim asked, and Margo could smell the hint of a cigarette he'd smoked a half hour ago.

"It's good," Margo said, and she meant it. "I hope that doesn't sound egotistical, but it has life, and movement. You can almost see her gold hoops swinging."

"You can thank the fixed shutter speed for that." Slim settled back into his seat. "And you're right. The image is all about Lilly in motion. A perfect moment, captured at the perfect time."

Margo inspected the picture again, seeing Peter and Lilly with fresh eyes, though she'd taken the shot.

"I'm proud of you." Slim squeezed her knee, and Margo got choked up. "Oh, Good Lord. You're not going to cry on me, are you?"

"I'm not sure," Margo snuffled, reaching into her purse for a tissue. "I'm just not accustomed to receiving compliments from you." She blew her nose and Slim pulled away, his face wracked with horror.

"Jesus, you sound like a foghorn!"

"I'm sorry." She shoved the tissue back into her purse. "We've had a busy week and I haven't had enough sleep, apparently." Margo felt something dribble from her nose. She'd grab another tissue, but Slim would probably abandon her right there in the terminal if she did. "It's so overwhelming, but in a good way." Margo fanned her nose, as if this might dry the tears. "Just ignore me! I'm being silly."

Margo was on the brink of having it all—a handsome man, a commendable skill, and, if they liked the photos as much as Slim did, the respect of the two most important people in Palm Beach. But the closer Margo got to what she wanted, the more likely that one wrong move could unravel everything. There was no Dutch without Lilly, and no photographs of Lilly and

Peter without Slim's concerns about Dutch. It was all so tightly connected, and Margo didn't know how long she could keep a grip on the strings.

—

George Huntington Hartford II was the leathery, tall, fifty-something A&P heir who'd purchased a deserted island occupied by pigs, bribed the Bahamian government to declare it an "out island" to reduce his taxes, and then built an eight-hundred-acre resort. This weekend, one thousand of his closest friends—plus Slim—would celebrate the grand opening of the island's Ocean Club, the former residence of a deceased Swedish industrialist that Hunt had transformed into a "resort within a resort."

Planes and helicopters were allowed on Paradise, but automobiles were not. As Margo and Slim toured the grounds via horse and buggy, Slim couldn't get over how much it reminded him of prewar Bermuda, which was a perfectly Slim Aarons observation. The resort had, among other features, a seven-hundred-foot, white-sand beach, formal gardens overlooking the harbor, and fifty-two luxury suites, each with its own balcony and ocean-view terrace.

Guests arrived in the late afternoon via private plane, or personal yacht, or in one of the jets Hunt chartered from Pan Am. After retiring to their rooms for several hours, they trickled back outside in jewels and tuxedos, gathering beneath candy-striped tents, beside lavender-lit gardens.

With music rippling over the lagoon and a full moon overhead, Hunt Hartford held court, working the crowd, regaling friends with the party details, like how he'd flown the chefs over from France and the fireworks crew from Monaco. Guests trilled and cooed, until he turned his back. Once he was out of earshot, they added up the cost of all this, concluding that even if his island was at capacity 365 days per year, Hunt would never make a dime, tax break or not. What was he trying to prove, anyhow? That he was on par with a Kennedy or Rockefeller? Since working for Slim, Margo had come to understand that when a person reached a certain level of wealth, aspiration wasn't a positive trait. You couldn't be seen yearning, wanting anything.

They moved through the crowd, Slim dapper in his tuxedo, Margo dolled up in a red satin dress to stand out for once, in this sea of guests. Right away she noted a full complement of Palm Beachers—Chris Dunphy, Cleveland Amory, Peter Lind Hayes—and countless Brits with titles. One table was reserved for bishops and two for United States senators, with stars and starlets and legends of all stripes scattered throughout.

"Go away!" Zsa Zsa Gabor shrieked at Slim as they descended upon the actress's table. She wore a gold beaded dress with a deep décolletage, though almost no skin was visible due to her thick diamond-and-emerald necklace. "Darlink, get back! Not even Elizabeth Taylor is attractive that close up."

Slim laughed but eventually wheedled her into submission. "Zsa Zsa, when are you ever going to turn forty?" he asked, snapping away.

"Never," she sniffed, though she'd been biologically well past forty for some time.

As Zsa Zsa giggled, Margo's eyes roamed the tent. Across the way, Tony Randall was talking to several men, among them Walter Cronkite. After sportingly slapping Tony on the back, Cronkite stepped to the side to reveal a tall, dark-haired man with a very strict part. It was Dutch. Margo's breath caught.

Dutch glanced over. She lifted an arm to wave, and he crinkled his brow, confused. The point of Margo's dress was to make her highly visible, but maybe she was too far away to be recognized. She took a step forward, just as Dutch turned to rejoin his group. The ground seemed to drop out from beneath her feet.

"I need to say hello to some folks," Slim said, startling Margo. "Everyone's here. *LIFE*, *TIME*, *Newsweek*, *Vogue*. Why don't you mingle?" He jammed a cigarette between his teeth.

"Mingle?" Margo yelped as panic surged through her. "Who would I mingle with?" Slim tried to walk away, but Margo leeched on to his side. "Don't leave me. Please! I'm not ready." Whatever confidence she'd built of late was now shot to hell.

"What is with you?" Slim said, shaking her off. "I can't babysit you all night. Go. Have fun. Act like a guest."

"Slim, please—" Margo said, but he was already gone.

In her glaring red dress, Margo felt overly conspicuous, like a beacon of the down-and-out and also-ran. When the ground refused to swallow her up, Margo shuffled to the party's perimeter, closed her eyes, and pretended to be somebody else.

"Is there a reason you're hiding behind a purple-lit statue of FDR?" someone said.

Margo jolted as if kicked in the shin. She flipped around and found Peter Pulitzer, dressed to the nines.

"Good Lord! Why'd you have to sneak up on me?" she said, and instead of slowing down, her pulse picked up extra beats.

"Sorry," he said, "but you looked like you needed a friend. Or someone to put you out of your misery."

"Ha. Well. You're not wrong," Margo said, quickly taking him in. Despite the dirt in his nail beds, and the red slash on his chin where he must've cut himself shaving, Peter was elegant in a tux. She recalled the first party they'd shot at the Pulitzers, when Slim told her all women—including Rita—agreed he was the dreamiest man in Palm Beach. "Never mind what I'm doing," Margo said, batting away the memory, and this foregone conclusion. "I don't think I've ever seen you so dressed up."

"I do like to take the old penguin for a walk every now and again," Peter said, "to check that he can still do his job." He reached out to jostle the big, floppy bow on Margo's left shoulder. "Love the dress. You always manage to do things differently, to make a splash."

"Thanks," Margo said, adjusting her red satin belt, which felt tight, though she hadn't had a chance to eat today. "So, what brings you to the former Hog Island? I thought you hated these fancy affairs?" It was well-known that Peter Pulitzer so detested parties and charity balls that he often didn't bother attending. Usually, Lilly took some beefcake friend of hers as an escort. The man wasn't interested in women, so no one questioned the arrangement.

"This isn't a regular party," Peter said. "It's the sort of event that you want to be able to say you were there. Not to mention, my wife would be apoplectic if I missed it."

"Is she here?" Margo asked.

"Probably? That woman is impossible to keep track of these days, especially now that she has every fabric known to man at her disposal. Speaking of Key West." He grinned. "Any idea when you'll get the photos back? I've been dying to see them."

"They are back," Margo said, beaming as she pictured them. "And they turned out great. Even Slim said as much, as he's *never* satisfied."

"That's amazing," Peter said. "Though not unexpected. I hope your success won't ignite Slim's world-famous jealousy, though. He can't stand any photographer with a speck of talent."

"Oh, no, the results have nothing to do with me," Margo said, not because she fully believed it, but because it seemed like the right thing to say. "I had the best subjects." This was true, but some of the credit *was* hers, she had to believe.

"It definitely wasn't just us," Peter said. "Slim wouldn't have sent you if he didn't think you had the chops. So, where are they?"

"With Slim, actually. He's right over there." Margo stood on her tiptoes to check, but instead of Slim, she spotted Dutch, who was cutting a straight line in their direction, as hell-bent and determined as an assassin. Margo's stomach coiled into a knot.

"Well, well, well, look who it is," Dutch said. His gray eyes had gone black. "The legendary Peter Pulitzer." Dutch gave him a robust thump on the back, and Peter coughed. "It's good to see you out of dungarees. And you!" He kissed Margo on the cheek. "You're more ravishing than usual."

"Typical Elkin," Peter clucked. He reached for a cigarette but didn't offer one to Dutch. "Compelled to intervene any-time he sees someone else with a pretty girl."

"She's more than a *pretty girl*, Pulitzer. She's the loveliest broad in the joint." Dutch fixed his sultry gaze on Margo, who was too stunned to speak. Ten minutes ago, he couldn't see her, and now she was the *loveliest broad*? He'd called himself scatterbrained, but she was the one who felt mixed-up. "I've been making my way to beautiful Margo all night, but keep getting waylaid."

"You waylay yourself," Peter said. "You're perpetually dis-tracted. Out to lunch. Don't have two brain cells to rub to-gether."

"I must've really hoodwinked those folks at Yale. Where did you get your degree from again?" He smirked. "Anyhow, I'll admit it. I can be distracted. That's what happens when you're a world-famous artist who keeps thousands of songs in his head."

"I'll give you that," Peter said, and Margo braced, waiting for the insult. "I've been meaning to tell you, congrats on the success of your record. I hear it's really killing the charts."

"Appreciate it, but all credit to my producer. I'm only along for the ride."

"We should celebrate," Peter said and invited him out to

his hunting cabin. The last time they were there, Dutch shot twenty-five quail and one hundred doves, which Peter considered an "okay start."

As the men spoke, Margo swiveled back and forth between them, unsure what the hell was going on. Why were they suddenly acting like the best of pals? Why were they even together in the first place? Had Peter been right? Did Dutch come over because she was talking to him? Margo had heard of girls flirting with one boy to get the attention of another but assumed that was what people meant by *feminine wiles*.

"Margo!" someone shouted. "MARGO!" It was Slim, speed-walking toward them, his long legs as graceful as ill-fitting stilts. His overall bearing was that of an outraged clown, but Margo was delighted to hear him screeching her name. "I told you to mingle," he said, panting on the approach, "not loiter about, flirting with celebrities and old men."

"Hey!" Peter groused.

"Thank you," Dutch said.

"I'm not flirting with anyone," Margo insisted.

"If you gentlemen will excuse us, my assistant needs to work." Slim pivoted and took off again.

"Er, I guess that's my cue to leave," Margo said, and gave the men a meek farewell. She'd taken no more than two steps before something tugged on her wrist. When Margo looked back, it was directly into Peter's brown-green eyes.

"Yes?" she said. Behind Peter, in the near distance, Dutch was walking away, sidewinding across the dance floor, left hand in his pocket, right hand waving to each person he saw.

"Sorry to bother you one last time," Peter said. He smiled, his lips stretching to expose every tooth. "But I had to tell you before you go. You look absolutely smashing in red."

42

Margo plodded through the lobby of her hotel, shoes in hand, feet aching, eyes stinging from the wind and sand. They'd spent the day on Lyford Cay, shooting a luncheon attended by a bevy of bold-faced names like Ladies Anne Orr-Lewis and Oakes, Buzzy Warburton, Henry Ford, and some auxiliary Kennedys—in this case, Pat Lawford and Steve Smith. Tomorrow it was back to Palm Beach for one day, and on to Katonah and Washington, DC. Another Palm Beach season in the books.

On her way to the elevator, Margo passed the patio restaurant, where the band was already playing. She groaned quietly, despising every person who *didn't* get depressed by calypso's chipper, syncopated beat. Of course, most guests weren't here to work and therefore not hamstrung by early wake-up calls.

Margo peeked through the double doors. Several stools at the bar were unoccupied, and she thought, why the hell not? Slim was dining with one of his magazine friends, and hadn't specifically told her to go straight to her room. Margo slipped on her shoes and strode outside.

One of the men at the bar glanced up, and Margo's heart kerplunked. It occurred to her in that moment that handsome

Peter Pulitzer carried the undeniable aura of a sneaky little boy three seconds from trouble. In the end, you'd forgive him, because he was so dang adorable.

Margo walked up to him, astounded by her own brass. "This is a pleasant surprise," she said, trying to play it cool but swinging up onto the stool so casually she nearly fell off the other side. "What are you doing here?" she asked, brushing the hair from her face.

"It's a hotel? And I'm staying in it?"

"Yes, I know. I thought…" Margo's voice drifted off. How to explain that while she'd assumed mainly Lords and Sirs were staying at the Ocean Club, she'd expected Hunt to put people like the Pulitzers in one of his other hotels on the island? "Well, it's nice to see you again," she added, hastily, as Peter motioned the waiter for another drink.

"Did you have fun at the party?" he asked. "You missed the fireworks. It was quite the show. The pyrotechnics were flown in from Monaco."

"No expense spared," Margo said. The bartender set a drink in front of her, and she held the glass up to the light. It seemed innocuous—like iced tea garnished with a slice of pineapple.

"It's a Goombay Smash. Mix of pineapple juice, orange juice, apricot brandy, both dark and coconut rum, plus a splash of grenadine syrup."

Margo sipped her drink and shivered from the kick. "Well, the party was fabulous," she said. "Kudos to Hunt for corralling one thousand people onto a deserted island. How did you and Lilly get there? Boat? Pan Am jet? Blimp?" She took another sip.

"I came alone, and via speedboat," he said. "Not the most luxurious choice, but Lilly was traveling over with her parents. Maybe you've heard…" He leaned closer, and the scent of rum blew in like a stiff wind. Margo guessed he'd already enjoyed a few drinks. "I'm banned from stepping foot onto any piece of property the Phipps family owns. That includes homes, boats, planes. Private train cars. You name it."

Margo feigned great shock, but it *was* shocking, even the second, third time, and she still couldn't get over the fact that Lilly went along with it, repeatedly leaving her husband high and dry. "I'm sorry, but I find that impossible to believe. What could they have against you?" she asked.

Peter responded with a bawdy laugh. "My thoughts exactly. I'm *wooooooonderful!*" he sang. "Seriously, though, it probably started when their daughter went to visit an aunt on Long Island but instead eloped with some boy she'd met on vacation. In which case, can you blame them?" His eyes danced as he spoke. "They also were not overjoyed to discover I'd traded newspaper mastheads for orange groves, or that we had kids so quickly and so close together. And then came the nervous collapse, and now one could argue that *Lilly's* the primary breadwinner."

"Wait," Margo said, brows pushed together. "Who had a nervous collapse? Her mom?"

Peter laughed again. "I was referring to Lilly's breakdown."

Lilly's breakdown? Margo replayed the words but could not take them all the way in. Lilly, who was perennially sunny, like any given day in Palm Beach? Then Margo remembered Rita's comment from Christmas night. *What you see is not what you get.*

"I'm surprised you didn't know about this," Peter said, clocking Margo's bewilderment. "Lilly tells it to everyone she meets, views it as part of her origin story. It happened about five years ago."

After giving birth to three kids in four years, he explained, Lilly lost the bounce in her step. It didn't help that they were living in Florida year-round by then, and off-season Palm Beach was a special kind of purgatory. Seemingly overnight, streetlamps were removed, and Fords replaced Rolls-Royces in the parking stalls. Storm shutters covered the windows, and almost every shop closed.

Lilly always had a touch of the postseason blues, but that year was different. She stopped speaking and brushing her hair. "Her sisters tried, I tried, but Lilly's mother was the only person who could convince her to get help," Peter said.

Ultimately, Lilly was sent to a psychiatric hospital in Westchester, where a doctor diagnosed her as a tad depressed but otherwise fine. To return to 100 percent, he recommended she find a hobby, and a fruit stand was born.

"I knew the fruit was supposed to be a hobby…" Margo said, putting the pieces together. "But Lilly told me the idea hit her when she was at Bloomingdale's?"

"Ah. We've found the point of confusion. *Bloomingdale's* is her nickname for the whole adventure. Lord knows why."

"Oh my God," Margo gasped. "Peter. That's awful." She'd never been inside a psychiatric hospital but pictured Lilly in a beige room, wearing beige clothes, drugged to the hilt. The image was so bleak she could hardly stand it. Tears began to well.

Peter picked up on this, right away. "Oh, Margo," he said, "it wasn't as bad as all that. The facility was top-shelf, and she got better. All's well that ends well, right?"

"It's just…" Margo snuffled, waving a hand in front of her face. "I don't mean to—"

"And you know Lilly. She adores *anything* that can be parlayed into cocktail fodder. Don't cry." Peter rubbed her arm and goose bumps rippled across her skin. "God, you're so sweet. But, please, you're breaking my heart."

"Stop being so nice!" Margo said, laughing, still crying a bit. "I am not the person who needs comforting!"

"No one needs comforting. Honest. It's all a huge giggle to

Lilly. I'd call it making lemons out of lemonade, but that's a stitch on the nose."

"Or else it's perfect," Margo said. "Lilly is amazing. Of course she'd go through all that and come out on the other side, sunnier than ever, ready to set the world on fire. Jiminy Cricket, she's even stronger than I thought. You must be in constant awe of her."

With this, Peter's forehead crunched. A look crossed his face, but Margo could not read it. "She is awe-inspiring," he said, in some other, harder man's tone. As he took a tight-lipped sip of his drink, Margo tilted her head, trying to figure out what had changed. "It's funny." Peter set down the glass and studied his hands. "Lilly's accomplished great things, but sometimes I feel sorry for her. She's kind of...stuck."

Margo balked. *Stuck?* That was the last word she'd use. People who were stuck weren't called whirlwinds. They didn't have the word *incorporated* tacked to the ends of their names. "How is she stuck?" Margo said. "From where I sit, Lilly Pulitzer is all movement."

"Well, she's stuck in Palm Beach, for one. Stuck being married to me."

"That doesn't sound too bad!" Margo warbled, wondering what'd come over him, and whether she was to blame. After all, she'd made him go into all that detail about the asylum, and then had the gall to get teary about it.

"Don't get me wrong," Peter said. "Marriage is a bum deal for *any* woman, even in the best circumstance. That's half the reason I'm so hard on you about Dutch. He's slick as a seal and I'm afraid you're gonna end up buying the bum package he's attempting to sell."

Margo blinked. *Dutch?* The name ran through her like it belonged to someone she'd known once but hadn't seen in years.

"It goes like this," Peter continued. "A girl spends weeks,

months, possibly years of her life being courted by a flounder-
ing, artless creature, a character so amusingly desperate that it's
downright endearing. Then they get married and it's the ol' bait
and switch. He's busy toiling away, *striving*, and she's saddled
with the house and kids. Gradually, she becomes a nonperson,
merely an extension of him, and their household. Before long,
she's happiest when he's gone, or when she's with her girlfriends, and they can play bridge and pretend they didn't trade
their great lives for some shitty arrangement with no benefit."

"I'd reckon there are some benefits," Margo said. "And your
marriage isn't like that. You're not a middle-rung manager and
Lilly's not a bored housewife with no life of her own."

"Sure, our circumstances are different," Peter allowed. "But
Lilly endures the same old bullshit, and is mostly defined by
her relation to everyone else. She's forever Mom to Liza, Minnie, and Pete. Wife to Peter."

"Lilly is more than somebody's wife."

"Yeah, but the name *Pulitzer* hangs on the shingle outside
the business *she* built."

"That's because the Pulitzers are a team," Margo said, more
mixed-up by the minute. Maybe Peter was one of those grumpy,
unreasonable drunks. At least this would make sense. "You encouraged her to open the shop. You're the oranges, the fruit
of the operation."

"And she's everything else," Peter finished. "At this point,
the oranges are obsolete. She doesn't need me. She doesn't even
like being in the same room, yet I can't free her—can't free either of us—because we're permanently linked. She's 'Mrs. Herbert Pulitzer Jr.' in the Shiny Sheet, and on every invitation in
the mailbox. And who is that guy, anyway? A college dropout
who's happiest when he's dirty and sunburned, a loner who
somehow ended up in a house that's too big, wearing clothes
that are too neat."

"Your clothes aren't that neat," Margo blurted, and Peter's expression cracked.

"Touché," he said, a smile dribbling out as Margo's insides turned to mush. Being the recipient of one of Peter Pulitzer's glittering, luminous grins was like sitting in the warmest ray of sun, on earth's prettiest beach.

Shit. What was she doing? What was she thinking? Absolutely nothing good. The wires between them had crossed and Margo needed to bail out, sooner rather than later.

"Sheesh. That's one hell of a strong drink," she said, shoving away the glass. "I'm already loopy!" She made a joke about sunstroke and the Bahamian heat, and scrabbled to her feet. "I should go. No doubt Slim's called my room forty-seven times. Always prattling on and on about his damned curfew."

"You're leaving?" Peter said, frowning. "Oh. That's too bad." He looked like the saddest, loneliest boy in the universe, and Margo wanted to cry.

"Yes. I'm sorry. I really must go," she said. "It was fun to run into you. I guess I'll see you next season!" With that, she sped off, just in the nick of time.

—

Margo stepped into the elevator. With a quaking finger, she pressed number four. As the doors were about to meet, an arm shot into the gap. They opened again, and Peter dashed through them.

"Hello there," he said. Margo was too addled to speak, and so she didn't. "I'm on the fourth floor, too. Fancy that."

The lift rose sluggishly, and Margo pretended to hunt for something in her purse, remembering what Lilly told her at the fashion show, about how men got lost in Palm Beach. She was starting to see it.

"Hey, sorry for all that," Peter said as they arrived at the fourth floor with a ding. "That was uncalled-for. I basically dumped a bag full of hang-ups and gripes onto you, completely without warning."

"Not a problem!" Margo said as she leaped out of the elevator. "Don't give it another thought." She zipped down the hall. "We've all been there! And it's nice to discover you're not perfect."

"Perfect?" Peter laughed dryly. He was hot on her heels. "Who gave you that idea? Certainly not Lilly. Again. I'm sorry. I shouldn't have unloaded that onto you. It wasn't fair."

"Oh. Well. What's fair, anyway? Blame it on the booze." That's what Margo planned to do, in any case.

"Hey, will you slow down?" Peter said. "Please?" Finally, Margo did slow down. She stopped, in fact, because they were in front of her room. "Do you think you could turn around? Or should I finish apologizing to your hair?"

Margo closed her eyes for a beat. Though she no longer trusted her own mind, or the effects of a Goombay Smash, Margo exhaled and rotated to face him.

"That's better." Peter gave a smirky, quiet smile, and Margo's stomach tumbled. "I'll try to explain this and not scare you off, but I was in a *mood*. I'd been sitting at that bar for an hour, gearing up for the monumental task of returning to my room and resuming the never-ending role of Peter Pulitzer. An extremely minor part, to be sure." His eyes slid to the left and Margo noticed for the first time they were more green than brown. "Then you walked into the bar, and I felt instant relief. You were an excuse to stay."

"I hope you didn't stick around solely on my account," Margo said, like a fool. His staying was not the part of the conversation flustering her.

"That's not it." Grimacing, he ran both hands over his head. "With you, everything's easy, and I don't have to pretend. I saw you and realized, hey, a few more minutes of normalcy, of being me, of what I wish was my real life. I'm so damned weary, Margo. The people, the parties, all the Palm Beach, jet-setter bullshit. I know you get exactly what I mean."

Margo nodded, though she didn't get it. Not at all.

"I want to live a regular fucking life," he said. "I want to work in the orange groves, and fly my plane, and have normal conversations with normal people. That's why I like your company. It may sound strange, but you make me feel at home."

"You make me feel at home, too," Margo said, out of nowhere, surprising them both. It was the perfect wrong thing to say, and her cheeks turned to fire.

"Really?" Peter said, as a questioning look passed over his face. All at once, Margo saw his confidence slip, and this unguarded version of Peter left her weak.

Suddenly, the elevator pinged. A man said something, and his companion giggled. Margo shook her head. She'd forgotten they weren't the only ones in this hotel.

"Around you, I'm *too* comfortable," Peter went on, oblivious to the other guests. "As I just demonstrated. I never talk that much. But. Again. It's you. Swooping in like someone I've always known, from a different, better world. A world that's real, and true. I'm jealous of whoever gets to live in it with you. I'm jealous of your entire existence."

"Peter..." Margo's breath had quickened. *Hurry. Open a door, an escape hatch. Throw some light into this room.* "I must say, it takes a lot of nerve to claim you're jealous of a Slim Aarons employee!" she said, lifting her voice, so he'd see it as a joke. "If you had my life, you wouldn't be flying planes, or speed-boating to a millionaire's island for a party. I wasn't kidding about the curfew, either."

"But it'd be *my* life," he said, "and I'd be able to do what I want."

"I definitely don't do what I want."

Peter leaned forward, and she caught a whiff of his boozy, loamy scent. "Then tell me, Margo. If you could do anything at this moment, what would it be?"

"Um, I'm not sure?" Margo swallowed, hard.

Peter moved closer and Margo felt the heat of his skin, though they were not yet touching. She knew then that he was going to kiss her. The only thing worse was how much she wanted him to. "Come on, Margo," he said. "You really don't know?"

Without a thought in her empty little brain, Margo popped up onto her toes and landed her mouth on his. Peter reacted naturally, easily, kissing her with such unexpected tenderness that Margo could nearly convince herself it was a dream.

"We shouldn't be doing this," Peter said, pulling away, though not by much. His breath was on her face, his fingers still knotted in her hair. "You can tell me to stop." He didn't mean it, and Margo didn't reply. Peter drew her in again, kissing harder, more forcefully, as he pressed her against the door.

Now his tongue was in her mouth and Margo tasted cigarettes and rum and all she imagined she would. No one had ever kissed her like this, and a thrill rose in her body, spreading, hitting every nerve.

When Margo's back hit the doorknob, the truth crashed into her like a wave. She couldn't do this. It'd ruin everything, and for what? Given who Peter was, and who she was, she'd never be more than a mistress. That wasn't the destiny Margo saw for herself. She put her hands on his chest and pushed him away.

"What?" Peter said. His complexion had gone white. "Did I do something wrong?"

"No, of course not," Margo said, whirling around. "That was my fault. My mistake." Her hands shook as she wrestled with the key and lock. Peter started to speak but stopped when a pair of feet clomped down the hall. *Saved by a stranger*, Margo thought.

"Well, look who it is." At the sound of Lilly's voice, Margo almost jumped out of her skin.

"Hi, sweetheart." Peter stepped away, and the air between them went cold. "Guess who I found at the bar! Couldn't let her walk to her room alone. This hotel is chock-full of wolves."

"Yes, it is," Lilly agreed, as Margo forced herself to turn back around.

"Hi, Lilly," Margo said, heart thundering. *Oh God, what had Lilly heard? What did she see?*

"Hello," Lilly greeted Margo lightly, without direct eye contact. "Glad you made it safely," she said. "Peter, you are ever the gentleman. The perennial knight in shining armor."

"You're the only one who thinks so, dear," Peter said, emanating joie de vivre, like the past five minutes hadn't happened at all. "Most see me as that strange fella who mucks about in the soil." His lips were an unnatural shade of pink, and Margo touched her own, trying to remember what color lipstick she had on.

"Isn't that the truth." Lilly sighed wearily, as though she'd just lugged every trouble she had up four flights of stairs. "You really are a—" she began, but hesitated. Lilly swung her gaze first to Margo and then to Peter, whom she drank in with one long sweep. When her eyes reached his shoes, something behind them clicked. Her face brightened, flipping like a switch.

Lilly released a high, tinkling giggle and gave Peter a frisky smack on the chest. "Oh, Peter," she said. "You're right, everyone does think you're a filthy beast! Anyhow, we should let our friend get to bed. She looks plum exhausted. Margo, dear, I hope you can excuse my sloppy ol' lug." She rumpled Peter's buzzed hair. "He can be such a stinker sometimes. But we adore him, don't we? My love, my one and only, my darling Sneaky Pete."

FASHION

The Lilly

She has the face of Hazel Brooks—with a dash of Joan Collins—and a Rubenesque figure ("I look kinda round, not lean and lanky"). Her home is magnificent, and located in Palm Beach, and she's married to a minor legend of a husband—Herbert ("Peter") Pulitzer Jr., 32, grandson of the publisher, who spends his days picking and packing oranges. There are also three kids and a menagerie of pets, but somehow Lilly Pulitzer, 30, has found the time to become a fashion magnate.

Mrs. Pulitzer's fame was built on a single dress, appropriately called "the Lilly," which she designed as a uniform to wear while making juice in her husband's Pulitzer Groves Fruit Shop. But customers liked it so much that they wanted to buy the dress off her back. Like any decent friend, she made a few more and, it's safe to say, people don't come for the oranges anymore.

Somewhere between a chemise and a muumuu, a Lilly hangs straight to just above the knees, and costs anywhere from $25 to $45. There are now six variations: five have mandarin side slits, and one comes in floor-length. Says Lilly: "It's the easiest way to get dressed, which is why people wear them day and night."

Lillys are made of cotton fabric, which is "hand-screened, hand-printed, hand-blocked, hand-somethinged" by Key West Fabrics. The dresses are fully lined, and Lilly cheekily insists that she makes purchasers sign a contract promising not to wear anything underneath. Apparently, it's a free-wheeling bunch down there in Palm Beach. Lilly claims she doesn't even own a pair of shoes.

Her customers include Jackie Kennedy ("She has quite a few of them, but I hate to use her name as a drawing card") and Wendy Vanderbilt. She's recently signed several contracts for nationwide distribution, with big orders from I. Magnin and Henri Bendel, and announced plans to introduce other designs: "the Minnie," a children's version of the Lilly, and a nightshirt for men.

"Naturally we'll call that one 'the Sneaky Pete,'" she says.

43

KATONAH / JUNE 1962

Margo was supposed to be writing captions but couldn't think straight, hadn't been able to think straight for the past three months. It didn't matter whether she was in Slim's farmhouse in Bedford, or Washington, DC, or glorious Kashmir. Peter was everywhere.

Mud tracked into the home. Cigarette smoke. The scent of any type of citrus. Margo had replayed the kiss a thousand times. Not to relive it, she told herself, but wear it out, whittle it down to nothing. Of course, this was just an excuse.

No matter how great it was, or how body-wracking the thrill, the kiss couldn't happen again, *wouldn't* happen again. They'd return to Palm Beach in November, so Margo had five months to convince herself it never did.

Five months seemed like forever, but then the magazine arrived, and "Sneaky Pete" was a spear aimed directly into her gut. Had Margo irrevocably bungled everything, from her friendship with Lilly, to the natural rapport with Peter, to the sparks of a possible career? Margo would never be able to look at the pictures she'd taken of the Pulitzers without exploding from shame. And what might happen if Lilly told Slim about the encounter and whatever she'd heard or seen?

Be reasonable, Margo reminded herself. She was inconsequential, a nobody, just flat-chested, stringy-haired Gogo Hightower. Half the people she'd met in Palm Beach wouldn't remember her by next season. Meanwhile, Lilly was an heiress and mogul who had a fabulous, decidedly un-*stuck* life. She'd married "a minor legend of a husband" and was therefore used to women fawning over him.

Would Lilly even care about a single kiss between Peter and some lowly assistant? It was nothing compared to the antics of her inner circle. Flo Smith thought monogamy was a joke and Jackie's husband was known throughout Palm Beach as Mattress Jack. Once, Margo asked whether Jackie was aware of the rumors, and Lilly snorted in response.

"You're very dear to call them *rumors*," she'd said. "Jackie is fully apprised. She's cunning as a shark and is happy with the deal she's made. All marriages have their headaches, and you must decide what you're willing to live with, and at what cost."

Her words left Margo confounded, but maybe this was what Rita meant when she mentioned tricks up sleeves.

What had Margo done? Why had she done it? How could a body switch so quickly from desire to regret? More than ever, Margo needed Dolly's counsel. Unfortunately, she'd relocated to Europe with Don.

"The wheels are coming off the bus," Dolly had said, the only time in months that one of Margo's calls got through. In this case, the bus was America, and it was carrying riots, protests, and Kennedy's profligate spending. "I can't raise my children here," she added, which was Dolly's way of announcing her pregnancy. Though she'd expected it, the news flattened Margo.

Thinking about the people in her life who were falling away, an awareness hit Margo with the force of a truck. Dolly, Lilly, her mother, even Crim—they shared one common trait, and it was *her*. Was Margo bad at relationships, or was she unlovable? If she went around kissing other people's husbands, then the answer was yes.

"Hello, hello," Slim said as he stomped into the sunroom, temporarily rescuing Margo from her black hole of despair. "How's the latest batch coming?"

Margo glanced at the slides on the table, reorienting herself. "Fine, so far," she said as Slim lowered into a chair. "Very Washington, very nation's capital." In truth, Margo hadn't cared for DC. The city was stony and gray, a real nonplace. She didn't give a whit about important monuments or men, but Slim expected her to contribute. "This could go in the magazine," Margo said, pushing an image across the table. "It's of the French ambassador's wife."

Most photographers wouldn't dream of shooting such an elegant woman in a dim, ornate parlor, but Slim's lens picked up all the light it needed from the woman's pink satin dress, white opera gloves, and smooth, alabaster skin.

"It was a clever suggestion you had," Slim said, "to turn the chandelier lights *low*. Most people would've gone in the opposite direction, but the speckled pattern overhead reads like stars."

Margo bobbed her head. She still had one thing going for her, at least. "I knew madame couldn't be the only bright spot in the frame. A tidbit I picked up in interior design school. I probably got lucky it worked."

"There is *some* skill involved in this job. I may regret saying this, Old Bean, but you might have a knack for this business."

Margo felt a sniffle coming on. *Old Bean* was a term of endearment, usually reserved for Slim's favorite people. How could a person feel like a million bucks and utterly useless at the same time?

"What's the matter?" Slim said. "*Old Bean* is a good thing."

"Yes, I know. Thank you. It means a lot." Margo looked away. *Stop complimenting me*, she pleaded. *I don't deserve it.*

"You're not upset about Kashmir, are you? I'm sorry I didn't give you the camera, but we were short on time and this was a one-shot deal. It might not be safe to return in the near future, given the border dispute." Slim exhaled dramatically and removed an orange from a bowl of fruit on the table. "If I'd known you'd be so pouty about it, I would've left you behind."

"No," Margo said. "I might've complained a little at first—"

"A little? Ha! Twice you called me a crankpot—not even under your breath."

"I was just being grumpy. Acting out. I loved Kashmir. It was magical."

So magical it allowed Margo to temporarily push thoughts of Peter to the back of her mind. With its misty waters, floating lotus flowers, and the Himalayan peaks in the distance, Dal Lake had been a fairy tale, the Shalimar Gardens pure romance. Built by a Mogul emperor three hundred and fifty years ago as an expression of love for his wife, the grounds were filled with elaborate fountains, marble pavilions, and more flowers than Margo could name. Tulips, daffodils, petunias. *Lilies*, of course.

Margo and Slim visited Hindu temples and mosques and the Oberoi Palace Hotel, where they photographed the maharajah and his family. One afternoon they had drinks with a North Carolina debutante on her canopied houseboat and spent the next day knocking around golf balls with Prime Minister Nehru. The week passed like a dream, and it was almost enough to convince Margo that she could recover from all this. Then they landed back in the States. *TIME* magazine hit Slim's mailbox, and Margo was forced to contend with real life again. *Real life.* She didn't know why Peter was so keen on it.

"I'm pleased that you don't consider traveling to one of the most beautiful places on earth *too* arduous." Slim dug into the orange and removed its peel in one long strip. "Now that we've settled that, let's discuss our next assignment. We're going to the city for a few days."

With this, Margo perked up. "The city?" she said. "As in New York?"

"What other city is there?" Slim bit his orange and juice sprayed onto his shirt. *Someone could use a Lilly*, Margo thought. "We'll be shooting a bunch of radio guys, and a few newsmen. The Flair Ladies, too."

Margo didn't know who the Flair Ladies were and didn't ask, because her mind was leaping five steps ahead. An idea began to form, a potential solution to the problems she'd bumbled into, and those she'd created herself. If a gal was in New York City, she had to take in a show. The Dutch Elkin Orchestra was playing the St. Regis all summer.

As far as potential husbands went, Dutch remained a compelling but extremely borderline prospect. He was easily distracted, a little beef-brained, and Peter said all those things about how he'd make a dreadful beau. *(Stop thinking about Peter!)* Dutch had his faults, but a person could argue that *Margo* was the fickle one. The reason they hadn't spoken since the awkward encounter at the Ocean Club was because of her onerous schedule and even more ornery boss. If she wasn't at the Pennsylvania, Dutch had no way to reach her, not after Rita warned him about Slim's certain wrath if anyone ever called and asked for Margo.

She had to think practically. With Dutch, the good far outstripped the mediocre. He was charming, gallant, and talented, and wholly unbothered by Sandy LaSalle and the ignominy that threw Margo into his path. It'd been six months since their first date—half a year!—and now was not the time to give up or, God forbid, start over.

Margo wasn't attracted to Peter Pulitzer, she assured herself, night after night. She was attracted to the *idea* of him, and the connection they'd made. *Every woman is a little bit in love with him*, Jackie Kennedy once said, and there was no reason to give him another thought. Margo had to move on and show Dutch she was serious about their fledgling romance. What's more, if everyone knew she was full steam ahead on Dutch, there'd be nothing sneaky about Pete.

44

NEW YORK CITY

Margo tucked an off-white sleeveless blouse into her kelly green skirt and knotted a geranium-colored sash around her waist. She added a cropped jacket—if something with no sleeves could be called a jacket—and grabbed her purse. *Pretty cute*, she thought, consulting the mirror.

Once downstairs, Margo canvassed the lobby and found the coast clear. After slipping on a pair of red, round-framed sunglasses and a flipped brim hat, Margo dashed out onto the street. She was taking a risk, but this was her best and only chance to give their relationship a kick in the pants.

Margo booked it up Seventh Avenue toward West 56th Street. It took ten forevers for the world-famous beaux arts building to come into view, unmistakable with its arched windows, carved friezes, and ornate cornices. After ducking beneath the marquee and stopping a second to air out her pits, Margo yanked on the center door handles, just about pulling both arms out of their sockets when the doors didn't budge. She tried the others, but those were locked, too.

Margo stepped back. Fidgeting with the six faux jade bangles on her left wrist, she stared at the entrance for five minutes, ten, fifteen, like the universe might realize she was waiting and let her in. As Margo weighed throwing in the towel, one of the side doors opened and out walked a man toting a guitar case. He had longish black hair and a face covered in stubble.

"Excuse me!" Margo said, scurrying up. "Hello!"

"Hello there." The man examined her head to toe, nodding in approval. "Can I help you?"

"Yes! Can you tell me how to access the apartments?" She pointed to the building. "I'm visiting one of my friends."

He peered over his shoulder. "Sweetheart, this is Carnegie Hall."

"Yes, I know," she huffed. "He specifically told me he has an apartment here." Margo hesitated, and thought back. *Had* Dutch said that? She recalled the words *Carnegie* and *hall*, but could've mixed up the details. "Or was it close to Carnegie Hall? He's a musician."

The man's face brightened. "A few artists do live at Carnegie, but if your friend is in the music business, he's probably at the Osborne," he said and crooked a thumb across the street. "Some people call it 'the Residential Carnegie Hall.' Who are you trying to see?" Margo told him, and as it happened, the man knew Dutch Elkin and offered to personally escort Margo to his pad. His name was Steve, by the way.

Margo followed Steve across the street, toward a Renaissance-style building that sat catty-corner from Carnegie Hall. The Osborne's lobby was dark and woody and lavish, with stained glass windows, mosaic-covered walls, and slick marble floors.

"This place is something else," Margo said as they passed a grand oak staircase.

"So ugly it's beautiful," Steve joked. "The walls are four feet thick." He knocked on one, as if to demonstrate. "Which is why musicians gravitate here. You can rehearse day or night without irritating the neighbors."

After pressing the button for the lift, Steve explained that, earlier in the year, the Osborne had been slated for demolition, but the residents were turning it into a cooperative, a movement spearheaded by Dutch. "He's very frustrated by those of us unwilling to buy our apartments. Sometimes he forgets we're not all highfliers like him," Steve said with a laugh.

They took the elevator to the ninth floor and hooked right. Two doors down, Steve knocked. "Come in!" said a muffled voice. "It's open!"

Steve opened the door and stepped aside. "After you, young lady," he said, sweeping a hand.

Margo offered a weak smile. She walked through, praying Dutch didn't mind surprises.

45

"Margo Hightower! I can't believe it!" Dutch sprang up from a yellow cushion on the floor. He wrapped his arms around her and squeezed. Margo nearly crumpled in relief.

"Found her wandering around outside Carnegie Hall," Steve said, flopping onto a rattan chair. "Methinks somebody tries to impress girls by implying that his living quarters are more impressive than they are. Carnegie Hall. Like you're the genius-in-residence."

"I didn't say anything like that," Dutch insisted, though he had a hint of the devil in his eyes. "Here! Sit, sit," he said, clearing newspapers off a patchwork leather pouf. "Let me get you a drink."

Margo smoothed the back of her skirt and sat down, while Dutch introduced the two men on the couch. Bobby, a pasty, brown-haired fellow in wire-rimmed glasses, sang cabaret. The man beside him in the yellow, red, and green dashiki was Isaac, a jazz pianist. Steve played in a folk band.

As Dutch hurried over to the bar cart, Margo took in the apartment with a single long glance. It was more modest than she might've anticipated, consisting of only the room they were sitting in, a kitchenette, and a small flight of stairs that led to a sleeping loft. Beyond the impressive stone fireplace and a huge set of windows overlooking the roof next door, the decorations were bare-bones, with a smattering of mismatched furniture and a baby grand piano.

"You've stumbled into a heated discussion," Dutch said, handing Margo a heavy, cut-glass tumbler. She sniffed the amber liquid and took the babiest of sips. Scotch, she concluded. "I was minutes from having my neck wrung."

"Heated? Who's heated?" Isaac asked. "I'm cool as a cucumber. I merely think Kennedy's not doing shit when it comes to addressing segregation and discrimination. He's trying to appease one side instead of *defeating* them."

Did anyone like Kennedy? Margo wondered.

"Listen, we're on the same page," Dutch said, "but it'll take time for everyone in the country to catch on that integration isn't just a moral imperative but an economic one."

He went on about national security, and how the United States would fail if complete swaths of the population were excluded from full participation in society. As Dutch spoke, Margo's eyes flew around the room. Was this conversation *appropriate*? How and when to discuss civil rights was never broached during debutante training, and although Margo unequivocally agreed with equal rights, she didn't want to weigh in and sound like a buffoon. Her efforts to keep up with the news remained extremely touch and go.

"The South needs to act," Bobby chimed in. "Too many of them are silent. They're sick down there. They've let racism thrive."

Isaac snickered. "Don't get it twisted. You pro–civil rights, white northerners are a pain in the ass, too. New York ain't such a utopia. Can't get a house in most neighborhoods. Can't get a job."

New York really was a different world. No one—absolutely *no one*—talked about these things in Palm Beach, and certainly not in mixed company. Once, Margo asked Slim to explain the seemingly unfair voting laws in some states, and he'd mockingly called her a *civil rights warrior* and told her to *just stick to photography.*

"For what it's worth, I'm always encouraging St. Regis to hire more Black performers," Dutch said, "but I'm only one guy."

"Yeah, you're a real hero," Isaac said good-naturedly.

"As much as I'd love to argue all night," Dutch said, pushing himself up. "We'll have to continue this discussion later. I've got to get ready for my gig."

"The bastard always splits right before he's about to be beat," Isaac said. "Break a leg out there tonight. Make us proud."

The men stood in unison and Margo did, too. They proceeded to the door and she followed.

"Hey! Where are you going?" Dutch said, reaching for her hand. "Don't you want to stick around? Keep me company while I get ready?" He lifted his forehead sweetly, pleadingly almost.

Margo pretended to consider it for a beat—*this* they taught in debutante school—before breaking out in a grin. "I'd love that," she said. "I'm so glad you asked."

—

Margo shifted and wiggled to find a comfortable spot, but Dutch's mattress seemed to be comprised entirely of lumps and springs. It didn't help that she was so goosey and consumed by nerves. She'd never been in a man's bedroom before, never mind his sleeping loft.

"You haven't told me why you're in New York," Dutch said as he ran a badger-bristled, ivory-backed brush through his hair.

"For work," Margo said, feeling rather cosmopolitan. "This

morning we shot at ABC." She told him about the other places she'd been since Palm Beach, like Washington and Kashmir.

"You're living the life, I'll tell ya what." Hair now lined with hard grooves, Dutch set down the brush. "When did we last see each other? Other than way too long ago."

"The opening of Paradise Island," Margo said, her tone snappish. It was Dutch, so he likely wouldn't notice, but she was sick of reminding him of every little detail. *Get over it, Margo. He has two thousand songs in his head.* "What about you?" she said. "Where have you been these past few months? According to the papers, this is your first time in New York since January. I wish we were able to talk more often. When I want to know what Dutch Elkin is up to, I consult the society pages."

Dutch laughed and kissed the top of her head. "You must stop reading that junk," he said. "Most of it is bull. Though, I suppose, not in this case. I have been on the road nonstop."

From the Bahamas, Dutch had traveled back to Miami for a stint at the Fontainebleau, followed by a two-month gig in Los Angeles, at the Ambassador Hotel. He went to San Francisco and then tore through a list of states, from West Coast to East, playing fundraising events and debutante balls and anniversary parties.

"The swing ended with back-to-back-to-back bat mitzvahs," he said, tugging on his suspenders. Dutch loved a good mitzvah, the only downside being he had two sacks of fan mail to read, 90 percent of which was probably from thirteen-year-old girls.

After adding the finishing touches—a cummerbund and dinner jacket—Dutch walked over to the bed. Smiling, he gently flicked one of Margo's apple-shaped earrings. "These are adorable," he said. "So playful and fun. Damn. Even your jewelry makes me happy."

"Thank you," Margo said, blushing fiercely. Her eyes were presently at crotch level, and she didn't know where to look.

"This is last-minute, but any chance you're free tonight?" he said. "Someone told me of a great band playing nearby and its bandleader could use a date."

—

The event was sold out and so Margo watched from backstage, otherwise known as a locker room behind the bandstand. No matter. Margo would've hung from the damned ceiling if it meant spending more time with Dutch. Everything was going as planned. Already she felt closer to him, and Peter didn't cross her mind once. Until she realized he hadn't, that is.

The Dutch Elkin Orchestra began the night with "Make Someone Happy," and followed it up with "Maria," and "Nice Work if You Can Get It." For "Everything's Coming Up Roses," Dutch played with his eyes closed, intensely feeling every beat. The audience stayed on their feet from the first song to the last and it all ended in a flash. Before long, the orchestra had finished its encore. The lights went up and Dutch's manager was leading Margo to his dressing room.

"Oh, Dutch!" Margo said as she swept in. "You were fantastic! The whole place was twisting, and everyone crowed about how great you were."

"Your review is the only one that matters," he said, sauntering up to her. His forehead was glistening, and his tie was askew, but every strand of hair remained in place.

"In that case, you were perfect," Margo said, feeling faint and swoony. Peter was not the only man who could make her heart flutter.

"Any chance I can convince you to come back to my place?" Dutch placed both hands on her hips, and when he drew her against him, Margo felt the bump in the front of his pants. "Come back to my place and stay the night?" he added in case it wasn't clear.

Margo smiled and tried not to *turn turtle*, as Dolly might've said. A nice girl would demur, but she wasn't all that nice. She'd kissed Peter, after all, and had shown up at Dutch's apartment unbidden, which meant she'd *made a move* on a man. Worse still, inside Margo's purse was the honest-to-God pessary that Rita had given her after their date at La Petite Marmite.

"Psssst," she'd said, discreetly handing Margo the white bag. Accompanying the pessary was a white tube of spermicide (written in mortifyingly bold letters) and directions explaining that the small, rubbery object covered the cervix, and was designed to prevent sperm from reaching the egg. Margo's face flamed as she absorbed the words, but she'd kept the "gift," just in case. While there was no guarantee she'd need it, Margo took a risk by coming here, and might as well see where the night led.

"Wow, that's a helluva pause," Dutch said, after some time. "Should I be worried?" He pretended to whisk sweat from his face.

Margo opened her mouth, but the words refused to come out, and so she slid her hand into his, nodded toward the door, and followed him home.

PART 3

46

PALM BEACH / NOVEMBER 1962

Staring at the yellow door, Margo struggled to accept that eight months had passed since she'd last been in Palm Beach. She had no way to gauge what had changed, or what hadn't, or whether she was welcome in this shop. Alas, Margo was here, and there was nothing left but the doing.

She flung open the door and stepped inside. "Hello?" Margo called out, glancing around. Under a table, a dog snored.

"Ciao," someone said from the couch. It was Wendy Vanderbilt, barefoot and wearing a bright yellow Lilly. A small, compact object rested in her lap. It wasn't a magazine, for once. "Did you just get into town?" she asked.

Margo nodded and moved farther into the shop, hoping to project a nothing-to-hide confidence. Surely they'd all moved on. It was a brand-new season, and there were so many problems in the world. They'd managed to avoid that Cuban missile situation, for one. The threat of nuclear annihilation really put things into perspective.

"How is everyone?" Margo said, and Wendy answered with a grunt.

The door sprang open again, and a dazzling gale whipped into the room.

"Took you long enough!" Wendy griped.

"Somebody has to tend to the children." Lilly pitched her cigarette case onto the counter. After kicking off her shoes, she spun around, eyes landing on Margo. "Oh. Hello! I'd heard you were back. Kiss, kiss," she said. She flipped back to Wendy. No hug? Margo tried not to read into it. "Have we finished settling the accounts?" she asked.

"You tell me," Wendy said. "Elizabeth and Robert McCarty. Check. Ruth and Robert Price. Check."

"Bad year for Roberts." Lowering onto the arm of the couch, Lilly pulled her waist-length hair over one shoulder. "We're conducting our annual marital audit," she told Margo. "Everyone divorces after the season ends in April, and it's imperative to update our address books before the new one begins."

"Swear to Jesus, people are only getting married for five minutes these days," Wendy said, and Margo thought of Dolly, wishing she'd been on the five-minute list. The MacMasters had welcomed their first child in September, a girl named Marguerite, born in Switzerland. After taking three days to drum up the guts for a congratulatory call, Margo rang the Huntington, only to be refused Dolly's forwarding information.

"Mr. Alphonso Calhoun Avery III and Velma," Wendy continued. The actress Gregg Dodge was asking for $15,000 per month. Elinor Udell was getting $300,000 in one chunk.

"She deserves more," Lilly said. "Twenty-three years is an awfully long time to be tied down to that man."

As the women traded names, Margo let out the breath she'd been holding. Everything was basically the same, aside from more dresses, and the fact that swatches and drawings covered every available surface. Yellow stripes with green butterflies. Green-and-white stripes with blue butterflies. A turquoise background with a bold rose print. Lilly's cookie jar was gone, replaced with a bona fide cash register.

"What about you, Margo?" Wendy said. "Are you still on the hunt for a beau? There are some fresh-on-the-market options." She waggled the address book.

"Oh, well. I mean, not really," Margo stuttered. "I'm in touch with Dutch Elkin?" She'd have to tread carefully here, using the right words to convey her interest in Dutch while preventing news of her transgressions from getting back to Slim.

Speaking of things that hadn't changed. Although their relationship progressed *physically* in New York, Margo's visit hadn't sped up much. "I'll be in Katonah these dates," she'd told him, writing them down, alongside Slim's phone number. "Call between one and three o'clock in the afternoon. That's when Slim is usually out on his mower. But hang up if anyone other than Rita answers."

Operating under these strict instructions, Dutch managed to ring every few weeks, always overflowing with apologies and a promise to do better. In turn, Margo would apologize for her own limitations, and they'd stay on the phone for up to an hour.

"You're the best listener," he said, during their most recent conversation. "My whole life, I've never had anyone to talk to. Suddenly, here you are. You're terrific, Margo. The absolute most."

She enjoyed Dutch's company. That sexy mug and smoldering voice could make Margo's heart skip more than one beat, but it was hard to perpetually wonder how long she'd have to survive on his crumbs. She had to constantly remind herself that Dutch *was* recording a new album, and had to work around Slim. Leeway needed to be granted.

"Dutch Elkin. Good for you," Lilly said with a wink.

"Gotta swing for the fences!" Wendy sang.

"Oh, please," Lilly said. "They make a darling pair. Anyway, if that doesn't work out, Margo's young and flirty and cute. The world is her oyster and the right one will come along eventually."

"Or the right one will get divorced!"

Lilly bopped Wendy on the head. "You can't *wish* it on people," she said as a parade of women entered the shop. With Palm Beachers up from their naps, Worth Avenue and the Vias were getting crowded. The door to Lilly's shop was opening and smacking shut every twenty to thirty seconds.

"What happened to the seashell print?" one woman asked. "With the red and pink?"

"If you like a particular pattern, you'd better snatch it up. Nothing lasts around here." Lilly turned back to Margo. "Somehow, during the off-season, this little dress endeavor really snowballed. Or avalanched. Is that a word? Either way, I was tickled to death the first time I saw my name in a major magazine. Who knew that'd amount to small beans compared to the rest?"

While the *TIME* article garnered Lilly heaps of acclaim, her business truly went through the roof over the summer, after Jackie Kennedy was photographed greeting the presidential helicopter in a daisy-print Lilly and a second time in Ravello, Italy, while wearing a different pattern. Now, whenever and wherever women gathered in Palm Beach—on the golf course, in a social club, waiting outside the Palm Beach Day School—they always did so in a rainbow of bright prints. There was no denying the island belonged to Lilly Pulitzer.

Lilly hadn't merely created a fun and easy way to dress, she'd launched a movement. Whereas bored wealthy wives were once expected to buck up and get to the business of country clubbing and playing bridge, Margo read no less than three articles insisting women could and should do more, maybe start an enterprise, like that wonderful Lilly Pulitzer. "The Modern Day Woman Must Be Included in the GNP!"

"While I adore the recognition," Lilly said, "I've been forced to convert my project into an actual *business* with a charter and board and everything. Ugh! It's so dull." She'd hired eighteen seamstresses and set up a board of directors. Lilly was CEO, Peter the vice president, and Lilly's old friend Laura, a former *Harper's Bazaar* fashion editor, served as secretary and treasurer. Now Lilly traveled to New York every month, a Miami factory twice per week, and to whichever department store in whatever city, whenever they called. "On the plus side, the world appreciates what I've been saying all along. Life is better in pink!"

A man poked his head through the door. "Lilly!" he said. "I need a fruit basket, stat. Can you help me out?"

"I'm sorry, I'm fresh out of fruit," Lilly said. "But you can try on a frock. Fair warning—the dressing rooms are packed." She gestured to three women who were at present dropping their trousers right on the floor. The man yelped and scurried off. Lilly threw back her head and laughed. "Peter is *furious* that I don't care about the oranges anymore."

The oranges are obsolete.

"I'm sure he's happy your business is doing well," Margo said, fumbling her words. Each time Lilly said the name *Peter*, she flushed. "He's always bursting with pride for you."

"Hmm. Perhaps." Lilly frowned and put a hand on her hip. "I do worry that all the success is getting to him. He likes to feel useful and *loves* being the center of attention." She chuckled again, but her voice was tinged with something less sweet, bitter rind fallen into the juice. "We women stay busy like beavers, but men get so easily bored around here."

"Hence the divorces," Wendy said, holding up her address book. "Leaving wives qualifies as a hobby."

"It's not as dire as all that, but Palm Beach husbands do act like naughty children when they're at loose ends. Even mine! Thank goodness the sugar plantation is harvesting next week, and his business is about to explode, too. Peter tends to get into so many pickles when he's not properly occupied." Lilly locked her eyes on Margo. "You must understand *exactly* what I mean."

47

Palm Beachers couldn't resist a party theme. The first major event of this season would be a Bums' Ball, held at the Bath & Tennis.

Slim and Rita scored an invite and brought Margo along as their guest. As much as she preferred hobnobbing over work, she was iffy from the word go. The theme seemed unnecessarily callous, and Margo wasn't especially jazzed to return to the place where she'd been dumped.

Almost two years had passed since Crim Pebley ruined her life, and when Margo tried to picture him, she couldn't remember the details of his face. Everything had slipped away like water through her hands—from the color of his eyes, to his smile, to his personality, if he'd had one. As Margo entered the B&T, she felt nothing, not a twinge of regret. It was as though that cursed event happened to somebody else.

Walking toward the ballroom, Margo struggled to fathom that this had been the location of Sibley and Dean's elegant wedding. Railroad tracks ran down the once satin-lined halls, and instead of lush, fragrant roses, the main room was decorated with soiled underwear dangling from clotheslines. Guests wore patched blue jeans, coveralls, and clown tramp shoes and slugged cocktails from rusty soup cans. Six minutes in, Margo was ready to leave.

"I need to make the rounds," Slim said, right on time. He was always working, even when he wasn't. "Why don't you ladies get a drink while I mingle?" He pulled a packet of cigarettes from his coat and Margo smirked, thinking how fortunate it was that his signature ratty blue blazer fit the theme.

"I'm glad that one of my dates likes to throw back," Rita said, and dragged Margo across the room, where she snagged two cups of punch from a waiter. "Bottoms up!" She lifted her drink to the sky.

Margo clinked her soup can to Rita's and took a swig. It tasted like how varnish smelled, but with a dash of cherry. She drank more because it wasn't awful and what else was she going to do.

Out of nowhere, a man came rushing through the party, bumping Rita from behind. She lurched forward, dousing Margo's smocked blue gingham in the red liquid. "Oh no!" Rita cried. "Your darling top. I'm so sorry. Hey, jerkface!" she shouted over her shoulder. "Pay attention!"

Margo watched the man charge onward in a pair of loafers so worn the bottoms flopped against the tile. "Hold on a minute…" she said, and her heart jumped. "Is that Peter Pulitzer?"

"The one and only," Rita said, dabbing Margo's left breast with a seltzer-soaked napkin.

"I thought Lilly was supposed to be in New York?"

"What does that have to do with anything? He and Lilly aren't joined at the hip."

"You've got that right," Margo mumbled. Rita gave her a sharp look and blotted harder. "Why do you think he's so steamed?"

"I saw him with Enrique Rousseau," she said. "So, problems with the sugar business, I'd wager. I'll never get why Lilly is so keen on everyone working together. Rousseau and Peter. Putting her friend Laura on her board. Opening a shop in Cocoa Beach for Dysie to run. These rich people love to make things more complicated and for *what*? Why not relax and enjoy life? Instead, her husband is getting into it with their friend at some party."

One eye trained on Peter, Margo took several glugs of her drink. It was already going to her head. "Rita?" she said, reaching for another can, weary from months of stewing, of trying to keep a lid on her worries and fears. "I need your opinion on something."

"What's up?" Rita said. Satisfied she'd done as much as she could to Margo's stain, she lobbed the napkin into the trash.

"It's a long story, but last season, when Slim and I were in the Bahamas, I ran into Peter at the hotel bar." After several deep breaths, Margo offered what she could. It was an ordinary conversation, she explained, until Peter started talking about marriage, and how bad wives had it.

"Complaining about marriage to a single broad? What an ass."

"He wasn't an ass," Margo said. "Peter was complaining about *himself*, and how he'll never hold a candle to Lilly. He thinks by marrying him, she signed herself up for a bum deal. You wouldn't believe how sad he was, how insecure. Peter Pulitzer without the swagger. It could break your heart."

"Oh, brother. Peter Pulitzer is the last person you should pity, I promise you that."

"We finished our drinks," Margo continued, glowering, "and Peter walked me to my room. When we were at my door, he apologized for the bellyaching. He couldn't help it, he said. Around me, he's too comfortable. Gets ahead of himself."

Rita rolled her eyes. "What a line."

"It wasn't a line," Margo said, though she wasn't sure, either way. "He called me *normal*. I'm pretty sure that's just a nicer word for *unimportant*."

"I doubt that's what he meant. Listen, sister, I don't know where you're going with this story, but all I see are flashing lights and danger signs."

"Will you let me finish? God, it's like talking to Slim. Can't get a word in." Margo let out a puff of air. "Eventually, Lilly came around the corner. She was polite as ever, but the whole encounter was awkward, like she'd caught us in the middle of something. Which wasn't the case!" Not at that exact second, anyway. "Lilly wasn't visibly mad, but she seemed...kinda ticked."

"How unreasonable," Rita said with a snort. "It wouldn't bother me *at all* if Slim were hanging around some girl's hotel room."

"We were staying on the same floor!" Margo protested and then unfurled the rest, from Lilly calling Peter a stinker, to the Sneaky Pete comment, everything but the kiss. "Since we've been back, I'm constantly on edge, wondering what they're thinking, or saying behind my back. There's an undercurrent of *something* in the air, but I'm overreacting, right? They probably haven't given me a second thought?"

Rita shrugged, which was supremely unhelpful. "Who knows? The most asinine things can irk a Palm Beacher," she said. "I've seen lifelong friendships implode because three men were interested in the same boat. Obviously, I can't read their minds, so what are you really asking?"

Margo mulled this over. "There's no way to avoid the Pulitzers. Should I attempt to clear the air? Apologize for whatever anyone thinks I did so we can all move on?"

Lips pinched together, Rita sized her up. "I've already told you what I think. Mixing in with these shiny, pretty folks is a gamble, on a bet that will never pay out. You're not going to win because the game is rigged. Personally, I wouldn't bother clearing the air. Your best move is to grab your cocktail and split."

—

With Rita and Slim off twisting, Margo downed a third cock-tail, grabbed a fourth, and ventured outside to where she'd last seen Peter. Despite Rita's "advice," the season had just started, and Margo refused to spend the next three to four months creeping around Palm Beach. She had to say something, what-ever that something was. Not even Margo knew.

After taking one last sip for courage, she stepped onto the veranda to where Peter stood, staring across the black Atlantic. Legs trembling, Margo walked toward him. "Hello," she said, her voice a high-pitched squeak.

"Margo!" Peter said, and his face lifted with surprise. "How are you?"

"Doing well. Lovely evening, isn't it?" It *was* a perfect Palm Beach night. Warm, but not sticky. A mild breeze but no chill.

"Doesn't get any better. You make an adorable scamp, by the way."

"Thanks, although it's hardly a costume compared to every-one else." Margo paused, debating whether to remark on Peter's getup. It might've been a costume, or what he'd worn to work.

"I think it strikes the perfect note," he said, and treated her to one of his big, showy smiles. Peter was his same old self and thank God for that. "It's great to see you. It's been ages. What have you been up to?"

"The usual. Work. Travel."

"Ah, very nice," Peter said, each word out of his mouth po-lite yet unsettlingly banal. Margo felt the life seeping from their conversation. This was not how she wanted this to go.

"So," she said. Margo looked around, trying to come up with more. After many awkward seconds, she spit out the first thing that popped into her brain. "Have you been keeping up with all the news? Nixon lost."

Peter tilted his head, smiling with only the left side of his mouth. "What now?"

"The California gubernatorial candidate?" Margo clarified.

"Um, yes. I'm aware of Nixon. Wouldn't have pegged you as a fan."

"I'm not!" she said. "It's just, that was an awfully sour speech. *You won't have Dick Nixon to kick around anymore.* He's lost to Kennedy *and* Pat Brown. I guess his political career is over." Margo kept talking even though every sentence was off.

"Are you okay?" Peter asked, laughing.

"No, I'm not," Margo said, deciding to go all in. "That's why I came out here. I hate to bring this up, but sometimes it's best to lay your cards on the table." She was jabbering like a deranged bird while Peter just stood there, staring. "As you may or may not recall, last March, back in Nassau, you walked me to my room. And then, well…" Rather than spelling it out, she cleared her throat. "Anyway. I'm sorry for my part in it. And I'm sorry for any fallout. I adore Lilly and have the utmost respect for both of you."

"Aww, kid." Peter squeezed her arm. "I hope you haven't been fretting for all these months. First, don't apologize, because I wouldn't say I *regret* that night. In fact, I'll always remember it fondly."

Margo responded with a gulp. Her breath was suddenly loud in her ears.

"But what's that you said about sunstroke and folks becoming slightly unhinged in the Bahamian heat?" Peter threw her a wink. "Stuff happens. People give into urges they shouldn't. No one's immune to it."

"Okay." Margo bobbed her head, flustered. Although she'd cleared the air, she still couldn't see through the lingering fog of confusion. "Also. One other thing." She winced. "When Lilly ran into us. In the hallway. She seemed…peeved."

Peter chuckled lightly. "*Peeved* is not in Lil's vocabulary. She's more of a silent seether who quickly forgets. Jeez, you've got a lot going on up there." He tapped her head. "Don't think so hard about stuff."

"But she named her new line the Sneaky Pete," Margo went on, unable to stop, "and though she's charming as ever, I have to wonder whether she's eyeing me with suspicion. Not that there's any reason to be suspicious! All that to say, I apologize for contributing to any disharmony, and if I can make it better, please let me know. I only want the best for you both." Margo exhaled. *There.* It was all very clumsy and artless, but she'd gotten it done.

"You really are too sweet," Peter said, "but, I promise, if Lilly was ever upset, she forgot within a day. And you did nothing wrong in the first place. Consider it water under the bridge."

Margo smiled, relieved she wasn't on anyone's bad side, and hopeful they could all move on from here. "Well, thank you," she said. "I appreciate it." She sipped her cocktail, which was better and better, the more she had. The rare drink improved by its aftertaste. "Now that we've put that hiccup in the rearview, what about you? What are you doing out here? Contemplating how you'll barnstorm the sugar world?"

"Something like that," he said, his lips tightening. "Caca Rousseau will be the death of me. That man." He clenched his fists for a second before releasing them. "Never mind. I won't bore you with all that. You haven't told me what's going on with you. Aside from your musings on Dick Nixon." He stepped closer and Margo's stomach flipped.

"Ha! Well! Not much is happening," Margo said. She panicked and poured the rest of the drink down her gullet. "This is quite tasty. Would another be one too many?" She glanced back and noticed Wendy Vanderbilt standing less than five yards away. Wendy was with George Hamilton, but 100 percent watching her with an expression that said "I understand exactly what you did." Margo's pulse began to race. "I should go," she said. "It's getting late, and I haven't seen Rita and Slim in a while. Can't have them leaving me behind!"

"Hold on. Wait. I need to say something." Peter brushed his fingers against hers. "About that night."

Margo hopped back. "Peter!" she yelped. Now Wendy was cutting a hot path in their direction, fingers curled like she wanted to strangle someone, which she no doubt did. Just as Margo contemplated her ability to fake a cardiac event, Rita appeared, planting herself between them.

"There you are!" Rita said. "We have an emergency."

"We do?" Margo said, hoping she didn't seem too bright-eyed and bushy-tailed about it.

"Slim snapped his ankle whilst doing the Broadway, and we have to leave."

"Shit," Peter said. "Is he okay?"

"He'll be fine. His ego is more hurt than his foot," Rita said, her countenance plainly on the perturbed end of the spectrum. If Slim had attempted a newfangled two-step, an injury was the only result that made sense. Margo would have to thank him later. "We need to get him home," Rita added, rooting around in her purse. "The doctor will meet us there. Would you mind driving, Margo?"

"Of course not," Margo said, taking the keys from her hand. "I've only had four drinks."

"Please ring if you need anything," Peter said, and the women turned to go.

As they took off toward the exit, Margo glanced back one last time. Wendy was gone and Peter stood alone, hands in his pockets, eyes fixed on the floor. Something was bothering him deeply, and Margo sensed it had little to do with Caca Rousseau's sugar.

48

Margo stood in front of Charles Amory's flower stand. Surly, grizzled Slim didn't really scream "zinnias!" but a get-well carton of cigarettes seemed inadequate.

The errand was taking longer than Margo planned. With everyone back for the season, Worth Avenue was teeming, and negotiating the flower stand was an act of extreme patience and tact. She'd had to beg the pardon of seven people just to access one bucket of sunflowers.

"Ladies!" Charles Amory called out to someone. "What are we looking for today?"

"A few blooms to brighten the shop," someone said, and Margo was besieged by a case of the cramps. The voice belonged to Wendy Vanderbilt, and she was accompanied by the devastating Hitchcock blonde Margo knew to be Lilly's new business partner, Laura.

"Some pinball wizards just came in," Charles said as Margo arched backward, hoping to fade into the shadows of the red-and-white canopy. "They're Lilly all the way. I'll grab them from the office."

"What about these?" Wendy said to Laura, as Charles scurried off. "Or this?" She picked up an orange rose by its flower.

"Stop that!" Laura said and whacked her wrist. "You're going to ruin it. Do you have to manhandle *everything*?"

"I didn't want to get pricked!"

"I should've come alone. I wouldn't have to babysit, and I already do everything by myself."

Wendy crossed her arms. "Just because you're mad at Lilly, don't take it out on me. *I'm* the one who's with you right now."

Laura sighed. "You're right," she said and stepped closer to Margo. "I'm sorry. It's exasperating. We're Lilly Pulitzer, Inc., but Lilly's *never* around."

"Well, it's incredibly time-consuming to be featured in every magazine ever printed," Wendy joked. "Who knew there was so much to say about a shift dress? It's not rocket science."

"The business bears *her* name, and either she wants it to succeed, or she doesn't. Being the CEO isn't all photo shoots and cocktails, or whatever the hell she's doing when she disappears for entire afternoons. There's no halfway anymore and she can't just expect it to work out. Actual effort is involved. We've had this discussion a thousand times, and she swears she understands, but nothing ever changes."

"Don't bother," Wendy said. "Confronting Lilly never works. Either she'll ignore you completely or say *thanks, sweetie, I'm so glad you expressed yourself! I love your passion!* Meanwhile, she'll keep doing what she's doing, possibly boiling with anger, though she'll never make a peep. She's the quintessential Scorpio. Her true thoughts and emotions are always close to the vest. We're all used to it."

Laura nodded. "The reason you call her the Sphinx."

"It's best to accept it and move on. I was telling Dysie the other day—" Wendy halted. Her face turned to stone. "Margo?"

She craned around a bucket of pink-tipped yellow carnations. "Is that you?"

"Oh! Hi!" Margo said, nearly popping out of her flats. "I didn't see you there. I was looking for some flowers for Slim." She grabbed a handful of carnations as sweat percolated on her brow. "He's recovering from an injury." For the love of St. Pete, why hadn't Margo listened to Rita? She'd "cleared the air" for a second that night at the B&T, then promptly contaminated it. *I need to say something about that night.* Margo couldn't stop wondering what Peter planned to confess.

"I heard about the ankle," Wendy said. "Poor Slimbo."

Saving them from a conversation no one wanted to have, Charles swung around the corner, arms overflowing with pink flowers. As he got closer, Margo noticed the zebra-like flecks and lines on the petals. They *were* perfect for Lilly, just as he'd claimed.

"Excellent, thank you, Charlie," Laura said. "You've made my day easier. Please put it on Lilly's account."

"If we're using Lilly's account," Wendy said, "I want to pick up some roses for the house." She whirled around. "Hell's bells!" she shouted, slapping her chest. "Margo! Why do you sneak up on people? You almost made me pee my pants!"

"I haven't moved…"

"You're such a chameleon," Wendy said. "Materializing from the ether and/or slithering your way into every scene. What a handy trait."

Margo didn't know how to take this, but with Wendy Vanderbilt, it was probably best to let things slide. "Yes. Well. Slim pays me to blend in," she said with a curt smile, passing Charles two dollars. "Have a nice day."

49

Slim tossed the flowers onto the table. "I'm allergic," he said.

"You're welcome. It's my absolute pleasure." Margo hadn't expected him to be overcome with gratitude, but a thanks would've been nice. "I don't suppose Rita is here?" Rita wasn't going to be pleased about her chat with Peter, or the run-in with Wendy, but Margo had to talk to somebody.

"She's at the beach with Mary," Slim said, plonking around the kitchen like a pirate with a new peg. According to the doctor, the fracture was minor, and he should be cane-free by next week. "I'm glad you're here. I need a favor. An old friend from *LIFE* wants me to shoot Lilly for an upcoming issue, but the woman's real hard to pin down these days."

"Yeah, I've heard…"

"She gave me one time slot." Slim flipped open his camera case. "Thursday afternoon, on her parents' boat. Obviously, I'm not going out on the water anytime soon." He spun the case to face Margo. "Congratulations. Your second assignment."

"The Leica?" Margo said, head swimming. "I don't have the first idea how to use it."

"Which is why I'm about to give you a lesson. Listen closely because I'm only doing this once."

Before Margo understood what was happening, Slim raced through the specifics, like how to change the shutter speed and aperture by moving this lever and that. Longer shutter speeds let in more light, which also meant a greater chance of blurring. That's why she should use 1/500 for action shots and 1/50 for wider-angle portraits.

"What about speeds in between?" Margo asked. "For instance, 1/100. When would I use that?"

"Let's not get ahead of ourselves. Just stick to action shots and wide-angle portraits." To avoid confusion, he said, Margo should think of aperture like a fraction. One half was bigger than 1/16, which meant an aperture of f/2 was larger, and let in more light, than f/16.

Margo nodded as though she'd always had a firm grasp on math.

"Shooting manually is more difficult," he said, "but it forces you to think about light, and what specific people or objects are important to the shot. Putting that much thought into it usually makes the image better overall." Slim covered several more technicalities, and Margo tried to concentrate while she buzzed with nerves.

"That's all there is to it," Slim concluded.

"You make it sound so easy," Margo said with a jittery smile. It'd been an awfully fast tutorial, and the only detail that'd stuck was the tip about fractions. "Maybe I should bring the Brownie, too?"

"Don't second-guess yourself. Unlike me, you don't need to rely on a crutch." He exhaled. "Look, is this my first choice? It is not. But when Lilly calls, we answer. All you can do is believe in what little skill you've developed and try not to fuck everything up."

50

DECEMBER 1962

If Margo hadn't known what she was walking up to, she might've mistaken the Phippses' home for a sprawling, Mediterranean-style hotel. It was twice as big as she'd imagined, and she'd imagined a lot.

Stomach churning, Margo approached the house, feeling insignificant, like a resident of Lilliput in the shadow of a castle. *You can do this*, she told herself, gripping the handle of the camera case. She'd written down everything Slim had said, but there was no telling whether any of it would translate.

Up ahead, two women stood beside a blue Buick convertible, talking animatedly, flinging around their hands. One was Lilly, wearing a white shift with blue palm fronds and a blue scarf tied around her bouffant. Her companion wore a rose print, and her hair was shellacked and neat. It took a minute for Margo to recognize her as Julia Rousseau. *Better than Wendy Vanderbilt*, she thought.

"Hello!" Margo called out, relieved she wouldn't have to find a front door. "I'm here for the shoot. Hopefully Slim told you I'd be filling in—"

The women turned. Julia glared, her forehead deeply lined,

lips pinched. Margo froze, trapped in the quicksand of whatever she'd interrupted.

"Hello, Margo!" Lilly sang, her voice thick with honey as she rushed to Margo's side. "You arrived at the perfect time. We're about to set sail. Julia can't join us. What a pity. Bye, sweetie!" she hollered. "You'll feel better after a nap."

Julia remained by her car, arms crossed, feet planted like redwoods.

"Right in the nick of time," Lilly hissed, clutching Margo's hand. "I think someone might need a trip to Bloomingdale's." She loosened her grip and her tone relaxed into a laugh. "She's so dang wound up about this sugar thing. But that's how Julia is, very *flappable*. She keeps accusing me of interfering—sabotage, even!—when my money's invested, too. Thank God her husband is rational. Anyhow, never mind all that. We have some boating to do."

———

Vergemer, the Phippses' 113-foot diesel yacht, was docked behind the house. The skipper, a *LIFE* reporter, and several of Lilly's friends were already aboard.

"Thanks, everyone, for coming," Lilly said as the boat pulled away from the dock. "I get so antsy when someone tries to make *me* the main subject. I'd much rather be at the shop, ringing up dresses. It's marvelous to have the moral support." She plopped down beside a blonde woman Margo deduced was the oft-mentioned Dysie. "Have you all met Slim's darling assistant, Margo? *She's* the photographer. Look at us! A real boobsville today. Who even needs men?" She giggled and flipped her attention back to the interviewer, who was the lone man, absent the skipper. "Except for you, Mister Reporter. I hope you can handle all this feminine energy."

"I prefer it," the man said, removing a voice recorder from his coat pocket.

"Gosh, Margo," Wendy said, and Margo was amazed that it took her a full ninety seconds to go in for the kill. "I'm seeing you *everywhere* these days. What are the chances?"

"Pretty decent," Margo said tightly.

"Tell me about Lilly Pulitzer, Inc.," the reporter said, saving the day. He licked a finger and opened his notepad. "You designed the dresses because of the stains from juicing your husband's fruits, is that right?"

Lilly chortled. "You make it sound so dirty," she said. "It was to hide the splotches but also my thick waist. I was merely solving my own problem—or *problems*, as it were—but then everyone went mad for the cut and colors, and the business took off!"

As Lilly prattled on in her miles-per-minute way, Margo set down the camera case and snapped open the top. The boat rocked and she grabbed a handrail for balance. It'd be difficult to keep the camera steady if Margo got seasick, or fell overboard. Running a hand along rails, furniture, anything she could touch, Margo circumnavigated the boat, on the hunt for a good place to shoot.

"We should get started!" Lilly called out to her. "Before the wind and sea air render me too horrendous to document on film. Did you pick your spot?"

Margo was eyeing the seating area at the rear of the boat with its blue-and-white cushions trimmed in white fringe. "I think maybe the—" she began. What was it called? The stern? "Would you mind if we relocated to the rear of the yacht?"

"Sweetie, you can just call it a boat," Lilly said, and the group moved en masse to join Margo, like a synchronized team.

When they reached the back, Lilly plunked down. "How's this?" she said, leaning into the cushions, stretching her arms.

Margo cocked her head, pondering whether the fabric's pattern clashed with or complemented the palm fronds on Lilly's dress, especially with the noise from other blues, like her turquoise scarf and the ocean itself. The contrast would either make the picture work, or ruin everything. There was only one way to find out.

Hands shaking, Margo rested the Leica against her hip. *Have confidence. Remember how well the Key West photos turned out.*

Under Margo's instruction and of her own accord, Lilly whipped through several poses, from relaxed to ramrod straight. "I'll need to do this, of course," she said, and clapped her knees together. Everyone laughed. "Lillys do not require underwear, but I don't need to prove it in a national magazine!"

With her kohl-rimmed eyes, loud red lips, and hair as shiny and deep as velvet, the lens found Lilly easily in the sea of blue. Margo saw right away that the composition was perfect, especially with Lilly's tan and the flapping American flag at the top of the frame.

After fifteen, twenty minutes, Margo set the camera down, breathless. It was exhausting to concentrate that intently for such a long stretch of time. "Take five, everyone," Margo said, for her own sake. She flopped down onto one of the cushions beside Lilly and pushed the hair out of her face.

"Being a photographer's assistant must be the neatest job," Wendy said. "Go out on a boat, snap a picture or two, and work is done for the day!"

"Oh, I'm sorry," Margo stammered, as a gaggle of beady, inquisitive eyes stared back. "It's just a break." Had it been too familiar of her to act like she could take a load off whenever she pleased?

"Don't listen to Wendy," Lilly said. "She's always a crab."

"A crab? *Moi?*" Wendy placed a hand on her chest. "I was giving a compliment. Who wouldn't want to sit on yachts and go to parties without having to suffer any of the boring stuff like bridge groups and charity fundraisers?"

"Working for Slim can be very boring," Margo said. "Rest assured."

"Speaking of parties," Lilly said. "Peter told me that he saw you at the B&T."

"*I* told you that," Wendy snipped.

"Sounded like a fun night." Lilly scowled. "Except for poor Slimbo getting hurt. What did you and my husband chat about anyhow? Did he talk your ear off about the damned sugar plantation?"

"Oh, um, no, he didn't mention it," she said, choking down the butterflies. She should've listened to Rita, Margo thought for the three hundredth time. Better yet, she should never have kissed Peter in the first place. "Mostly we talked about current events. We also briefly discussed Dutch Elkin—" They did not discuss Dutch, but it'd send a message and sound more believable than politics.

Lilly looked at Wendy. "Didn't I just read that Dutch is dating Jackie's press secretary, Pam?"

"I saw them at Toots Shor's last time I was in New York," Wendy said.

"She is such a cutie pie, and Jackie handled her with such shrewdness." Lilly swiveled back toward Margo. "Pamela was *Jack's* secretary first. Naturally, they were having an affair, so Jackie hired her away from her husband. Brilliant and diabolical." Lilly cackled and Margo wanted to die. "Oh! Margo!" Her eyes widened. "Wait! Weren't you into Dutch for a second?"

"We saw each other over the summer? And we've spoken a few times. He's busy. He's recording a new album, and it's about to be released. Next week, I think."

"Don't worry for a minute about the Pam thing!" She threw out a hand. "I'm sure it's a rumor. Jackie probably planted items herself, to detract attention from Jack."

"So Dutch is still on the table, huh?" Wendy said. "I've never seen you two together…"

Lilly gave a heavy roll of the eyes. "Wendy believes she's being paid to get everyone's goats." She shimmied closer to Margo and took her hand. "Ignore her," she said. "Just stay next to me. Stick close to my side."

For a second, Margo felt better, but the relief soon morphed into a faint, creeping terror. The physical contact wasn't altogether friendly, or warm. Instead, it was like Lilly was holding her there, keeping her in her place.

51

HENDRY COUNTY, FLORIDA / CHRISTMAS 1962

As if trying to put gossip about Pamela Tenure and Toots Shor's to rest, Dutch swooped in five days before Christmas, after weeks of silence.

"Let's spend the holiday together," he announced.

Margo pulled the phone away from her ear and stared into the receiver, mystified. Spend Christmas together? How? Where? Also, what about his new album? Didn't he need to promote it, or something? Naturally, Dutch hadn't thought about any of this. All he knew was that the album was out, and he wanted to make up for lost time.

"Please, Margo," he begged. "I need a getaway and know of a cabin within driving distance of Palm Beach. Let's go there. Tell Slim you're visiting family."

At this, Margo prickled. How could he forget that, like him, she had no real family? Unlike him, she didn't have anyone to play the part.

"Listen, I get it," he'd said, when she returned only static. "It's hell being with a guy like me. I'm gone all the time and awful lies are written in the gossip rags. Girls get sick of my deal, and I don't blame them. Please, hang with me a bit longer and I swear it will get better, when life settles down. A cabin, Margo. Can't you picture it? It'd be so romantic."

She could picture it, in fact. As Margo's head filled with fantasies of crackling fires, thick blankets, and potbelly stoves, she softened. Why was she so hesitant? Margo wanted more of Dutch, and this was her chance. She even had a decent reason for leaving town. Sandy LaSalle had turned himself in, and was being extradited through Miami. Margo's mom was scheduled to meet him.

"It's time," Antoinette said on the phone. "You can't fight city hall, or the federal government. It's the noble thing to do." In Margo's opinion, the noble thing would've been not to commit crimes, but sometimes a person could only work with what they had.

When Margo told Slim she was "thinking of seeing" her mom, he didn't bat an eye, and her plan was set. On the twenty-fourth, Antoinette would be in Miami, waiting for Sandy, while Margo waited for Dutch in West Palm Beach.

As she rode the elevator down to meet him, Margo's mind entertained a long list of potential calamities. Dutch wouldn't show. Slim might catch wind of the plan. A hunter could accidentally shoot Margo, or she'd get eaten by a bear. Were there bears in Florida? She didn't know. But whatever misgivings Margo had fell away the second she stepped into the lobby and saw Dutch leaning against a marble pillar looking heaven-sent.

"Uh-oh, someone's brought out the big dogs," he said, eyeing Margo's very reasonably sized suitcase. "For the record, this is an *actual* cabin. Not like when New Englanders call their country estates *camps*. I hope you're not expecting much."

"I'm not expecting anything," Margo said, then paused to weigh whether this was true. She *had* envisioned cozy blankets and potbelly stoves. But if Dutch was driving there in the Whitneys' Rolls-Royce, it couldn't be too chancy.

The cabin was an hour away, close to Lake Okeechobee, smack in the middle of twenty thousand acres of Florida scrub crawling with deer, turkeys, boars, and alligators. "It's a wild, wild place," Dutch said, and Margo's spirits flagged with each new detail. They keeled over and died when they finally rolled to a stop. This was not a cabin but a shack—a shack seemingly built with termite-ridden wood and no more than three to four nails.

"Goodness," Margo said with a gulp. "How rustic. It's safe, though, right? No creatures can get in?"

Dutch laughed and kicked open the door. "I'll protect ya."

Margo lumbered out of the car, twigs crunching beneath her feet. "You said this is a friend's cabin? Which friend?" She swung her gaze to the left and saw an airplane parked nearby— gold belly, dark green stripe, beige curtains in the windows. Margo's stomach dropped to the dirt. She'd flown in it before. "Peter—"

"How'd you…?" Dutch turned around. "Oh! Wow. Looks like he's here, too."

Pulse racing, Margo gawped at the cabin. Never mind the Peter factor, could this place *fit* three live adult humans? She imagined all of them piled into a rickety bed like Depression-era sharecroppers. "Is he staying…with *us*?"

"I assume so," Dutch said. "Sorry. I wasn't aware he'd be here. Obviously."

"Maybe we should leave?" Margo said, but Dutch was already on the front porch.

"Knock, knock!" he hollered. The cabin rattled as he pounded the door. "Dutch and Margo have arrived!"

—

"Sorry, guys," Peter said from where he sat on a lump of foam on the floor. A couch, perhaps? It was impossible to distinguish furniture from random detritus in this room. "I know you weren't expecting company."

"This is your place, so we're the company," Dutch said amiably, though his expression dimmed.

"When you suggested taking a breather, it sounded like a hell of an idea," Peter said. "Lilly invited her parents and the Rousseaus for the holiday and I'd prefer to avoid the topic of frostbitten sugarcane for one day. Anyhow." He thwacked Dutch on the back, and Dutch pitched forward. "I'm sorry, pal. You didn't mention a date."

"You didn't tell him I'd be here?" Margo cranked her head toward Dutch.

"I'll stay out of your way," Peter added. "I've got a sleeping bag in the plane so can shack up out there. You two, please, take the bedroom."

Margo smiled, though it probably read as a gritting-of-teeth. His offer might've been generous if the "bedroom" was more than a narrow, wafer-thin mattress hidden behind a black-lacquered screen. It was a handsome, out-of-place piece, likely filched from their home in Palm Beach.

"You know what?" Peter said as he popped onto his feet. He planted himself between Dutch and Margo, one hand on each. "The three of us are going to have a blast. This isn't the fanciest house in Florida, but it sure is fun. What do you think, Margo? Are you game for adventure?"

"Game as can be," she said, her smile wide and strained and cracked at the edges. What other choice did she have? "We're all here, and that's what counts."

52

"I'm a miserable failure," Dutch wailed. "I've never been so down in my life."

It was Christmas, and the second night in a row of this. According to Dutch, his album was a bust. It'd taken off like a bag of concrete, had all the zing of a dead trout. Margo already regretted the trip, not to mention wasting a lie to Slim on a getaway that had nothing to do with her. It didn't matter that Peter was with them. Romance had never been on the menu.

"Listen, buddy, I get it," Peter said, rubbing Dutch's back with one hand while swilling whiskey from the other. Margo was glad someone understood, because she did not. "It's hard to be in the limelight. A million ups and downs. But let's step back for a minute. Is there a chance you're being overly sensitive?"

"It's called facing the truth."

"It can't be that bad," Margo tried.

"Yes, it is. It's curtains for me!"

Margo sighed and glanced at Peter, who shrugged help-lessly. "Even though it's against your policy to read what they say about you in the papers," she said, "maybe you should. The reviews have been positive. And from what you've told me, you're still booking gigs."

"Who gives a shit about all that?" Dutch grouched. "What good is the praise of some eggheads or earning a few dollars at bar mitzvahs when I'm barely hanging on to the middle of the *Billboard* charts?" He grabbed the bottle of whiskey by its neck and glugged it all the way down. Between his wailing and the stubbled face, greasy skin, and crooked part, this version of Dutch was unrecognizable.

"No, thanks, I didn't want another drink," Peter said.

"And Margo!" Dutch cried. "My Margo! The one person I thought wouldn't view me with disgust, but you see me as a failure, the biggest zero around."

"I've never seen you as a failure. Not even close!"

"Look at you. You're standing ten feet away, like you might catch something."

"I'm right here." Margo touched his shoulder. "See? This proves you're overreacting. There isn't room in this cabin for anyone to keep ten feet of space." She met eyes with Peter and cringed. "Sorry," she said. "I didn't mean to imply that—"

"How dare you besmirch my grand palace!" he joked.

"If you're not repulsed by me," Dutch said, "then explain why we've been here for over twenty-four hours and haven't had a single roll in the sheets!"

"Dutch!" Margo snatched away her hand. "There's no need to be crude. But since you raised the point, you don't seem especially primed for romance. And Peter's been here the whole time."

"Hey." Peter put up his hands. "Don't let me stop you. I can leave for a bit if that'll cheer everyone up. A Christmas present from me to the two of you."

"No!" Margo yelped, and Peter gave her a look she could not read. "I doubt either of us are in the mood," she added.

Indeed, Margo *wasn't* in the mood, and she couldn't imagine Dutch was prepared for that level of physical exertion.

"I get it," Dutch said, hunching his shoulders, sinking into himself. "Who'd want to fuck a massive loser like me? I should go to bed so you don't have to suffer my company." With great, wailing, moaning effort, he rose to his feet, but his legs wouldn't hold him. He collapsed, landing on the floor like a bag of wet bones. "Even my body is betraying me!"

"Nah, pal. I think that's just the booze," Peter said and moved behind him. He hooked both arms beneath Dutch's pits and gestured for Margo to take his feet. "Think we can get him all the way there?" he asked, and she nodded.

Together, they heaved him into bed. "That wasn't too difficult," Margo said, pulling the sheet to cover Dutch's hulking body.

"The benefit of my dismally minuscule cabin," Peter said.

Dutch blasted out a loud, rumbling snore and they laughed.

Peter put his hands in his pockets. Margo crossed her arms. They stared at each other over Dutch's body, the only light coming from the moon in the window and the lamplight dancing on the other side of the screen.

"Need help with anything else?" Peter asked, and Margo shook her head. "Good night, Margo."

"Good night," she said.

53

Margo woke up the next morning alone in the cot. Dutch's bag was gone, likewise the Rolls when she peered out the window. Her initial reaction wasn't one of anger, or even surprise. Mostly she was grateful for the sound of Peter's snores on the other side of the screen. Thank God she wasn't stranded.

After slipping into Bermuda shorts and an old sweater, Margo made a cup of Nescafé, and padded outside to the camp chairs on the porch. As she settled into her seat, she felt oddly hopeful, filled with something like peace. She'd been foolish to put so much hope in Dutch. It was never going to work, and it was strangely comforting to acknowledge it.

The cabin door creaked. "Good morning," Peter said as he timidly crept outside. He lowered into the chair next to hers with a groan. "We don't have to discuss what happened, but I'll make sure you get home. If you can stomach flying with me again."

"Better than staying out here and being attacked by wild boars."

Peter lit a cigarette. "Might depend on the day. Anyway, I'm glad *that's* over," he said, not specifying which *that* he meant. "I won't say I told you so."

"I appreciate your thoughtfulness," Margo said with a smirk. "It's nice that you don't enjoy kicking people when they're down."

"Who's down? I'd reckon you're on your way up. I've always suspected he'd make a terrible beau, but I'm truly sorry he pissed up a storm." Peter took in a deep inhale of smoke and let it all out. "What a night. This proves, once and for all, that Christmas always blows."

Margo looked at him. "Not a big fan of Christmas, huh?"

"Last year's was okay," he said with a sly glance. He took another drag before speaking again. "On the whole, however, the holiday is nothing but high expectations, followed by swift letdowns. Relentless grinning and small talk and hanging around family members you're pretending to like."

"You don't get along with your parents?" Margo said. This surprised her.

"No. I meant…" Peter laughed, but the humor didn't reach his eyes. He leaned forward, resting his elbows on his knees. "I was referring to the people who pretend to like *me*. My in-laws, in other words. Though they don't really pretend much anymore, unless the kids are around. My parents might've qualified once, but they are dead."

"Oh, Peter," Margo said, swallowing a gasp. "I'm so sorry. I wasn't thinking." She'd known his parents were gone but lost the story somewhere along the way. As Margo remembered it, Peter's mother died when he was little, and his father more recently. Herbert Pulitzer Sr. was a notorious character in Palm Beach, infamous for his eye patch and wearing silk pajamas in public. "Your dad passed recently, right? The holidays must be difficult."

"A few years ago," Peter said, mashing his cigarette into the ground. He leaned back into his chair. "That didn't really affect anything, though. I barely knew him. Or my mom, for that matter. She was sick with tuberculosis from the time I was born." Because of her illness, Peter's father kept her away from the kids, sending him and his sister to boarding school at age seven while he combed the world for a cure. She eventually succumbed to the disease, his dad went off to war, and Peter didn't see him again until his graduation from St. Mark's. If not for the eye patch, Peter never would've picked him out of the crowd.

Margo thought about what Lilly said at the fashion show, how Peter hadn't ever learned how to be loved. Now that she'd heard his story, it made sense. There wasn't anyone around to try.

"I didn't mean to get into all that," Peter said. "The Pulitzers are screwed up, just like everyone else. It's so mundane, the oldest tale in the book, especially for Palm Beachers."

"What do you mean, *especially for Palm Beachers*?" Margo said, lifting a brow.

"Haven't you heard? In other parts of the country, the children are delinquents. In Palm Beach, it's the parents." They're the ones who stayed out all night drinking and wrecking cars, Peter explained. The ones who mired themselves in sexual misadventures that two times out of three led to a half-hearted attempt at suicide. Even the people they hired were all kinds of hinky. Most wealthy parents brought in competent governesses to tend to their kids, but Palm Beachers left it to whatever housekeeper or gardener, or off-duty cop, happened to be around that day.

"The children are horrifically malnourished," Peter went on, delighted by Margo's stunned disbelief. "The richer the family, the worse the food, and it's really an all-or-nothing situation." At best, a kid arrived at school with a flimsy sandwich that was never cut, simply torn in two, or a whole roasted grouse, which was awfully inconvenient to consume at the lunch tables. "Most

teachers pack extra food for their starving little charges," Peter
added, and Margo could not believe her ears.

"You must be exaggerating," she said, starting to feel mildly
less embarrassed about her own childhood. She'd been casually
neglected, but never to this degree.

"Not at all. If anything, I'm downplaying it so as not to hor-
rify you, or chase you away," Peter said. "Of course, Lilly's not
like that. When she's in charge, nothing ever falls through the
cracks. It helps that *her* parents were on the better end of things.
They were never willfully cruel and managed to acknowledge
her existence more than once per season."

"Is that why she's so close with them?" Margo asked.

Peter nodded. "Lil thinks they walk on water. Indeed, compared to the others, they're basically saints. You should probably call your own parents tonight. Thank them for not being
complete derelicts."

Margo snorted. "Oh, they're derelicts, just in a different
way."

"Well, you *are* from California," Peter teased.

"True, but not every West Coast family has a patriarch who's
been on the lam in Brazil for two years." The admission appeared from nowhere, and Margo was shocked that she didn't
have the urge to take it back.

Peter's eyes widened. "No!"

Margo bobbed her head. "It's true," she said, astonished by
the smile inching across her face. After the incident in the Bahamas, and the encounter at the Bums' Ball, it was nice to feel
relaxed around Peter again. She spooled out the rest of the story.

"I'm sorry you've had to go through that," he said, when
Margo was done. "What does your mom think about it all?"

"To this day, she swears it's a 'misunderstanding,' despite the
fact that he's turning himself in…" Margo pretended to check
a watch. "Right about now. I can't believe it's finally over. Not

that it's really *over*. He has to be sentenced, and my mom has to figure out what to do next." Antoinette had spent the past fifteen years putting Sandy first, rotating around him like the moon, and the last few waiting for him to come back. Margo couldn't imagine what'd become of her.

"Wow. That is some story," Peter said, and took a drag of his cigarette. He hadn't smoked it in two or three minutes, which must've been a personal record. "I've known loads of cheats and scamps and ne'er-do-wells, but never someone on the bona fide *lam*. Congratulations." He raised an invisible glass. "You win this round."

Margo rolled her eyes. "Lucky me," she said, debating whether to confess that she might've known *two* people evading the fuzz, now that Rita was thoroughly convinced Dolly had gone into hiding. There were two warrants out for her arrest thanks to some missed court dates—one to fight off her mother's $20 million claim on her estate, and a second to face Prince Gonzalo, who accused Dolly of stealing her own $100,000 engagement ring. These transgressions didn't seem that dire, and running away wasn't Dolly's style, but the Huntington had been awfully cagey about her forwarding address.

"Hey, I had a thought," Peter said, dragging Margo's focus back to the porch. "If you don't have anywhere to be, it might be fun to stay another night or two? No monkey business, I promise!" He placed a hand over his heart as Margo's threatened to break through her chest. "What do you think?"

"Um. Yeah. Well," Margo stuttered. Her internal organs were tumbling around each other like Keds in a washing machine. Could she? *Should* she? No monkey business, he swore. Margo went to speak, but her voice was drowned out by the roar of an engine, and a Rolls-Royce barreling up the dirt road. Time seemed to drag as they watched the car thunder toward them and grind to a halt.

"Look who's back," Peter said.

The driver's-side door flew open, and Dutch stepped into the swirling dust. "The villain has returned to the scene," he said. "I'm sorry to both of you. I was a complete ass. Margo, I assume it's over between us, but I didn't want to abandon you. Please, let me drive you back to Palm Beach. Let me cling to the belief I'm a decent person."

Margo inhaled. Her eyes darted back and forth between Peter and Dutch. She didn't want to go but couldn't stay, now that Dutch had gallantly returned. Slowly, she rose to her feet. "Um, let me get my things," Margo said, her voice so thin it could break. She packed up and left the cabin without so much as a final glimpse at Peter.

As they drove back to Palm Beach, Margo rested her head on the window and pretended to sleep. She was upset with Dutch, for more reasons than she dared name, but tried to convince herself that one day she'd forgive him, and be grateful for this interruption.

54

What in God's name was Margo doing at Ta-boo? Why was she with Lilly and Peter and Caca Rousseau, eating Caesar salad beneath huge clusters of plastic-grape lights?

Margo knew the answer from a factual perspective. While shooting the Royal Poinciana Playhouse opening two nights before, Lilly asked Margo and Slim to dinner, but Slim canceled last-minute, citing a cold. Whether this was a nightmare or what she'd always wanted, Margo didn't know. Wendy Vanderbilt wasn't there, so thank God for small mercies.

"Digging for information about the *LIFE* article, no doubt," Slim said, after Margo asked why they'd been invited. "When's it coming out, is it coming out. If she asks, tell her the truth. You're not aware of any update. It's only been a month and these things take time." So far, Lilly hadn't mentioned it.

As the others discussed the famed New Year's party held by the Cocoanuts, a subset of the Old Guard men, Margo picked at her salad, a dozen questions circling her head. Had Peter mentioned the hunting cabin to Lilly, or the breakup with Dutch? Should Margo say something? Also, where was Julia tonight?

"It's a shame Slim is under the weather," Lilly said, forcing Margo back to the table. "What did he come down with?"

"I'm not sure? Whatever it is, he probably got it in Hawaii," Margo guessed. They'd spent the New Year in Waikiki, which sounded dreamy, until they arrived and it rained for seven straight days. Whatever visions Margo had of catamaran rides, hikes to Diamond Head, or swimming in Hanauma Bay were whisked away in the storm and she spent most of the time drinking Cokes in the Captain's Galley at the Moana-Surfrider while rain streamed down the windows. "It was pouring all week," she added. "There were three tsunami warnings."

"That's the pits," Lilly said with a mild pout. "Granted, the weather hasn't been brilliant around here, either, which is an outrage. This is Florida, for Christ's sake."

"You can blame your government for that," Caca said and took a sip of wine. "When they experiment with the atomic bomb, it disturbs the Gulf Stream."

Lilly nodded. "Too true," she said.

Margo hadn't heard this before, and she found herself sneaking a peek at Peter as if to confirm, but he hadn't said much all night. He seemed distracted, half-engaged, the opposite of his regular self. At least he and Caca weren't arguing.

"Speaking of absolute paradise," Lilly said, swinging her focus back to Margo. "Peter told me you were forced to suffer several nights in that god-awful cabin of his. Over Christmas! Talk about coal in your stocking."

"The cabin wasn't that bad," Margo said, cautiously. Lilly was cheerful as ever, but this didn't amount to much, given what Wendy and Laura said about her being the Sphinx. "In fact, it was quite peaceful until Dutch lost his head, and we were forced to split. After all that commotion, Peter must've been thrilled to be rid of us." Margo's gaze slid toward Peter, who was now on his feet.

"Please excuse me," he said, tossing his napkin onto the table. "I see Henry in the lounge, and we are overdue for a chat."

Caca also hopped up. "I'll join you," he said. "My apologies to the ladies. It pains me to leave two gorgeous women alone, but business calls."

They hurried off and Lilly craned to see where they'd gone. "Oh." She frowned. "It's Henry Ford. Money talk. Real dull stuff." She returned her attentions to Margo. "Okay, let's dish. I presume Slim doesn't know about your little jaunt to Okeechobee. What a sneaky minx you are!" Lilly tickled the top of her hand, and Margo practically vaulted out of her seat. "Sheesh! Relax! I'm only joshing. I won't utter a word. Although I'm so incredibly sorry Peter decided to grace you with his untimely presence. No wonder Dutch was in such foul spirits."

"His grumpiness was not about Peter," Margo said. "He doesn't think his album is doing as well as it should. And you can't blame Peter for showing up. It *is* his cabin..."

"No, no, no," Lilly clucked. "Don't make excuses. I'm *sure* Dutch told him you'd be there. My husband can't resist the allure of a pretty girl, and so he ruined your whole damned weekend. I swear Peter has a crush on you." She narrowed her eyes, zeroing in on Margo, silently demanding a response.

"Oh gosh, no, that's not true at all," Margo spluttered, feeling like a spooked bird thrashing around its cage. The last time they were together, on the boat, Lilly gave off an aura best described as *flinty*. Now she was joking and laughing about Peter's pursuit of "pretty girls." Margo didn't know what to think. *Typical Scorpio.* "I'm convinced Peter sees me as a sister type," she added. "Maybe the annoying little girl next door."

"I wouldn't bet on that," Lilly said. "It's like I told you before, Peter gets into such jams when he's bored. And he doesn't always think straight. It's worse when he's under stress. You've probably heard." She nodded toward the bar, where Caca and Peter remained in a heated, arms-throwing, feet-stomping discussion with Henry Ford. "But Talisman Sugar Corp. is struggling. One complication after another."

"He mentioned something about the cold snap?" Margo knew this was a subject so touchy even the Shiny Sheet was writing about it, but she was delighted to move on.

"Frostbite," Lilly said. "*Cut the cane before the cold weather*, I told Peter, but he was too slow to get the mill up and running." By Lilly's telling, the freeze damaged the sugarcane before they could grind it, leaving Talisman Sugar with no sugar to sell. Now Henry Ford was ready to pull his money and swap out the entire board. "The boys are running around like chickens with their heads cut off," Lilly said. "But there *are* solutions."

"Really?" Margo said, perking up. Though she wasn't especially concerned with the sugar trade, she'd prefer that Peter return to his sunnier self. His unsettling bitter streak was setting her on edge.

"Damaged cane can be used for molasses, but it's like Peter can only see *sugar*. Men are so prideful and single-minded. Why are women always viewed as the unreasonable ones?" Lilly shook her head. "None of this falls on Caca, though. I blame Peter, and pray he hasn't led that nice gentleman irrevocably astray. It's no surprise that Julia isn't speaking to me."

Margo squinted, confused. Wasn't Caca the sugar impresario and Peter the one who came in later, to help with financing, and the securing of land? If anything, it seemed to Margo that Peter had been led astray by Caca, not the other way around.

"Naturally, the frost was also murder on the citrus," Lilly went on. "And Peter is spinning, certain he's about to have two businesses in shambles. He's downright hysterical. Thank God no one must stew about my enterprise. Oops!" She slapped a hand across her mouth. "Speak of the devil. Here he comes! Hello, darling!" She fluttered a hand overhead.

"Christ on a bike," Peter groused as he stormed up. He flung himself into his chair and knocked back the rest of his drink.

"Did you make any progress with Henry?" Lilly asked with a wince. She peered around Margo to where Caca sat alone.

"We're past the point of making *progress*, Lilly," Peter growled. "Rousseau with his damned imperiousness just pissed off the last remaining investor. Now we wait to see whether I'll lose my pants, or only my shirt." He guzzled down Lilly's drink, too. "I should just hand the business to the trustees and be done with it."

"You will do no such thing," Lilly said, pushing herself away from the table. "Looks like I'll have to intervene once again. You two entertain each other while I check on Caca. I'm sure you'll *relish* the one-on-one time."

—

Margo stared beady-eyed at the morass of dressing and soggy lettuce on her plate while Peter clanked around the ice in his otherwise empty glass. "I'm sorry about the frost," she said at last. "What a drag." It was the best she could do.

Peter glanced up. "It's not just about the freeze."

"Yeah, I picked up on that," Margo mumbled.

"Absolutely everything is going to shit."

"Lilly's business is gangbusters," Margo said, and Peter gave her a look so withering she was surprised she didn't die on the spot. "Not that this eliminates all the problems but…"

"Yeah, yeah. Lilly's success is absolutely fucking fantastic," Peter said, and Margo intuited he was being sarcastic. "How lucky for her. She doesn't even need to fake the perpetual rainbows and butterflies. She has the perfect excuse for nonstop happiness."

"People need an excuse for that?" Margo said, crinkling her nose.

"That woman can only abide sunshine. Why do you think she lives in Palm Beach year-round?" Peter shoved his empty glass aside and reached for his cigarettes. "You know what I realized recently?" he said, lighting up. "That picture you took, after our trip to Key West. You captured our dynamic perfectly. Lilly lunging out of the plane, me staring at the ground, defeated, as she runs away."

"Running *away*?" Margo was completely beside herself. "That's not what I saw," she said. "Not at all. I saw Lilly's determination. Your admiration and pride. An appreciation of her business savvy." And her backside.

"Oh, I appreciate her alright," Peter said. "But sometimes I wonder." He paused and proceeded to suck the dickens out of his cigarette, like he only had one smoke left. After it burned to his fingertips, he dropped it into the ashtray. "Sometimes I wonder what I'm doing mixed up in all this, mixed up with *her*. Lilly Pulitzer is beloved, spectacularly adored, but am I capable of loving her as much as everyone else does? Anything I could possibly give her feels minuscule. And, believe me, she agrees, and relishes reminding me of it."

"That's ridiculous." Margo's eyes flew toward the bar, where Lilly was listening to Caca with a sympathetic tilt of the head. "You have endless love for Lilly. Your pride is palpable."

"Pride and love are not the same," Peter said with a sigh. "Lilly is incredible, but she's a lot to live up to. She consumes all the space and there's hardly a spot left for me."

"What space?" Margo asked. "Where?" Once again, she was scrambled, all mixed-up, dropped into a story she didn't recognize.

"Any given room. The house. Our marriage. You name it." Peter laughed ruefully and lifted his hand, as if he'd wanted a smoke but had forgotten his cigarette was gone. "Just look at her over there, smoothing over what I messed up, making me feel small once again. Everyone would be so much happier if I just got out of the way."

"I think she intervened because of her faith in you," Margo said, even as she questioned the statement. Lilly called Peter unreasonable, after all. *Hysterical.* "She just wants everything to work out." This had to be true.

"Fuck me!" Peter said, and Margo jumped. "Fuck fuck fuck." He stopped and locked his eyes on to hers. "I'm sorry, Margo. I apologize for being so candid, yet again. But it's a relief to say it out loud."

"I understand." Margo did know what it was like to feel small, knew it like the back of her hand. But Peter had a place in this world, even if he couldn't see it. He was Tarzan, and Lilly was Jane. This was the natural order of things, and if that was muddled, there wasn't much hope for Margo, or anyone else.

55

Eventually, Caca and Lilly returned to the table. The meal ended, and Lilly picked up the check. They said their pleasant goodbyes and Margo rode the bus home in a daze. When she reimagined the night—the past three months—as a series of photographs, the pictures were blurry, double exposed. She couldn't make out a damned thing.

At the Pennsylvania, Margo greeted the night desk staff and took the elevator to her floor. Shuffling down the hall, she noticed a tall figure lurking outside her room, enveloped in a cloud of cigarette smoke. "Slim?" she said, squinting in the dim light. "What are you doing here?"

"Do you have a minute?"

"Of course." Margo hurried to his side. "You must be feeling better. You don't look sick at all." She opened the door.

"False alarm," Slim said, sauntering into the room. "How was your dinner? Breaking bread with the cream of the crop. Don't say I never did anything for you."

Margo offered a strangled kind of smile. For once, she wouldn't have minded a chaperone, someone to help her read between the lines. "It was fine," she said, generously. "Talisman is in hot water, from the sounds of it. It kind of put a damper on the night. In fact—"

Slim wasn't listening at all. "I'm not really sick," he said. "I was expecting a phone call and didn't want to miss it." He dropped a stack of photographs onto the table. "These are the pictures you shot, on Lilly's boat. They're going to use them in *LIFE* magazine."

"They're *what*?" Margo glanced down. Staring back was Lilly in her blue-and-white shift, knees pushed together, feet splayed. Her expression was beguiling, secretive, quietly dangerous, and totally absent its usual bubbly pink effervescence.

"I had other photographs ready to go," Slim said. "But you did an excellent job. So good that I have *two* pieces of news." *LIFE* was also planning to use the photograph she took of Lilly leaping out of Peter's plane, bolts of fabric in her arms. "I've asked the editors to give you the credit. The copyright will belong to you."

"Thank you," Margo whispered, as she continued to examine the images. She was happy, and aghast, and a little uneasy. How would Peter feel about seeing the photos in *LIFE*? "Thank you for the compliment, the chance, all of it. I never imagined this was a possibility. I didn't even think to wish for it."

Slim chortled. "You were too busy looking for a man," he said. "But you're less focused on that now, which has opened a whole new world of possibility. Thank God all that husband-hunting is out the window."

Margo made a face. *Was* it out the window? At first, this didn't seem accurate, but Margo couldn't recall when she'd last agonized over her marriage prospects. She hadn't even second-guessed herself after walking out on Dutch.

"You keep doing things like this..." Slim said, tapping Margo's head. "Someone might mistake you for a professional. You've surprised me, Old Bean. Not only are you developing a perspective, but you've managed to ingratiate yourself in their world. These people trust you, and that is no small feat." He gave Margo a hardy wallop on the back. "If you get any better, people might consider picking you over me. I'll have to sabotage you, of course, but I'm pleased. It's about time you started betting on yourself."

56

FEBRUARY 1963

Slim rarely shot portraits.

"People hire me because I can take someone and put them in a setting," Margo heard him say on her first day of work and approximately one hundred times since. Anyone could do a portrait, and while Slim did not see himself as "anyone," he sometimes made exceptions, such as agreeing to photograph the Rousseaus' daughter, Sandra, for her society debut.

"Not my first choice," Slim grumbled. "Not by a mile. But Lilly promised Julia I would do it. To make it more interesting, I'll let you hold the camera today."

Margo wasn't above portraits, of course. In the wake of the *LIFE* magazine news, she was thrilled to shoot any damned thing and, on the day of the session, woke up feeling jazzed, refreshed, brand spanking new. This shiny attitude carried her all the way through morning, until they entered the Rousseau home.

"Wow, okay," Margo said, stumbling down the hall, looking around as her excitement drained away. The house was oddly familiar, though she'd never been here. It was also inexplicably sad, a place in which nothing could be trusted and everything was suspect.

"Impressed with the digs?" Slim asked, over his shoulder.

"Um. Yes. Sure."

Objectively, the house *was* grand and elegant, a prototypical Mizner Mediterranean with a white stucco exterior, red-tiled roof, wood beams, and dramatic Moorish flair. Yet Margo couldn't shake the sense of a cold wind having rushed through, nor the reverberations of impending doom. She might chalk it up to last month's awkward meal at Ta-boo, but Caca had one of those handy, companionable personalities that smoothed any situation, and he was unlikely to be around anyway.

Perhaps the problem was Julia, who they could hear relentlessly haranguing her daughter about not frosting her hair. Why she so desperately needed highlights, Margo couldn't begin to guess. With her deep chestnut locks and dark, ethereal stare, Sandra Rousseau was objectively beautiful. She looked like the sort of girl who might've escaped a revolution with a suitcase packed full of diamonds, which was exactly the case.

But Margo would have to ignore the foreboding, and stuff it down, far as it'd go. They were there to work, and she was a professional, according to Slim. Or was it that she could be mistaken for a professional? No matter. Today he'd put her in charge, and soon, Margo's name would be in *LIFE*. It was one of the best things that'd ever happened to her, even if the victory didn't feel cleanly won.

Slim applauded Margo for doing her job, but if she was supposed to present the Pulitzers as they saw themselves, then she'd failed—with Peter at least. Readers would see a handsome, adoring man supporting his wife, while the man saw something else. How could one photograph embody two ideas that lived so many miles apart?

"None of this works," Slim said, sidling up to Margo, who was ruminating beside the ballroom's stone fireplace. *Stop think-*

ing about the Pulitzers, Margo reminded herself, touching the Leica, which hung from her neck. *You're the photographer today.*

"I had the same thought," she said, reorienting herself. "We've cleared out multiple rooms, brought everything in here, but it's still not enough."

"Why don't you poke around? See if you can find something else? Maybe a musical instrument or two. A nod to the girl's burgeoning career."

Sandra Rousseau was the music critic for the *Palm Beach Daily News*, though most likely because of her connections as opposed to any actual ability. But it was worth a shot, and Margo did recall Lilly saying that Caca played the maracas and something called a *thumb piano*.

"I'll see what I can find," Margo said, and went off to search.

Treading gently down the echoing hall, Margo peeked into one room, and the next. She didn't spy a viable piece of furniture, or photographic knickknack, not a single object to bring back to Slim. In a derelict, table-less dining room at the end of the hall, dark squares on the walls marked where art once hung. The windows were bare, the curtains pulled from their rods. What happened to all their stuff? Why was it gone?

Margo took in a sharp breath as the facts slammed together. Her first instincts were spot-on. She *had* recognized the home, because it looked like hers, right before they'd lost it for good. The rumors must've been true. The Talisman Sugar Corporation was going belly-up. Instead of fat city like Lilly promised, their goose was cooked.

"I'll be damned," Margo said as a figure appeared in the doorway, enveloped in a musky cloud of perfume. It was Julia Rousseau. "Oh, hi!" Margo blushed hard, as though she'd been caught red-handed, not that there was anything to steal. The most valuable object around was the camera dangling from her neck. "Slim sent me to find a musical instrument. We thought it might be fun for Sandra to pose with one? Do you know of any we could use?"

Julia pursed her lips, as if weighing whether Margo was worthy of the effort of more words. After taking her in with one long, cutting glare, she finally spoke. "Try the pool house," she said. Then she vanished like a ghost.

———

The door to the pool house was wide open. Margo tiptoed inside and scanned the room, from the unmade bed to the discarded Cuban guayabera and crumpled blue Lilly on the floor. Something slowly dawned on her, and Margo didn't like the weight of it. She rattled her head.

As she took another step, Margo heard the thump of water being cut off. She looked at the floor again. Without knowing why, she lifted the camera and snapped a picture of the shucked-off clothes.

A woman laughed. "I swear! You're the only person in the world who can make a shower *dirty*!" she said. It was Lilly Pulitzer's voice.

Margo froze. She was a fly trapped in amber, feet stuck, wings unable to flap. Her mind thought *leave!* but her body seemed intent on seeing this through.

Eventually, inevitably, the bathroom door opened. Lilly appeared in the doorway, wearing only a towel. Caca stood behind her, naked all the way down.

"Margo! What in the hell are you doing?" Lilly said, and all time seemed to stop. Margo would only partially remember what happened next.

She must've turned. She must've raced back to the main house, and thrust the Leica into Slim's hands. "For the love of Christ," he barked. "What the hell are you doing?" It was the same question Lilly had asked.

"I have to go," Margo said. She was hyperventilating and

could barely get the words out. "I'm not feeling well." She heard Lilly's voice in the near distance, coming from somewhere inside the house. "I have to go," she repeated. "Now. I'm about to be sick."

"Then, go," Slim said, throwing out an arm. "Get out of here. I don't have the patience for histrionics today."

Margo didn't need to be told twice. "I'm sorry," she whimpered, and grabbed her purse. With her lips clamped and stomach clutched, Margo sprinted outside, down the road, and all the way to the bus stop.

57

The next day, Margo woke up from a nap to the sound of knocking. Groggy and fuzzy-headed, she opened her door, without checking first.

"You're welcome for saving your hide," Lilly said, sweeping in, her scent so much like Peter's that Margo thought she was still asleep. Why had this been such a surprise? Peter and Lilly lived together. They smoked the same cigarettes. They were husband and wife. "Slim was absolutely livid that you took off like that." Lilly plopped down on the bed and pulled out a cigarette. "I took the fall. Told him that we got into an argument, and it was entirely my fault."

"It *was* your fault," Margo pointed out. She pictured the guayabera and the Lilly on the floor and wondered what Slim would make of the image once he developed it. Margo didn't know what to make of it now, or why she'd taken it in the first place. Had she sensed, deep down, what she was about to witness? Had she wanted to document it, to convince herself that it was true?

"Well, I suppose you want to give your opinion or something," Lilly said, lighting up.

Although she'd envisioned many conversations she might have with Lilly, covering dozens of topics, Margo never planned for this. *Caca Rousseau?* It still didn't seem real. *"Why?"* she said at last. "Why would you do that?"

"The real question is why you're bothered by it," she said. "You're not involved. It's not personal."

She was right, of course. It wasn't about Margo, but she loved Lilly, same as everyone who'd crossed her path and, justified or not, felt betrayed. All this time, Lilly pretended to be Jane, blissfully married to Tarzan, yet it was a facade, and the lies only multiplied the more Margo pondered it. Every day, Lilly lied about where she was going, and what she was doing. She lied about being friends with Julia Rousseau, and she lied about small things, too, even in lighthearted articles for the *New York Times*...

"I can't remember attending a charity ball, but I must have been to one once."

"I don't always know what people are talking about."

"I'm dumb when it comes to questions."

The interviewer called Lilly a "fragile, little-girl intellectual" on one line, and "a strapping, thirty-three-year-old Gauguin woman whose major concern is television" on the next. When Margo read the article, it'd gotten under her skin, and now she knew why.

Was Lilly's entire persona an act? Was it a game, a charade, an image to sell? Or was this life in the jet set? Palm Beachers lived like they were constantly setting up for one of Slim's shoots, lugging their possessions and poodles onto the lawn, showing their best angles, waiting for the best light. Slim didn't do portraits and wasn't that the damned truth. Portraits were too honest. They revealed too much. Margo had been chasing a life that wasn't real.

"It doesn't change anything," Lilly said. Another lie. Not that Margo was counting. Not that she could.

"It changes everything," Margo said. "You're a scammer, a swindler, no better than Sandy LaSalle."

Lilly scrunched her forehead. "Sandy who?"

"All Peter wants is to be part of your life. Meanwhile, you ignore him constantly, and are sleeping with somebody else. His business nemesis, no less!" Margo remembered what Lilly said at Ta-boo, how she blamed Peter for "leading that nice gentleman irrevocably astray." Caca was no gentleman, and he was apparently not very nice. And, yes, Margo kissed Peter, but it was only once, and she hadn't been sneaking around.

"Don't worry about Peter," Lilly said. "Rest assured, he's glad to have me out of his hair, occupied by some other man so he doesn't have to do it."

"Peter would love to spend more time with you. He's always going on and on about how proud he is, how you're so remarkable that his biggest concern is he's holding you back."

"My husband *is* dreadfully insecure. He doesn't have the slightest idea who he is, which is why he is currently on to business number three. Building hotels or some such nonsense, who can keep track?" Lilly exhaled, running a cigaretted hand over her bouffant. "Listen, sweetie, if you're looking to get involved on the charity scene, there are far worthier causes than white-gloving Peter Pulitzer's ego. He *wants* to be the person you think he is," she said, and pulled on her cigarette. "But sadly, he is not."

"What person is that?" Margo asked.

Lilly blew out a long stream of smoke. "The guidepost, the rock, the man of unwavering support. It's a noble aim but he's too easily threatened. That's why he treats me like a flighty young girl and my company like a hobby I'll tire of soon."

"Peter's been behind you since the beginning," Margo said.

"That's what I've seen personally, and it's the story everyone tells—including you! He's the one who insisted you sell dresses in the first place. Remember? You asked him if you could hang a few in the shop, and he told you to make eighty." And Lilly told *him* he was out of his mind. Margo knew the legend by heart.

"Don't give him credit for my hard work," Lilly said, nostrils flaring.

"I'm not—"

"I built that business, and he only encouraged me because he didn't think it'd amount to anything," Lilly said. "Now I'm a raging success and he halfway pretends Lilly Pulitzer Incorporated doesn't exist. He doesn't even bother to attend board meetings. With Laura back and forth between here and New York, he makes it impossible to have a quorum. I swear he'd sabotage the whole deal if he could get away with it."

"Even if that is true," Margo said, but couldn't see how it was, "how does taking up with Caca Rousseau fix it?"

"What's there to fix? I'm enjoying myself with a man who understands me. As opposed to Peter, he's great fun, and his ego is intact. Also, darling..." Lilly tilted her head and frowned. "It sounds very silly when you call him 'Caca.' That's for those close to him."

"Fine. *Enrique.* What about Julia? I thought you were friends, but you're lying to her, every day." Although, Julia *had* told Margo to go to the pool house. Was it possible she knew, and wanted to let someone else in on the secret?

"Golly. I didn't realize you had such an affinity for Julia Rousseau."

"I don't! I just fail to see the point." Margo stomped across the room and threw open the window. All that smoke was giving her a headache. "Why sneak around? If Peter is so terrible, and you'd rather be with Ca—with *Enrique*—then be with him and let Peter and Julia off their hooks."

"Are you suggesting I divorce?" Lilly said in mock horror.

"Why not? Everyone else around here does!"

At first, the ubiquity of divorce in Palm Beach confounded Margo, but after two years of working for Slim, she now understood. It's not that the jet-setters wanted to divorce more often than their lower-class counterparts, it's that they *could*. Divorce was a luxury item. Lilly and those like her could cut the cord and give up nothing in the process—not a dime, not an iota of social standing. They had their own bank accounts, their own lives, and weren't forced to ride out unhappy marriages, white-knuckling it to the bitter end.

"Oh, precious Margo," Lilly said with a long cackle. "Telling me to divorce? You must recognize how self-serving that sounds. Don't make that face. I've seen the way you look at Pete, all starry-eyed and gaga."

"That's how everyone looks at him!"

Lilly laughed again, but this time in her genuine, full-bodied way. "You've got me there. I have always enjoyed your sense of humor," she said, and Margo ached, recalling how good it'd felt to view Lilly as a friend. "You have a crush on Peter. It's obvious. And who could blame you? The man's a hunk, but there is no scenario in which you two end up together."

"I never imagined that," Margo swore, even as her mind faltered, doubling back to check whether this was true. She liked Peter, she respected Peter, and maybe she had developed a crush. But as much as she'd fallen for him, Margo had also fallen for Lilly, drawn in by her panache and humor and light, seduced by her world and all that came with it. Bohemia and bare feet and spraying champagne on the floor to do the twist. Lilly with a monkey on her shoulder, and everyone talking about how Peter would get eaten by a shark. Would he be the same person, if he were with somebody else?

"I hate to burst your bubble," Lilly said, "but I don't want to get divorced, and neither does Peter. So you'll have to put that dream to rest." She ground her cigarette into the ashtray by the bed and stood. "I see you remain unassuaged. So what are you going to do about it? Make a big fuss, pull off the veil? I assure you that will harm you far more than me."

Lilly was right. Margo couldn't tell anyone what she'd seen, not even Slim. At the very least, he'd scream at her for not blending in. At worst, he'd fire her or call *LIFE* and tell them the copyrights were his.

"Far as I can tell, you have two choices," Lilly said, one hand on the door. "Nothing's really changed for you, and you can carry on, same as before. If that's too much, if you don't care about Slim or your job, then leave. Go back to California and let the rest of us live our lives."

58

Margo arrived at the party in a bad mood. The theme was "baby," and guests were wobbling around in diapers and one-sies, gnawing on teething rings. She hated everything about it, and since this was a reconnaissance mission for Slim, Margo would have to endure it alone.

The party's hosts were new to Palm Beach, having given up on Acapulco (too many reminders of poverty and potential revolution) and Jamaica (too much "culture") before. Slim hoped to add the couple to his client list and dispatched Margo to observe them in their natural setting.

"See who they want to be," Slim said, "and how they want to appear to the world." Like infants, apparently. The wife spent the party in the back of a baby carriage, sucking on a red lollipop while a maid wheeled her from guest to guest.

The whole island was losing its damned mind, and for the first time, Margo couldn't wait for the season to end. She'd finally accomplished something and now was forced to smile and pretend all was swell. Lilly said it herself. *If you don't care about Slim or your job, then leave.* Unfortunately, Margo cared about both, and her recent success seemed precarious, hanging by the finest of wires.

Margo meandered through the party, grumpier with each step. It was all the same players, and all the same talk, the only difference the baby bottles in their hands, and the diapers on their rears. The hosts wanted to be part of the Palm Beach set, which meant they'd ask Slim to shoot them, eventually. Margo didn't need to stick around.

As she turned back to the house, Margo spotted Peter Pulitzer headed her way. He was tanned and glossy as ever, like he could summon the sun to shine at his command.

"Margo?" he said, flipping up his aviators. Margo's heart jumped. "What are you doing here? Lured by the promise of grown adults spitting up and crapping their pants?"

"Scoping it out for Slim," Margo said as he tramped across the grass toward her, destroying a flower bed in the process. The closer he got, the breathier and hotter she became. *Act normal. Act like you don't know about Caca Rousseau's belly paunch, or the length of his member.* "What's your excuse? This isn't your scene."

"It's certainly not," he said. "I thought I'd had an aneurysm when I first read the invitation. Speaking of babies. You didn't happen to see Jim Kimberly around?"

"Ew. No," Margo blurted. The notion of Jim Kimberly in a diaper was revolting.

"My sentiment exactly," Peter said with a chuckle. "Alas, he's why I'm here. The bastard owes me money and has been avoiding me for weeks. Want to help me track him down? I would love the company. That is, if you weren't leaving?"

Margo considered this for a second before deciding to stay, lest news of her early departure wind its way back to Slim. It was the excuse she gave herself, in any case. "Um, sure," she said, after a beat. "Why the hell not?"

⌒

Jim Kimberly owed Peter twenty-five hundred clams.

Together they owned *Rum Runner*, the yellow-hulled, thirty-one-foot runabout that Peter had taken to the Ocean Club opening. Last month, they'd entered it into the Miami-Nassau powerboat race, and covered the 160-mile course in four hours, fifty-four minutes, which to Margo seemed like too much time on a boat. Regardless, they won, and Jim hadn't given Peter his share of their earnings. It's not that he cared about the actual dollars and cents, Peter simply didn't want *his* money to end up in the hands of Jim's next ex-wife.

"I don't see him anywhere," Margo said, after they circled the party three times. Being with Peter was so easy, she'd almost forgotten what'd happened, and what she knew.

"This is classic Jim Kimberly," Peter said. "He's always late so people can herald his arrival. Why don't we wait it out by the lake?"

"I should probably get going," Margo began, but Peter had already swiped two cocktail-filled baby bottles from the bar. He motioned for Margo to follow, and instead of heeding her better sense, she trailed Peter down the grassy slope toward the dock. He plunked onto the end and reached up for Margo's hand, guiding her down beside him.

"I'm not drinking out of a damned nipple," he said and inspected the bottles. After unscrewing both, he pitched the tops into the lake.

"What is this?" Margo asked, sniffing the thick liquid.

"Pink squirrel. It's Crème de Noyaux, white crème de cacao, and cream."

Margo took a sip. The taste was cool and almondy, like melted ice cream. It reminded her of the afternoon they spent wandering the streets of Key West exactly one year ago.

"Huh. Weird." Peter squinted out across the water. "These

people have a dock but no boat." Margo nodded obligatorily, figuring this was some kind of insult. "You're probably curious about where Lilly is today," he said, and Margo's nerves instantly spiked.

"Not especially," she croaked.

"She claims to be in New York, meeting with a department store." He chugged his squirrel. "But I swear she's met with all of them."

"There are always more dresses to ship!" Margo sang.

"The CEO does not need to be handwriting orders with ongoing customers."

"Oh," Margo said.

Peter was quiet for several minutes, staring at the boatless water in front of them, swinging his legs. Occasionally, he'd hit the post with the back of his foot, and Margo would jump, then be compelled to guzzle the pink, goopy liquid to steady herself.

"I'm so tired of it all," Peter said at last. "So tired of living this life. *Acting* this life. It's all such a sham."

"Peter, let's not—"

He looked at her. "Did you know that people call us Tarzan and Jane?"

Margo gulped. "Do they? How strange."

"Sometimes I want to run away," he continued. "I doubt Lilly would notice, or care. Unfortunately, this is the life I'm roped into, and I can't just *split*. What excuse would I have?"

Margo threw her gaze toward Peter. Lilly said that neither of them wanted a divorce, but why? They weren't happy, and didn't seem prepared to fix things. Weren't they the perfect candidates? "Are you *looking* for an excuse?" Margo asked, as her pulse did a quickstep.

"Yes. No." Peter exhaled. "Who the hell knows? Why do I keep telling you this stuff? Forget I said anything?" He gave a smile so weak his eyes hardly crinkled.

"Perhaps you should talk to Lilly?" Margo said, scratching the back of her neck. "Some of your problems might be solved if you spent more time together. Forgive me for chiming in, but..."

"Talking would be great if either of us remembered how. I can't recall the last time we had a conversation, or even looked at each other, much less touched."

Margo shivered at the word *touch*. "But it can't hurt to try..." she said, half-heartedly.

"All the talking in the world isn't going to help," he ranted on. "Lilly is incapable of saying the word *problem* and I'm 90 percent sure she's having an affair. I suppose it was inevitable since she considers me such a dud of a husband."

Margo made a choking sound, and Peter whipped in her direction.

"What was that?" he said. "Are you okay? You're breaking out into hives."

"What? No, I'm not." Margo's skin was so itchy she could've screamed. "First of all, from what I can tell, you're a great husband." Lilly said otherwise, but Margo chose to believe her own two eyes. "You're thoughtful, and supportive. How many men would wander around Key West while their wife browsed fabrics?"

"I enjoyed doing it," he said, sadly.

"You love Lilly, just as she loves you. You make each other better, and you're meant to be together. I'm *positive* she'd never want a divorce."

Peter jolted, and a shadow passed over his face. "Who said anything about divorce?" he said and studied Margo, with great intensity. She babbled some excuse about her tendency toward dumb assumptions, flailing as she tried to cover her tracks. "What's going on, Margo?" he pressed. "What's up?"

"Nothing's up! I swear!"

"Lilly mentioned an incident between the two of you. A run-in at Julia Rousseau's."

"Julia's?" Margo squawked. "Well, that's rich!"

"She didn't provide many details. I only know because she came home flustered, in an extremely un-Lilly-like state. Margooooooo," Peter said, drawing out her name. "What have you seen? What do you know? Please. If you respect me at all, I'm begging you. Spill it. Tell me the truth. You're one of the few people in this world I trust."

Margo was defeated, thoroughly backed into a corner. She should've been more circumspect, but it was too late. Peter had seen through the cracks, and she refused to add to the lies. "You're right," Margo said. "Lilly's having an affair. I'm sorry to be the one to tell you."

"I knew it," Peter said. "Who is it? Who is fucking my wife?"

The word *fuck* jarred Margo, and giving Caca's name wasn't likely to engender a better response. But Peter wanted to live in the real world, did he not? There was no going back, and so Margo braced herself, and spoke the secret out loud. *"Enrique Rousseau,"* she said.

"What. The. Fuck." Peter launched himself onto his feet. "She's sleeping with Caca Rousseau? Of all the goddamned people in Palm Beach. In the world! No wonder she was so adamant about making Talisman work. No wonder she suggested he manage the Howard Johnson's I'm building on Miami Beach."

Margo blinked. "Wow," she said. "That's not very nice. Congratulations on the hotel, though!"

Peter glared at her with a wrath so violent Margo was shocked she didn't burst into flames.

"I'm sure it's just a fling," she added hastily. "A way to pass time." It was possible Margo was making this worse. "He can't mean that much to her. Lilly told me she loves you and doesn't want a divorce. She was very clear on this."

Peter's ears reddened, and his eyes bulged. She'd been wrong to think he was mad before. "You spoke to Lilly about our *marriage?*" he boomed. "Why, in God's name, would you do that?"

"I didn't mean to. It just came up. Because of—" Margo stopped. She'd lost control of this conversation and needed to reel it back in. While she'd made her mistakes, Margo wasn't the bad guy here. "Let me get this straight," she said as she stood. "You're not upset about the affair, but the fact Lilly and I discussed your marriage?"

"I'm upset about both!"

"Meanwhile, you've blabbed to me about your marriage on multiple occasions."

"That's different," Peter snapped. "Jesus Christ. What is wrong with you? Hasn't anyone ever taught you to mind your own business?"

If Margo weren't so humiliated, she might've laughed. She'd expected sorrow from Peter, heartbreak, and even harbored the distant fantasy he'd thank her for exposing the lies. But none of this was playing out how she could've predicted. "Please stop shouting at me," she said. "I'm not the villain and never wanted to be involved with any of this."

"Then, why did you get involved?" Peter had the gall to ask.

"You asked me to tell you the truth," she reminded him. "To *spill it.* And so I did. I can see it was a mistake. Don't worry, I'll happily stay out of your business. Good luck to you both."

Margo stomped back up the hill, incensed, and with her little soul stinging. Sure, Peter had spun a good story about himself— lover of the real world, desirer of truth—but Lilly was right. He was the same as every other man in Palm Beach. Bored. Insecure. Confused. Unwilling to stand near anyone else's sun.

Slim built his career on helping the Beautiful People maintain their charade, and Margo was furious to realize she'd signed up for the same fate. Slim had known what he was getting into and was happy to play along, using a camera to keep his distance. Meanwhile, like a dope, Margo bought the whole enchilada. She'd gotten too close, just as Rita worried she might.

Now Margo was stuck, with no way to start over. She liked photography, was even halfway skilled at it, but the only reason LIFE wanted to publish her images was because she'd worked with the best. Slim taught her about aperture and shutter speed, but also to believe in fairy tales. He taught her how to harness the magic of Lilly and Peter and sell it to the rest of the world.

59

"Hello, Slim. Hi," Margo said, rushing up to the entrance of a new condo complex on Ocean Avenue. "I'm sorry I'm late. The bus stop was farther than I thought."

The stop was one block away and the real story was that Margo almost hadn't come. For a month, she'd been biding her time, calculating her next move, to precisely no success. It'd been easy enough to fake it around golfers and vacationing princes and Guests and Toppings, but today they were shooting Lilly's latest collection. While Lilly wasn't scheduled to be there—*too busy*, with what, Margo didn't inquire—she'd asked her closest friends to model the clothes.

Margo dreaded seeing these women, especially Wendy, and spent so much time hemming and hawing that she'd missed the bus that'd get her there on time. A late-breaking illness might be in order, she decided, and for a minute, Margo felt better. Then she remembered the facts of her life. If she truly wanted to be a photographer, she'd need Slim on her side. He could make or break her with one phone call. The same could be said for so many people in Palm Beach.

And so, Margo pulled herself together, and threw on one of

her only clean pieces of clothing—a floor-length, pink-and-white Lilly she'd never worn, one of four she'd bought. Sadness swept over Margo as she slipped into it. Lillys really were ingenious, and the absolute easiest way to dress.

After catching the late bus, Margo arrived fifteen minutes past due, with a face crying out for makeup and hair pinned atop her head in a manner best described as "deflated mushroom." Not even a works-for-every-woman Lilly could improve her ghastly state, and when Slim gave her a once-over, he made a face like he'd detected a whiff of something foul. "So glad you were able to join us," he said. That he made no direct assault on Margo's appearance meant it was worse than she'd thought. "Let's get to work."

Margo trailed Slim through the shiny, marbled lobby and back outside, to where a group of twelve women in Lillys and a handful of children in Minnies gathered around a fountain. In the middle of the water was a white stucco planter overflowing with ferns and palms, as though the fountain had its own island.

Slim directed the women into position. Some waded, while others stood on the planter's low, rounded edge, gossiping, half listening to Slim. Were any of them thinking about Lilly and Caca? Margo wondered. Did any of them know?

"Ugh, Palm Beach is so much more crowded lately," someone complained, the same old routine. "Brutally nouveau. I can barely stand it." The woman's name was Porter Malone, and from what Margo had gleaned, she spent most of her time trying to climb ladders while pushing other people down.

"I feel sorry for her," Wendy once said. "It must be difficult to always be the least attractive and least interesting person in the room." All of it, par for the course.

"Palm Beach is crowded because of the tourists," another woman said. "You can thank the Kennedys for that."

"Honestly, I hope he doesn't have a second term."

"Don't we all. I've had enough of that family. Jackie included."

In an unexpected turn of events, Wendy wasn't gossiping. She was off to the side, teaching three others how to do the surf. "Just stand in one place and pretend you're on a surfboard and losing your balance. Sort of like this." She flailed her arms.

"Even a man could do that," one woman noted.

"Can we save the dance instruction for *after* the shoot?" Slim griped.

"What's wrong, Slimbo? You don't care for my moves?" Wendy said, swinging her hips, waving her arms. He shot her a hard look. "Fine. I hate people in the daytime. Where do you want me?"

Slim placed her on the planter, seated off-center, to the right. With her deep tan, brilliant white smile, and canary yellow dress, Wendy was in danger of becoming the main subject in what was intended to be a group shot.

He turned to a different woman. "You, over there," he said, gesturing with a freshly lit cigarette. "And you—" Someone else. "Go here." After situating everyone, Slim inspected the scene. "What are your thoughts, Miss Hightower?" he asked.

Margo stepped up beside him, relieved he'd asked about setup, instead of handing her the camera. When it came to this group, her perspective was off, her point of view inexorably skewed.

"The colors are terrific, of course," she said. "Quintessential Lilly Pulitzer." With the soft pinks and yellows and light greenish blues, the tableau was sweet like a candy store, but the composition didn't jive. "Maybe we should group the yellows together?" Margo suggested. "Like the center of a flower? Then arrange the other colors out from there?" She checked Slim for a reaction, and he told her to go ahead.

First, Margo moved a tall blonde to the middle—her dress

was the boldest, with petals of turquoise, yellow, and raspberry pink—then layered in the others, one by one. Taking inspiration from Wendy's hot pink headscarf, Margo snagged somebody's similarly colored sunhat from a table and asked a girl on the end to wear it. The shot was getting close but wasn't there yet.

"I think *more* pink might be in order," Margo said, consulting Slim. "Like maybe in the middle? By those two." She made a circle in the air, indicating the open spot between the tall blonde in the center and a brunette in light yellow. "I wonder if we could find another pink accessory?"

"That isn't what this shot needs," Slim said.

Margo slid him a look. She couldn't remember the last time he contradicted one of her suggestions. "I do think there's a hole," she said, between her teeth. "And this is Lilly Pulitzer, so the solution should be *more pink*."

Slim turned toward her and raised his brows with a devilish flair. "I agree. Which is why you're going to be in the shot."

"Slim!" Margo gasped. "No! I can't—" Slim gave her a small shove. "Lilly wanted her friends in the shoot."

"Surely you qualify," Slim said, and Margo couldn't tell whether he was being truthful or sly. "And you are perfectly attired. Stop wasting my time and *go*."

Margo inhaled. Smiling blankly into the crowd, she lifted the hem of her dress and put one foot and then a second into the water. She slogged forward, feeling all the pairs of eyes on her, and dying a thousand deaths inside.

"Get in the planter!" Slim called out, and Wendy extended a hand to help her up.

"Someone's moving to higher ground," she said.

"Further back!" Slim said as ferns crunched beneath Margo's feet. "Further! Stand on the tree roots, so you don't seem so short." Finally, he told her to stop. Margo was so removed from the group that she questioned whether she was still in the frame. "Perfect. Wow. You're sort of hidden away, like a secret," he said. "I love it."

Wendy sniggered. "Oh, Slimbo, you really are the genius everyone says you are."

"Can we get a smile back there, Margo?" Slim called out. "This isn't so bad. Aren't you excited to be in the shot? It's you and the rest of Palm Beach young society, exactly where you've always wanted to be."

—

As Slim packed up, and the women filtered away, Margo ducked into the empty lobby, taking a minute to enjoy the air-conditioning and the cool marble against her feet. The day was over, and Margo had managed not to die of shame or heatstroke. She'd become quite deft at pulling back from the brink of ignominy. What a shame she couldn't put this on a CV.

Just as Margo finished applauding herself, a bolt of yellow cracked into view. "Jesus Christ!" she said, jumping back. "Wendy! Hello. I didn't know anyone was here." Damn it all to hell, she'd nearly made it.

"That must've been fun for you," she said. "Gogo Hightower got to be part of the crowd. Lilly would be so proud."

"Yes, yes, I know," Margo said. She was exasperated, pushed to the limit, and whatever sheen of politeness she'd once clung to was now razor-thin. "Lilly loves her projects, her impossible tasks. None more so than me. I suppose her work is finished, and she'll have to find someone new."

"It really is too bad," Wendy clucked. "You've been such an excellent diversion for her—for both of them. Until you blew it up so spectacularly."

"Excuse me?" Margo screwed up her face. "*I* blew it up?"

"Knowing Lilly, she'll count it as a success anyway," Wendy mused. "And I must hand it to Peter. He saw his opportunity and took it. He isn't usually so light on his feet."

"Wendy," Margo said, closing her eyes, and wishing for a spaceship, any preternatural force to swoop in and whisk her away. "I don't have the faintest idea what you're talking about."

"The way Peter flirts with you," Wendy said. "Or flirted, I guess. Lilly found it the most hilarious thing on earth. You were a good sport, though. Entertaining it, playing along, even though he was only ever trying to get Lilly's attention."

Margo crossed her arms. "Are you implying that Peter's been using me as a pawn?" she said, glaring, unwilling to let Wendy get to her in this way. Peter wasn't the exact man Margo thought, but whatever did or did not happen between them had been about more than Lilly.

"You've been a pawn for both," Wendy said, doubling down. "Peter got his wife to glance in his direction for once, and Lilly found a project *and* a decent way to deflect suspicion when people started questioning her closeness with Rousseau. *If you think that's flirting, you should see how Peter acts around Slim's assistant!*"

"Why would she bother?" Margo wondered out loud as Dutch's handsome mug popped into her head. Lilly had worked hard to push them together. Was that part of her schemes, too?

"Don't kid yourself," Wendy said. "Even Lilly Pulitzer cares what other people think. And look at you! You got... So. Much. Attention. From the spectacular Pulitzers! If you weren't so enraged by Lilly's extracurricular activities, you could've kept it going."

"Her *cheating*, you mean?"

Wendy tossed her eyes. "I never took you for a prude," she said. "Make no mistake. Enrique Rousseau is the best thing that's ever happened to Lilly. He shares her passion, her zest for life. Peter has none of that. So, what does a gal do if she needs an essential item and is fresh out of stock? She acquires it somewhere else. The arrangement worked. Everyone was happy, blissfully following the script, until you decided to in-volve yourself."

"I question the 'everyone' part," Margo said. "Peter was—*is*—extremely unhappy. And you're not going to put this on me. He asked for the truth, and I gave it. No one can blame me for what came next."

"Can't they?" Wendy said, crossing her arms to match Margo's.

"Peter already suspected an affair. My information changed nothing."

"Other than Peter is filing for divorce," Wendy said.

Margo's stomach crashed to the ground. "He is?" she said and, for a second, flirted with hope. Maybe Peter really was something like the man she'd come to adore. Maybe he'd fi-nally live the life he wanted.

"It won't be a workaday divorce," Wendy added. "He's plan-ning an obliteration. You may think that man is all charm and charisma and toothy grins, but remember where he works. *How* he works. Peter Pulitzer likes to get down in the mud. Thanks to your untimely, baffling intervention, he's vowed to ruin Lilly. All because you couldn't keep your mouth shut."

"That's absurd!" Margo cried. "First of all, I'm not the one who had an affair. And this is Lilly Pulitzer. She can't be ru-ined. Peter knows that better than anyone." Lilly was a mogul, a figurehead, the most successful person Margo had ever known. How could Peter, or anyone, erase all of that?

"Don't be so sure. He's threatened to hire every lawyer in the book," Wendy said, "to guarantee that Lilly will have to give back the Pulitzer name. If Peter gets his way, every morning, tens of thousands of women will wake up, and put on dresses that bear the signature of a person who doesn't exist."

"That's not going to happen," Margo said, the panic building in her chest. "No judge would agree to it!" Not that a court-room verdict would matter in the end. A long-drawn-out fight would kill the name, either way, especially if a woman was always "stuck" in a marriage, as Peter said so long ago.

"The courts always favor the men." Wendy's eyes glistened as she spoke. Her love for Lilly was at once laid bare, and it socked Margo in the gut. The affair was wrong, but Lilly did not deserve to lose it all. "Goodbye to Lilly Pulitzer," Wendy said. "Goodbye to her entire life."

"It's not her entire life," Margo insisted. "Lilly was someone else before she got married, for more than twenty years!"

"Oh, really? Do tell, Margo, what's her maiden name?" Wendy waited while Margo searched the furthest recesses of her brain, if the information had been there in the first place. Lilly's mother was Lillian Phipps, but Phipps was *her* husband's name. "It's McKim," Wendy said at last. "Ever heard of her? I didn't think so."

She's so much more than that, Margo was desperate to say, but she wasn't going to tussle over the importance of surnames with a Vanderbilt. "I'm sorry," she said instead. "But this didn't have to happen. Peter and Lilly are two of the most dynamic, incredible people on earth. They're beautiful and brilliant and universally beloved. Why lie? Why sneak around? Why search for something they didn't need? If they were honest with each other, completely up-front, they could've avoided all this. Instead, they chose to cheat and lie and pretend to want one thing when really they wanted another."

"Please," Wendy scoffed. "Spare me the moral high ground. You're always up-front, is that right? You agreed to work for Slim because you just *love* photography?"

"I do like photography," Margo snipped. "My pictures are going to be in *LIFE.*"

Wendy wasn't interested. "You can't blame people for going after what they want," she said. "Isn't that what you've been doing all this time?"

Margo opened her mouth, then snapped it shut. She studied Wendy, and slowly, the anger that'd been balled up inside of her started to unravel. "You know what?" she said, astonished by this new sensation. "I can't believe I'm saying this, but you're right."

Wendy pulled her chin into her neck. "Huh?"

"Thank you," Margo said. "Until this moment, I didn't appreciate that I actually *like* you. I respect you, too. You're the only person around here who isn't full of shit."

Wendy ogled her, and Margo smiled, her heart and mind freer than they'd ever been. In this open space an idea sparked, the formation of a plan. It couldn't happen right away, but Margo knew exactly what she needed to do next.

60

MARCH 1963

The bell jangled as Margo walked into the shop. A woman behind the counter looked up, peering over the top of cat-eyed specs.

"Hello, good afternoon," Margo said. "How are you? It's my first time here." This was a habit of hers, announcing her history with a place as soon as she entered it, lest she encroach upon any more members-only territory. Of course, Margo didn't anticipate any problems today. This wasn't Au Bon Goût but a secondhand shop. "I heard about your store from a friend."

"Buying or selling?" the woman asked, rising from her stool.

Margo set her suitcase on the floor and flopped a Gristedes bag onto the counter. "I'd like to sell these," she said, and pulled out five Lillys, every Lilly she'd ever owned.

The woman's eyes bugged as she took in the prints, from Margo's first (the butterflies) to the pink-and-white swirl she'd worn two weeks ago. She fingered the fabrics, doing little to suppress her gasps. "I've never heard of anyone reselling a Lilly," she said. "You do realize her shop is a few blocks away?"

"Yes. That's where I bought them." And was given one, Margo thought with a pang. For all her talk of mistakes and giggles and happenstance, Lilly knew what she was doing. They were great dresses, and Margo would miss them.

"She'll hear about this," the woman warned. "She'll know exactly where they came from."

"That's okay," Margo said. "I need the money." And she couldn't worry about what Palm Beachers thought of her anymore.

The woman clucked and shook her head. *It's your funeral*, her face seemed to say. "These are in excellent condition." She examined each one, turning them inside out, checking labels and zippers and seams. "I'll give you seventy-five dollars for all five."

It was a steep discount, but Margo didn't want to drag this out, in case the visibly spooked store clerk changed her mind. She agreed to the price, and the woman opened the till, paying her out in fives.

"Thank you," Margo said, cramming the bills into her purse. "Have a nice day." She grabbed her suitcase and hustled out of the shop.

When the door clapped shut, Margo exhaled. She'd done it. She'd made her last stop and would escape Palm Beach without further accusations of interfering, or ruining lives. Aside from her conversation with Wendy, there'd been no rumors of a pending divorce, yet the anticipation was pushing Margo to the brink. Finally, she could let it go.

"Hello, Margo. Going somewhere?"

Margo spun around, her confidence faltering for the first time since deciding to leave. "Rita," she said. "What are you doing here?" In her little white shorts, snug red top, and cropped, stylish hair, Rita resembled a high-cheeked Parisian doll.

"Slim told me you'd quit," she said, "but I had to see it for myself. I went to find you at the Pennsylvania and rolled up just in time to see you boarding a bus headed for town."

"You followed me? That's so sweet," Margo said, and Rita put up a hand. She wasn't here for a chat.

"So, you're doing it," she said. "You're really leaving."

Margo bowed her head, a confirmation. The latest issue of *LIFE* magazine was newly out, and her name was in print. With the beginnings of what some might consider a portfolio in hand, Margo acted on what she'd been planning for weeks. Last night, as they drove home from the Breakers, she told Slim it was her last shoot.

"I won't be talked out of it," Margo said, though he hadn't tried. "I've bought a bus ticket to New York, departing tomorrow afternoon. I hate to miss Marbella next month, and every trip after that, but this is for the best."

Instead of screaming his head off, Slim remained uncharacteristically silent. He barely acknowledged when Margo got out of the car. Whether this painted the interaction in a better or worse light, she hadn't decided.

"You weren't going to tell me personally?" Rita said. "I'm hurt." She smiled as she spoke, and Margo didn't know how to take it.

"I really wanted to, but thought if I had to face you, I'd chicken out. A very reasonable assumption, as it happens," she added in a mumble.

"No. No." Rita slapped the air. "You're doing the right thing. And listen, I get it, you're sick of Slim's shit. Who wouldn't be?"

"It's not about Slim. It's about what he shoots," Margo said. "He's good at what he does—the very best, in fact—but I can't stand the front, the facade. I want to shoot things that are real."

"To be fair, it *is* pretty 'real' to openly telegraph how you see yourself, how you want to be seen by the world," Rita said. "Jim Kimberly, for instance, is photographed with cars and yachts but rarely a human. That tells you all you need to know."

"Maybe you have a point," Margo said, and then thought, *Wait. Was* she doing the right thing?

"Did I understand correctly? You're going to try to make it as a photographer?" Rita said.

Margo nodded, sharply, though she was riddled with doubt. How would she find a photographer willing to hire her, or a newspaper, or magazine? Were two measly *LIFE* magazine clippings enough of a résumé? Margo hadn't asked Slim because she feared the answer.

"This is terrible news for me," Rita said. "You know how impossibly jealous Slim gets when he realizes anyone else has talent. I warned him not to let you use the camera. *This girl is different than the others*, I said. He certainly won't make *that* mistake again."

Margo smiled as tears pricked her eyes. She'd chosen to leave, but the notion of a replacement left her weepy.

"Hopefully the next one won't meddle in the lives of the most prominent people in Palm Beach," Rita added with a wink. "Or see clients naked."

"Oh God!" Margo groaned, and Rita snickered.

"Don't worry about it. They've made their beds, and now they'll have to screw other people in them. I'll miss you, kiddo." Never a hugger, Rita patted her arm. "Good luck. Take care of yourself, and I'll see ya around." With that, she popped a stick of Beemans into her mouth, and strolled off.

61

MAY 1963

New York was expensive, even though Margo lived in a dingy bedsit in a dicey part of town and subsisted primarily on crackers, bologna, and gum. In hindsight, maybe the Pennsylvania really *was* Breakers West. Margo wished she'd been more grateful to Slim for covering the cost of her very nice room.

Margo started out in the city with a healthy stash of dough, between years of squirreling away chunks of her salary allotment from Slim plus the seventy-five dollars from selling her Lillys. But getting basic photography work wasn't a snap, and Margo didn't have enough irons or any fires to put them in. After a month with no prospects in sight, she had to enact her backup plan. It took her three days to gin up the guts to dial the phone.

"I was wondering when you'd call." There was no mistaking the glee in Slim's voice. "You want your money, yes?"

"Yes," Margo said. "I'm sorry to bother you. I thought you might just…keep it."

She'd hoped to get by on what she'd banked, and would eventually earn, even if her roommate, Doris, thought abandoning her hard-earned scratch was *certifiably bananas!* But Margo felt like she owed Slim something after quitting without notice, and to compensate for the mess she'd stirred up with the Pulitzers. Alas, it was either this or work with Doris at the diner.

"You thought I'd *keep* the rest of your money?" Slim said. "I told you I was saving it for you. Jesus, what kind of jerk do you take me for? I'm glad you rang. It's your cash, and it would've been a pain in the ass to track you down. I'm happy to sign off on the withdrawal. When can you meet me in Bedford?"

The following Tuesday, Margo walked into the Country Trust Company and spotted Slim with the teller, a cigarette dangling from his mouth. "Here she is!" he called out. "As always, flirting with the very line of what could be considered on time." Slim turned back to the teller and slapped the passbook onto the counter. "I'd like to make a complete withdrawal."

"Yes, sir," the man said and began removing bills from his drawer. Two and a half years of hard work, all of it shoveable into a single envelope. Would it be enough, Margo wondered, to chase this dream of photography without resorting to some other career to get by? Margo wasn't necessarily opposed to flipping grilled cheese, but it seemed like one of those jobs that could trap a person longer than they intended, or forever.

The teller slid the envelope back across the marble countertop. It was thicker than Margo expected. Slim tapped the number written on the outside. "This is the total," he said. "I didn't count it, but tell me if you think you're short."

"*Short?*" Margo gaped, unable to comprehend the amount. "There must be some mistake. It's too much."

"It's what you saved," Slim said. "And that reaction—" he pointed with his cigarette "—is exactly why I never let you do anything. It's why I had so many NOs."

"*So* many. Some people count sheep, but I recite your NOs in my head," Margo said, not entirely joking. *No tennis, no hair appointments, no minibar tabs. No shopping, no dry cleaning, no days off, no boyfriends, no sightseeing, no cameras.* "Puts me right to sleep."

"Very droll." Slim turned toward the exit and Margo scrambled after him.

"I just don't understand how I accumulated this much," she said as Slim threw open the door.

"It's not complicated, Margo. You earned money and didn't spend it, and on top of this, there's the concept of compounding interest. I don't have time to explain it."

Margo never would've contemplated letting Slim keep it if she'd known the total. Whatever mistakes she'd made, they did not add up to *that* much.

"A little advice, though?" Flicking his cigarette into the street, Slim looked back over his shoulder. "You shouldn't walk out of a bank waving around a wad of cash and complaining about how you think it's too much."

Margo crammed the envelope down the front of her blouse, which was hardly subtler.

"I know you consider me a tyrant of the highest order, but I had those rules for a reason," Slim said as he lengthened his stride. "Well, many reasons, but mainly so you wouldn't have to marry some idiot just to get a nest egg. Divorce is no fun. Just ask Lilly and Peter."

"Wait! What?" Margo said, panting, struggling to keep up. Luckily Slim's beaten-up old wagon was ahead, parked beside the village green. "So, they *are* getting divorced?" Margo thought that since she hadn't heard anything, it might've blown over. If they divorced, she'd harbor some guilt, and even now, she wasn't fully prepared to give up on the myth of Lilly and Peter, or Slim's entire world. Margo wanted to open magazines, see Slim's shots, and think, *You were there, and it's mostly a true story.* "Did they say why?" she asked.

"I think you know the answer." Slim unlocked the car and Margo peered through the window at the clutter of discarded notepads and old newspaper circulars in the back. Some things

never changed, she thought, sadly. There were parts of this
job—even Slim's idiosyncrasies—she'd miss. "I have one more
present for you," Slim said, grabbing a box from the passenger
seat. He whomped it onto the roof of the car. "Do you know
what this is?"

"One of your storage boxes?" Margo said.

"Indeed." He flipped it around. Instead of "Gstaad" or "Palm
Beach Golf Club" written on the outside in thick, black print,
it was labeled MARGO. "Your images." He pushed it toward
her. "For your portfolio."

Heart galloping, Margo removed the lid. There weren't
many slides, but she'd only just started using the camera. "Slim,
this is too generous," she said and withdrew an image. PALM
BEACH—ARTS FESTIVAL PROCESSION—MH was
scrawled on top, the date on the bottom. Who was labeling
his photographs these days? "Are you sure?" she said.

"It's your work."

"Sort of. You paid for the film, and to have it processed.
They were taken on your camera."

He smirked. "On my metaphorical back. There are some
good ones in there. My personal favorite is Clothes in Repose.
Or maybe we should rename it Doing the Cuban Salsa?"

Margo's cheeks flamed bright red. "God, that was awful," she
muttered, more embarrassed for herself than for Lilly and Caca.

"Don't beat yourself up about it," Slim said. "Divorce is no
laughing matter, but Lilly is already giggling about how it all
went down. You catching her and Caca bare bottomed, then
exposing the affair to Peter, and ultimately winding up in her
first catalogue, wearing one of her favorite prints."

"I really did prove to be excellent at *blending in*," Margo said,
and Slim snorted. "You're not bothered by any of this?" She
gestured to the box of photos and pictured Lilly laughing off
impending disaster. "Your photos are beautiful, aspirational, but

don't you ever want to tell your subjects to—I don't know—tone it down a notch, so people don't get the wrong idea?"

"I capture people's lives as they want to present them, which means never pointing out the ugliness or forcing them to confront things they don't care to face. I'm a storyteller, not a documentarian, or a therapist, or priest."

"What about truth?" Margo said. "What about the real world? Aren't you concerned about that?"

"I've had enough of the real world to last twelve lifetimes."

"The war. Bombed-out villages. I remember."

"Yes. But also." Slim bit down on his lip, ruminating, deciding whether to carry on. "Do you ever wonder why I don't talk about the rest of my family?" he asked but didn't wait for an answer. "Here's the short version. My father split when I was eight, my brother shot himself a few years ago, and my mother has been in a psychiatric hospital on the Lower East Side for years. If that's the real world, then no-fucking-thanks. I don't care to suffer my brother's fate, and I'll say no more on the topic. It's over, the end."

Margo opened her mouth to protest, to ask how this was possible. What about his boyhood shenanigans and the Huck Finn childhood he was forever yammering on about? Then Margo replayed the words Slim just said, the words he always said. *I'm a storyteller, not a documentarian.* No wonder his clients felt such an affinity. Slim understood them in ways much deeper than anyone suspected.

Though Margo wanted to comment, to express sympathy or ask a question at least, she followed Dolly's advice from all those years ago. *For God's sake, Gogo, know when to shut up.* She studied the box again. "What am I supposed to do with these?" she asked, and Slim rattled his head, startled that she hadn't pestered or pressed.

"Er. Well. That's up to you," he said. "You'll need to purchase a pocket light or something."

"No, I meant—" Margo began, suddenly gummed up. Though she'd quit a month ago, it didn't seem final, not while they still shared a bank account, and hints of Margo lingered in Slim's workroom, and in rolls of undeveloped film. "I meant, where do I go from here?" she said. Margo lost her tether and was about to float out to sea. She couldn't have stayed with Slim, but that didn't mean she'd been ready to go.

Slim leveled his gaze on hers. "Margo. You will figure this out. Despite your occasional…lapses in judgment…you know what you're doing as a photographer and in life. Thanks to my tireless efforts and training, of course."

Margo chewed on this. She had Slim's faith, if nothing else. Could she really do this on her own? There was only one way to find out.

"Thank you, Slim," she said. "Thanks for all you've done for me."

"It was my absolute pleasure."

"Wait!" Margo chirped, as Slim went to get into his car. "What about my silverware set?"

Slim rolled his eyes. "It's back at the house. Safe and sound. The minute you're ready to host a dinner party for twelve, give me a jingle, and I'll make a personal delivery." He spoke in a teasing tone, but Margo truly believed that, if asked, he'd bring the silver all the way to her front door.

"When I first started working for you," Margo said, squinting against the morning sun, "you told me I'd love you and I'd hate you, but these would balance in the end. You were wrong." She offered a watery smile. "My feelings very much favor one side."

Slim looked away. "Margo Hightower, my work here is done, and so is yours. You have the money. You have all the tools that you need." He took in a deep, quivery inhale. "Now, get out there and do something with yourself. And don't sully my good name."

EPILOGUE

PALM BEACH / JULY 1965

The taxi whisked Margo through the white brick columns flanking the Palm Bay Club entrance, then along a curved road lined with palms. After passing a parking lot packed with Ferraris and Fleetwoods, the car stopped beneath a covered portico. A bellman opened Margo's door and she introduced herself as one of the photographers there to shoot Mrs. Dinkler's grand opening.

"Right this way, miss," the man said, wiping the sweat from his top lip. He led her through tinted glass doors, across an avocado-and-brown lobby, and into an office where a petite blonde woman sat behind a desk. "Miss Hightower has arrived," he announced. "The first of the reporters."

"Photographer—" Margo corrected, but the man was gone. "Hello, Mrs. Dinkler. I'm with *Sports Illustrated*." The words felt made-up, but here she was, on assignment for a major national publication for the very first time. As a stringer working primarily for New York–based newspapers and regional magazines, her work had gone mostly uncredited, but Margo's name would be attached to this.

"I'm so glad you're here!" Connie Dinkler said as she leaped to her feet. "I know what you're thinking. Why the heck did Connie D build the Palm Bay Club right *next* to Miami, and so close to Palm Beach?" She lowered onto the corner of the desk. "Those places are *over*. Miami Beach makes Palm Beach seem chic and Palm Beach is basically Milwaukee now. A bunch of rusty, dusty people you've never heard of who've chased all the interesting people away."

If Margo hadn't sold her Lillys, she might have worn one today, instead of white waffle pants and a blue-and-white-swirled Pucci-like top. Lilly Pulitzer was popular as ever, but Margo sensed Connie Dinkler wouldn't have approved.

"We needed a club that caters to swingers," Connie continued, "not the people who sit in wicker chairs leafing through Lloyd's Register." When this property came up for sale, the Dinklers bought it and set about building a place where friends and friends of friends could vacation in the utmost of luxury, on Biscayne Bay.

"The government spends all this time fretting about the poor," Connie said, "but the rich are on their own." She believed the people paying for household help and private school should be able to afford a nice vacation. Her "Play by the Bay" was for the younger set, the wealthy, *and* the potentially rich. She wanted this to be the most exclusive club on the planet, not the most expensive.

"This is about compatible people spending time together," she said. "When accepting new members, I don't give a rat's ass about money, religion, or race. No segregationists, though!"

Margo smiled. When she was first given the assignment, she'd hesitated, worried it'd be like resuming her old life, but Margo was in no position to be picky. It'd taken her a year to find employment beyond assisting a rheumy, handsy photographer in his dank portrait studio in Queens, and most of her recent work involved shooting fashion shows and high teas. It was a big opportunity, even if it was perilously close to Palm Beach. But this seemed like a different gig altogether, and Margo liked Mrs. Dinkler already. The fast-talking, tiny New Orleans native was someone she could look up to—but not too much. She'd made that mistake before.

"Since you're the first one here," Connie said, "do you want to wander the grounds and meet me in the Terrace restaurant at—" she checked her watch "—one o'clock? In the meantime, I'll have your room prepared. Oh, Miss Hightower, wait until the weekend kicks off. You might think you've seen it all, but I'm doing something new."

Margo stepped out into the brilliant sun. Camera case in hand, and a pocketbook under her arm, she put on a pair of big, round sunglasses and turned toward the pool. On the other side of a row of neatly trimmed shrubs, a tall figure smoked a cigarette. When Margo called out Slim's name, he did a double take.

Margo had considered the possibility that he might be here but decided probably not. There was his searing hatred of *nouveaus*, which was the very definition of Connie's ideal crowd. Beyond that, Slim was loyal to the core. He loved Palm Beach and Palm Beachers, both of which Connie Dinkler ripped to shreds whenever reporters gave her the chance.

"Margo?" Slim said, craning.

She took off her sunglasses and lifted her white, floppy hat. "It's me!"

"Stay right there. I'll come to you." He tossed aside his cigarette and hurdled over the shrubs. "I didn't recognize you. Your hair is so dark."

"That's what happens when you spend more time in New

York than Palm Beach. I'm living at the Martha Washington. Working as a stringer." She put her hat back on and smiled. "Exactly how you started out. So, where's my replacement?" Margo made a big show of looking around. "It's been two years. You must have a new girl by now. Or has my replacement already been replaced?"

"Yes, I have an assistant. Flo Smith's niece." He glowered. "She's in the lobby. Gets sun sick and can't be out certain times of the day."

"Sounds like a match made in heaven."

"There aren't too many Gogo Hightowers in the world." He exhaled. "So."

"So," Margo answered.

They stood awkwardly for several seconds, until finally Slim broke the silence. "I was doing a walkabout," he said. "Care to join me?"

Margo bobbed her head. As they headed toward the marina, she asked about Rita and Mary. Both were doing swell. Margo told him that Antoinette was living in Palm Springs with her new paramour, another man with dubious business connections. He also came with a longtime "houseboy" who Margo suspected was more than an employee.

"And what about the...?" Margo couldn't find the right word. "Did you spend the season in Palm Beach?"

"Wouldn't miss it," he said, and flashed a smile. "If you've been following the papers, you're up on the news. It's all the same, maybe even better than when you left."

Margo knew what he meant. Lilly and Peter were still together, and "Lilly Pulitzer" continued making a splash. Caca was managing Peter's recently completed Howard Johnson's in Miami Beach, and the Rousseaus, after losing their home in the Talisman debacle, were living in the Pulitzers' guesthouse. *All marriages have their headaches*, Lilly said all those years ago about Jackie Kennedy, *and you must decide what you're willing to live with, and at what cost.*

Margo would never understand the arrangement, but she didn't have to, and she could finally view it with a sense of detachment. The idea of being anyone's *pawn* no longer rankled and one could argue that she'd used them, too. After all, images of Lilly and Peter put Margo on the path that'd led her here.

"Since you're in New York, you should come up to the farm for dinner sometime," Slim said, breaking into her thoughts. "Rita and Mary would love to see you."

"I would love that, too," Margo said with a heaviness in her chest, a combination of nostalgia and something else, possibly a twinge of regret.

"Not for nothing," Slim said as their feet slapped against the freshly laid dock. "But I'm friends with *gobs* of people at *LIFE* and am happy to make introductions. Remind them you've been in their magazine."

"I might take you up on that," Margo said, not sure that she would. When she was dumped at the B&T all those years ago, Margo thought her life was over. Now she felt as though she'd just reached the starting gate and was proud of herself for snagging this job on her own.

"Let's talk about this shoot," Slim said. "What do you plan to focus on?"

"I was taught to explore a place with an open mind before I form an opinion." If Margo weren't mistaken, Slim was beaming. "I'm intrigued by tennis, though," she said. "All that politeness and etiquette juxtaposed with competition, and an underlying, seething hatred."

Slim chuckled. "I'm glad I never allowed you to play," he

said. "But I like where your brain is headed. Shall we check out the courts?"

Margo nodded and they walked away together, two photographers getting the lay of the land.

★ ★ ★ ★ ★

CHARACTER POSTSCRIPTS

Slim Aarons

Slim spent the rest of his life photographing high society, to varying degrees of success. When he published his first book in 1974, *A Wonderful Time*, it was considered a flop. By then, much of America felt like Margo. They hungered for something "real."

The *Boston Globe* deemed the book obnoxious, with no point other than to highlight "the era of America's social elite." The *New York Times* used the word *repelling*, and the overall take was that Slim Aarons and his gaggle of aging, sunburned friends were grossly out of touch. Were they not aware of Vietnam? Who wanted to observe others eating, drinking, and being merry in the age of stagflation?

Times had changed but stubborn Slim did not, and the former war photographer continued photographing "attractive people doing attractive things in attractive places," even after the notion was passé. He served as *Town and Country* magazine's roving editor (often called *the raving editor* given his colorful, demanding personality) for many years until he was fired in

1990, when the editorship changed hands. He supported himself by selling pictures to magazines, though viewed this as very much beneath him. There were too many women in the business, for one, and he was "sick to death of being asked to shoot stories for publications that tell you How to Have Multiple Orgasms While Camping."

Everything changed in 1997 when Mark Getty founded Getty Images and came knocking on Slim's door. By then, the pendulum had swung back around to glorifying the rich. Having waited it out for so many decades, refusing to change, Slim sold the thousands of pictures in his catalogue to Getty for an undisclosed but very large sum.

When Slim died in 2006 at age eighty-nine, he was a "respected" photographer again. Over the years, many leading designers and artists have cited him as a muse, including Katy Perry, Tory Burch, Michael Kors, Rachel Zoe, and First Lady Michelle Obama's designer, Barbara Tfank. When Ralph Lauren launched polo.com, Slim's photographs were on the landing page.

After Slim died, it was discovered that the classic New Hampshire childhood he claimed, along with his Huck Finn tales, were as aspirational as the scenes he photographed. Slim had been born to a Yiddish-speaking immigrant Jewish family that lived on Manhattan's Lower East Side. His father was absent, his mother committed to a psychiatric hospital, and his brother died by suicide. This background was a secret Slim kept from everyone, including Rita. Along the way, the couple separated, but never divorced.

Photographs of Slim and Rita (all can be found on gettyimages.com):

It's a Hard Life | Photographer Slim Aarons riding a Huffy bicycle along the quayside with cameras slung round his neck. Editorial# 2695077.

Slim's Helping Hand | Society photographer Slim Aarons helps his daughter Mary to sustain a headstand, Bedford, New York. Editorial# 71995170.

Rita Aarons | Rita Aarons, wife of photographer Slim Aarons. Editorial# 674395267.

Christmas Swim | Rita Aarons, wife of photographer Slim Aarons, swimming in a pool festooned with floating baubles and a decorated Christmas tree. Editorial# 51220667.

The Pulitzers

Lilly and Peter divorced in 1969 and Lilly married Enrique "Caca" Rousseau only weeks afterward. Yes, Peter invested in Caca's sugar business, and hired him to manage his Howard Johnson's. Yes, Lilly moved her lover into her family home. When Lilly filed for divorce, she cited "extreme cruelty." The Tarzan-and-Jane era was over.

By all accounts, Caca and Lilly had a happy marriage. Enrique was known to be cultured, funny, and filled with old-world panache. He had a calm temperament, was very protective of Lilly, and enjoyed her zest for life. They remained together, living in Palm Beach, until his death in 1993. Julia Rousseau married Charles Amory, the flower stand owner and Peter's stepbrother.

In the mid-70s, Peter married Roxanne Renckens, a spirited, curly-haired blonde from Buffalo, twenty-one years his junior, whom the papers described as having a "carbonated glucose giggle and Windex-blue eyes." When they met, she was living in a trailer court and attending Palm Beach Junior College.

Unsurprisingly, Roxanne didn't fit into Peter's world. Palm Beachers considered her a gold digger and invitations sent to their home were addressed to "Mr. Peter Pulitzer" with a "P.S. Please come alone" tacked on to the end. After giving birth to twin boys, Roxanne grew restless. Mistakes were made, and raucous fights were had, and eventually, the couple was embroiled in a sordid, very public divorce that inspired multiple books and a television miniseries. Hunter S. Thompson reported on it for *Rolling Stone*.

Though Lilly found success in her second marriage, the same could not be said for her business. As with Slim's glitzy photographs, the Lilly Pulitzer look went out of style when her ebullient, colorful spirit collided with the staid, shoulder-padded '80s. She declared bankruptcy in 1984 and focused on being a grandmother until the 1990s, just as Slim's work came back into vogue. Around this time, three men who were raised by Lilly-wearing moms wanted to revive the brand, and they did, to great success. As the barefoot tycoon said herself, *The world is ready for Lillys again. It's goony to have them back.* Lilly passed away in 2013 and Peter in 2018.

—

Peter Pulitzer | Peter Pulitzer, grandson of press magnate Joseph Pulitzer, in Palm Beach. Editorial# 135862517.

Peter Pulitzer | Peter Pulitzer, grandson of press magnate Joseph Pulitzer, in Palm Beach. Editorial# 135862506.

Pulitzers in Florida | Peter Pulitzer, grandson of press magnate Joseph Pulitzer, with his wife Lilly at Palm Beach. Editorial# 3438326.

Top Lunch | Mrs. Bedford (Dysie) Davie, Mayor Earl E. T. Smith, Charles Munn (Mr. Palm Beach) and Lilly McKim Pulitzer Rousseau, lunching at La Petite Marmite. Editorial# 3088785.

Dolly Fritz

Dolly divorced Don MacMasters in 1966 but was forced to endure his repeated kidnapping attempts (some of them successful) of one or both of their daughters. He was later jailed for a diamond swindle.

Dolly went on to marry Newton Cope, a restauranteur from San Francisco, and had two more children. At age forty, Dolly was found dead in her dressing room, but curiously, the coroner found no cause. At the time of her death, Dolly owned the Huntington Hotel, as well as dozens of properties and pieces of land from Santa Barbara to San Francisco, and Newton was elevated to "real estate magnate." His 2005 obituary called him "one of those larger-than-life figures who came from a humble background in Bakersfield and Sacramento and used his manners and charm to move in the best San Francisco social circles." Of course, everything he "built" was Dolly's first.

Dutch Elkin

Although Dutch Elkin is a fictional character, he was inspired by the big band leader Peter Duchin. The men share the same career trajectory and tragic backstory—the real Dutch was also raised by his mother's wealthy friend and her husband, in this case, the statesman and JFK confidant, W. Averell Harriman. In 1964, Peter married Cheray Zauderer, a divorced Manhattan socialite. As of this writing, he is eighty-six years old.

Wendy Vanderbilt Lehman

From what I've read, Wendy had a spicy and fun personality. While she probably wasn't as cutting as depicted in this book, I needed a good foil for Margo, someone wise and suspicious to keep her on her toes. The real Wendy was close friends with Lilly and did share my fictional Wendy's colorful dating history, from Lilly's brother to Rhadamés Trujillo.

Greatly inspired by her mentor, Georgia O'Keefe, Wendy became an artist who worked in several mediums, including wood and aluminum sculpture, acrylic, and watercolor. Some of her work is displayed in the National Gallery of Art.

Wendy was known for her wry sense of humor and, later in life, sending political commentary and dirty jokes to everyone on her extensive, high-powered email list. In 1970, she married Orin Lehman, longest-serving commissioner of New York State Parks, Recreation and Historic Preservation. The couple had two daughters before divorcing in 1995. Wendy died from heart failure in 2016, at the age of seventy-two.

—

Wendy Vanderbilt | American socialite Wendy Vanderbilt at home in Palm Beach. Editorial# 674383389.

—

An important character in Lilly Pulitzer's life who does not receive mention in this book is her designer, Suzie Zuzek. I wanted to keep the focus on Lilly, and Zuzek's influence didn't come to the forefront until later in the 1960s.

Lilly met Zuzek on that fateful trip to Key West, when she marched into Key West Hand Print Fabrics with a Gristedes bag full of patterns and asked, "Is this your shit?" She purchased all they had on hand, and eventually, Zuzek and Lilly designed patterns together, although I suspect Zuzek had the brains behind the designs. By 1966, Lilly was using more than five thousand yards per week and Zuzek continued working for Lilly until the bankruptcy.

Zuzek did not get due credit in her lifetime, even though

she was arguably one of the most collected artists of the twentieth century. It was assumed that her archive was lost to history until a few years ago, when twenty-five hundred original drawings were found in a basement. Soon thereafter, dozens of her watercolors and vintage Lilly Pulitzer pieces were put on exhibit at the Cooper Hewitt, Smithsonian Design Museum.

SELECTED LIST OF SOURCES

Magazines and Newspapers:

"Palm Beach's Barefoot Princess" by Laura Jacobs, *Vanity Fair*, July 19, 2011.

"Fashion: The Lilly," *TIME*, June 1, 1962.

"A Barefoot Tycoon Makes Lillies Bloom All Over," *LIFE*, February 8, 1963.

"A New Kind of Pulitzer Prize," *LIFE*, February 8, 1963.

"Lilly's Life as Casual as a Lilly Dress" by Charlotte Curtis, the *New York Times*, March 13, 1965.

"Suzie Zuzek Was a 1960s Icon Who Never Got Her Due" by Andrea Whittle, *W* magazine, May 8, 2020.

And dozens of issues from 1955 to 1965 of *HOLIDAY* magazine.

Books:

A Wonderful Time: An Intimate Portrait of the Good Life by Slim Aarons.

Once Upon A Time by Slim Aarons.

A Place in the Sun by Slim Aarons.

Poolside with Slim Aarons by Slim Aarons.

Women by Slim Aarons.

Lilly Pulitzer by Nancy MacDonnell.

Lilly: Palm Beach, Tropical Glamour, and the Birth of a Fashion Legend by Kathryn Livingston.

Palm Beach: The Place, The People, Its Pleasures and Palaces by John Ney.

Who Killed Society? by Cleveland Amory.

The Last Resorts by Cleveland Amory.

Essentially Lilly: A Guide to Colorful Entertaining by Lilly Pulitzer.

Suzie Zuzek for Lilly Pulitzer: The Artist Behind an Iconic American Fashion Brand, 1962–1985 by Susan Brown and Caroline Rennolds Millbank.

The Prize Pulitzer by Roxanne Pulitzer.

Palm Beach Babylon: Sins, Scams, and Scandals by Murray Weiss and Bill Hoffman.

The Season: Inside Palm Beach and America's Richest Society by Ronald Kessler.

INDEX OF SELECTED SLIM AARONS IMAGES

Chapter 3

Dolly Fritz | Socialite Dolly Fritz enjoys a cigarette by the lagoon-rimmed Palace of Fine Arts in San Francisco. Editorial# 52171094.

Chapter 6

Sunbathing At Palm Beach's Colony Hotel | View of sunbathers beside the outdoor pool at the Colony Hotel. Editorial# 166899883.

Poolside Promenade | A fashion show at the Colony Hotel. Editorial# 605352843.

Leisure and Fashion | A woman watching a poolside fashion show at the Colony Hotel. Editorial# 77442874.

Chapter 7

Poolside Musicians | Musicians at Lilly Pulitzer's pool party. Editorial# 77442809.

Chapter 8

Lilly Pulitzer | Fashion designer Lilly Pulitzer attends a poolside party in Palm Beach. Editorial# 3230590.

Florida Pool Party | Guests at a pool party, Palm Beach. Editorial# 77550151.

Poolside Secrets | Flo Smith and Lilly Pulitzer at a pool party. Editorial# 77442804.

Chapter 10

Mr. Palm Beach | Palm Beach resident, and patent holder of the racing ticket "totalizator," Charles A. Munn. Editorial# 51428807.

Chapter 14

Slim's Helping Hand | Society photographer Slim Aarons helps his daughter Mary to sustain a headstand, Bedford, New York. Editorial# 71995170.

Poolside Bar | Mrs. Charles Rogers sits on a submerged bar stool in the club at Acapulco. Editorial# 3165306.

Hibiscus Flowers | A woman surrounded by red hibiscus flowers in a swimming pool in Acapulco. Editorial# 669617899.

Chapter 17

All Mine | Jim Kimberly and his wife, with his white sports car and white boats moored on Lake Worth. A Palm Beach socialite, he acts as Honorary Consul of Jordan. Editorial# 2665700.

Chapter 21

Jackie K | Jacqueline Kennedy (Jackie Onassis) (1929–1994) wife of Senator Jack Kennedy at an "April in Paris" ball. Editorial# 2668217.

Chapter 30

Florida Businessman | Citrus grower and restauranteur, Peter Pulitzer on the patio of his home in Palm Beach. Editorial# 3088846.

Chapter 31

Lech Ice Bar | The Ice Bar at the Hotel Krone in Lech, Austria. The mountain in the background is the Omeshorn. Editorial# 113911979.

Ice Bar in Lech | Customers at the Ice Bar at the Hotel Krone in Lech, Austria. Editorial# 135464432.

Curling | Heinrich Dite and Leonie Heller play a variety of curling in Lech, Austria. Editorial# 3165410.

Chapter 32

Flo Smith | Model Florence Pritchett Smith (1920–1965), wife of American diplomat and former ambassador to Cuba, Earl E. T. Smith. Editorial# 763492907.

Earl E. T. Smith | United States foreign diplomat and former ambassador to Cuba, Earl E. T. Smith and his wife, model Florence Pritchett Smith with their son. Editorial# 674395673.

Chapter 40

Pictures from Lilly's trip to Key West can be seen in the February 8, 1963, issue of *LIFE* magazine:

https://tinyurl.com/LillyPlane

Chapter 41

Ocean Club on Paradise Island | A waiter serving drinks at The Ocean Club on Paradise Island in the Bahamas. Editorial# 77442718.

Chapter 43

Jhelum River | A luxury boat trip on the Jhelum River near Srinagar, in Jammu and Kashmir, India. Editorial# 166899857.

Diplomatic Wife | Mme. Hervé Alphand, wife of the French ambassador, in the grand salon of the French embassy in Washington. Editorial# 3089117.

Chapter 48

Sweet Smelling | A socialite who has gone into trade, Charles Amory outside his flower shop on Via Mizner, off Worth Avenue, Palm Beach. Editorial# 3089668.

Chapter 50

Pictures on Lilly's yacht can be seen in the February 8, 1963, issue of *LIFE* magazine:

https://tinyurl.com/LillyYacht

Chapter 59

Young Society | Young matrons of Palm Beach, Florida. Most of them are wearing a gaily colored Lilly Pulitzer shift. Editorial# 3089116.

Pulitzer Fashions | The young matrons of Palm Beach wearing designs by Lilly Pulitzer. Wendy Vanderbilt is wearing a yellow dress and pink headscarf. Editorial# 51246655.

Epilogue

Palm Bay Club | A young woman at the Palm Bay Club, Miami, Florida. Editorial# 88997148.

ACKNOWLEDGMENTS

Nonwriters are always surprised by the length of time between a book's first draft and publication. That's because there are a million parts that go into the finished product, and a team of dedicated people making it all happen. Thank you to the awesome folks at Graydon House—I've been lucky to be with you for three books now. From spectacular cover designer Kathleen Oudit, to copy editor Jerri Gallagher, my publicist, Justine Sha, Diane Lavoie and Ambur Hostyn in marketing, and everyone who works behind the scenes in the sales, production, art, channel marketing, and subrights departments—it's truly a remarkable group.

No thank-you could be complete without mentioning my editor, Melanie Fried. Thanks for your unsurpassed work ethic and for always pushing me to be my best. As ever, a trillion thanks to my agent, Barbara Poelle. Fifteen years ago (and fourteen, thirteen, twelve, eleven, ten…) you were the only person in the publishing world who believed in me, and I'll be eternally grateful for your faith.

Thank you to my family for always cheering me on. Dennis, there's no better rock or dad in this world. Paige and Georgia, the only reason I've been able to have my career(s) is because you're such great kids. By the time this book comes out, you'll both be "adults" and the thought of it makes me cry buckets of tears. I've loved every second of being your mom.

Finally, a big thank-you to John Schnack for his photography advice (any error in that regard is my own!) and, of course, to Lilly Pulitzer and Slim Aarons for inspiring me, and millions more.

THE
BEAUTIFUL
PEOPLE

MICHELLE GABLE

Reader's Guide

GRAYDON
HOUSE

1. Consider the novel's title, *The Beautiful People*. In what ways do the characters demonstrate, defy, and twist ideas of beauty?

2. Who was your favorite character in the novel? Why?

3. Discuss Lilly Pulitzer's surprising business success and her invention of resortwear. Why do you think she downplayed her success? How did her more practical (though colorful!) designs help women of the era?

4. Look up some of the Slim Aarons photos mentioned in the novel. Which are you most drawn to? Why?

5. What was your favorite setting in the novel? If you could "jet set" anywhere, where would you go?

6. Discuss Lilly and Peter's complicated marriage and the way that gender and money shaped it. Did you think their marriage would last?

7. Trace Margo's journey over the course of the novel. Do you feel she ultimately landed in the right place? Do you expect she'll stick with her photography career?

8. What new or unexpected information about the 1960s or Palm Beach did you learn from the novel?